Paper
&
Blood

Paper & Blood

BOOK TWO OF THE INK & SIGIL SERIES

KEVIN HEARNE

DEL REY

NEW YORK

Published in the United States by Del Rey, an imprint of Random House, a division of Penguin Random House LLC, New York.

Del Rey is a registered trademark and the Circle colophon is a trademark of Penguin Random House LLC.

LIBRARY OF CONGRESS CATALOGING-IN-PUBLICATION DATA
Names: Hearne, Kevin, author.
Title: Paper & blood / Kevin Hearne.
Other titles: Paper and blood
Description: First Edition. | New York : Del Rey, [2021] |
Series: Ink & Sigil ; book 2
Identifiers: LCCN 2020047856 (print) | LCCN 2020047857 (ebook) | ISBN 9781984821287 (hardcover) | ISBN 9781984821294 (ebook)
Subjects: GSAFD: Mystery fiction. | Fantasy fiction.
Classification: LCC PS3608.E264 P37 2021 (print) | LCC PS3608.E264 (ebook) | DDC 813/.6—dc23
LC record available at https://lccn.loc.gov/2020047856
LC ebook record available at https://lccn.loc.gov/2020047857

Printed in Canada on acid-free paper

randomhousebooks.com

2 4 6 8 9 7 5 3 1

First Edition

Book design by Caroline Cunningham
Title page: antique pen: iStock/InaSchönrock; Flourish: iStock/Terriana; Pen and ink pot icon within the text: iStock/kite-kit

for Aussies

AUTHOR'S NOTE

Since Al MacBharrais (pronounced as *mac VARE ish*) and his companions are Glaswegians and have a particular way of speaking, I've provided some guidance here as to how their speech should be pronounced, in case you want it. I haven't tried to reproduce the Glaswegian Scots dialect in all its glory but rather chosen to focus on a few phrases and words that provide the general flavor of their speech. While it may seem disorienting at first, you do get used to it and will find the rules are pretty consistent. There are, as well, some specific words from the Irish language that probably need some helpful hints, since their pronunciation would not be immediately obvious to English speakers. So here we go:

Caoránach = CARE ah NACH, an Irish name, where the final syllable would rhyme with *rack*, except that the *ch* sound is more like a guttural German thing instead of a hard *k* sound.

Oilliphéist = UHL ih FISHT, because that *i* before the *s* means it's a slender vowel and turns the *s* into a *sh* sound. First syllable would rhyme with *dull*. That's your other Irish word.

Okay, now to the Scots! First, and most important: *Ye* is not pronounced as *yee*, with a long *e*. No, no, no. Weegies are not speaking lines from old-timey pirate movies. *Ye* is pronounced like *yuh* and used in place of *you* in most cases. Sometimes they will take the trouble to spell and pronounce *you* the standard way, just for emphasis, but when they are calling someone a name, as in *you jammy bastard*, the vowel shifts differently to a short *a* sound, so it would appear as *ya jammy bastard*. For extra credit, you can combine them in repetitive phrases, as when a parent might call their mildly misbehaving child *you rascal you*; a Weegie would say *ya rascal ye*. In the same vein, *yer* is used in place of *your* and *ye're* in place of *you're*, and again, there's no long *e* sound in either of those. The long *e* is next!

Tae is pronounced like *tee* and is used in place of *to* in speech. *Happy birthday to you*, therefore, would be *happy birthday tae ye*, pronounced as *tee yuh* (except, I imagine, when it is sung).

Gonnay is the same as *gonna* in English slang, but the vowel at the end is a long *a*, so the spelling reflects that.

My is typically pronounced as *ma* in speech and is therefore spelled that way, as in *I'm gonnay call ma mum*.

Head and *dead* are pronounced like *heed* and *deed* but spelled as *heid* and *deid*.

Polis is the *police*, but it's pronounced like *POH-lis* rather than *poh-LEASE*.

To avoid using contractions like *didn't* and *couldn't*, the Scots often use *nae* in place of the *n't*, pronounced like *knee*. So he *didnae* run far because he *couldnae*, since his shoelaces were tied. If the word *not* is to be used by itself, the *t* at the end is often dropped, resulting in phrases like *I'm no gonnay pay for yer booze, ya wanker. Ye should pay ma bill instead.* An interesting exception to the rule is the use of *don't* instead of *dinnae*; while *dinnae* is commonly used on the east coast of Scotland, it isn't used at all in Glasgow, and since Al, Buck, and Nadia are using Glasgow Scots, you'll see *don't* throughout. (There are actual linguistic papers that detail the "Glasgow Dinnae Gap" and yes I have read them, because I geek out on linguistics a bit.)

Ooyah! is an exclamation equivalent to *ouch!*

Haud is used sometimes in lieu of *hold,* and it's regionally accented, meaning it might be pronounced differently depending on where in Scotland the speaker is from. In this case we're using the Weegie accent, so *haud* is going to rhyme with *clawed.* Overheard in Glasgow: *Oi, ye only got two meters in distance pissing? Haud ma beer while I unroll ma firehose.*

A *stooshie* and a *rammy* are both Scots terms that refer to a violent confrontation. I take particular joy in these words, since they sound adorable but in practice involve the spilling of blood and the breaking of bones.

A *walloper* is something big enough to give you a wallop, but the standard implication is that it might just be a huge dick.

A *pile of jobbies* means a *whole lot of turds.*

A *jammy bastard* is a person who's extremely lucky but with the implication that maybe they don't deserve to be.

Gallus is an adjective that means stylish and impressive.

Wot is just a shorter, vowel-shifted *what,* almost exclusively used by Buck Foi.

The phrase *nae danger* can mean either *no worries* or *no chance.*

A few Scots words that need to be broken down:

Milngavie = *mil GUY.* Yeah, I know. That looks like three syllables and you're wondering why the *n* and the *v* are silent, so that's why I provide these guides. I'm told that in the extra-credit Weegie pronunciation, when it's spoken quickly, the first syllable will vowel-shift to a short *u,* so it sounds like *mul GUY.*

Bardowie = *bar DOW ee,* rhymes with *Howie.*

Weans = *waynes.* But that there is a noun, my friends, not a verb. In Scotland it's a contraction for *wee ones* and therefore refers to children. At one point in Glasgow, there was a baby clothing shop called Weans World.

And, since this novel is mostly set in Australia, there are a few Aussie slang terms that might need some elucidation: *Arvo* is a term that means *afternoon. Unco* is a shortened version of *unco-ordinated. Flat out* means *incredibly busy.*

Also, you will find that there is a location named Donnelly Weir and an associated park and picnic area as well, but the road to it is named Donnellys Weir Road and the creek is Donnellys Creek. This is not an inconsistency or an editing error but rather reflective of how those places are spelled in Australia. The inconsistency exists in reality, in other words, and we are being consistent with that.

Hope that all helps! And thanks for reading.

THE STORY SO FAR

In *Ink & Sigil,* we meet Al MacBharrais, an aging sigil agent who would very much like to train an apprentice to take over his territory so that he can retire, but they have a worrisome habit of dying. Six of them, in fact, have died in apparently freak accidents.

When his seventh apprentice, Gordie, is found dead in his Glasgow flat, Al hurries over and discovers that Gordie had a hobgoblin imprisoned in one of his bedrooms. The hobgoblin informs Al that Gordie had been trafficking Fae, including a pixie, to some unknown buyer, and he escapes shortly afterward. Al finds a note that says the hobgoblin was supposed to be delivered to a ferry at eight P.M., and Al is determined to find out who's behind it.

He clears out Gordie's flat—all the inks and papers, plus his phone and laptop—and takes the cage that the hobgoblin escaped from, leaving the one the pixie was in. He goes to see a hacker, rather outrageously named Saxon Codpiece, to see what info can be gleaned from the laptop. The information gleaned reveals that

Gordie had sold six Fae creatures to someone over the past months and been paid a hundred thousand pounds for each.

When he returns to his printshop, Al is met by the hobgoblin, who asks to be called by the name of Buck Foi. Buck claims he was lured to the plane by a fake offer of contracted service from Clíodhna, one of the Tuatha Dé Danann and Queen of the Bean Sídhe. Al offers him a legitimate contract to be his hobgoblin, and Buck accepts. Together they go to the ferry to meet whoever was supposed to buy him.

It turns out to be three Fae acting on behalf of the actual buyer, a shadowy figure named Bastille. They kick Al and Buck's asses for them and they manage to escape, but not without multiple injuries.

Al informs the four other sigil agents—Eli, Diego, Mei-ling, and Shu-hua—that his apprentice is dead and was trafficking Fae to Bastille. They are mightily annoyed but will look for the dastardly villain. He also informs Coriander, Herald Extraordinary to the goddess Brighid, that someone is trafficking Fae. Coriander tells Al to expect a meeting with Brighid soon.

When he does meet Brighid, she examines Al's aura and informs him that he has not one but two curses on his head. The first curse he knew about: If he speaks too long to anyone, they begin to loathe him like no other. He's lost his family to that curse and, as a result, communicates via a text-to-speech app on his phone with everyone he wants to maintain a relationship with. But the other curse is more subtle and more deadly: It waits for a year or so and then kills whoever's in his service, in what seems like a fatal accident. Which means his seven dead apprentices were indirectly murdered and he didn't know. It also might mean that Buck Foi is imperiled by the same curse.

With the help of a couple of clues and the hacking skills of Saxon Codpiece, Al figures out that Bastille is the alias of Simon Hatcher, a CIA agent who resides in Reston, Virginia. He flies there with Buck, teams up with Eli, and they make the accidental discovery that hobgoblins can get high off salsa.

When they go to Hatcher's home to interrogate him, they get confirmation that Clíodhna is indeed behind the trafficking from the Fae planes. And what she wants from Hatcher is a way to make the Fae immune to iron, subjecting them to experiments that alter and corrupt their bodies and minds. Armed with why if not how and where the dirty deeds are being done, Al and Buck return to Scotland and contract a barghest—a ghost hound—to track the pixie that Gordie had sold just prior to Buck. Climbing into the wizard van of his manager and accountant, Nadia, they follow the barghest to a secret underground facility in the hills above a wee village east of Stirling. The pixie, Cowslip, warns them of danger ahead and that the corrupted Fae have all gone quite mad. There, Al, Nadia, and Buck confront the corrupted Fae and ultimately the evil scientist behind it all. Clíodhna, however, is beyond Al's power to punish, and he must take what comfort he can in foiling her plans and forcing her to cease her trafficking scheme. Cowslip is sent to Taiwan to recover, with the aid of Mei-ling, the sigil agent there.

To celebrate their victory, Al, Buck, and Nadia hop in the wizard van to steal a barrel of Highlands whisky and bottle it under the label Buck Foi's Best Boosted Spirits.

Paper
&
Blood

CHAPTER 1

A Call from the Land Down Under

If you have to tell someone they're going to die soon, it's a good idea to buy them a whisky first. That way they can drink it or throw it in your face and feel a tiny bit better either way. It's only polite.

Buck Foi thought about throwing his dram at me—his hand drew back, ready to strike—but he reconsidered and tossed it down his throat instead. It was getting on toward bedtime on a Sunday night. It might help him to sleep.

"How long have ye known this was gonnay happen?" the hobgoblin demanded. He had a new waistcoat on, a subtle black-on-black pattern that amused me. He would never admit it, but I think he was either trying to impress my manager, Nadia, or else he was impressed by her and emulating her fashion philosophy that all colors were excellent so long as they were black. The stated reason for wearing it, however, was that he needed to wear something appropriate to the Glasgow Necropolis, since we had gone there for a nice gothic sulk that morning while the organ droned in the nearby cathedral. It was a thirty-seven-acre city of the dead set upon a hill, populated by solemn mausoleums and weathered markers commemorating the lives of Victorian well-to-dos, and the gravitas it exuded did tend to make one feel that at least a nod to formality was required. Without walking it myself, I taught him the winding steps of the Old Way hidden in the grass between the graves, which would let him go to Tír na nÓg if he ever found it necessary. He already knew the steps to the Old Way in Kelvingrove but not to this one or the one in Virginia Court.

I replied to him via my text-to-speech app—the good one on my laptop, which at least sounded Scottish, albeit from Edinburgh instead of Glasgow. [Brighid told me about the curse shortly after you signed up to be in my service. We had more pressing matters to attend to at the time—a goddess trying to kill us and an utterly mad man-eating leprechaun and all that—so I waited just a wee bit.]

The hobgoblin teleported himself up to the kitchen island next to my laptop and waggled a pink finger in my face. He was only about two feet tall, so he liked to stand on the counter and look down at me instead of up when he had an important point to make. "That was a couple of months ago, ol' man!"

[Aye, but I also wanted you to enjoy bottling and distributing Buck Foi's Best Boosted Spirits. A nice soft time, a short span of happiness to enjoy and remember before I laid any more stress on you. Wasn't that nice, giving away all that whisky to the Fae Court?]

"Aye, it was a good laugh." His expression relaxed for a moment, recalling it. Two hundred bottles of ten-year-old whisky made from an honestly stolen barrel from the Highlands, given for free to the faeries and the Tuatha Dé Danann themselves. "Did ye know, MacBharrais, they composed songs in my honor on the spot? I mean, half of it was howled, because ma whisky kicked off an epic drunken orgy, but still: They sang me songs. I'm no a culture hero yet, ye know, not like Holga Thunderpoot, but it was quality all the same, and I think I have a legitimate shot at achieving that rare status someday if only I don't *die first*." He practically shouted the last two words, and I received a few wayward flecks of manic spittle. I cringed a little more than I might have a few years ago; echoes of the coronavirus pandemic bore heavily on everyone's psyche, though hobgoblins were not known to transmit viruses to humans.

[I'd like you to live to achieve that status, believe me. Not just because I care about you, though I do. If I can get rid of these curses, I can talk without this app. I'll be able to speak with people again for more than a few days or weeks without causing them to hate me. I'll get my family back. And I can finally train an apprentice to replace me so I can retire. An apprentice that won't die of a sudden accident, like you're apparently fated to do.]

"Come on, now. There has tae be a way around this, right?"

[Several ways, yes.]

"How many is several, again?"

[More than two, I think, but less than a half dozen.]

"Three tae five, then. Let's hear them, ol' man."

[One is that I die. I have to be honest: That's my least favorite way out.]

"I understand."

[Two is that the person who cast the curse on me dies. I like that much better, but, unfortunately, I don't know who did this to me. Brighid said it might be someone with god-level powers, so even if we do find out who did it, killing them might be impossible.]

"That's bitter news, so it is. Like fast-food coffee with no cream or sugar."

[Three is that you leave my service, cancel the contract. There are risks to that, however.]

"Like wot?"

[Like the curse might still go off in any case, now that you've been exposed. There's simply no way to know. But also, if I release you from your contract, you'll need to return to the Fae planes unless you can get another contract to remain. I'm not sure you'll be able to. I'm pretty certain none of the other sigil agents are in the market for a hobgoblin.]

"Hold on, now. I know the man in Philadelphia isnae—Eli whatsisname—because he made it clear he doesnae have use for hobgoblins. Plus he let his dog hump me while I was unconscious that time and he took pictures. Wot about the others?"

[Diego is extremely handsome and doesn't like anything that distracts from that. He has his own personal gravity and doesn't want anything to yank people out of his orbit. Shu-hua tends to avoid the company of men, and Mei-ling is so old that she thinks that I'm young and rash at age sixty-three. So: no. I'm the only one daft enough to draft a hobgoblin into service.]

Hearing it spoken aloud—that I was daft—caused an unexpected self-inflicted wound. Or, rather, tore the bandage off a wound that had not healed. The fact that I'd been so slow to discover the nature of my curses and completely missed the criminal activity of my last apprentice still stung. I was long past the time when I was supposed to have my shite together, yet I very clearly did not.

"So that's all the options?" Buck demanded. "I'm boned like a fish on Friday?"

I couldn't resist ribbing him. [Well, option four is that you die somehow completely unrelated to the curse, and then you wouldn't have any worries.]

"Oh-ho." He narrowed his eyes and shook his head. "Ho-ho-hooooh. The revenge I'll have on ye for this will be written down, MacBharrais. Written down in the anals of history, it will, whispered in the dark as a warning to wee weans—"

[I think you meant to say *annals*. The extra *n* makes a small but vital difference.]

"Don't interrupt me! The anals of history is what I meant!"

[That's not even a thing.]

"It's gonnay be! Sign me up for service and then tell me two months later I'm gonnay croak like a choir of bullfrogs? That shite belongs in the anals if anything does!"

[Okay. Let's focus on how to fix the problem, shall we?]

"I thought ye basically said it cannae be fixed in any way that works out well for us."

[We have a year to work on this. Every apprentice made it at least a year before an accident befell them. If we can find out who put the curse on me, we might find a solution.]

"How long have ye been living with it so far? Eleven years? What makes ye think ye have a shot at figuring it out now?"

[I'm properly motivated. I didn't realize that there was a second curse killing my apprentices until Brighid told me so. When I thought I was the only one suffering, I could live with it, because I'm Scottish. Now it's different because there's vengeance—or at least justice—due for my apprentices. And saving you.]

The hobgoblin deflated and sighed. "Gods below, I could use a beer. Ye want?"

I nodded at him, and he hopped off the counter and disappeared from my view. But I saw the refrigerator door open, and then he nimbly leapt up to snag a growler of stolen ale. A few more leaps around the kitchen and he had a couple of pints set before us. He stood on a stool next to mine and grabbed his pint with both hands. It was quite nearly half his height.

"G'wan, then. Dazzle me with what ye have so far."

[If we are looking at pantheons that are traditionally known for curses, the Olympians and the Egyptians were both known for bestowing curses upon mortals, and both happen to be in my territory as a sigil agent. I have no doubt annoyed them both just by doing my job.]

"But those each have, wot, fifteen gods or more?"

[Easily more.]

"Well, that's sobering. But this should fix that." He promptly drained half his glass at one go.

[There's also the infernals. They quite enjoy a good curse.]

"Who are they?"

[It's a catchall term for any of the demons in the various hells.]

"Why would they want tae curse ye?"

[I've killed a couple of them in my time. They might have had friends, if demons have friends. Not too clear on that.]

"Is that it?"

[Not remotely. I could be collateral damage. Someone who was mad at Brighid might have discovered they couldn't curse her directly, so they hurt me to hurt her. Or it's payback for some slight I committed in my youth, by some entirely different pantheon, and it only seems unconnected because gods have plenty of patience.]

"Wait. So it could be anyone? Ye haven't really narrowed it down at all?"

[Well, it's probably not someone mortal.]

"Still, MacBharrais. Still. Ye're telling me this business is wide open and insane, like yer maw."

Before I could summon an appropriate response to his inappropriate jibe, my phone rang, which meant I'd probably need to answer it. I had it set so that only known numbers in my contacts would make it ring; unknown numbers automatically went to voicemail. But anyone who really knew me would know that texting or email was a better option, since too much exposure to my voice would trigger the curse and that would be the end of our relationship. So it was with no little curiosity that I pulled out my phone and looked at the caller ID.

Chen Ya-ping, it said. I couldn't think of who the hell that was or why she would be calling me at first, but then it clicked.

[Pop away somewhere for fifteen minutes,] I typed quickly for Buck. [I need to take this.]

He teleported away without a word and I answered the call. "MacBharrais."

"Mr. MacBharrais, thank you for answering," a young woman's voice with an Australian accent said. "This is Ya-ping, Sifu Lin's apprentice."

I had many questions, like why Shu-hua's apprentice in Melbourne would ever have reason to contact me, but wanted to use as few words as possible to avoid triggering my curse, so I settled on asking, "How can I help?"

We had never spoken, and I only had her number in my contacts for emergencies. Whenever an agent took on a new apprentice, that apprentice's contact info was given to all the agents and vice versa, in case it was ever needed. I dearly hoped she simply wanted to surprise Shu-hua with a gift for an upcoming birthday or something and I could get properly miffed about the call.

"I wouldn't have called unless it was an emergency," she said. Well, fuck.

"Yes?" I asked, prompting her to get to it.

"Sifu Lin has gone missing."

"When?"

"She left Friday afternoon. It's now early morning here, six A.M. on Monday. We're nine hours ahead of you in Glasgow."

"And why are you calling me? Wu Mei-ling is in Taipei and much closer."

"She's missing too. I called her first."

"What's going on down there?"

"Well, it's summer for us right now, so like most summers, large parts of the country are on fire."

"Aye, I've heard. Bushfires are always a problem."

"Yes. As far as trouble is concerned, that's mostly it. But Sifu Lin realized that at least a small portion of the fires were being inflamed, if you will, by extraplanar visitors. The Iron Druid even came up from Tasmania to fight one in the Blue Mountains."

That sounded like an enormous problem right there. "She went somewhere with the Iron Druid?" Trouble seemed to follow him like remoras attached to a shark. A mortal who'd managed to extend his life past two thousand years tended to outlive most problems, but he also gradually acquired immortal enemies and therefore a class of obstacles most of us would never have to confront.

"No. She'd just heard from Coriander that he was on the mainland. But it got her thinking that there might be more problems out there like the one the Iron Druid had come to address—or that certain visitors were attracting yet more visitors—and she went to the Yarra Valley to follow up on a twinge to one of her territorial wards. She told me she'd check in twice a day, but she hasn't checked in at all."

"She left Friday afternoon, hasn't checked in like she said she would, and you haven't been able to get in touch with Mei-ling?"

"No, I just said she was missing too. I called and got hold of her and she said she was on her way, but I've heard nothing else since and she's not answering any more calls."

"What about Mei-ling's apprentice?"

"Hsin-yi is not responding either. And I'm afraid that Sifu Lin's partner may also have gone looking for her and not come back."

"Her partner? Remind me of who that is?"

"A woman named Sarasvati Ramamurthy, though she goes by Sara. She does IT work in the city but for the last three years has also done extracurricular work for Sifu Lin."

"In other words, she's your hacker."

"Yes. And very much in love with Sifu Lin."

"So that's four people missing all told. That's sounding pretty dire. All right. Let me make some calls and get back to you. Do you have the Signal app?"

"No. I use something else for texts."

"Signal is encrypted and all the agents use it, so you might as well download it now. I'll contact you through that from now on, soon as I can—but I'll probably use a different phone number than this one. It'll be a burner phone, because I can't bring this one instantly to Australia or someone will ask questions."

"Understood. Thank you, Mr. MacBharrais."

The first question I had when I hung up was whether I had actually been speaking to Chen Ya-ping or not. This might be a genuine missing-persons case, or it might be a trap—one that had already engulfed two sigil agents and maybe two other people as well.

I knew that Shu-hua was from a third- or fourth-generation immigrant family there and Ya-ping was as well, so the Australian accent fit, at least. But that didn't mean it had really been her.

Pulling up Signal, I fired a text off to Shu-hua: *Check in with me and your apprentice please.*

Next, to Mei-ling: *Are you okay? Worried about Shu-hua, and her apprentice says she can't reach you.*

Then identical texts to the American sigil agents, Eli Robicheaux in Philadelphia and Diego Salazar in Chattanooga: *Shu-hua's apprentice, Ya-ping, says Shu-hua disappeared two days ago. Mei-ling not answering calls. Do you know anything?*

Eli replied almost instantly: *WTF. I don't know jack.*

Diego a moment later: *I know nothing except that Santa Muerte seems happy lately, and that should worry us all.*

I replied to Eli: *Will you please call Ya-ping and ask her what's up? I'd like to see if you get the same story as me. Not entirely sure it's Ya-ping on the other end. If Shu-hua is compromised, then Ya-ping might be as well.*

Eli's reply: *Okay, Al, but I am gonna say right now that there is no damn way I am going to Australia over this.*

Understood. I would just like some sense of whether this is a trap or merely a situation.

On it. Stand by, he Signaled.

Just to be thorough, I checked my office email remotely to see if there was anything in there that landed after close of business on Friday. I tried to avoid the business email on the weekends, so it was conceivable that—yes. There was a brief email from Mei-ling dated Friday night, but it would have been early Saturday morning for her in Taiwan. It was informative but gave me no sense of urgency; I didn't know, however, that Mei-ling would ever try to characterize anything as urgent in written communication. If something was urgent, she tended to address it and then declare that the matter was taken care of, if she mentioned it at all.

Al,

I'm going to Melbourne to look into a possible problem with Shu-hua. I am taking Hsin-yi with me.

Mei-ling

It was an unusual missive in that Mei-ling rarely informed me of her movements—the five sigil agents operated independently in their own territories and traveled as needed. So the bald fact that she sent anything was an indication she thought this warranted my attention. But the addition of her apprentice was puzzling, since I didn't know if that meant Mei-ling thought it was safe or if she thought she'd need all the help she could get.

A knock at the door interrupted my thoughts, and I stalked over to peer through the peephole. Nobody there. No—wait. It was Buck. He moved into view by backing up in the hallway so I could see him down there. He had a brown paper bag full of groceries and a huge grin on his face, his pearly white caps searing my eyeballs. I opened the door and glared at him, raising my eyebrows in a question and chucking my chin at the bag.

"Awright to come in? Ye done with yer jawin'?"

I pointed at the bag and widened my eyes.

"Wot? This? Nothing here but a fine selection of wines and cheeses liberated from the kitchen of a smashing wee local eatery, where the capitalists go tae eat and chuckle smugly over how they're gonnay exploit the working classes tomorrow. Fancy a late-night hunk of Red Leicester?"

My thumbs flew on my phone to a saved and oft-used phrase on my speech app, which was sadly more of a UK accent than the app on my laptop. [Damn it, Buck.]

"Naw? Maybe a nice Spanish cheese, then. I got Cabrales, Manchego, and—"

[You can't spend fifteen minutes without stealing something?]

"Why should I waste time like that, is what I'd like tae know," he said, as he pushed past me into the flat and leapt up onto the kitchen island with his purloined picnic goodies. His vertical leap was truly impressive. "The Christians have a saying about idle hands, right? Something about the devil playing on their mounds."

[Idle hands are the devil's playground. There are no mounds.]

"More's the pity. So what's the problem?"

[The Australian sigil agent might be in trouble. Trying to confirm that independently now.]

"Is that sumhin we need tae worry about?"

[Yes.]

Buck froze, a wedge of Manchego in his right hand. "Let me rephrase. Is that sumhin we need tae *do* anything about?"

[Yes. We may need to go to Australia.]

"Where's that, again? I havenae been out of the UK except for that time ye took me tae Philadelphia and I got high on salsa."

[It's in another hemisphere. Bloody big spiders there, about your size.]

"Naw, ye're taking the piss."

[It's true.]

"It has spiders my size and people live there on purpose?"

[Aye. It's also on fire most of the time, lately.]

"Why do *we* have tae do it?"

[Because it might be a trap. And unlike the other sigil agents, I don't have family waiting for me to come home.] My son, Dougal, hadn't spoken to me in eleven years because of the curse on my heid. I'd like nothing more than to talk to him again without sending him into a murderous rage. A quick chat about the weather with him, normally meaningless, would mean everything to me now.

"Well, that's easily fixed. I could wait for ye here. How would that be, ol' man?"

[Come on, Buck, what's a little fire and spiders to a legendary hobgoblin like you?]

"I'm no legendary yet!"

[This will help, then, won't it?]

The wedge of Manchego was suddenly thrust at me accusingly. "Ye know what ye're like? That heavy-breathing space bastard in the cock helmet who's always changing the deal. Wot's his name? Dark Vaper?"

[Close enough. But you know I'm not altering our deal. I told you up front that being in my service would be dangerous at times, and it's written in the contract as well.]

"The contract doesnae mention fire and spiders."

[It says, *dangers, many and sundry*.]

"Damn it, MacBharrais!"

My phone pinged, forestalling any further ranting. It was Eli, confirming that he had spoken with Ya-ping and her story remained consistent. His attempts to call Mei-ling, her apprentice, and Shu-hua had all failed. *Straight to voicemail,* he Signaled.

They could all be asleep—it was still early there. They could be in the shower in some Australian hotel. Away from their phones for any number of reasons. It didn't necessarily mean they were dead. But it did mean I'd have to go down there to investigate.

[Pack your best flame-retardant outerwear, Buck,] I told him. [And whatever anti-arachnid weaponry hobgoblins typically carry with them. We're going to Melbourne.]

CHAPTER 2

Postponing Puissance

My ticket to Australia was through Tír na nÓg with a Fae
escort, but to get that escort I needed to make it to Gin71,
a bar in the Merchant City neighborhood, before it closed. It was
open until midnight on Sundays, so I had a couple of hours to
spare. The time would not go idly by. I needed to pick up some
sigils in my office and let some people know I wouldn't be around.

I fired off three Signals as we walked from my flat to the office
on High Street. One to Heather MacEwan, the bartender at Gin71,
whose real name was Harrowbean and who would arrange my
speedy passage to Australia through the Fae planes. Another to my
receptionist, Gladys Who Has Seen Some Shite, to let her know I'd
be visiting Australia on business for a few days and to reschedule
any appointments for the upcoming week. A third to my shop
manager, Nadia, letting her know that she was in charge until I got
back but that I'd contact her from a new phone number so she
could reach me while I was away.

Surprisingly, it was my receptionist who replied first.

*You know, Mr. MacBharrais, I've never seen Australia. I have
a feeling there's some shite there I'd like to see.*

Oh. Did you want to come with us?

Oh, no, I'll make my own way there, thanks.

You mean this week? So you'll be gone too?

I have plenty of vacation days saved up, sir. And I can email everyone who has an appointment with you now and take care of that online.

Right you are. Nadia will be fine.

Almost immediately after I sent that, Nadia replied to me.

No worries, boss. Gladys Who Has Seen Some Shite will keep things running smooth.

She won't be there, sorry.

What? Are ye joking?

No. She's taking annual leave.

Since when? I'm shop manager and human resources on top of being your accountant, and I wasnae told.

Since thirty seconds ago.

There was an ominous pause before the reply arrived. *Al? Do ye remember those yoga wankers in Colorado who aimed their arseholes at the sun for supposed health benefits?*

I sighed, and Buck picked up on it. "Nadia just starting tae chew ye out?" I nodded and he chuckled. "This should be a good one."

I do, I replied to her. *I expect an unkind comparison forthwith.*

It's not you, Al. It's me. I want ye to picture a tender vegan yoga arsehole that's been fed plenty of fiber and kale smoothies. Super-healthy arsehole, fantastic and elastic. Then one day, without warning, it's bathed in ultraviolet radiation until it's chapped and blistered and screaming WHY, GOD, WHY? That's me. I'm the screaming arsehole, Al, because that's what happens when ye dump surprises on me like this. I cannae believe ye would do this to me without a shred of warning or courtesy.

I grunted in amusement. Buck would enjoy that one. *I recently gave you a very nice raise above what you asked for, and that was pretty courteous.*

Fuck. That's a really good point.

Gladys Who Has Seen Some Shite will move the appointments around. You'll only have walk-ins, deliveries, and pickups to deal with.

Awright. I'll go back to being a healthy arsehole. Don't do anything in Australia that would need me there to save yours.

Thanks, Nadia.

Buck enjoyed a chortle at Nadia's comparison when I shared it with him, but he had a lot of questions about yoga afterward that I wasn't qualified to answer. When we got to MacBharrais Printing & Binding, we headed straight upstairs to my office. Buck glanced longingly at the whisky table, but I told him to lay off as he'd already had a shot and a pint and he was no doubt feeling fine.

[Just wait; I'll be as fast as I can. When we get to Gin71, you can have a drink if we have to wait for Coriander.]

"Oh, well, that's a sure thing, then. Coriander's too fancy to be in a hurry."

While Buck's observation that Coriander was very fancy could not be disputed, his fanciness was not the reason he sometimes made us wait. Brighid's Herald Extraordinary had permission to travel the planes freely and as such wound up escorting the sigil agents around the globe during emergencies. His privileged movement also made incredible demands on his time, and finding him with an idle moment simply never happened.

First thing I did was tear a new prepaid smartphone out of its packaging and plug it in to charge it, then tucked away a portable gadget that would continue to charge the phone from its own battery. I had several phones and chargers waiting in a drawer for situations like this. The ability to use the Fae planes as a travel shortcut in emergencies was a spectacular perk on one hand, but on the other it was astoundingly difficult to explain how a phone might ping in Glasgow one minute and then ping on a tower in Melbourne five minutes later. If sigil agents didn't take such precautions, we'd wind up with military and spy services investigating us, and we didn't want that. They always looked closely at financials, for one thing, and we didn't need the hassle. And we always had to use memory sigils on anyone who knocked on our doors to ask us questions about the strange jumping of our phones, and then we'd raid intelligence services to erase records so that there wouldn't be follow-ups. Wu Mei-ling was the one who'd had to deal with this first: Back in the early 2000s, the Chinese government wished to know how her phone had been in Taipei one minute and in Seoul three minutes later. The rest of us had taken the lesson to heart and established protocols for any traveling we did outside what humans believed possible. I printed a written list of numbers to program into the phone once I activated it in Australia—Nadia's, of course, but also those of the other sigil agents, their apprentices, and some others. Then it was time to leave my outer office and enter the real office—the hidden one behind the bookcase on the north wall. I pressed the button underneath my desk and it shifted aside, revealing my ink-and-sigil room. It was a glorious space of cubbyholes, inkpots, jars of ingredients, cooking and brewing equipment, and paper.

I grabbed stacks of all the prepared battle stuff I had available— sigils that would increase my strength and agility and so on—plus blank cotton cardstock and fountain pens filled with the proper inks to make more. These I stuffed into the many interior pockets of my custom topcoat. I didn't have a prepared Sigil of Unchained Destruction or the ink to make a new one, so I had to hope I wouldn't find myself in a situation where that was needed.

I also packed the required pens and materials to write a contract for the services of a barghest. A Fae ghost hound would be able to find Shu-hua as long as she was alive and maybe even if she was dead, but Ya-ping wouldn't be able to write such contracts yet.

I almost brought my inks for the wards used in the Chinese system of sigils but reasoned that Shu-hua would already have these available in her study, and I could borrow hers if needed. I settled instead on bringing my favorite calligraphy brush.

All told it took me only fifteen minutes, but Buck had begun to nod off in one of the plush armchairs arranged around the whisky table. He may have had another shot—I wouldn't put it past him—but he'd already had plenty for his size and it had been a long day besides. It was already his normal bedtime, and we probably had another full day ahead of us before we could properly rest. I shook the chair to jostle him awake.

"Waaugh! Huh? Fuck sake, MacBharrais, why do ye no just clap or sumhin? There's no need tae make me feel I'm gonnay die in an earthquake. I nearly shat myself."

I hooked my thumb at the door and he scooched himself off the chair, yawning, as I retrieved the new phone and made sure I had my passport and official ID with me. Chances were we'd never have to present our passport to anyone, but if we did, there would be questions about the lack of stamp in there from Customs, and then the official ID—which was not official at all but a trio of sigils that granted me authority in the eyes of the beholder—would come in handy.

I very purposely left my regular phone on my office desk. That particular tracking device needed to stay in Glasgow. I shooed Buck out, and he groused at me, "Do we have tae walk to Gin71 now?"

I nodded, and he sighed.

"I wish we could take Nadia's gallus wizard van. Whisky and cheese for the gob of Lhurnog and all that—I think it does sumhin grand for ma state of mind."

It suited me well that we didn't have that opportunity. Nadia's patron deity, a man-eating god named Lhurnog—which she'd made up—currently had only three worshippers, if one included Buck. The danger was that gods could actually manifest if they accrued enough genuine faith from human believers, but Nadia was thankfully unclear on that concept and not actively trying to recruit disciples. I'd rather such a god as Lhurnog remain entirely fictional, so it was important that he didn't collect enough psychic energy from worship to manifest. I didn't relish trying to make him sign a contract to leave the citizens of earth alone; from what

I could understand, he would no more sign such a contract than I would sign one promising never to eat chicken.

The cobbled square in Virginia Court was the site of the old Tobacco Exchange, and plenty of money had flowed through there in days of yore. Since its contours had remained stable for a good while, the Fae had bound it to Tír na nÓg via an Old Way, which allowed them to easily visit Glasgow—and me—at Gin71 on its perimeter. Buck and I entered the pub at a quarter to eleven, and I gave a thumbs-up to order my usual Pilgrim's G&T from Heather MacEwan, one of two bartenders working that night, and pointed at Buck to indicate he needed one too. She brought them to us at a booth, and I promptly steered one to Buck as she left the pub and walked the Old Way to Tír na nÓg. Her exit did not go unobserved, since she was Fae and possessed the sort of ethereal beauty that ensured she would be observed at all times. She habitually dressed as a Victorian gentleman would, without a jacket—that is, a white long-sleeved shirt with a pinned cravat covered by a silver-and-grey paisley waistcoat. She wore men's trousers and shoes as well, the first impeccably creased and the second polished to a soft shine. The subdued palette of her clothing only set off the fire of her red hair.

Her exit to the patio seating area, closed for winter, caused some confusion. "Where's Heather going?" I heard the other bartender say. Heather was Harrowbean now, and she quickly disappeared into the darkness and then, of course, from the plane entirely. She'd be back soon enough, with Coriander by her side, a being every bit as beautiful if not more.

Buck took advantage of the fact that, without a working smartphone at the moment, I couldn't tell him to shut it.

"We need tae plan a proper heist, ol' man. Another whisky barrel tae show the first one was no fluke. Ma second bottling of Buck Foi's Best Boosted Spirits will be twelve years old instead of ten. Ye have tae avoid the sophomore slump, ye see."

I nodded agreeably, because it was a subject I could safely put off until later. I took out some blank cotton cardstock for new work and found the proper pen to draw up a few Sigils of Restorative Care. I had a feeling we might need them—and if we didn't, Shu-hua and Mei-ling might. I also took out the seal for the Sigil of Postponed Puissance, which allowed me to preserve the sigils for later use, together with some red wax shavings that I set to melting in a spoon over the flame of a lighter. I had a collapsible brass stand that held the spoon steady over the lighter, and deploying it usually drew a few stares, but people lost interest once assured I wasn't melting down heroin. While the wax dissolved into a puddle, I pulled out a twenty-five-millimeter-square dry-ink pad for the seal. It was one of only two dry inks we used as sigil agents—the other was for the Sigil of Binding Law, applied to contracts. This was a golden ink that required the carapace of golden tortoise beetles, which were ubiquitous in North America and easy to obtain in the summertime. But decocting the creatures down to isolate the gold pigment was the trick. It required some lengthy lab work to distill it; their golden shells dulled to brown upon death, but the chromatophoric dyes still existed in their bodies. Luster was achieved with the addition of ground pearls, and grinding them to a sufficient fine powder was a chore in itself. A liquid version of the same ink could be created and drawn on top of something like Sellotape, and while that was occasionally convenient, it was inelegant and aesthetically unsatisfying compared to pressing an inked seal into hot wax. (The liquid ink was also prone to clogging up a pen because of the ground pearls, in which case it was not so convenient.)

The reason such a production was necessary was because sigils activated within a few seconds of completion, unless they didn't have a target. That was denied them by folding over the top of the card. Still, the sigil would continue to search for a target, and its potency would fizzle out if not preserved, so I had about thirty seconds to pour the wax, ink the Sigil of Postponed Puissance, and press the seal into it, effectively delaying the underlying sigil's activation until the seal was broken and a target was presented. It was a bit of a process to make a few sigils, but as Buck had said earlier, there was no use in wasting time.

The hobgoblin gulped down his gin and tonic, not bothering to savor it, and kept talking while he watched me work.

"Last time we hit the Highlands, but I'm thinking something Speyside this time. And after that we'll get some ridiculously old and peaty Islay stuff and tell everyone tae slow down and sip it for once, give yer gob a chance tae taste it before it sluices down the throat."

I dearly wished to point out that he had not taken the opportunity just now to taste his drink, so I did my best with a raised eyebrow and a nod at the glass full of lonely ice, while I raised my glass to draw in its carefully distilled aromas. Pilgrim's offers base botanicals of juniper, coriander, and angelica root, which are earthy notes common to many gins, but it layers hints of licorice and grapefruit on top and blends in a soupçon of black currant at the finishing stage. Heather had garnished it with three plump blackberries, which had no doubt been flown up from the southern hemisphere at this time of the year. Why Buck would rush past all those glorious goads to the senses was beyond me.

"Oi, don't gimme that look. I know ye like both gin and whisky, and good for you, ye're a man of the world. But the Tuatha Dé Danann and the Fae prefer three drinks: ales, whisky, and whiskey with an *e*. Everyone knows that gin smells and tastes medicinal, and ye don't stop tae savor medicine."

I responded with a snort. There was no judgment of taste that mattered except one's own. Shunning food and drink because of what one was *supposed* to like was nonsense. That was the sort of hidebound thinking that gave us gender roles. If Buck truly didn't like gin, then fine. But he had also just drunk some gin without visible disgust. He could like the things he liked if he would only grant himself permission—no other permission was required. If he limited his pleasure of simple things because of some external imposition of acceptable bliss, then he had let someone else build a ceiling over his life's joy.

"Wot? Why ye snorting at me?"

I shook my head as if to say it was nothing and continued sealing fresh sigils with wax and golden ink, to be popped open later when needed. He continued to lay out a series of ever-escalating heists to improve the brand of Buck Foi's Best Boosted Spirits.

When Heather MacEwan and Coriander entered from the patio door, conversation stopped and mouths dropped open. One remarkable beauty in a waistcoat was bearable: two of them together somehow inspired a deep insecurity, a sudden desire to buy a raft of cosmetics and schedule elective plastic surgery.

Coriander wore a lavender ensemble with a paisley waistcoat of shimmering silver and purple. He was attractive to all beings, so far as I could tell, regardless of orientation.

He nodded a greeting at me and remained by the door, clearly not intending to sit down.

I hastily put away my sigils and paraphernalia and slapped down twenty pounds on the table for Heather. She waved as she returned to the bar to resume her earthly duties.

"Good evening, Al. Buck," Coriander said, his Irish lilt smoothly welcoming. "I would appreciate a modicum of haste, since I have much else to do."

We exited to the patio and through the gate that gave egress to Virginia Court. Coriander walked to a seemingly random spot that was not random at all but a sort of planar off-ramp, which would extend all the way to Tír na nÓg if one walked it in just the right way.

The Herald Extraordinary walked a few millimeters off the actual ground, fully enveloped by kinetic wards. He was impervious to most harm, including the everyday shocks that the skeleton took from merely walking around. "Stand behind me, please, single file, and follow closely and precisely, stepping forward with your left foot first."

We stepped and turned and doubled back on an invisible maze-like path, and gradually the cold pavestone court in Glasgow faded out as a bright-green sward surrounded by leafy oaks faded in. It smelled of grass and pepper and the light floral kiss of daisies. Bumblebees hovered over poppies and other wildflowers growing amongst the grass and clover, almost frozen with indecision over which blossom's pollen to plunder first. Songbirds chirped happily because there were plenty of insects and worms for them to eat and no cats to eat them.

It was always a pleasant summer day in Tír na nÓg, and my infrequent visits reminded me for a brief instant of a trip I once took to Massachusetts with my family, a vacation during which I spent only a short time harvesting some ink ingredients I required. I needed to collect monarch butterfly cocoons shortly after the gorgeous creatures emerged, and there was a meadow of wildflowers and milkweed in the middle of the state where many of them took their first flight and then lingered, supping delicately on various nectars. When we saw the riot of colors—the butterflies dancing over the wildflowers in front of a line of green trees that brushed a heartbreakingly blue sky—the three of us gasped our wonder into the air and then breathed in peace. Here, we thought, was something unequivocally good. My dear Josephine squeezed my left hand and said, "Oh, Al, isn't that beautiful? I don't think I've ever seen anything so wonderful." And Dougal, who was only ten at the time, squeezed my right hand and said, "Wow, Dad, look at that!" It was a moment as perfect as one could wish for, where you feel the love from your family and feel that the world loves you too and you know, if for only a few seconds, that you belong here after all. That's what I felt every time I came to Tír na nÓg: that sense of peace and perfection, followed by a reminder of that time with my family, and then, hard afterward, a reminder that such times were long gone, for Josephine had passed in a motor accident and Dougal could not bear the sight of me anymore.

It was a bittersweet return, therefore, every time. A memory of bliss and a pang of loss. And I got maybe three seconds to experience it before someone tried to kill us.

A *whoosh* and a clipped wooden *snap* followed by the sight of a tumbling stick in the air was my first clue that we were targets. Coriander shouting, "Down!" was my second. Someone had fired a projectile at us, and Coriander's wards had deflected them.

"Oi!" Buck said, and he popped out of sight to appear shortly afterward in the branches of an oak tree, attacking a figure of his own diminutive stature. That figure winked out of sight the way Buck often did, indicating that the would-be assassin had been a hobgoblin. We heard Buck curse and then he popped back in front of us.

"He ported away somewhere. Didnae recognize him, though he had a nose like the Fullbritches, or maybe the Snothouses."

"His weapon?" Coriander asked.

"One of those mini-crossbows."

"He could return to try again, so be on your guard, Al."

I pointed at myself in surprise, as if to say, *Me?*

"Yes, you. You were the target. The bolt glanced off the wards on my shoulder but was aimed over it, at you. No one would try to attack me with such weapons. It is well known that I am invulnerable to them."

I grunted and could almost feel the lines in my face carve a little deeper. To set up such an ambush, one would have to know I'd be coming through that particular Old Way. One would have to know I'd be traveling through Tír na nÓg at that time. It seemed likely that it would be someone connected to the disappearances of the sigil agents in Australia.

"Come, let's move quickly to the transit point and get you to Australia. Single file, once more. Right foot first this time."

This second walk was longer, the path more sinuous, as Coriander led us through a shortcut of Tír na nÓg, a process that I did not understand fully, except that the plane was porous and veiled, the space and time all warped and diaphanous, like a sodden paper towel folded into strange origami. After a few steps we left the sward and saw different landscapes with every footfall, a bog here and an old-growth pine forest there, a vast plain followed by a bramble-choked riverbank, and then a cliff overlooking a stormy sea right before a hill with an easy slope down to a beach with gentle whitecaps lapping at the shore. There we stopped.

"Excellent. From here we take the Old Way to Melbourne. We will emerge in a green space called Fitzroy Gardens, which I believe is rather popular with the public, and we may be seen. Once there, Al, I will wait just long enough for you to get your mobile device working so you can speak to me, and then I must return to attend to a long list of errands, which has just been made longer. I'll be reporting to Brighid that a hobgoblin took a shot at you in our lands."

"Here's wot I don't understand," Buck said. "He obviously could have teleported behind us tae get a better shot, but he didnae. He took a low-percentage shot instead. Why bother? Was that just a warning?"

"Perhaps. Or it was meant to be deadly and the hobgoblin wasn't into it," Coriander mused. When we gave him blank stares, obviously not following, he explained: "I may have skipped some steps. If we assume that Al was the target, we can also assume the hobgoblin was hired rather than pursuing some personal vendetta. His behavior suggests that he couldn't refuse the job, but he didn't want to follow through either. So he took a terrible shot and now he can say he tried but I foiled him. This sort of thing has happened before."

"Aye, hobs will do that sometimes," Buck confirmed. "We're very reluctant tae be used as assassins. But people try tae rope us intae the job anyway, so we try tae be terrible at it when we cannae say no. Which means the relevant questions are who hired the hob and why—and why would they even go for a hob when we never kill anyone we didnae want tae kill in the first place?"

"A problem for the road ahead." Coriander led us a few paces away to a knobby rock outcropping on the hill. "Behind me once more, please, and left foot first this time. Here we go."

The path was a rigid one of frequent ninety-degree turns, and after twenty steps or so, the nice hillside overlooking the ocean dissolved in our vision and the silence filled in with the low-level industrial hum of a major city, though the replacement landscape remained at least somewhat bucolic.

Fitzroy Gardens was a garden in the sense that there were some planted and groomed areas around the walkways crisscrossing the expansive lawns; it was truly more of a park where some people also did a smidgen of gardening. People typically went there to enjoy a picnic and let their children work through their sugar highs so that they'd nap later, a process I thought of as "nap farming." Before my time, there used to be a bound tree in the park. The Iron Druid had bound the native gum tree to Tír na nÓg in the nineteenth century, but it died in the early twentieth century and a decision was made to create an Old Way that emerged near the old stump instead of binding another tree. The Australians, curiously, had preserved the stump and carved fantastical creatures into it in the 1930s, one artist's imagining of what fairies must be like. They were cute and friendly-looking and wholly unlike the actual Fae. Coriander laughed out loud when he saw it, for which he apologized.

"Sorry. It gets me every time. They're just so adorable and unthreatening."

There was a wrought-iron fence surrounding the stump—pretty inconsiderate if the carved figures were supposed to be true Fae— but it was there to prevent vandalization of the artwork.

We had emerged from Tír na nÓg in a small square of grass near the old tree, a space ringed by hedges and a sidewalk, and there we paused, half-expecting someone to gasp and wonder aloud where we'd come from. But despite it being rather busy with morning joggers and businesspeople urgently muttering into their Bluetooth headsets as they cut through the park on their way to an office, trying to project an aura of wealth and importance, no one appeared to have noted our arrival. Everyone was in their own world, paying attention to their phones or occasionally watching someone else's dog chase a Frisbee, and therefore not looking in our direction. Since no one saw us actually appear from nothing, when they did notice us, they assumed we had been there all along and hadn't just come from Glasgow via the Fae planes.

I immediately powered on the new phone and began the activation process. I wouldn't be able to talk until it was finished and I had a text-to-speech app installed.

"Arse biscuits, what's that thing in the sky?" Buck asked, wincing and holding up his arms to shield his face.

"That's the sun," Coriander explained.

"Gah! It's rude and brash here, not shy like it is in Scotland. Do they have a law here against clouds or sumhin?"

"Opposite seasons. It's summer here in the southern hemisphere."

"Still, it feels like a different summer somehow. And we are unprepared. People are gonnay wonder what ye're hiding underneath that topcoat, MacBharrais. It's gonnay get awfully warm."

I merely nodded, since I could do little else.

"What sweet unholy bollocks is that?" the hobgoblin said, pointing across from us to another iron-fenced area, through the bars of which one could see small, brightly colored houses about three or four feet high.

Coriander snorted. "That's what the humans call a 'fairy village.' Human children are led to believe that the Fae either live there or in homes very similar to it."

"And the children believe them? Even I couldnae fit into those things."

"It gets better. These modern humans have imagined the fairies to be incredibly small, but then they tell tales of an enormous rabbit that visits one Sunday in spring and hides eggs and chocolate— and sometimes, chocolate eggs—for the children to find. They call this monster the Easter Bunny."

"Wot? Now, why would a rabbit take the trouble tae swell up tae such a size and then use its time tae hide food for human children?"

"A crucial question that the children never ask! Especially since the food is so often poorly hidden. But they are feeble-minded when they are young. And—rumor has it—delicious."

That sort of conversation was precisely why there were treaties keeping the Fae and humanity apart. The two of them strolled over to the fairy village to take a closer look while keeping a safe distance from the iron, chatting amiably about roast-baby recipes, while I waited for technology to catch up with me.

Eventually it did, and the clock revealed that it was eight A.M. in Melbourne, two hours after Ya-ping had first contacted me. Not bad.

I punched in the numbers I'd brought and sent off Signals to Nadia and the other sigil agents that this was my contact info for the near future. I downloaded a speech app after that and moved closer to Coriander.

[May I send you off with a contract for a barghest?] I asked.

"To find Shu-hua? I don't recommend wasting your time," he replied. "Mei-ling already contracted one and it disappeared. So there won't be a packmaster willing to send another hound on this mission."

I frowned and typed, [Ya-ping didn't tell me about that.]

"She may not have known anything about it."

[You have been gracious with your time,] I said, because a statement like that was always preferable to saying *thank you* to the Fae and thereby implying you were in their debt. If you owed them anything, they might just ask for a baby. [Should I need you again, I will call Harrowbean from this number.]

"I wish you well," Coriander said, and he turned to leave. I waved to stop him and typed out one more thing.

[I was told by Ya-ping that the Iron Druid was in the country recently, addressing an extraplanar visitor. Was that true?]

"Yes. There was an infernal of some sort in the Blue Mountains near the east coast. That was only a day or two ago, I believe."

[So he's still here?]

The herald shrugged elegantly. "Somewhere on the continent, I'm sure."

[Is there any chance you could reach out to him for us? He may be able to help us find Shu-hua or, barring that, eliminate some possibilities.]

"I could do that. Are you sure you want him to get involved?"

Buck tore his eyes away from the ridiculous fairy village before I could answer. "Haud the phone, MacBharrais. Are ye havin' a laugh? Ye're actually asking for the Iron Druid tae come pal around with us? The Iron Druid whose touch would turn me tae ash?"

[Not pal around. Help the agents who are basically doing the job Druids should have been doing all along.] I said *Druids*, plural, but I supposed I was being unfair. Back in the nineteenth century, there had been only the Iron Druid, and he was in hiding and unable to do much of anything without attracting the attention of a deity who wanted him dead. That was why Brighid had bothered to create sigil agents in the first place—she had work that needed doing on earth and no one to do it.

"Sounds like he's daein' his job if he just got rid of an infernal. Let's let him do his thing in peace."

[He might be able to help, Buck, and we need help. Coriander, please contact him.]

The faery bowed, a small grin on his face. "As you wish." He turned and strolled down the invisible path that would take him back to Tír na nÓg, and Buck waggled a finger at his fading form.

"That was some ominous fucking agreement there, ol' man! Do ye no see how bad this could be? Allow me tae translate: When a faery asks ye if ye're sure ye want something, he's flat-out saying that ye really *don't* want it but he's interested tae see if you'll be daft enough tae insist. And that bit where he gave a tiny smug smile at the end? That smile silently means, *You will die a horrible fucking death, but* . . . and then he finishes with *As you wish* out loud. I feel it's ma duty tae point out tae ye as yer hob that this is a bad move."

[Your concern is noted,] I said. [But if two sigil agents every bit as capable as I am have gone missing, we may be dealing with a problem that requires a heavy hitter. The Iron Druid qualifies.]

"Sure, he might hit whatever we're up against. He might hit us too, though."

[If it eliminates the threat to sigil agents, that's fine.]

"Fine tae put ourselves in an iron hell? Was that in ma contract?"

[*Dangers, many and sundry.*]

"Oh, I'm gettin' tae hate that phrase. Where are all the fires and the spiders ye promised me, then? It doesnae look so bad here. Lookit all these birds and dugs and people walkin' about, none of them on fire or being sucked dry of their juices by great bloody arachnids."

[Give it time.]

CHAPTER 3

Flat Whites

It was time to contact Chen Ya-ping.

This is MacBharrais. I'm in Melbourne. Where are you?

Her reply came quickly. *You're here? Oh. You took the Old Way. Okay. Directions incoming.* There was a small pause as she composed her next message. *Take Clarendon Street north a couple of blocks until you reach a small café called Square and Compass. It'll be on your right-hand side. If you reach Victoria Parade, you've gone too far. I'll meet you there.*

I didn't know where Clarendon Street was in relation to where we stood, but a map app solved that easily enough. I pointed to our right for Buck's benefit, indicating that we'd be walking that way. My topcoat gathered stares as we walked, and I began to sweat, so I took it off and held it draped over my forearm. We passed an old rotunda that a plaque identified as having been built in the nineteenth century, a white-pillared Greek shrine-like structure that the British seemed incapable of leaving out of green spaces back then. A lawn or two later, a similar period piece advertised itself as a bandstand.

Once we reached Clarendon Street, we turned left on the advice of my app, and at the intersection that marked the corner of the park, we had to cross the road twice to get to the corner diagonally across from us. Continuing north from there would bring us to our destination, and it hove into view after a couple of blocks, a red-brick establishment sandwiched between others, with large windows and a glass door once we passed a fenced outdoor-seating area. A glass pastry case greeted us when we stepped inside, along with a menu above it and, shortly thereafter, a friendly employee.

It became apparent that we'd arrived before Chen Ya-ping, since no one hailed us inside. I took the liberty of ordering a flat white for Buck and another for myself. When in Australia or New Zealand, that's what one does. The flat whites in most of the rest of the world do not fare well by comparison.

We picked up our order at the counter and had just taken a seat when a young Chinese Australian woman entered. She spied us quickly, as my formal dress and mustache tend to make me stand out somewhat, and Buck stood out even more, being an extraordinarily pink and diminutive person dressed in black. She had her hair pulled back in a simple queue and wore blue jeans, a yellow blouse buttoned up to the neck with a white collar and tiny white flowers all over it, and canvas shoes that I believe are commonly referred to as "Chucks."

Before she could say anything, I raised a hand to stop her. She paused with her mouth open and was very patient as I quickly typed into my app.

"Hi, I'm Buck," my hobgoblin said into the silence. "He'll be with you in a moment."

She did not respond verbally, I noted, but did give Buck a tight nod and small grin.

[Hello, Ya-ping. I don't know if you were going to say this, but I need to warn you: Do not, for any reason, address me as sifu or master, because I am not yours and that may trigger a curse on your head. Call me Al, please.]

Her eyes widened the tiniest bit in surprise, and then she spoke, thankfully the same voice and accent I had heard on the phone. "No worries. Pleasure to meet you, Al and Buck. Thanks for coming. We should take the train out to Sifu Lin's place, but maybe first I'll get a flat white to go. Those look good."

Once we were out the door and happily sipping our coffees, albeit squinting in the sun, Ya-ping led us to Parliament Station, a decent stretch of the legs back along the top of the park and circling around a building until we descended some steps into the underground to get tickets. We had no idea what to do or even where we were going, so I handed over some cash to Ya-ping and she took care of it with her bank card. Then we stepped onto an insanely long pair of escalators—the longest in the southern hemisphere, according to Ya-ping—which conveyed us deep into the bowels of the continent.

"Glen Waverley, Platform Four. That's us. About twenty-five minutes or so once we get on, and then a walk to Sifu Lin's house."

[Ah, so that's where we're going. I had wondered if we might be going to an office at one of her businesses.]

"Oh, no. Years ago, before my time, she used to have a sigil room in her laundry and dry-cleaning place but discovered that the steam and general humidity were curling her papers and messing with some of her ingredients. She couldn't have that, so now she's got some dedicated space for ink-and-sigil work in her house. It's really cool, actually—hidden entrance and all that. It's like going to a mad scientist's secret laboratory, except with none of the madness or stained surfaces or scraggly whiskers." She cupped a hand over one side of her mouth, as if to tell me a secret, but whispered it loud enough that anyone could hear if they wished. "Sifu Lin is very tidy. You will find zero whiskers in her sigil room."

I chuckled at the absurdity of that—it was such a profound statement of the obvious to anyone who knew Shu-hua, and Ya-ping tittered too, out of fondness for her master's foibles. But then she gasped and covered her mouth, her expression falling and her eyes downcast.

"I shouldn't be making jokes at a time like this. It's disrespectful. Sifu could be injured or even . . . worse."

"Aw, well, that's bollocks," Buck said, and I nodded while I typed up something more and my hobgoblin continued. "That's about as mild a pisstaking as I've ever seen—it doesnae even qualify, really—and it's yer duty tae shovel a wee bit o' shite on yer master's shoes from time tae time. Firstly so they're reminded they're no so high and mighty and they'd look good dressed in a bit of humility, and secondly because play is creative and vital to growth and a fairly big reason why we enjoy living at all."

The depth of his answer surprised me, but I added, [I saw no disrespect at all. Only great admiration and even affection.]

She searched my face quickly to see if my expression matched the words coming out of the phone, and I nodded my sincerity.

"You're both kind. But I am nervous and frightened and perhaps talking too much out of a sense of relief. You got here very fast and I'm so grateful."

[I need you to talk much more, Ya-ping. We have a ride ahead. Tell me more about your education thus far and your situation.]

Ya-ping's shoulders fell at my words, and the train was pulling up to the platform, so I didn't pursue it. But she said, "I knew we'd have to do that. Might as well be on the train. It is a liminal space, and within we shall move from being unacquainted to acquainted."

"Wot, now?" Buck said. "MacBharrais, wot was that she just said? Subliminal? Did I just get hypnotized? Ye'd tell me if I was, right?"

I shook my head at him to dismiss it, but he didn't take it in the manner I intended.

"Ye mean ye wouldnae tell me? That's no very bloody nice. I'd tell ye if *you* were hypnotized. I'd say, *Oi! MacBharrais! Ye're hypnotized! Now get me a scone!* Or sumhin like that. A scone sounds good right now. But no with raisins in."

A small quacking noise emanated from Ya-ping's pocket and

she checked her phone, the noise evidently being an alert of some kind. Whatever she saw there, she dismissed with a shake of her head. We boarded, taking three seats out of four that faced one another in pairs. The empty chair next to Ya-ping struck me as symbolic; it was why we were there, and she followed my gaze and sighed as we got under way, a breathy hiss over the rumbling white noise of the train.

"I graduated from Glen Waverley Secondary College a couple of weeks ago, just before Christmas. In a few months I'm supposed to complete my training to be a sigil agent, the youngest one in quite some time, I'm told, because I'll still be eighteen."

That was interesting. Shu-hua had begun her training while she was still a minor. It wasn't impermissible, but it meant that there were potential conflicts with the parents and the necessity to let them in on the secret that gods and monsters were real, just drowned out by the noise of modern living and the grind to pay the mortgage or talk about the new thing on the telly. Popular culture's embrace of science, too, tended to make people dismiss the mystical or magical almost by reflex. Ya-ping lifted a hand and cocked it at me like a pistol.

"And now's the part where you ask about my parents."

"Wot about yer parents?" Buck asked, saving me the trouble.

"They're dead. No need to get their permission. Sifu Lin has been my legal guardian for the last two years and a better parent in every way than my real ones were."

My surprise must have been plain.

"Yeah, she didn't share that information with the group. I know how it goes. She just said, 'This is my new apprentice,' and none of you asked any questions, because it's not your business, right? But I guess it's your business now. You want to know what happened."

[In case it proves relevant later.]

"It won't. But I'll tell you so you won't worry. My father was an alcoholic. Not physically abusive but certainly not shy about hurling verbal abuse in my direction. A couple of years ago, as I was finishing up grade ten, they went out for a Christmas party and got lit up. And then Dad tried to drive them home. Instead, he drove right off the road into a tree, maybe three hundred meters from where he'd parked. Mom was killed instantly. Dad lived long enough to realize what he'd done, decided he couldn't live with the shame and guilt, broke a whisky bottle, because of course he had one in the car, and sliced open his throat with the glass. So that was a pretty terrible holiday season."

"I'm sorry," I said aloud, not bothering with the app.

"Me too," Buck added. "Gods below."

Ya-ping closed her eyes for a moment, acknowledging our words, and continued. "My mom was good friends with Sifu Lin. Like, childhood friends. She was already a huge part of my life. I called her Auntie Lin while I was growing up, even though there's no blood relationship. She was at all of my birthdays and all of my mother's birthdays, and I'd see her two or three times a month. And, as it turned out, she was the person to whom my mother had legally entrusted my life should something catastrophic happen. I was with child services for like, a day, when Auntie Lin came in with the documents. And once I moved in with her, she couldn't pretend that she did anything normal anymore. When I was young, she told me she did paralegal work. Ha! Paralegal. I didn't realize at the time it was a pun."

"Wot?" Buck said.

"Because she writes legal contracts for paranormals—never mind. My sense of humor is a bit nerdy."

"Ohhh. I get it. Yeahhh, ha ha!"

I was pretty sure Buck did not get it.

"So I was at a place, mentally, where I did not want to do anything my parents ever imagined for me, and Sifu Lin needed an apprentice she could trust who didn't have a lot of family entanglements. It sort of worked out best for both of us. Auntie Lin became Sifu Lin."

[Are you still in that place? The one where you do not want to do anything your parents imagined for you?]

"You mean, would I rather be a dental hygienist or a vascular surgeon? No. I want to be a sigil agent."

[Good. How far along are you?]

"I know one hundred percent of the Chinese sigils and maybe half of the Irish ones. I just learned Iron Gall and painted it on my weapons."

[I see. And Hsin-ye was . . . ahead of you in her studies?]

"Yes, by a month or two. She likes to tease me about what's coming next, always texting that something she's learning is really awesome or bloody awful. She's also older than me. She's twenty."

It took me some time to type my next sentence. [If all three of them are lost . . . you might be the last true adept of the Chinese system.]

Ya-ping dropped her face into her hands. "I don't want to think about that."

[We must. The inkmaking in particular would be a tragic body of knowledge to lose. A priceless cache of lore. I learned to make the inks in my training long ago but have since traded Mei-ling and Shu-hua for everything I needed, since their ink sticks were flawless and mine were . . . not.]

"The procedures can be time-consuming and exacting for sure. But that's not our worry for now. We are going to find them."

[Yes. Can you walk me through what happened when she disappeared?]

"Sure. She loaded up with battle sigils—all the Irish ones, you know—plus some extra cards and pens. That by itself told me she was expecting trouble—or at least preparing for it. She said there was a twinge to a ward she wanted to check out in the Dandenong Ranges. That's about forty minutes northeast, depending. Plenty of settlement in the foothills, suburbs, and what have you, and then, *blam,* you're in the bush."

[Which ward specifically?]

"The Ward of Imbalance."

That relatively vague title was one of the oldest mystical wards, used to detect the arrival of gods and demons on the plane. If yin and yang were in balance on the earth—an admittedly dubious proposition—the sudden appearance of a powerful being from another plane would be like dropping an anvil on one side of a seesaw. Or, viewed as a membrane, the plummet of a stunt professional into an air mattress. Such wards had, in the old days, let seers and magicians of all stripes warn the Middle Kingdom of threats or give them hope that help was on the way.

They were passive sensors and lasted for years when painted properly. The wards did have a limited range, however, and didn't always pick up the arrival of low-level visitors. A pixie could slip in and out of the plane without us ever knowing. A single ogre could sneak in, even—they were brutes, sure, but there were plenty of human brutes too, and they didn't represent a significant deviation from normal.

A web of such wards could provide a fairly decent early-warning system, but it was a constant game of updating them and hiding them so that the Fae didn't know where they were; they would regularly destroy them on sight to blind us and keep their movements secret. Whenever a sigil agent showed up too fast to confront them in the middle of some shenanigans, the Fae knew we had learned of their presence through the Ward of Imbalance.

[Did she say anything about the twinge to give a sense of how powerful the being was?]

"No. I haven't felt these twinges yet, because I guess I'm not attuned."

[It's like a sudden chill along your spine and then someone screaming at a very high pitch in one of your ears, though it is thankfully brief. Which ear varies.]

Ya-ping grinned. "That's very similar to how Sifu Lin described it. But, no, she didn't say. Only that it was in the Dandenong Ranges, and then she loaded up for a fight."

[Did she take a Sigil of Unchained Destruction?]

"I don't know. I saw the Sigils of Agile Grace and Muscular Brawn for sure, but there were others."

The train emerged from its underground track to the daylight, having completed a gradual hill climb, and we were rocking along the suburbs. Buck was immediately distracted by the prospect of people to mess with and counting which of their possessions he could easily steal.

[You only recognized two sigils? No more?] What Shu-hua took with her might give me some clue as to what she thought she was facing.

"Just those two were all I saw for sure, but I know the others she took were also Irish ones because of where she reached in her sigil drawer—you'll see how it's organized. I'm sorry I can't be more specific. At the time it seemed routine and nothing to worry about, so I wasn't paying close attention, until she told me about the note."

[What note?]

"When Sifu Lin is going on a mission or errand that she believes could be potentially dangerous, she establishes a dead drop somewhere just outside the engagement zone and leaves a note for me there. She's done this several times in the past and always returned, so I never had to go find one. This time, she packed up everything and then told me that there would be a note for me at the Healesville Grand Hotel if she did not check in or return."

[Have you been there yet?]

"No. I called Sifu Wu when I first became worried, and she said she was on her way because she felt the twinge too."

[She felt it in Taipei?] That didn't bode well. Coriander didn't set the wards off, which was a blessing, since he came and went all the time. Likewise, contracted Fae like Buck and Harrowbean, as well as other beings who had permission to be on earth and to come and go, didn't set off the wards. So whoever had tripped the wards definitely had no permission to be here, and it was someone rather powerful.

"Yes, all the way in Taipei. So I waited for her to look into it. But when she disappeared as well, I called you, because I figured that if two sigil agents couldn't handle what's out there, I couldn't either, and the note would most likely tell me to call you and the others anyway."

[So that's a solid clue. We have a starting point.]

"We do."

[Do you know where the Ward of Imbalance is located? That would give us the center of a circle to search.]

The young woman shook her head. "Dandenong Ranges is all I know, because that's what she said aloud. I haven't felt any twinges and don't know where any wards are painted, other than the ones I did myself in my studies. I think attuning myself to them is supposed to happen in a few months."

I nodded. That was true. Introducing the apprentice to the surveillance net was one of the final tasks before starting them on the ink for the Sigil of Unchained Destruction. The Ward of Imbalance was an excellent start, but it worked in conjunction with the Sigils of Gentle Alarm and Ethereal Scriving, which Brighid had designed to provide a picture of extraplanar comings and goings we could consult as needed, without our nerves jangling at every little thing. Jangling nerves were sometimes useful—they provided a certain motivation—but they could affect sleep patterns after a while.

A portion of my sigil room held a pigment-soaked map of my territory, which was, in many ways, a priceless gift. It would be the chief treasure I'd pass down to my apprentice, if one ever made it to mastery. Shu-hua had one, Mei-ling had one, as did Eli and Diego, each map made by Brighid. As a rule, the pigments in the map appeared as a neutral brown, the way all colors turn to a slurry of brown when mixed together. But disturbances to the web of wards and sigils we made were bound to the Sigil of Ethereal Scriving in the map, which updated every hour: Dots of color appeared where some being entered or exited the plane, according to the wards and sigils we had out there. A bright-red dot meant an infernal of some kind had arrived; a soft pink meant an infernal had exited. Kelly green and hunter green indicated the comings and goings of most Fae, and white paired with grey tracked the arrival and departure of beings many would consider to be gods.

[Have you checked Shu-hua's map?] I asked, because everything else had been a prologue to that.

Ya-ping nodded, her entire body tensing at the question. She'd been expecting this one and had not been looking forward to delivering an answer.

"Sifu Lin did when she felt the twinge. She said there was a white dot in the Dandenong Ranges."

"Wot? Is that bad? It looks bad," Buck said. "Lookit her, MacBharrais. She's clenched up tighter than a rich man's bum when ye mention paying taxes. What's a white dot on a map mean?"

[It means there's a god of some kind out there.]

"A god? Ye told me it was all fire and spiders in this country, and now it's a god? Ye're a damn Dark Vaper, I swear."

I ignored him and typed to Ya-ping, [We'll need to drive out there after I check her map for myself. Do you have a car?]

"Yes. But it's tiny, a two-seater. I mean, Buck would need to sit on your lap."

"He'll never let that happen. He knows I'll piss on him, see. And he'll *deserve* it," the hobgoblin said, standing on his chair and pointing at me, "because of fire and spiders and gods and a curse on ma heid because of the curse on *his* heid and that time he gave me a nasty drink called a negroni and said it was popular!"

Ya-ping arched an eyebrow at me and flicked her index finger a couple of times in Buck's direction. "I'm picking up on a low-key current of repressed hostility from your hobgoblin. Are they all like this?"

"Naw, there's no any as fine as me. I'm gonnay be a culture hero, if I live that long."

[Buck, the solution is clear. We need you to acquire us some alternative transportation.]

His annoyance melted away from his features and was replaced by a childlike excitement. "Ye mean grand theft auto?"

[Or the theft of a grand auto, yes.]

"Can it be a van? A *wizard* van?"

[If you wish.]

His arms shot up in triumph. "Ya beauty! Yessss, ha ha ha!"

CHAPTER 4

The Gallus Wizard Van

All vans, Buck explained, had the potential to be wizard vans. They were like hunks of marble before the sculptor took a chisel to them. But the best hunks of marble, in this metaphor, would be windowless vans that were kind of tall so one could stand up in them, the sort that plumbers and electricians often used.

"You mean a tradie van," Ya-ping said.

"Wot?"

"As in tradesmen. We call them tradie vans. They get to park anywhere, and it drives us mad. Anyone else would get a ticket for parking the way they do."

"Right. Those. They have the largest surface area tae paint, so we want one of them."

When the train arrived and we emerged from the Glen Waverley station, we had to walk a few blocks to Shu-hua's house, on Florence Street. Glen Waverley was an older neighborhood, which continued to thrive because of the school Ya-ping had just graduated from. It was an extraordinarily good one and everyone wanted their kids to go there, so property values were up, and it seemed they were always cramming in some high-rises or remodeling old houses to accommodate demand. As a result, Ya-ping observed, she and Buck would have little trouble finding a tradie van parked somewhere. Stealing, however, was not her specialty.

"Don't worry about that," Buck assured her. "I'll steal it, you drive it."

Ya-ping shot me a glance. "Mr. MacBharrais, you're okay with this?"

[We'll return the van. It will no doubt be in a much different condition from when we took it, but it will be returned with some monetary compensation as a sort of rental fee. They will be inconvenienced a brief while but not suffer any permanent harm.]

The houses along Florence Street had been built before the idea of tract homes had taken hold, and as a result there were some rather grand aging places along its length, some that were not so grand, and some that had been torn down and rebuilt to be bigger.

From the outside, Shu-hua's house looked to be two stories, though it may have also had a basement. It sported a red-brick façade and a black-shingled roof, and there was a balcony above the entrance with a pair of wide French doors. There wasn't a front yard, exactly, but rather a cement courtyard leading to the garage and entry; lining the edges were little half circles of shrubbery, sprouting out of beds of cedar chips alongside some crepe myrtles and Japanese maples. Along the front was a wrought-iron fence interrupted periodically by four-foot brick columns, each capped with a flat white hat of cast stone. The sides of the property, however, had a more traditional wooden fence for privacy.

"Swank," Buck commented.

"We say *swish* here," Ya-ping replied. "Sifu Lin's house is very swish."

Ya-ping opened the front door with a key, turned off an alarm system, and asked Buck very politely not to steal or break anything.

"Aww. I was hoping ye'd forget tae ask. Awright, ye have ma word."

The interior was modern and uncluttered and looked clean enough to show for an open house. There were some stunning pieces of art on the walls, but the furniture was nondescript, as if trying not to be noticed or at least not to distract from the art. My quick impression of the kitchen as we passed through was that it was designed to draw attention to the porcelain tea set, which rested next to the kettle on an island—the stove being installed there, rather than along the wall. Nothing else mattered but the tea set.

Ya-ping led us upstairs without giving us much of a tour, except to say, "The downstairs is where we entertain guests, so it's kept pretty bare. All the good stuff is upstairs."

She pointed to closed doors on our left and right once we reached the top floor, emerging in a sort of pleasant reading area with comfy chairs and tables in front of the French doors and balcony we'd seen from outside. "Sifu Lin's private rooms are to the left, mine to the right. The magic is at the back."

It was indeed. There was a simply magnificent private library with floor-to-ceiling shelves on all four walls. There was even a line of books placed above the door.

"Ahh, ink and glue and paper." Buck clapped his hands together in appreciation, and his nostrils flared as he inhaled. "Lots of dusty ideas, but not much actual dust."

"No, dust is not tolerated here."

[How is it organized?] I asked, indicating the shelves.

"Author's home country, then alphabetically. Australian authors kept separate from the UK, Americans, and so on, Taiwan from China, and all the Spanish-language stuff is broken out too. Spain is separate from Mexico, Peru, and so on."

[I didn't know Shu-hua was into Spanish literature.]

"Very much so. Are you familiar with the work of Sor Juana Inés de la Cruz?" Ya-ping asked, crossing to the opposite wall of books.

[No, sorry.]

"Remarkable woman from the colonial period. Hieronymite nun. *Primero Sueño* is Sifu Lin's favorite."

She plucked out said volume from the stacks, thereby causing the entire bookcase to rotate clockwise, allowing us to see that there was a secret room behind it. "And here is Sifu Lin's ink-and-sigil room. Please, go ahead."

Buck spread his arms wide in admiration. "Oh, that's very fine—pure class. I like the rotating thing. It's better than yer sliding door, MacBharrais."

[Outstanding,] I agreed. The room was a white minimalist space with framed art prints of calligraphy on the back side of the bookcase, but those would have to be appreciated later. [Where's the map?]

Ya-ping pointed to a white-paneled workbench with a wide top drawer of the sort one might store blueprints in. "She keeps it in there."

[Okay, I'll be fine here. You can go and get us a van.]

The two of them left and I immediately sought out the map. It was set into the top drawer, as promised, and it was mostly clear at the moment. There were a few green dots in Madagascar, a couple of red ones in Australia, but no telltale white dots that would tip me off to a god nearby. That didn't mean much; the god could very well still be on the plane. The wards detected the arrivals and departures as a flux in extraplanar energy. Once the flux faded, so did the marker of their whereabouts. The god who'd arrived may have departed and Ya-ping missed it, or they might still be on earth somewhere, perhaps nearby. It was a far-from-perfect system, for all its magic and power; still, it was better than simply wondering.

I shut the drawer; it would not tell me anything new for a while. I turned to see what else I could discover, besides the obvious fact that Shu-hua preferred an immaculate environment.

Her ink cakes, pots, brushes, and pens were on the same wall as the bookcase, though obviously not on the rotating part. The ink was displayed in a wooden lattice of shelves and labeled in Mandarin. Higher up, centered and in a larger space, a porcelain vase that I suspected might be a priceless artifact from one of the old dynasties gleamed under soft light behind a pane of nonreflective glass. It was easy to see and admire, impossible to accidentally knock over or splatter with ink. She had been very careful with its placement. Beneath this wall of open-faced cubbyholes was a flat writing desk and a stack of precut cardstock for creating sigils. She used a bright-white linen fiber rather than the ivory cotton I preferred. Her waxes, matches, melting spoon, and candles were tidily lined up on the right side.

On the opposite wall, she had jars of ink ingredients that she used to make the finished cakes, and a distilling and brewing setup similar to mine, except that it all looked brand-new. The one nod to modernity was a small Bluetooth speaker so that she could enjoy her playlists while she worked. She was a fan of Indigo Girls, if I recalled correctly.

Where were her other materials? This stash of sigils that Ya-ping mentioned?

I began opening drawers, finding stacks of handmade paper and some correspondence that I ignored. But then I spotted another wide drawer like the one across the room, and when I pulled it open, I discovered an organizational marvel. Rows of bamboo, the thickness of a finger, stretched across the width of the drawer, while columns of much thinner balsa wood formed rectangular compartments. At the top of each compartment, a white label had been placed on the bamboo, indicating in both Mandarin and English which sigil was stored below. Then, inside those compartments, she had her prepared sigils stacked but set flush against the bamboo at the top, leaving a finger's breadth of blank space at the bottom of each one, allowing her to easily pluck out whichever sigil she needed. She had organized them so that the modern, Irish sigils were on the left-hand side, and the older, Chinese sigils were on the right. She had copies of most every sigil waiting in those compartments, and the ones required for wards were either full or nearly so; the ones for battle were entirely depleted. She had taken everything. That included the contents of the compartment labeled SIGIL OF UN-CHAINED DESTRUCTION. That didn't mean she had one or more on her—she might, like me, be fresh out—but it made it possible. And if Shu-hua thought she needed one of those, then we could have a problem out there too big for the standard bag of tricks.

Which I had already concluded must be the case. I didn't yet have a full set of pieces to this puzzle, and I didn't have a convenient reference photo of the big picture, but I had put together enough around the metaphorical edges to know that it was going to be a dire scene when completed. More like Munch's painting *The Scream* than *A Sunday Afternoon on the Island of La Grande Jatte* by Seurat. Missing sigil agents and an unnamed god on the loose in the Australian bush were probably not going to be elements of a tranquil tableau.

I Signaled Eli and Diego before I went any further: *Unidentified god arrived in the Dandenong Ranges in Australia on Friday. Both Shu-hua and Mei-ling felt the twinge from the Ward of Imbalance and went to investigate. Now both are missing. I'm going in. If I disappear too, do not come after me. Send in the big guns.*

Eli's reply: *Yes! Dive into that shit! You're white! What could go wrong?*

Diego's answer: *Hey, Al, can I have all your stuff when you die?*

I blinked. Ah, well. Americans.

If a god was involved in this, then any actual confrontation was almost impossible to prepare for. But what I could prepare for was the absolute certainty that regular folks might witness something they couldn't explain and would need to forget promptly. Paradigm shifts are rough on the psyche, and most adults are unable to process that there's been a hidden world around them since they were born, that science is only half the story. For their own safety, sanity, and future employment prospects, it would be best for them to unsee what they saw. I borrowed some blank cards, located the proper ink required, along with sealing wax and her dry-ink pad for Postponed Puissance, and even found a number of empty fountain pens without too much difficulty. She had Platinum and Diplomat pens in there, but I selected a Pilot Metropolitan model in turquoise—since they weren't terribly expensive, she probably did not have a sentimental attachment to it. I filled the converter with the ink from the pot and prepared two dozen Sigils of Lethe River, which would make the target forget the last hour of events and, in the resulting disorientation, be open to the suggestion that they go home and rest. After the gods had battled in a short-lived Ragnarok in Sweden about a year or so ago, I'd had to use plenty of those sigils to keep the story from hitting the mainstream press. They'd done their job, and as a result most of humanity was blissfully unaware of how close they came to being wiped out by an army of draugr. The few who did know either weren't talking or weren't believed. If I didn't wind up using them—well, they were endlessly useful, and I could give them to Shu-hua since it was her ink anyway and represented a good deal of time and effort on her part.

There was no time to lose; we needed to get hunting, and I had seen all I needed to see— Wait. I checked the map one more time to see if it had updated, and it had. The Fae dots had darkened, indicating their exit from Madagascar. Probably a raid on vanilla beans; Brighid liked homemade ice cream and had been sending faeries to fetch her ingredients ever since humans had invented the process—she actually had an Official Ice Cream Ogre with the unfortunate name of Yark. But nothing new in Australia. I did not believe for one second, however, that there wasn't a problem here just because I couldn't see it yet. The map did have its limits, and we routinely missed comings and goings.

Carefully attempting to put everything back precisely the way it was and knowing that I was failing, I resolved to simply apologize to Shu-hua for the terrible mess and hope she forgave me. I replaced the volume of *Primero Sueño,* the bookcase rotated closed, and I thought it best to go outside to see if Buck and Ya-ping had enjoyed any success.

They had.

A tall black tradie van with KAUFMAN ELECTRIC emblazoned on its side sat parked in the driveway.

Buck was dancing in his excitement. "Oh, good, ye're here. Lookit this beautiful canvas, ol' man! We can make this so wizard. Do ye want a pointy hat?"

[I'm not the wizard, Buck. You are.]

". . . I am?"

[You're the one who has innate actual magic. So make this your wizard van.]

"Are ye serious?"

"Do it fast, please," Ya-ping said. "Anyone could see it here and report it later."

That was an excellent point. With the van parked outside the garage and parallel to the street, the logo was plainly visible. The iron fence with occasional low brick columns did nothing to conceal it from drivers or pedestrians.

"Right, right." Buck clapped his hands together, then rubbed them in a fit of glee. "First the disguise, then we tackle the interior. But registration first, eh? That's how they find ye. See, MacBharrais? I listen to yer rules and bollocks sometimes."

He separated his hands and curled his fingers toward the rear bumper. The numbers on the license plate shifted and changed in response.

"There. Now, a background—I know just the place. The Glasgow Necropolis. Victorian boneyard for the win! And a threatening sky, a circling of clouds that might be a tornado forming or a portal to a plane of horrors."

He made a noise that sounded something like *Zoop!* and contorted his arms and legs, spun about, then leapt in a series of twirling kicks, his hand shooting out. Entire sections of the van's side suddenly appeared fully painted by an exceptional artist. It was a view of a gloomy necropolis, and not the logo of Kaufman

Electric. To look at it from the outside, this van couldn't possibly be the recently stolen one that authorities would soon be looking for. It was remarkable and eye-catching, though.

[Buck—that's art right there. It's beautiful.]

"Aw, g'wan now, ol' man. I'm just getting started. How can it be beautiful yet if I'm no on there? Zoop!" He flailed his arms again, then shot them out, held close together with the palms open toward the target, like a popular martial-arts videogame move. As a result, a painted Buck—dressed incongruously like a seventeenth-century musketeer—appeared on top of a sculpted tombstone, his right arm raised and fingers clutching as if to pull down lightning from the sky, for that is what he did. His expression, lit by pure electricity, was noble and righteous, and that too was incongruous.

[That's fantastic,] I told him. [What is that thing you keep saying? Zoop?]

He scowled, casting his eyes sideways at me. "Ye cannae ask me that. Zooping is very private."

[What? Zooping is not even a thing.]

"It's a private thing. A hobgoblin thing. But the details are juicy, just like yer maw."

[Fine.] I knew what this was. He'd promised to get me back for that small matter of the death curse, and pretending to have a sacred secret so that I'd worry about it or waste my time on it was just an overture to the aria of his revenge.

Buck turned to Ya-ping, whose mouth had dropped open in shock. "Wot? No, don't bother tae float any moralizing meward for talkin' tae him that way. Now, look, ye're a part of this, so ye need tae be in the picture. What do ye want tae be wearin'?"

"Oh? Oh. Uh. Well, I don't think you should be able to see my face. People might recognize me because I live here. So maybe something with a mask."

"And yer sai?"

"Oh, yes."

[What sai?]

Buck zooped again and Ya-ping appeared in her current clothing—no historical anachronisms or superhero outfit— holding sai in a defensive position as she faced the unknown threat in the sky. She had a simple black mask over her eyes and nose, her lips pressed together in grim determination.

"That's brilliant," Ya-ping said.

"In't it, though?" To me, Buck explained, "I asked her what she'd bring tae a fight in case we got caught boosting the van. She said she'd use sai if she had them."

[Oh! Are you proficient?]

"Yes. And I think I should get them before we go—they're inside."

"Aye, but not yet; the van's no finished. We have two heroic figures here, but we need a contrast tae set them off, a sidekick who can spotlight their bravery with his cowardice. Zoop!"

I abruptly appeared on the side of the van, behind Buck and Ya-ping and wearing my black derby hat. My mouth yawned in terror as I pointed to some horror in the sky. And I was nearly buried in a pile of something: Only my head and my pointing arm were visible.

[What is that? Coal?]

"Naw, turds. Ye're up tae yer neck in shite and screaming, which is an apt summary of how most days go for ye by noon."

[I don't think I scream very much,] I said, but had little defense for the first accusation.

"Awright, I know ye're in a hurry tae get moving, but the inside of this thing is basically metal and plastic and a significant copper-recycling opportunity. We need tae fix that too. So I'm gonnay get some appropriate furnishings and I need you two tae clean out all the sparky bollocks."

"And put it where?" Ya-ping demanded.

"It doesnae matter. Don't worry 'bout the polis; ol man's got a goat that'll get them out of our hair pronto."

"What did you even say just now?"

"Ta!" the hobgoblin said, and popped away somewhere, leaving me to explain.

[He meant we shouldn't have to worry about the police; my goatskin sigils will take care of them.]

Ya-ping sighed, but then fairly hopped into the van. "I'll grab a couple of things now, but I'm going to get some boxes from the garage. We can just cram it all in there."

I don't hop anymore unless I'm enjoying the aid of a Sigil of Agile Grace, but once I got myself up into the rear of the van and Ya-ping brought some boxes, I filled them with parts and tools and wires while Ya-ping shuttled them to the garage. Her two-seater car was parked in there.

Buck reappeared briefly to dump a glossy black pleather love-seat on the lawn. He was breathing hard but promised he just needed one more trip.

"Wait! Where did you get that?" Ya-ping asked.

"Furniture-store showroom, so it's only been sat on by show-room arses, only five tae seven farts on it at *most*—practically new!" He was gone again before Ya-ping could muster a reply. He'd need some time to recover after depleting himself so much, and I was worried that he might not get any. I thought he was spending an awful lot of his juice on a frivolous undertaking, but if I voiced that concern, he'd tell me to shut it and then argue that it was absolutely vital to have a proper wizard van, and we'd just waste more time in the process. He was, at least, trying to be quick, and for a hobgoblin, this was extraordinarily helpful be-havior. Apart from depicting me up to my neck in a pile of job-bies.

I began a sporadic conversation with Ya-ping while we divested the van of its electronic components and waited for Buck to re-turn. The next time she came back with an empty box, only to haul away another, I had a sentence or three ready on my phone and pressed PLAY.

[I lost my wife in an automobile accident too. Thirteen years ago. Not precisely the same thing, of course, but I can empathize with the suddenness of the loss and the disorientation of it.]

"Oh," she said. "I'm very sorry to hear that, Mr. MacBharrais."

I nodded in acknowledgment, and she took away the next box while I began filling the empty one. When she returned, she had a question, as I thought she might. She looked down into the empty box as she spoke and pushed it gently toward me, filling it with words.

"Did you . . . ? Forgive me for asking, but after the accident, did you spend some time adrift? Unmoored, purposeless, and just, I don't know, unsure how to get under way again?"

[I did. Months of grieving and depression. It comes back and flattens me from time to time, years later.]

"So it's normal."

[Very normal.] She had frozen, staring at me, her eyes welling a little bit. I nudged the full box to her and a tear spilled out of her right eye, which she dashed away before clasping her arms around the box.

"Right. Work to do."

She was off, because she knew how to work and it had doubt-less been what had gotten her through the intervening years, but I knew she'd be back with another question.

"Does it get easier?" she said when she returned.

[Grief is never easy. But it gets softer around the edges, smoothed over like a river rock given time enough and water. It's still a rock and it's heavy and dangerous and capable of hurting you. Just not immediately to the touch, if that makes sense.]

She sniffled and curled her arms around the new box like she was hugging something important. "That sounds like a true thing," she murmured. "Thank you."

I nodded and busied myself with clearing off the last of the items from the grey metal shelves bolted to the interior of the van, because it was a true thing I knew too well. It was odd how some-one's absence could feel so heavy. Some days I missed Josephine so much I could barely walk, and if I dwelled on her now, I might

lose track of what needed to be done today. With the shelves emp-
tied, I realized that they were an obstacle in themselves. Getting
those out would be a hassle.

A loud but muffled clanking of glass alerted me that someone
had returned. That, and ragged breathing.

"Gods below, ol' man!" Buck said, sagging next to a pair of
very full shopping carts. "Is this what it feels like tae be old?"

[No,] I said. [It's mostly low-level joint pain and unwelcome
ear hair.]

"Aw, man, I don't—" he gasped. "Don't know. How I can finish this. Must . . . fortify!" He plucked a bottle of whisky out of
one cart and popped it open, pouring some down his throat. He
choked, coughed, and laughed. "Ah ha! Ha ha haaa! Fire in the
hole! Yeah. That'll do it. Some more would be good." He repeated the exercise and spat out half of it, but he was able to
stand up straight afterward. "Awright. Way I see it, the major
difficulty we have left are those shelves and that wall separating
the cargo area from the cab. We gotta get them outta there."

He raised his hand, and with a *spung!* and scream of sheared
metal, the shelves were abruptly gone, as was the panel separating
the cab from the cargo space. A crash from the neighbor's yard a
moment later announced where he had teleported them. He wob-
bled and fell on his back after that.

[Buck!]

"Oh, my gods, did you seriously dump shelves in the neighbor's yard? Like that's not going to attract attention?" Ya-ping
grumbled.

"Just get the whole shebang in the back and we'll go. Fix it on
the road," Buck said. "Rugs first."

He had several rolled-up lengths of carpet stashed in the shopping carts, and we spread those on the floor of the van before
maneuvering the loveseat in there and then simply piling the rest
of his ill-gotten goods inside. He was passed out on the loveseat
when we got rolling in the general direction of the dead drop
Ya-ping had mentioned. The apprentice brought her weapons, a

few sigils, and some essentials, but she said we could stop to buy whatever else we needed on the way.

She turned in her seat to look back at the snoring hobgoblin, who was surrounded by a mess of fabric, scrap metal, tools, and a black metal bistro table on its side, as well as far more whisky than we could reasonably expect to consume in the next few days. Her eyes narrowed.

"I dislike drunken stupors," she said, and held up a hand when I reached for my phone in an attempt to reply. "No need to comment. I'm sure you understand why. Just . . . maybe you can tell him, when you feel the time is right, that there are monsters lurking in that darkness he's sleeping through. They're waiting for their moment. And they'll follow him into his waking hours and consume him if they can."

I nodded. It was an easy promise to make, and to keep.

CHAPTER 5

The Hitchhiker

The drive to the dead drop would take a small amount of time, but we had a significant stop to make first.

[Where do I go to get some clothing more appropriate to this climate and what we're walking into?] I asked Ya-ping.

"Kathmandu—I mean, not the actual city in Nepal, but a chain store that sells outdoor gear down here. It's in Knox City. I'll give you directions."

It was a pleasant drive there, and while it was the sort of modern western suburbia one finds in many places, I cannot express how wildly different Melbourne was from Glasgow in every shred of affect. The sandstone tenements were missing, the pavements looked strange without cigarette butts mashed into them, and simply existing outdoors felt like being put inside a kiln that *could* bake my bodily clay to a dry ceramic if it wanted to, but it was too relaxed right now to put in the effort.

The establishment itself was located in a business zone with a strip of stores on either side. It had large floor-to-ceiling windows with painted bits in a pink-grapefruit color shouting about what else shoppers might find if they just walked through the door, but you could spy some fit mannequins modeling clothes inside and figure there would be more of the same. We got plenty of stares when we exited the van, which Buck appreciated.

"That's right, Aussies," he said. "Ma wizard van is the dug's bollocks."

"*Bollocks* is a good word," Ya-ping agreed, and entered the store ahead of Buck's retort. It was an open space with racks of merchandise, circular racks of poufy jackets and rugged shirts, and a wall full of hiking boots opposite the checkout, which was backed by a panoramic photo of a likely rock-climbing site beneath a deep-blue sky. If you bought some gear, the photo suggested, why, you could just go jump around on those rocks like you've always wanted. We were there to do as the photo suggested.

Buck was disappointed that the children's section didn't have anything in black, but I didn't know why he expected anything else.

[Goths don't hike very much, Buck,] I said.

"How could ye possibly know that?"

[I've known Nadia a good long while. The only hiking she does is around the necropolis. She drapes herself artfully over tombstones for Instagram photos and wears platform shoes with unnecessary buckles on them. That's a nice day outdoors for her. Now, what you see here are brightly colored clothes for children so that their parents can spot them easily in the bush when they wander off. The only black clothing you'll find here is for men who like to think it's tactical.]

"Gods below, ye don't have tae be so smug about it."

He was probably correct, but I went ahead and felt smug anyway.

We got outfitted for a walkabout, with field jackets and khakis and boots and thick socks and so on. I basically asked an employee how I could leave the store with as many pockets as possible and bought items accordingly. Ya-ping did the same, but she also asked to know where the mozzy gear was, which completely bewildered Buck and me.

"Which gear?" my hobgoblin asked.

"Mosquitoes," she explained. "Shorten a noun, put a *y* or an *o* at the end of it, and you'll understand most of Aussie slang."

We caused a raised eyebrow by asking to leave the store wearing our new purchases but were allowed to do so, and we spent a few minutes secreting sigils, pens, and inkpots in our clothing before moving on. I carefully folded then rolled my topcoat into my new pack, for while I wouldn't be wearing the coat in this heat, I couldn't bear to part with it. Buck spent the time grousing that khaki should be illegal, looking down despondently at his muted outfit. I cheered him up by walking him down a few doors to a place called Gami Chicken & Beer. We got some Korean fried chicken to go, and he sounded pleased again until he fell asleep on the loveseat in the back, exhausted by his exertions on the van thus far and the enervating effects of consumerism.

The paved expanse of the suburbs dwindled to narrower roads as we hit wine country, and then it got greener and livelier as we hit farmland and pollinators chirped and buzzed in robust health. Cattle lowed in pastures, and occasionally there were some goats or alpacas ruminating on this and that.

Buck awoke from his power nap before we reached Healesville, and we tried to ignore the sounds of grunting, pounding, and clanking coming from the rear as he began to work on his wizard interior.

"I cannae match the glory of that altarpiece Nadia has in hers, but I'm gonnay have a run at this and make it the finest I can on short notice," he said. "Ye know, MacBharrais, I bet we could start a profitable side business in wizard vans if ye wanted. Think about it, awright? Because I bet ye can launder a suitcase or ten fulla cash through a business like that."

I blinked in surprise, because he had a point. We could indeed launder money effectively through a garage. Parts and labor and custom alterations were ripe for exploitation. I'd have to run the concept by Nadia.

A bright-green field dotted with contented cows beckoned to

me to come rest with them, like the lotus-eaters of the *Odyssey*, who encouraged Odysseus to sigh and be satisfied. A hitchhiker on the side of the road ahead caused me to check oncoming traffic to see if I could stray over the dividing line to give them a wide berth, but then I took a closer look at who had their thumb out into the wind. It wasn't a typical hitchhiker, whose fashion landed somewhere on the scale from forgotten dog-chew-toy to Army surplus. It was a well-groomed middle-aged woman in sensible tweed. She wore heels, stockings, a feathered bonnet, and large sunglasses with thick white rims. And she was on my payroll.

It was Gladys Who Has Seen Some Shite.

I pulled over shortly after passing her location and caught her smirking in the rearview mirror as she began to walk to catch up.

Snatching up my phone, I typed, [How the hell did Gladys Who Has Seen Some Shite get here so fast?] There was absolutely no way an international flight from Scotland could have made it to Melbourne in two hours, allowing my receptionist to mysteriously appear to hitch a ride on the precise road we were traveling. I twisted around in my seat to let Buck know my question was really addressed to him. The hobgoblin looked bewildered, as if the answer should be obvious.

"Ye mean ye don't know what she is?"

[I thought she was my Canadian receptionist.]

"Aye, sure, that's the truth, ol' man, but she's more than that. She's *also* a Canadian receptionist."

[What else is she, then?]

The hobgoblin shrank back, clutching a stolen whisky bottle in one hand and placing the other over his heart. He replied in a subdued tone, "It's no ma place tae say. Either she tells ye or no one does. But this isnae good."

[Why not?]

"The only reason Gladys Who Has Seen Some Shite would bother tae come here is tae see some more shite. And I don't mean scenery, awright? Sumhin's gonnay happen. This might be why she's been slumming it in yer office all this while."

Slumming it? I didn't get a chance to inquire further, because three smart raps on the back door announced her arrival. Buck opened the rear door and my receptionist beamed at him. "G'day, Mr. Foi. Kind of you to stop."

He bowed briefly and extended a hand to help her up into the back, then gestured grandly to the stolen showroom loveseat.

"Thank you," she said. "Hello, Mr. MacBharrais. And hello to you," she added, nodding at Ya-ping. "I'm Gladys."

"I'm Ya-ping. It's a pleasure to meet you, Gladys."

She smiled beatifically and crossed her legs, adjusting the hem of her skirt over her knees. "It's all mine."

"Can I get ye a dram?" Buck asked, his tone solicitous. "I have many fine whiskies here."

"That sounds wonderful. Something Speyside if you have it, please, but don't worry if you don't. I'll drink whatever you think is best."

"Right ye are!" My hobgoblin immediately dove into his hoard of purloined whiskies to find the perfect dram for my receptionist, giving me an opportunity to ask a question.

[Gladys, how did you get here so quickly?]

"Well, sir, I was motivated, don'tcha know. I've been wanting to take a vacation for *ever* so long."

[But getting here that fast is impossible.]

"Oh, surely not, Mr. MacBharrais. I mean, here we all are. Isn't this cozy?"

A cold thrill of fear radiated from the base of my skull, where the lizard brain had woken in response to a surprise. It was the sensation one gets of suddenly spying something that has been in a blind spot for a long while, and its abrupt appearance was threat enough to pump adrenaline into the system and speed up the heart.

[Who are you really, Gladys? Buck tells me it's more accurate to say you're *also* Canadian.]

My receptionist turned her face to Buck, the pleasant expression briefly turning to steel, a flash of warning in her dark eyes. "I hope for your sake, hobgoblin, that you did not tell him what I am."

"Naw, miss, nae danger! I know it's for you tae say or no as ye please." His politeness in the face of such a direct challenge chilled me more than anything else thus far. It occurred to me that Buck had not once tried to mess with Gladys since he'd come to be in my service. I had thought in passing it was because she wasn't enough of a challenge, but now I saw that I was mistaken. She obviously was going to dodge any direct questions about her true identity, but this deference my hobgoblin paid to her was similar to what he would reserve for a god, so that made me wonder.

[Tell me, Gladys: Are you the one who cursed me?]

She smiled. "Oh, no, sir. I don't even dabble in such things as curses."

I wanted to ask what she *did* dabble in but supposed she'd say something vague in reply, and I had a specific follow-up in any case: [Do you know who did, then?]

"No, sir. I'm truly curious about that myself. I'm waiting to see what happens when you find out who it is. Ah, thank you, Mr. Foi," she said, as Buck handed her a finger of Balvenie Double-Wood neat in a stolen rocks glass he'd torn from a swaddling of bubble wrap.

She took a sip and sighed appreciatively while I typed. [Whenever you're ready to tell me what else you are in addition to Canadian, I'm ready to hear it.]

"Understood. I'm not ready for that yet, sir. I'll understand if you want to fire me now."

[I do not want that. I want you to be safe. What we're heading into could be dangerous.]

"Ha! I certainly hope so. It's an awfully long way to come if it's no more interesting than running out for groceries."

[I might not be able to protect you,] I said, aware that I probably sounded unnecessarily patriarchal.

Gladys tittered. "There's absolutely no need for that, Mr. MacBharrais. Let me put your mind at ease: Once we get to this place you're going, I'll get out and disappear and you won't give me another thought. I'm very Canadian in that regard."

[Wait: You'll disappear?]

"I'm not sure you'll see me again until you're back at the office, eh? If you get back."

Buck stopped breathing and I said, [Gods below, that was an ominous afterthought.]

"Oh? Oh! I'm sorry, Mr. MacBharrais. You're right, that wasn't a very sensitive thing for me to say, was it? I'd buy you a maple-frosted apology donut right now if I could. Or a can of Moosehead if you weren't driving. I'm sure it'll be—I mean I'm certain that you'll be—well. You might be fine."

[I might be?]

"Yes, I'm absolutely positive that you might. But if you dwell on how you might not, then that could affect your readiness to meet the mortal peril ahead."

[What?]

"It's why I showed up on the road to get a ride. Didn't want to land smack in the middle of an abattoir. Best to approach that mess from the outside."

[What kind of mess?]

"A deadly one. You know what Canadians do to take their minds off mortal peril? They talk about hockey. We could do that."

My enigmatic receptionist clearly wanted to steer the conversation elsewhere, so I put the van in gear and steered us back onto the road to Healesville.

Buck said, "But aren't Canadians always talking about hockey?"

"Well, there's a lot of mortal peril in Canada, so it works out, doesn't it? I'll tell you what isn't working out: the Toronto Maple Leafs' second and third lines. Am I right? There's just no balance to their roster, and they don't have a decent forecheck. If they're ever gonna beat the degens from the States, they gotta get that figured out."

"Degens?" Buck asked.

"Degenerates, Mr. Foi. Like your mother."

We all gasped aloud in surprise, including Buck, but then the hobgoblin laughed until he had tears streaming down his cheeks.

"Tits and biscuits, ol' man, we have tae talk hockey with Gladys more often!"

Ya-ping wasn't laughing, and my hobgoblin noticed.

"Wot? Did I say sumhin wrong? Was it the tits or the biscuits?"

"No, it's just that I don't think I can talk about hockey very well," she said. "I haven't studied that game yet. But I agree that sports are an excellent distraction that allows people to avoid talking about anything real. I can pretend to care about footy if you want. I can drape the words around me like social camouflage and seem cool while concealing my tender nerd feelings. Here, I'll show you: What do you guys think about the Hawks' prospects next season? I think it's obvious they've got to find a decent small forward somewhere, and it'd be nice if someone taught the back line what pressure means; otherwise . . . Nope, sorry, I've already lost interest."

"Oh, I hope you won't mind if I gently disagree with you, Ya-ping," Gladys Who Has Seen Some Shite said. "I think sports are extremely real. They are socially acceptable ways to channel human territorial urges as well as aggression, violence, and the psychological will to dominate, while also providing the comfort of tribalism and partially satiating the greed of owners, players, and merchants."

"Hmm. I had never thought of it in those terms."

"They do seem to be crass affairs on the surface, but I find that sports condense humanity into its essentials, including its tendency to indulge in magical thinking. If you have ever seen a peak performer give credit to a deity for his or her achievements, you know what I mean. This person, usually between twenty and thirty years old, has spent at least half their life working relentlessly during their waking hours to fine-tune their body with exercise and diet until they earn a spot on an elite team and then score a goal or prevent one from being scored, thereby earning an interview on television where they assign all the credit for their achievement to a deity who is most likely unaware that they even live and is more interested in kumquat marmalade toast than whatever that human did that day."

It took some time to digest all that, but Ya-ping eventually replied, "So you think I should pay attention to sports?"

"Not if it fails to fulfill any of your needs. Simply recognize that they do fulfill many people's needs—even if they just need to say something before a conversation gets awkward. But in this case, you really need to talk about footy so you won't think about the terrible peril."

"What peril, exactly? And how do you know?"

There was no way she would answer that. Whatever Gladys Who Has Seen Some Shite was in addition to being Canadian, she was obviously one of those beings bound by rules. Rules that said she couldn't be too specific about the dangers she saw ahead of us, because that would risk changing the outcome of events and she might be blamed for it. Someone else with deity credentials might cry foul, say that she had interfered somehow in our fates or our delicate illusion of free will or some such nonsense, but, regardless, she'd pay a price for it, so a vague warning was all we were going to get. But we got it twice. She wasn't kidding around.

"Oh, look, isn't that the hotel? We're here!" she said. "It was lovely to meet you, Ya-ping, and I hope you will survive so we can talk of safer things, maybe over a yummy cup of tea. Sweetened with maple syrup instead of honey, you know, for a proper Canadian cup."

"You'd really do that to tea?" Ya-ping replied, incredulous, while looking out the window to confirm our arrival. We were indeed at the hotel, and I braked in the loading area across the street. Then we heard the back door open and my hobgoblin exclaim in surprise. When we turned around, Gladys Who Has Seen Some Shite was gone, her empty rocks glass perched on the arm of the loveseat.

"I didnae know she could do that!" Buck exclaimed. "I just

blinked—a single blink, mind, a fraction of a second—and off she fucked!"

"She's your receptionist?" Ya-ping asked. I nodded, and she began to tick off points on her fingers: "Let's recap: She came here from Scotland at the same impossible pace you did, except not actually with you, and then she hitched a ride with us on the road to where we were going when she could not have possibly known where we were going because she wasn't there when I said where it was, and after that she spoke some cryptic doom, threatened me with maple syrup in my tea, and disappeared?"

"That's about it," Buck agreed.

"That might be Canadian behavior—I don't know, since I haven't been to Canada. But it is definitely not human."

[I've just now come to the same conclusion,] I replied.

"Hate to say it, Mr. MacBharrais," Ya-ping said, sliding her eyes to the back and hooking a thumb at Buck, "but that painting of you up to your neck is starting to look pretty accurate."

INTERLUDE

———— • • ————

Papermaking

I think people take paper for granted these days, not realizing how much time and energy and resources are consumed to make it. I also think whoever was chiseling records into clay tablets a few thousand years ago would rank it as one of our finest achievements, if they could peek into the future at modern miracles. I think of the process as a journey to clarity and creation.

At least, the old handmade process is. Modern processes are journeys to pollution and poisoned rivers.

Plant fibers are required. Wood is most common now, but hemp, cotton, and other fibers work too—like the flax fibers of linen—and ancient papers were made from bamboo and rags rather than trees. I personally prefer cotton or linen paper; my sigils are drawn on cotton cardstock, and I take a day or two out of the year to make it myself. All one needs is cotton, water, sunlight, and a few tools.

But, ye gods, it can be a slow and soggy business. I suppose patience is needed also—especially since sunlight can be hard to come by in Scotland.

The tearing and shredding of the cotton is a comfort. I actually speak to it as I break it down, reassuring it that it will be a vessel for magic someday rather than somebody's underwear, and isn't that a kinder fate?

Put the pulp in a tub of water, submerge a mold and deckle with a wire frame stretched across it, and witness the cloudy mess of the pulp suspended in the water. It's like looking into the future, ill-defined.

Pull the frame up a bit, try to distribute the pulp as evenly as possible across the screen, and, Bob's your uncle, you already see the outline of a sheet of paper, which will dry out and accept whatever correspondence or grocery lists or sigils you choose to write on it someday. I like that process, that clarity, that simplicity. I love that the results are predictable and reproducible. But I especially treasure what it does to my mind.

As I make sheet after sheet and hang it up to dry, I plan out my next year, visualize my goals, think of the most orderly way to proceed, how to give shape to a formless void. My summertime papermaking winds up being when I make resolutions for the year ahead. And, sometimes, I can also gnaw at any questions or problems that have been bothering me. I already knew what question would dog my hours:

Who or what the living fuck was Gladys, really?

CHAPTER 6

The Dead Drop

The Healesville Grand Hotel was a three-story affair built more than two hundred years ago. It had Tudor-ish towers at either corner, the kind with grey-shingled roofs that wanted to look like steeples someday and swooped up in that direction, but then the architect had mercy on the tradies who'd have to build them and just squared them off before they got too pointy. Arched windows stared at us from the expanse of roof between the towers, and then the bottom two floors were painted a chalky white with four pillars supporting a second-floor balcony. That balcony wall was painted a burnt sienna so that some thin white letters could declare the building GRAND HOTEL, and it also provided shade for the entrance below. Near the street, some landscapers had planted and pruned what the wags of Monty Python might declare to be "a shrubbery!" Posters on the windows shouted in bright colors about upcoming festivals and events in town.

Inside, a young woman in a burgundy hijab smiled and greeted us. "G'day. Checking in?"

"I am here to see if you're keeping a message for me. The name's Chen Ya-ping."

"Oh! Yes. I have that right here." The woman opened a drawer and produced an envelope made of a lavender-colored artisanal paper. I clearly saw *Chen Ya-ping* written on it in black ink, but above and below that were Mandarin characters. Ya-ping took it with both hands and stared at it. Her fingers began to tremble. A couple of them curled, hesitantly, toward the Mandarin characters, as if to affirm they were real by touching them.

[What is it?]

"It says to imagine she has written my name in red ink." I didn't know what that meant but supposed it must be bad, judging by the way she said it. "And this paper."

[What about it?]

Ya-ping didn't answer but opened the letter, breaking the wax seal and unfolding it with an exquisite whispered rustle. I saw just enough from the side to recognize that the letter was written in Mandarin, mostly in red ink except for a couple of lines on the left.

[What does it say?]

Ya-ping took a breath and translated: *"If you are reading this, then we are having a lovely time somewhere on the Bicentennial National Trail, which begins at Donnelly Weir with the section marked Mount St. Leonard."*

[Oh. Well, that's nice.]

"No, it's not. It means they are in deep trouble."

[It does? Read it again, please?]

"The words aren't the message. The message is how the words are delivered."

[Explain it to me.]

Ya-ping's eyes slid over to the hotel clerk, and it was fairly clear the young woman was listening intently while pretending not to.

"Okay. Let's go have a seat in the bar."

The remodeled bar had kept very little of the original structure, except for some ancient exposed brick behind the liquor bottles displayed on its shelves. The rest of it was a straight bar with a lacquered pine top over a grey-tiled front. The tables varied in size from two- to six-seat high-tops with grey metal stools. We chose a larger table near the window and consulted menus in anticipation of the bartender's arrival. He was an affable sunburnt fellow with sleepy eyelids and tight brown curls on his head. He had some stubble on his chin that appeared curiously to cultivate a rugged devil-may-care affect, for which I may have judged him slightly. But he also wore a navy-blue pinstriped waistcoat, for which I forgave him all minor faults since so few people bothered to wear them anymore.

I ordered a finger of Limeburners Sherry Cask, which I had never tried before. It was a whisky made in western Australia, so I was delighted to have the opportunity to try something new. Buck ordered the same but groused that it would taste better if he just stole it. The bartender simply nodded, proving to be as affable as he looked. Ya-ping asked for an iced tea.

"Red is a very positive color in Chinese culture," Ya-ping said in low tones when the bartender had retreated, "except when it's used for the name of a living person. Then it's like an ill omen—the very worst kind of bad luck. That's because the names of the dead are often written in red on tombstones. She would never actually write my name in red, because that would be like assigning me a death curse. But telling me to imagine my name in red is a warning of extreme danger. And she left this here for me before she went off to find whatever she found. She knew she was heading into something dangerous."

[Oh, no.]

"But that's not all. This paper? I watched Sifu Lin make this paper herself. I helped make it, in fact. She told me it's her emergency paper and she only uses it for dead drops like these. I've never seen it actually used before, because of course this is the first dead drop I've had to retrieve. But it signifies a code: Any message she writes on this paper in red ink is supposed to be the opposite."

[Locations too?]

"What? No. That part is correct—she wanted me to know

where she was. But the part about having a lovely time? That's false. She is having an absolutely terrible time somewhere out there on the trail. Following her could be life-threatening. Which matches up with what your receptionist said."

Buck raised his hand. "Sorry tae ask this, but given wot we've heard and now wot ye've seen, wot do ye think are the chances of her still being alive?"

"I . . . I couldn't possibly say. I'm going after her, though, whether you come along or not."

"Can ye say if there are any huge fucking spiders out where we're going?" Buck asked, and Ya-ping shrugged.

"It's Australia, mate. So, yeah, probably."

"I cannae believe I signed up for this," he muttered.

[We're coming with you, of course. What do those lines on the left say, in black ink?]

"Oh. They say to be extremely careful if we follow. That part's true, because it's in black ink. Looks like . . . huh. She used an iridescent! Something glittery in there, a magenta or a lavender sheen when the light catches it. I love when she does that."

[That's showing off.]

Ya-ping flashed a grin. "I know. Isn't it fabulous?" The grin melted away suddenly, and her bottom lip quivered once. "Gods, I hope she's all right."

Our drinks arrived, and the Limeburners was a soft golden color rather than a tawny amber. The bartender suggested a few drops of water to open up the flavors and I agreed, but Buck opted to drink his neat. We made appreciative noises and smiled at the young man to make him go away, and once his back was turned, Buck pointed at his glass and whispered, "I'm gonnay steal the whole bottle. It's the business. Apricotty! And don't ye dare tell me that's no a word, because it bloody well should be."

I shook my head at him.

"We need it for the wizard van, ol' man. Local mojo is important!"

Before I could answer, movement outside the window tore my

eyes away from him. Our table provided us a view of the street, specifically the spaces across the street reserved for taxis, where passengers were regularly disgorged and, I suppose, also gorged. (Or would it be *engorged*? I hope not.) A yellow taxi minivan rolled into one of those spaces, its hue screaming for attention, and I almost looked away, disgusted that my eyes had been drawn so easily to a marketing paint job. But then the sliding passenger door shot open and an enormous grey Irish wolfhound poked his head out and looked both ways before bounding out into the street, assured that no oncoming traffic would be a danger. He woofed once, over his shoulder, apparently sounding the all-clear. I hadn't seen such a smart hound since a peculiar early evening in Rome a few years ago. The hound in that instance had been wearing a curious teardrop-shaped hunk of iron attached to his collar, and . . . this one was too. Could it be the same hound? If so, then someone extraordinary would shortly follow.

I stood, eyes transfixed, and that caused Buck and Ya-ping to turn their heads.

"Wot is it? A huge spider? Aw. Naw, it's just a huge dug."

A smaller dug leapt out behind the wolfhound—a Boston terrier, who almost immediately began a sneezing fit after breathing the air outside the taxi. He hadn't been in Rome, so maybe this wasn't who I thought it was after all. But then a young man in blue jeans and sandals stepped out of the taxi, with a crown of soft wavy red hair and a straight beard falling from his chin; the rest of his face was clean-shaven. He was missing his right arm at the shoulder, his black T-shirt sleeve tied off there, and around his neck he wore a hammered-iron amulet with many silver charms on either side of it. He had a green khaki backpack slung over his left shoulder with a hatchet strapped to it.

"He's actually here," I said aloud, forgetting my speech app.

"Who?" Buck demanded.

"The Iron Druid."

CHAPTER 7

Way Too Many Legs

Buck pointed an outraged pink finger. "That's him? He can destroy me by shakin' ma hand! And ye invited him here!" He stomped a foot on top of the barstool and winced theatrically. "I cannae believe the *gall* ye have sometimes, ol' man!"

"That's him?" Ya-ping said, her nose scrunched up. "I mean, I expected a white guy, but I thought he'd look angrier, like an American complaining to a manager. He looks like a laid-back surfer dude."

[Looks are definitely deceiving in his case. He's more than two thousand years old and he's killed gods.]

"How do I address him?"

[Informally, I'm sure. He doesn't demand honorifics or even his proper name. He prefers to be addressed by a chosen alias. It was Atticus a couple of years ago, but I think he's committed to a new name lately.]

Once across the street, the Iron Druid pointed at a spot near the door and out of the sun, the balcony doing yeoman service there. The dogs obediently trotted to it and sat down, tongues lolling at him. He paused to pet them both briefly, then he moved to the lobby entrance and therefore out of sight until he cleared the walls. It was not long, however, until he appeared in the doorway leading to the front desk and his eyes landed on me. His head cocked to one side, and his jaw dropped then morphed into a grin.

"Al MacBharrais! It really is you! You look great."

"As do you," I said aloud, bowing in greeting.

"It's good to see you again. Wow, it's been a while. Rome, I believe?" He spoke with the same American accent that he had when I met him back then, though it was my understanding he could speak in many different languages and accents.

"Indeed. Welcome, and thank ye for coming. Let me introduce ye tae ma companions briefly, then I'll use ma speech app tae avoid this curse. This is Chen Ya-ping, apprentice to Lin Shu-hua, who is missing. And this is Buck Foi, ma contracted help."

The Iron Druid bowed back and smiled. "Ms. Chen, it is an honor. I go by Connor Molloy these days and ask that you call me Connor."

"Thank you, Connor. The honor is mine. Please call me Ya-ping."

Connor turned to my hobgoblin. "Hello, Buck. It's been a long time since I've met a hobgoblin and it's an honor. I regret the necessity to wear this cold iron—please be careful around my dogs as well, since they are wearing cold iron also. If there's anything I can do to put you at ease, please let me know."

"Just keep yer distance," Buck growled.

The Iron Druid nodded, his lips pressed tightly together, understanding that his very existence raised the hackles of the Fae. "I shall do my best. May I join you—carefully?"

"Of course," Ya-ping said, and I gestured to the seating.

Before moving, he turned his head to check on the clerk at the front desk, to see if she was paying attention.

"Do you think the staff here would mind if I brought my dogs inside? It's kind of hot out."

"If they do mind, I can take care of it with a sigil," I said.

"You can?"

"Sure. Not a problem."

Normally I would inconvenience myself rather than use a Sigil of Certain Authority on someone else, but there was no reason that the dogs should suffer outside in the heat when they didn't need to.

He opened the lobby door and the dogs trotted in, tongues dangling, nails clacking on the floor, and they purposely veered to the left and tried to sit under some chairs out of the way as soon as they were in the bar area. The wolfhound had difficulty getting underneath anything but curled himself into a corner and wagged his tail agreeably.

"The wolfhound is Oberon," Connor said. "He can understand everything you say and answer you, if need be, through me. He says hello to you all and wishes you happiness and sausage."

I grinned at the hound and noticed that sections of his coat were patchy and, in some places, missing, pink skin showing through.

"Hello, Oberon. Are you okay, pal?" I asked. The hound whuffed softly in reply, but Connor provided a full answer.

"Oh, yes. We just came from the east coast, where there were some fires in the Blue Mountains. Ran into a fallen angel there. Oberon saved us, but he got a little toasted. He'll be good as new soon enough."

"Fires, ye say?" Buck asked. When Connor nodded in response, the hobgoblin's eyes shifted to me. "So ye weren't just winding me up with that. Good tae know."

The bartender came over. "Sir? I'm very sorry, but we can't have the dogs in here. It's against health codes." I pulled out my official ID, the piece of goatskin parchment that had three sigils on it. One of them—the Sigil of Porous Mind—might mess with his memory, so I covered it with a finger, leaving only the Sigil of Certain Authority and the Sigil of Quick Compliance visible. It would make him assume that I was an authority figure whose word should be obeyed.

"It's okay for him to have the dogs in here a short while. It's hot outside."

The bartender blinked a few times, then smiled and relaxed. "Of course. Not a problem. Can I get you something to drink, sir?"

"Whatever whisky they're having would be perfect, thanks," Connor said.

We returned to our seats at the long wooden high-top, which had room for six people. Connor sat on one end and Buck purposely chose the seat farthest away and on the other side, standing on the stool and holding his rocks glass protectively in front of him. Ya-ping and I also sat across from the Druid, and I got out my phone to make sure I didn't trigger my curse.

"The Boston terrier is Starbuck," Connor continued, "and he can also understand most everything but is still acquiring language. He also says hello and says you smell like good humans. Except for you, Buck. He says you smell like dead leaves, but I think it's meant as a compliment. You smell like autumn to him, and he likes that."

We all paused to say hello to the dogs and welcome them, and Buck was gracious, telling them they were "good dugs" and he'd steal them something to eat when he could.

[You got here faster than I expected,] I typed into my app, and Connor nodded.

"I was already on my way to this general area when Coriander found me. The local elemental for this part of Gaia felt that something odd was going on around here and thought I should check it out. Since they also felt 'something odd' was going on where we found the fallen angel, I knew it was absolutely necessary to follow up. The elemental's not as sharp as they should be and has trouble being specific; the fires and the extinctions from climate change are seriously affecting their senses. But then Coriander found me on the way here."

[In your taxi?]

"No, we'd stopped to take a break. The dogs needed to say hello to some trees and I just wanted to reconnect to the earth. When I did, I got Coriander's message and he showed up soon afterward, explained to me that you have a situation here and you'd requested my help."

[How'd you know we were at this hotel, though?]

Connor flicked a finger at Buck. "Coriander's watching him."

Buck flinched. "Wot? Coriander is tracking me? Why, that gorgeous luxuriant bastard! I'd kick him in his golden junk if he weren't warded nine ways tae Nancy. I still don't know who Nancy is or why there are nine ways tae her, but ye get ma meaning."

"So you'll help us find Sifu Lin?" Ya-ping asked.

"Sifu . . . ? Forgive me, because I don't wish to assume, Ya-ping, but would you be comfortable catching me up in Mandarin on what's happening?"

They immediately switched to Mandarin and relieved me of having to follow the conversation. Rumor had it the Iron Druid spent more than a century in China during the Tang dynasty and picked up the language there.

As Ya-ping was between us, Buck caught my attention and leaned backward so we could have a conversation without intruding on her thing with the Iron Druid.

"Are we gonnay be leaving soon, then?" he asked. I nodded at him, and he spun a finger around in a circle. "Leaving with all of those iron creatures over there? In the wizard van?" I nodded again. "Awright, then. I call shotgun. Let them sit in the back, away from me." I gave him a thumbs-up, because it was honestly the best solution considering the space we had. We did need to give the Iron Druid plenty of room to make sure there was no incidental contact. The cold iron suffusing his very aura made any contact with him deadly to the Fae. It made him eternally hated by almost every creature in the nine Fae planes, but it also eternally protected him from their magic—and from mine. I hadn't actually tried it yet—and had no plans to try anything—but I was fairly certain my sigils wouldn't work against him. The iron protected him from magic and also divination, so that gods and other magic users couldn't find him. He was, for the most part, magically invulnerable and invisible, and it had kept him from dying by violence. A potion he brewed and called "Immortali-Tea" kept him from dying of age.

Which was not to say he was invincible. His vulnerability was exposed during Ragnarok a bit over a year ago and resulted in the loss of his arm.

"Right, so where's this trail?" Connor said, switching abruptly back to English.

"The trailhead's less than fifteen minutes from here," Ya-ping said. "We have to go the Donnelly Weir picnic area, where the trailhead is. There's a car park there for the van."

Connor raised his nonexistent brows—and I don't mean that in the sense that they were difficult to see in the way that many redheads' eyebrows are, I mean that in the sense that the hair had all been singed off in the fires he'd been fighting in the east. "The van?" he said.

"The wizard van!" Buck exclaimed, raising his fist in the air. "Yeah!"

[Is there anything left to do to make it appropriate for guests?] I asked him. The hobgoblin's eyes widened.

"Oh, bollocks. It's still no ready. Give me ten minutes!" Then he popped from sight.

We were soon on the road, after settling the bar tab. Ya-ping sat next to Connor on the loveseat and chatted as the dogs spread themselves out on the floor. The rear portion of the van was now transformed from an electrician's efficient workspace to a sybaritic lounge lined with black velvet and craft spirits. The overturned bistro table had been righted and furnished with bracketed cupholders for rocks glasses. The walls were draped with black velvet, and the one opposite the loveseat was given over entirely to mounted brackets for displaying whisky—mostly labels from Scotland, though a recently stolen bottle of Limeburners held the central position right above the bistro table. Three battery-operated mini-spotlights were also on the table and pointed in three directions at the bottles, giving the amber liquids a chance to shine and lending the place a rudimentary lighting concept.

Above the loveseat was a framed painting of Nadia's giant wizard lizard, the saddled one from the side of her van, looking somewhat bored without a battle to ride into. How Buck had managed to create that—and indeed the painting on the outside of the van—represented another business opportunity, because art was also an excellent vehicle for money laundering.

Connor spent some time showering Buck with praise for his efforts, and Starbuck asked permission to get up on the loveseat so that Ya-ping could pet him, which Buck allowed and for which he received even more appreciation. The Iron Druid was wise; a hobgoblin who couldn't touch him did not equal a hobgoblin who couldn't mess with him, and reducing Buck's impulse to cause mischief was a good call.

I thought the hobgoblin's mood improved measurably after the flattery. Or maybe it was the salubrious effects of the countryside we were driving through, for despite being rather hot, it was beautiful. We took Donnellys Weir Road, which was little more than a one-lane dirt track through a pastoral landscape quilted with small green pastures and rustic barns.

"Feast yer eyes on all this nature, MacBharrais," Buck breathed in wonder. "It's bucolic as fuck, as they say."

I had never heard anyone say that, ever, but nodded agreeably.

"We've got our share of bucolic scenes in Scotland—there's nothing like a flock of sheep in the Highlands tae turn the bucolic dial up tae eleven—but I'm liking this sunny southern version. Wot's that smell in the air, hey? Kinda minty but no, clears out the sinuses?"

Ya-ping answered from the back. "That's probably eucalyptus."

"The bollocks ye find in cough drops? Aye, that makes sense, then."

We crossed a ford in a creek and continued on until we reached a dirt car park, a rectangle of brown earth surrounded by green. Beyond was a lush space: The ground was covered in moss and grass and low-slung feathery ferns, while tree ferns stood above them like adolescents in a family photo. The adults in this flora portrait were eucalypts and gums mixed in with conifers.

We parked and climbed out of the wizard van, and I noted that there were probably ten cars there with room for ten more, so it wasn't deserted but not crowded either.

As we dragged out our packs full of water, food, and single tents, I noticed that the Iron Druid's hatchet had a Sigil of Cold Fire drawn on it, which would destroy most demons, regardless of size, a few seconds after it touched them. I was about to ask him if he'd drawn that himself, when he relayed a message from the hounds.

"The dogs smell something bad in the wind. Not like dead-body bad, but something weird. Something unnatural."

[Sulfur? As in demons?]

"A bit different. Unsavory, certainly, but not precisely infernal." He scanned the area for danger, but all appeared quiet at the moment. There were some metal posts and a dark-green-painted gate blocking the trail off to motor traffic, but there were walk-throughs for people to get by easily. There were also handy signs with maps on them, pointing out that we'd have a bit of a walk to get to the actual picnic area and weir and, oh, by the way, dogs weren't allowed.

"Not sure what you do to prepare for a scrap, but you might want to have your weapons in easy reach."

I hefted my cane, the end of which was a carbon-steel alloy, and selected a Sigil of Agile Grace from my bush jacket. A chorus of distant screams alerted us that something was indeed amiss.

"I think we should come back for the packs," Connor said, removing his hatchet and returning his pack to the back of the van. We quickly tossed our packs on top of his. "That's the trail-head there?"

Ya-ping nodded. "Yes, where the screams came from." She

withdrew her sai and checked her pockets for sigils; once satisfied, she began drifting toward the trailhead.

"I'll cast camouflage on myself and the dogs and come up on the flank," Connor said, and after speaking a few words in Old Irish, he and his hounds melted from view, taking on the pigments of their surroundings.

"I'll take the other side," Ya-ping called over her shoulder, leaving Buck and me to go up the middle.

We heard more screaming as I reached the trailhead. If it had been just birds chirping—a laughing kookaburra or a pied currawong—it would have been a magical place to meditate and enjoy the wonders of nature. The path from here to the picnic area was easily six feet wide or more, having been bulldozed, I imagined, decades in the past, but it had settled into a comfortable track of pine needles and old leaves and grasses. On either side, messmates, manna gums, and silver wattle trees stood proudly among a medley of cedars and firs. The path curved around to the right and disappeared after a couple hundred meters, and the picnic area and weir waited beyond. The forest around the area was filled with possums, sugar gliders, owls, cockatoos, parrots, and the occasional wallaby. And also, at the moment, pants-ruining terror.

A pair of white women, both blond and splattered with blood, appeared around the bend, crying for help. One of them had a significant limp but was not letting it slow her down; she just moved awkwardly, and I was convinced she'd run on a bloody stump if she had to. Neither carried a pack, which made me wonder if they had gone hiking without one or if they had ditched them back at the picnic area.

"Get out of here!" the lead one said, waving her arms to get my attention as if I simply hadn't seen her yet. Perhaps she thought I was distracted by something else, since I wasn't doing the sensible thing and running away.

She was dressed in those slick fitness tights that had become popular in recent years and wore brightly colored running shoes instead of hiking boots. Her wounded companion was dressed similarly but in a different color palette.

"Whoa—what happened?" I asked. She only slowed down minimally to answer.

"This thing, this creature, this monster—it killed Scott and Keith! It's coming! We have to go, come on! Run!"

I nearly told them to go, but if they had seen an actual monster and there were dead bodies ahead, I needed to contain the situation. I flashed my official ID at them, giving them the full force of its three sigils. "Go get in your car but do not leave the scene. I'll be by shortly to take your statements," I said, and they both nodded and said they'd wait for me, and then they were past.

Something large lumbered into view down the trail, coming around the curve. It was about the size of an elephant but not anything like the shape of one. Buck squinted.

"What in the name of sweet and salty sunburnt bollocks is that? A giant tortoise? Naw—it's got way too many legs."

It did indeed. And, I suspected, it would feature heavily in my nightmares in the coming months.

The thing approaching and picking up speed was a chimera in the classical sense that it was composed of the body parts of several creatures, but the combination of creatures was not classic at all. It was as if someone had grafted the head of a Komodo dragon and the forelegs of a praying mantis onto the chassis of a giant tarantula, except that the abdomen was covered in the armor of a tortoiseshell. All of it was far larger than any of the individual animals would be in nature.

The mantis limbs and the scaly dragon lips were clearly stained with human blood.

I opened that Sigil of Agile Grace and followed up with a Sigil of Muscular Brawn. To my left, perhaps twenty meters away next to a tree fern, Ya-ping was doing the same. The Iron Druid, I assumed, was also busy doing something, though I couldn't see him at all. There was no way to coordinate a strike, so I set myself and provided a target and hoped that Ya-ping and Connor would take advantage and attack from the sides.

"Are we just gonnay stand here like snack food on the shelf?" Buck said.

I chucked my chin at the thing, letting him know he could attack whenever he wanted.

"Ye know I'm still completely exhausted from decorating the wizard van, right? And I'm above the legal blood-alcohol limit besides. I havenae got the oomph for fancy shenanigans. Ye're lucky I'm even here for moral support."

In other words, he would be worthless in this fight, and I sighed.

"The van looks great though, eh? And so does yer mustache. Awright, that's all I have time for, good luck!"

The syncopated footfalls of eight legs coupled with louder hissing was unnerving, to say the least. And an additional vocalization erupted once a hatchet materialized on the right and lodged itself in the tortoiseshell. It didn't sink very deep, but it made a satisfying *thunk* and the creature felt it, giving rise to a tortured ululation and a pivot in that direction to meet the unseen threat. Connor and his hounds, however, wisely chose to remain unseen. Though I couldn't figure out why the shell had been the Iron Druid's choice of target.

But the distraction allowed Ya-ping to approach from the other side unobserved, and perhaps that had been the point. The way she moved made it clear she had been fairly modest about her training, and she was far, far faster than I was. Ah, to be young again!

Her running start and boosted strength allowed her to leap, action-heroine style, at the monstrosity's neck, behind the cocked mantis foreleg. She had the sai blade in her right hand tucked defensively along her forearm, but the left was poised to strike, and she struck, right at the base of the neck, plunging it in as deeply as she could from the side and leaving it there. The creature screamed and shuddered, staggering away from the hit, and before it could turn and locate her, Ya-ping wisely flipped away in another feat of acrobatic prowess. When the creature did turn, it failed to see her at all. But it sure saw me and figured I was eligible to receive all the blame for the pain it was feeling, along with all its wrath and vengeance. It thundered forward, its forelegs ready to strike.

"This is the worst job in the world," Buck muttered behind me, but did absolutely nothing to help.

The dragon head hissed. If it was anything like a real Komodo dragon, the globs of bacteria-filled spittle flying from its mouth would be incredibly dangerous stuff that killed more slowly but no less effectively than venom. If the wounded woman had been bitten at all, she'd need some powerful antibiotics soon.

It had been easy to be cavalier about the situation when the creature was a hundred meters away. It was like watching a cool CGI effect in the movies and saying, *Huh, isn't that something?* But up close, when you can hear it and smell it and see it fill your vision and know in every fiber of your being that it wants to disembowel you and enjoy the feeling of a full belly thanks to your own flesh, it's much different. And Buck may have had an excellent point about the job.

It tried to spear me with a mantis claw, and I batted it away, but just barely. It scratched my arm, tearing through the fabric and tracing a line of fire across the muscle. The dragon head, as I expected, followed up. It just needed a bite, a taste, to infect me, and then it could back off and consume me later when I eventually succumbed to fever and convulsions. But I whipped my cane back and caught it on the snout, and the reaction to that was much more severe than I thought the blow warranted. It wasn't a home-run swing, and it didn't have the sort of force one might consider a mortal blow, but the monster screeched and recoiled and began to steam, then smoke. It crisped and flash-fried, the entire bulk turning to ash and crumbling into a rather large pile of greasy dust. Ya-ping's sai and Connor's hatchet fell into the midst of it.

"Gods damn it, ol' man," Buck cried, "ye said the spiders here were *my* size!"

[I'm no expert, but I'm pretty sure that wasn't a native species.]

"Granted, but I'd still say ye undersold the spiders by orders of magnitude. That thing was the weight class of a bulldozer."

Connor and his dogs dropped their camouflage and appeared on our right.

"That wasn't a demon, Al," he said. "It didn't die from the Cold Fire on my hatchet. It died from iron. The tiny bit from my hatchet blade just annoyed it, but you two did the real damage, between Ya-ping's sai and your cane. Do you have sigils on those?"

"The Sigil of Iron Gall, yes," Ya-ping said. It accelerated iron poisoning in magical creatures. It was painted on my cane as well.

"Which means that thing—that turtle dragon spider—wasn't infernal. It was Fae."

I nodded in agreement, and Buck said aloud what I was thinking, getting faster and more manic as his adrenaline worked itself out.

"Now, I'm no census taker, mind, but I've never seen anything like that in Tír na nÓg. I mean, I've never seen anything like that *anywhere* without hallucinogens, on the kind of nights ye're wearin' incontinence trousers 'cause ye expect tae piss yerself before it's over. That wasnae the product of a furious faery hump 'n' pump, ye know what I'm sayin'? Unless there's some kinky shagging going on in one of the planes I don't know about. How does a thing like that even get born? What came first, the turtle dragon spider or the egg?"

Connor shook his head. "I'm not familiar with this either. The Dagda created many unusual Fae creatures but nothing that resembled such an organic scrapyard. There are layers of strangeness here. I haven't seen a chimera like this on earth since ancient days."

"If that's the sort of thing we can expect," Ya-ping said to me, "it's no wonder Sifu Lin warned of extreme danger. I hope she's okay."

[I need to make the witnesses forget this and heal at least one of them. Then we should get to the picnic area. This is going to be a containment issue.]

It was indeed an issue. Because while we had been dealing with the turtle dragon spider, the two women who'd lost Scott and Keith had been calling authorities on their cell phones and screaming about dead people at the Donnelly Weir picnic area. Dead bodies in a public place attract attention, and not just from police. The media love to report such things.

They had dutifully waited in the car for me to "take their statement," but I had forgotten to instruct them not to call anyone, so it was really my fault. The uninjured one was in the driver's seat with the window rolled down and was shouting at someone on the phone. "It was a wild animal! I don't know, but it was huge! And it just tore them apart! Send someone to help now! My friend needs an ambulance!"

I winced in dismay. She was smart and hadn't said the word *monster,* so that was going to mobilize a response. A large part of my job was not only making sure that the proverbial monsters stayed away but that their very existence could be easily dismissed and disbelieved by modern society. Getting police and media involved would make that difficult. There were ten cars in the lot, and that probably meant twenty people out there at minimum, if one assumed that no one went hiking solo, and perhaps more. If any of them were alive, they'd need to remember nothing, and if they weren't alive, they'd need to disappear, unfortunately. We couldn't have forensic investigation reveal an unnatural cause of death and unknown DNA—though I suppose, in this case, the DNA would reveal known animals. Just in combinations that should be impossible.

The injured woman did need an ambulance. She was sweating and trembling in the passenger seat, her hands curled into fists.

I pulled out my official ID and showed it to the driver again, letting the sigils work. "Ma'am, I need you to hang up and give me your phone."

She blinked. "Of course." She thumbed the call off and handed it over.

"Thanks. Did your friend get bitten?"

"Yes. Right on the bum."

"Okay. Wait a minute and I'll take care of it."

It was a good thing she was still conscious. I walked around to the passenger side and got her phone too, then had her look at a Sigil of Knit Flesh and another of Restorative Care. She sighed in relief as the pain eased. She'd nod off soon and her infection would subside, for the most part—though a follow-up with a doctor would be wise. But getting them out of there and not bringing any more people to the scene would require some stronger measures.

The Sigil of Lethe River is reserved for people who need to forget what they've seen. It basically attacks recent neural connections in the brain, making the person lose the events of the last hour. I don't like to use it, because sometimes very important things that need to be remembered get wiped out with the things that need to be forgotten. But in this case, I really needed Shouting Woman and Injured Bum to forget that they'd seen Scott and Keith get killed by a turtle dragon spider. They would, no doubt, endure an agony of not knowing what happened to their beaus, and I wished I knew how to fix that too, but at least I could save them from nightmares and possibly psychiatric evaluation.

Once both of them had a gander at those sigils, I pulled out my official ID once more and gave them some more instructions while they were open to suggestion. "Go home and get some rest. Get some new phones later, and don't worry about Scott and Keith. They're fine, wherever they are. And see a doctor about your injury."

They nodded, thoroughly confused about how they'd gotten to their vehicle and how one of them had sustained a bite on the arse, but they mumbled thanks and left the car park. I met up with the others at the back of the wizard van and handed the phones to Buck.

"Why ye giving me these?"

[Destroy them,] I said. [We can't have them traced or their data recovered.]

"I can unbind the interior components if you want," Connor volunteered. "Turn it all into a molecular slurry. The cases can remain intact and you can just toss them in the bin that way."

"Ye can do that?" my hobgoblin said.

"Sure."

Buck tossed them to him, one by one, and he spent perhaps thirty seconds just staring at them, though we heard muffled pops and hissing from inside the phones as the silicon and other metals melted and re-formed into a mess.

[So you still have most of your powers, obviously,] I said. I'd been curious about that, since the tattoos on a Druid's right side were bindings to the earth that allowed him or her to perform their duties. Losing his arm, therefore, meant losing some of his magical abilities.

"Oh, aye," he said, with a tiny grin. "Losing the arm was not nearly as bad as I thought it was at first. I can't shape-shift any-more and I can't travel the planes, and my ability to heal myself and others requires the help of the local elemental, but all the binding and unbinding remains intact. I'm lucky to still be here, frankly."

My sigils of strength and agility wore off at that point and I felt all my years again. Connor noticed, perhaps because my shoulders slumped perceptibly or the corners of my mouth drooped a little.

"Coming down from the juice is never fun, eh? But I think it's good to be reminded of our limitations. Keeps us humble." His head turned toward Oberon, the wolfhound, who obviously had something to say about that. "That's right, Oberon, you have nothing to be humble about. You are magnificent."

He tossed the phones back to Buck so that his hand would be free to pet Oberon. Starbuck danced around, wanting his share of attention, and Ya-ping said, "I'll pet you, Starbuck. You are magnificent too." The Boston trotted over to her and she gave him some scritches while Buck shook his head and turned to find a bin for the phones.

"If ye ever try tae pet me, MacBharrais, I'll punch yer stones up intae yer pelvis."

CHAPTER 8

The Case of the Abandoned Cheese

We had hoped to get moving quickly, but the raised alarm meant that we had to deal with arriving emergency vehicles, and that delayed us somewhat. I had Ya-ping practice on the ambulance, which arrived first, and she deployed the Sigil of Certain Authority very well and got them turned around. The police followed up soon after and were a bit tougher to convince that there was nothing for them to do there. They required a Sigil of Porous Mind to weaken their resolve and a Sigil of Quick Compliance to shut down higher cerebral function and open them to accepting just about any suggestion that wouldn't harm them; then Certain Authority could do its work.

Once Ya-ping got the police turned around, I typed, [You might wish to make an ID like mine with all three sigils on it and just hit them at the same time. The specially treated goatskin preserves potency when there's no target, so it remains useful for weeks or even months.]

"I've asked Sifu Lin before, but I'll ask you too: Why do they resist it so much?"

[Police tend to see themselves as the authority in most situations—and they are. And in your case, unfortunately, you're also fighting against your perceived age, in addition to whatever misogyny and racism lives in their hearts. It's going to be more difficult for them to accept you as an authority.]

A corner of her mouth quirked up, and I realized I'd just been tested.

[Did I get that right?]

"You mean the sigils would work better if I were an old white guy."

[Yes.] It was a sad and unfortunate truth.

"Good. I'm glad you're aware."

We needed to check the picnic ground but couldn't leave the car park unattended, so I left her my official ID to deal with any new arrivals while we were investigating. The Iron Druid went ahead with his dogs to check things out, but there was only carnage awaiting us.

Scott and Keith were easily found near the picnic-grounds rotunda: white males in their twenties, bodies pierced by mantis claws and partially gnawed on and undergoing further chewing by some carrion birds attracted by the blood. There were two other bodies as well, presumably an unrelated couple whose car would be waiting in the car park. Their picnic basket was undisturbed, except that their bottle of wine had spilled.

"Oberon and Starbuck, will you scout the perimeter and see if you can find out which direction the turtle dragon spider came from? But don't leave my sight—and if you smell or hear any more coming, let me know."

The dogs immediately fanned out and began to circle the area, noses to the green. It would be a beautiful area if it weren't for the bloody murder in the middle of it. Next to the picnic ground, Donnellys Creek fell over the low wall of the weir and exhaled a misty breath of white noise, and below that it chuckled over what great fun it was to have had that small adventure as it ran under a wooden pedestrian bridge. The air smelled of eucalyptus and the copper-penny tang of blood, though Buck picked up something else.

"I smell cheese. Abandoned cheese, MacBharrais, that needs tae be loved again."

He was looking at the couple's picnic basket, and I typed furiously.

[Don't you dare.]

"Wot? There's no sense in letting it go tae waste."

[We can't have anyone find the bodies, but their families need to assume the worst. Abandoned cheese will send the signal that something terrible happened and might provide closure. Don't take that away from them.]

The hobgoblin hunkered down and considered. "Huh. I would never have thought about it that way, but I think ye may be right, ol' man. Abandoned cheese is a sure sign that something's gone wrong. Like, it's so obvious ye would think it would be a clue in all the detective shows. An unseasoned constable sees a scene like this and suggests it might be a suicide pact, and then the detective walks in—it's you, MacBharrais—and he twirls his luxuriant mustache. *If it was a suicide, Constable, then why would they pack expensive cheese and no eat it? Naw, that's abandoned cheese, so it is, and that means it was murder!* And then ye would squeeze it, sniff it, and tell him it feels soft and smells funky, like his maw."

[I would not!]

The dogs reported that the monstrosity had indeed come from the direction of the Mount St. Leonard trail, so we had confirmation that the bad business was that way. But we still had a huge mess on our hands, which Buck pointed out.

"What are we gonnay do about them?"

"We'll hide them for now," Connor said, even though the question hadn't been directed at him, "and when the threat is taken care of, we can reveal their location and the families can have a proper farewell."

Buck raised his furry caterpillar eyebrows. "MacBharrais just said we cannae ever let them be found."

"That would be the right call if I weren't here," Connor said. "I can do some unbinding, though, remove the weird trace evidence that might point to a supernatural cause of death. It's still going to look weird—there will be investigations and so on—but no chimeric DNA." I nodded agreement, and then he added, "I'll need your help, though. Can you two bring the bodies up over there for me, away from the high-traffic area? I'll make a grave."

I nodded at him and turned to the bodies of Scott and Keith— I had no idea which was which without checking for ID, but if they had that on them, I was going to leave it for easier identification later. They both curiously looked like a lead singer from a rock band my son liked—American chaps, I believed, called Foo Fighters. They had dark hair, narrow faces, and goatees framing their mouths.

My hobgoblin sidled up to me and said in a low tone, "MacBharrais, what exactly do ye think I can do here? I'm no a muscle-bound ogre. I'm a wee hobgoblin."

[I'll take the head and you just keep the heels from dragging on the ground.]

"Can I just cheer ye on? I don't wannay get ma fine new clothes dirty, and I can be tremendously encouraging when I put ma mind tae it."

[It had better be legendary encouragement.]

And that is how I came to drag four bloody corpses about twenty meters while a hobgoblin complimented my extraordinary musculature and said, if only I'd take my shirt off, he could sell tickets to Aussies who'd line up to slather my ancient yet chiseled carcass in baby oil.

"Listen, MacBharrais: Glisten. That's where the money is. Niche markets are like shy veins of gold, but they can run deep, and I'm telling ye, photo ops with glistening old men are a niche that's about tae be golden in a big way, and it all starts today with yer oiled-up pecs. Now, I know we don't have any baby oil with us, but I could catch a trout in the creek and give ye a rub with it, how would that be? Ye would have the fish oil coating yer bod, see, all o' those omega-three fatty acids on yer nipples, and maybe some scales too, and they'd sparkle in the sun. People would call ye 'Fish-Tits MacBharrais' and ye never know, ye might even get famous for it in America, because I hear the Yanks are mad for tits."

Connor was doing a very poor job trying to disguise his laughter. But what he had done, with the help of the elemental, was roll back a six-foot-wide strip of turf, and then the earth underneath it compressed and deepened about three feet. I placed the dead in there, then Connor rolled back the turf, and the ground looked entirely undisturbed.

"It's kinda scary how well ye can hide a body," Buck observed.

"I've had more practice than I would like," Connor admitted, all mirth leaving his face. I felt mine falling too. It was a grim thing to see innocent life mown down like that, to think that those young men had been happy perhaps an hour ago, out with their girlfriends for a picnic in a pretty spot, and now they were dead. And there was a precipice overlooking a vast chasm of guilt too, and it began with *If only I'd* . . . Been faster. Shaved ten minutes off our time somehow and gotten here earlier. Felt more urgency than I already did. Then maybe those two men wouldn't be lying in a shallow grave.

But, like the Spanish Inquisition, *nobody* expects a turtle dragon spider.

Time was slipping away from us, midafternoon creeping toward the evening, and we still hadn't gotten on the trail yet. When we realized it was nearing five P.M. and no one else had come to enjoy the park for a while, we decided to gamble that no further hikers would arrive today. The nine cars remaining in the car park (besides our wizard van) suggested that there would be a terrible sight to behold on the trail, and we needed to get going. If one belonged to the pair who'd abandoned their cheese, and if another belonged to Scott or Keith, that was still seven cars and a minimum of seven people out there, but likely more.

Ya-ping had identified one of the cars as Shu-hua's and another as Sara's, which took the number of unaccounted-for vehicles down to five.

Ya-ping was visibly relieved to get on the trail. She set a rather quick pace, in fact, which had Buck complaining before long, as he had to break into a jog to keep up.

"Ye all have legs that are longer than ma whole body," he pointed out. "I should have stolen a motor scooter for this."

He was given a break after a kilometer or so when we discovered three more victims of the turtle dragon spider. A middle-aged married couple, judging by their matching wedding bands, lay sprawled on the path with their entrails yanked from their torsos; perhaps a hundred meters farther along was a younger man, dressed in the uniform of a park ranger. I mentally revised the number of mystery cars down to three, assuming that the ranger and the hikers accounted for two cars in the park.

Burying them, erasing evidence, and erecting small cairns to mark the spots for later took us past six, and the sun was flirting with the horizon. Ya-ping was mildly revolted by the proceedings but much more worried about her master and anxious to keep going.

[Any of these people might be missed,] I said, [but it depends if they told anyone where they were going. The park ranger will definitely be missed and looked for, because his colleagues would know he was out here and will miss him checking in either tonight or tomorrow morning.]

"I should have fetched the dead drop earlier. I should have called you earlier," Ya-ping said, her bottom lip quivering. She'd just witnessed some horror-movie levels of gore, and that wasn't common to the lived experience of people in Glen Waverley. She was looking over that Grand Canyon of *if only* that I'd been gazing into some minutes before and feeling the same doubts and guilt.

[Nonsense,] I told her. [You acted precisely as you should have. If you'd called too early and she proved to be fine, I imagine you would have been scolded for being alarmist.]

"But what if that thing—or some other things—tore her up and left her like these others? Or if she's trapped and needs help?"

[We can only hope we reach her in time.]

Unfortunately, another five hundred meters brought us to another pair of deaths. That one creature had been stupendously destructive. And after burying them in their turn, we were past seven and the light was waning. In theory we could have kept going, with sigils for night vision, but it had been an extraordinarily long day for Buck and me, since we'd begun it around our bedtime in Scotland. We agreed that we'd need to camp for the night and trudged another couple of hundred meters, worried that we'd find more bodies, but we instead found a nice level stretch where we could pitch tents.

Ya-ping got out her mozzy gear, but Connor waved that off. "Don't worry about that stuff. I've got you covered."

"How so?"

"I've asked the elemental to keep insects and spiders away from us. Small perk of traveling with a Druid."

"That trick only works on regular spiders, then? Not turtle dragon spiders?" she said.

Connor snorted. "No, they're Fae. We'll have to deal with them ourselves."

"Can ye sense any of the normal spiders around here?" Buck asked.

"Sure, if I wanted to have the elemental find them for me."

"Do ye know if any of them are as big as me?"

"Well, not quite. Huntsman spiders can get to be about half your size. Don't worry, none will bother you."

My hobgoblin looked up at me. "Ye've been telling tall tales, ol' man, and now they've come up a bit short. But I'm relieved. Ye had me worried that Australia was gonnay kill me. All I have tae do now is worry about unnatural causes of death, and I can most likely push you in front of the jaws first."

CHAPTER 9

A Campfire Story

Connor had a bedroll but no tent, since he never worried about the elements or things nibbling on him in the night. He was able to finish his preparations quickly and build a small campfire for us as we got our tents set up. With the elemental's help, he also managed to get some decent-sized boulders to scoot across the earth and arrange themselves in a circle, creating quite the comfortable campground for us.

We had nothing to cook, just prepacked meals that required no heat, so the campfire was for comfort, Connor said. Ya-ping didn't appear very comforted by it, but she did appreciate Starbuck jumping into her lap for pets.

Connor idly petted Oberon, who was curled up at his feet, and said that our current travails brought to mind echoes of days long past.

[How long past, exactly?] I asked.

"Long enough that I wasn't the Iron Druid yet. I was just a Druid who'd managed to live longer than he should have. It was two thousand years ago, or close enough to make no never mind."

Oberon woofed softly and wagged his tail, and Connor grinned.

"Yes, Oberon, it's story time." He looked around at us. "That is, if you're all in the mood for one."

We all nodded at him and he smiled.

"So be it."

 I left Ireland and came to the European continent in the first century of the Common Era. I was on the run from a fraternity of Irish gods because I'd stolen an enchanted sword they wanted to keep in Ireland. Every day I remained alive was a victory—and that's still true, honestly. But it was also true for everyone living at that time, because scraping out an existence was difficult. Gods, the air was so clean and easy to breathe back then. But everything else was hard. Life expectancy was low to begin with, due to malnutrition and disease, but a violent death could come at any time. Anyone could come through and put you to the sword or simply steal the food you were depending on to survive the winter. The Romans could come calling, and that was never good, because you'd always be poorer for the visit. You'd be robbed at minimum, even if they called it a tribute, but there was also a good chance you'd wind up being enslaved or killed. They called themselves civilized and everyone else barbarians. I wound up either avoiding them or fighting them until they fell, since vampires were the true power behind that empire. And if they didn't get you—or any other band of bastards that thought might made right—you could step into the wrong bog or forest and disappear into the belly of some monster or else some god or demon. Lots of lives ended too soon that way. It was still largely a pagan time, and many gods remained active across the earth. The veil between the planes was thin and easily passed through by all manner of entities.

I lived for a time with a tribe called the Chauci, who were settled near the Elbe River in what is modern-day Hamburg, Germany. They were eventually assimilated into the Saxons, but at that time they were sea raiders along the coast and cattle farmers in the interior—farming and raiding were the two main paths to prosperity, each with its own set of risks. If you farmed, you had to worry about protecting your crop, because raiders would try to take it. If you raided, you had to worry about well-defended farms. My own father, in fact, lost his life trying to raid another village. It was the way of things. And pretty much everyone tried to avoid the forests where possible; people too often disappeared. There were wolves, witches, wizards, and all manner of dangers hiding in the trees. These were not things that I feared, but I pretended to so that no one would think that *I* was to be feared.

I was already a stranger and didn't speak their language fluently and was barely tolerated. Only the facts that I could hunt well, shared my kills generously, and seemed to have a knack for taming horses allowed me a place among them. Even so, I farmed a plot far away from prying eyes, near a dark forest, where I could remain a harmless curiosity and hopefully avoid any village drama.

The village drama, alas, did not avoid me.

There was a single inn, and when I say *inn* I mean a slightly larger-than-normal lodge with a slightly larger-than-normal hearth and exactly one beer on tap. The menu was always stew and a hunk of bread, and while the quality and ingredients of the stew varied, the bread was always good. I ingratiated myself with the owner, Gebhart, by bringing him some herbs I'd grown to throw into his stews. He got such rave reviews for adding actual flavors to his cooking that he asked me for more, and gradually it spread throughout the village that I knew how to make one's sad vegetables taste less miserable.

Gebhart was a stout man in his mid-thirties with a bushy black beard going prematurely grey—he'd already lived longer than his own father had and counted himself as having lived a full life. He had a younger wife, named Gerlind, tall and pale and widely considered to be the beauty of the region. She was the one who baked the excellent bread and also looked after their children while Gebhart looked after customers.

Several men of the village, unfortunately, looked after Gerlind whenever she passed by, their eyes lingering longer than they should, and I noted them. One in particular was Behrtoald, who made little effort to disguise his lust. He made lewd jokes and suggestions to Gerlind, and for some while she attempted to laugh these off. Then she stopped laughing and told him it wasn't appropriate, and he laughed off her reaction. Eventually, however, he pushed it too far, and I was there to see it happen. I didn't understand exactly what he said to her as she passed by his table, but she whirled on him and shouted immediately for Gebhart. She repeated what Behrtoald had said, pointed to everyone in the room as witnesses, and demanded that he be banned forevermore from setting foot in the inn. Gebhart, of course, issued the decree, and Behrtoald's attempt to apologize was shouted down. He was escorted out rather forcefully by a trio of men, including Gebhart, and told never to return. And since Gebhart's inn was the only gathering place for literal miles, he'd essentially been cut off from the town's social life. I heard him cursing outside for a good while, but eventually he quieted and went home.

A few days later, Gebhart was at my home. He was taking a day off, as he occasionally did, to get out and enjoy some time for himself. He liked to hunt, and I'd told him there was good hunting in the woods behind my place, and he wanted to see my farm in any case. We had a nice visit in the morning, and then I sent him off with some suggestions while I worked in my fields.

About an hour later, a distant whinny caused me to turn my head from my fields to the sound, trying to spot the source, and I spied a cloaked figure on a horse entering the woods. I couldn't tell who it was and didn't recognize the horse either—it was only the rear view, after all. At first I didn't think much of it, because hunting in the woods was pretty common, but solitary hunters were less so. It gnawed at me, though, because with two solitary hunters in a forest, accidents could happen. And then, remembering the events of a few days before, it occurred to me that maybe it wasn't a coincidence after all. I began to worry: What if that rider had been Behrtoald, and the prey he was hunting was Gebhart?

I needed to check. I could do so fairly quickly, but I was paranoid about being seen, so I opened the back door, ran into my house, and shape-shifted into a wolfhound. I shot out into the forest from there, hopefully unseen, and quickly picked up the scent of Gebhart, who had left from the same place. I followed his trail, which angled a bit to the west, snuffling and noticing how the forest was either unnaturally quiet or else pierced by the warning calls of birds and squirrels.

I found Gebhart's body ten minutes later. He'd shot a stag and had just begun to dress his kill when someone shot him in the back. He was slumped over the stag, a small ragged hole between his shoulder blades that suggested an arrow, because the wound was too small for a spear and the edges too torn for a stabbing. I thought it rather brazen, because it was quite clearly murder and no accident, and no effort had been made to hide the body.

A chill shook me as I peered ahead into the future and saw a cold fact waiting for me; I was going to be blamed for this. The rumor would be that the strange foreigner who lived near these woods must have done it.

The murderer had to have left his own trail, however, and a little bit of casting about allowed me to pick it up. I'd come back for Gebhart's body later—I didn't want to lose my chance of finding the murderer.

It was only another ten minutes before the cloaked rider came into view. He was heading back toward the village and whistling tunelessly, if happily, and his bow and quiver were plainly visible. I cast camouflage on myself so I could draw alongside without being seen. The horse nickered nervously, picking up my scent, but the man astride the horse didn't react.

He was grinning, supremely pleased with himself. It was Behrtoald, as I'd feared.

I couldn't know exactly how he planned to make it work, but it was not difficult to assume that he would somehow lay Gebhart's death at my feet and then make a play for Gerlind.

I wasn't going to let him do either.

I reversed course and sped back to my farm. Once inside the house, I shifted to human and got dressed, strapping on my sword just in case. Then I got on my horse and used all the juice from the earth that I could to boost its speed, hoping to beat Behrtoald back to the inn.

Victory was mine by perhaps thirty seconds. I actually galloped past Behrtoald on the outskirts, and he belatedly realized who had passed him, where I was going, and what was at stake. But being first through the door made a whole lot of difference. My grasp of the language wasn't great, but I did manage to shout, "Gebhart dead! Behrtoald kill! I see him!"

That last part was a lie—I hadn't actually seen him kill Gebhart. But I'd seen him enter the forest after Gebhart and exit a while later with nothing to show for his journey but a smug smile. And I'd tracked him by scent, of course, from Gebhart's corpse, but I could hardly tell them that.

Then Behrtoald crashed in, obviously ignoring the fact that he'd been banned. He pointed at me and said, "He killed Gebhart!"

At that point there was a lot of shouting and determination to get to the bottom of this. The relevant information to Gerlind, of course, was not so much who did it as the fact that it had been done: Her husband was dead. While the people shouted, she came to me, quietly, and asked what happened.

"Gebhart come to hunt by my house," I said brokenly. "He go. Behrtoald go after him later. I worry and go too. Find Gebhart dead, shot in back."

"He's still there? In the forest?"

"Yes. I can show."

So a large portion of the adults in the village were soon on the road toward the forest. Some of them had already made up their minds as to who had done it, and I was worried that it wouldn't end well for me. I was still an outsider, and though Behrtoald was not well liked, he had a much better grasp of the language and was trusted more, simply because he was one of the tribe.

They tried to take my sword but curiously found that it was stuck firm in its scabbard and they couldn't remove it. I had bound it magically to prevent its removal, so they settled for tying my hands at the wrists once I got on my horse. Behrtoald was tied up too, his weapons removed, and we formed a group of about twenty men and five women out to recover Gebhard and figure out what exactly had happened. Behrtoald had either thrown away the arrow he'd used, somewhere along the trail, or fastidiously cleaned it before replacing it; they could not find a "smoking arrow" solution to the mystery.

I was not actually afraid for my life. I could unbind the ropes around my wrists at any time. I could communicate to all the horses and ask them to throw off their riders, leaving me a clear path to escape. I could cast camouflage and simply disappear. But that would mean that I'd lose everything I'd worked on for months, and I'd have to start over somewhere else. It would be a lean winter for me. Plus, I really didn't want Behrtoald to get away with it.

Neither did Gebhart, it turned out.

Once we entered the forest and the sunlight was obscured by the canopy of leaves, the temperature dropped significantly, which was expected, but it was by far more than ten degrees, which was very much unexpected. Our breath suddenly steamed out of our mouths, even though it was summer. We had entered an uncommonly frigid pocket of air, and I knew right away it wasn't natural. The others suspected but had their suspicions confirmed moments later, when an unholy roar erupted ahead and the horses startled.

A man's body—Gebhart's, in fact—with a stag's head charged at us. Some of the men who had their bows strung were able to get off a shot, and arrows thunked into the torso and remained there but caused no visible distress. The creature kept coming, snorting, grunting, and because of the way we'd been surrounded by the others, preventing our escape, Behrtoald and I were helpless to get out of its path.

It was what the Germans call a wiedergänger, a revenant, dead tissue animated by an angry spirit.

The vast majority of the time—more than 99 percent of it, I'd wager—spirits move on to wherever they're supposed to go when they're severed from their mortal coil. But sometimes, in traumatic circumstances, the spirits either can't or simply won't move on. And in those days, when people believed widely in ghosts and vengeful spirits, you tended to have a lot more of both, since people devoted so much of their belief to that reality. That collective belief *made* it real. So when Gebhart was ambushed and shot in the back, his spirit wanted nothing more than to meet his murderer face to, well . . . face, I guess.

The villagers who were crowded in front of us parted before the wiedergänger just in time to clear its path to us. We still could not move well to either side or backward, however. I very nearly took my chances by sliding off the saddle, but I realized that the stag's eyes were focused solely on Behrtoald, so I stayed where I was.

Behrtoald began to scream as he realized the enormity of what was happening. It was a reckoning, and there was no escape. He may have cried for help or uttered a prayer to his gods, I'm not sure—it was unintelligible terror.

He tried to goad his horse into charging the wiedergänger and got dumped on the ground for his efforts.

"No!" he cried—that much I understood—and then Gebhart seized him and yanked him to his feet. He bellowed his fury at Behrtoald, the murderer quailed and struggled to break free of an implacable grip, and then the stag lowered its head and very purposely thrust one of its antlers through Behrtoald's screaming gob and right up into his brain. We all heard the crunch and squish, the screaming ceased, and Behrtoald's body twitched, dangling on the end of an antler. The wiedergänger roared once more, whipped its head down and to the left, effectively flinging Behrtoald's corpse to the ground, and stood there staring at him with clenched fists. The stag's head jerked up only when Gerlind said, "Gebhart?" in a quavering voice.

The creature groaned and reached out a hand. She dismounted and went to him, crying, and someone tried to stop her, to warn her away. She brushed past them. Both arms were open for an embrace, and when she hugged him, fitting herself between the shafts of arrows sticking out of his torso, the stag head groaned once more, rested its head on her shoulder, and then all the strength left the body. The arms fell slack, the knees buckled, and Gebhart's revenant fell to the ground. When it hit, the stag's head disengaged from the neck, though it was a bloodless affair.

"Spirit gone," I said, and Gerlind wept. I hoped Gebhart's spirit went somewhere pleasant after it spent its rage, but I had little idea of what afterlives the Chauci imagined for themselves.

The villagers were pretty confident I hadn't murdered Gebhart, though, based on the witness of the revenant, so my bonds were cut and we put Gebhart's body on Behrtoald's horse, leaving the murderer where he lay. I led them to the murder scene, where we found Gebhart's head and the stag's body, along with Gebhart's bloody knife on the ground. (I didn't want to think too hard about how or why Gebhart's spirit would cut off his own head and replace it with a stag's, but perhaps it made some sense to the Chauci.) We had to shoo away some foxes, but thankfully the wolves hadn't arrived yet.

After Gebhart was laid to rest, I stayed in the area just long enough to bring in my harvest, sell most of it, and pack up a wagon for the winter. I headed upriver and settled with the Semnones—or the Juthungi, depending on who's writing the history—and remained with them long enough to absorb that language, a precursor to Old High German and maybe even Low German. They had a grove-based religion and I scrupulously avoided their ceremonies, for I knew they worshipped some god other than the ones I was used to, and powerful things could happen in a grove like that.

I knew that even without a grove—with just the love and will of a single man—extraordinary things could happen. Sometimes, the dead don't stay dead.

"To this day," Connor finished, "outside of vampires, that episode remains the only case of the dead avenging themselves that I've ever seen, though it's not the only case I've heard of."

We turned in for the evening, a bit unsure why he'd shared that with us. Usually there is a story behind the storytelling. Did he want us to think of vengeance or think of the dead coming back to life? Did we need to worry about Scott and Keith or the others?

It was too much for me to figure out. My brain felt fuzzy, since I'd been awake at that point for close to forty hours straight. With Connor assuring us we could sleep without fear, I drifted off to the sound of frogs and crickets.

CHAPTER 10

Two in the Bush

We woke at dawn on Tuesday thanks to unidentified bird-calls, and I had really needed that sleep. My joints creaked and complained, the sort of omnipresent agony that crept up on one with age, even when in fairly decent shape. Progressive cellular decay, as they say, is a wee slice of hell every day.

The bush off the trail afforded us a modicum of privacy for morning ablutions, and our breakfast was a quick and raw affair composed of trail mix and water. We packed up and got moving as quickly as possible, since we all felt the urgency of finding Mei-ling and Shu-hua.

The trail remained wide and easy to follow, occasionally intersecting with others but steadily climbing toward Mount St. Leonard. The bush underneath the trees was a mixture of ferns and thorny berry bushes, with lots of fallen eucalypts providing fodder for carpenter ants and shelter for normal-sized spiders and so on. There were snakes out there, though, Ya-ping warned me, the unfriendly kind. Brown snakes and tiger snakes and copperheads, all of which could ruin your day or maybe end your life.

We'd been climbing long enough to get mildly winded and were nearing the Mount St. Leonard summit when a mixed group of authorities caught up to us. There were six in total; two of them were mounted police on beautiful black horses, and four were in bright-orange jumpsuits with reflective yellow hazard stripes on them and caps with a checkerboard pattern reminiscent of those of constables in the UK. These last were riding two-seater four-wheeled all-terrain vehicles, so we heard them coming well in advance of seeing them. We moved over to let them pass, but they hailed us as soon as they came into view, and it looked like we were going to have a meeting.

[Who are the orange folks?] I asked Ya-ping while we waited for them to catch up.

"That's the Victoria SES. State Emergency Service. They coordinate with law enforcement and other agencies on all kinds of things like fires and earthquakes and so on, but they also help out tremendously in missing-persons cases. Which is probably why they're here."

[Yes. The missing park ranger, no doubt, and all the others. What's the top federal security agency here? Who'd boss around the SES and the local police?]

"AFP. Australian Federal Police."

"G'day," the first mounted police officer said to us. He was a tanned white fellow wearing mirror sunglasses, his muscles straining at his shirt and the cut of his jaw so sharp it probably wounded the air. "Very sorry, folks, but the trail's closed. We need you to head back and hike here another day."

"Oh?" Connor said. "We didn't see any signs saying the trail's closed."

"Closing it now. We're getting reports of dangerous conditions ahead and some people have gone missing, so we don't want you to go missing too. In fact"—he twisted in his saddle to look at the SES folks—"can one or two of you escort them back and make sure they get out of here okay?"

"Sure," one of the orange-clad people said, and hopped off the back seat of the two-seater ATV. He was a rangy lad with blond sandpapery stubble on his face; a patch sewn on his chest declared him to be RORY. He gestured to the person on the back of the other vehicle and we suddenly had two escorts to lead us out of the park.

"Thanks," the police officer said. Squinting at his name badge, I caught the surname of CAMPBELL. The other officer, also a white man, had a badge that read BASKIN. The badges of the ATV drivers read MARCUS and THEA. Campbell turned back to us and said, "Sorry again, everybody. Just want to make sure you stay safe today. You can come back another time to enjoy this area. And the dogs aren't allowed, honestly, so leave them home next time."

Ya-ping and Connor looked at me and I nodded agreeably, going along. Six people were far too many to try to sway all at once. I could get one or two, but the others would catch on that they shouldn't look at my ID badge or they'd suddenly change their mission priorities based entirely on my unqualified say-so. Even if they did look at my badge, they'd be warned against it and resistant. And, in truth, I didn't get a chance, because the officers and ATV drivers surprised me and advanced along the trail, clearly in a hurry, leaving us with Rory and the other SES volunteer, whose name badge announced her to be CHERISE. She was a Black woman who smiled at us very briefly, because she wasn't really interested in us at all.

"I know they're not supposed to be here, right, but I love your dogs." Her grin widened as she waved at Starbuck and said, a couple of octaves higher, "Hello, cutie! You're such a good boy! Yes, you are."

We all turned our backs on the trail ahead to make it appear like we were going to go with them, but after a few steps I pulled out my official ID and showed it to them, deploying a fake name.

"I'm Al Henshaw with the AFP. There is indeed a serious situation up ahead, and my colleagues and I are all undercover. We'll take care of it. We have resources incoming, and this needs to remain secret. You must head back now. We'll catch up with the others and send them back too, all right?"

Rory and Cherise not only blinked, they winced. This was a lot for them to process. "You just . . . want us to go back by ourselves?" Cherise asked.

"Yeah—can't we help?" Rory added. Bless them both, that's all they wanted to do: help.

"No, there's some national security involved as well. For your safety and ours, I need you to leave now. We'll get the others. Don't worry. Go."

"Well, we can just call them on the wireless—" Rory began, trying to help anyway by busting out a walkie talkie, and I cut him off.

"No, that would compromise the operation. We need radio silence, because others may be listening—the terrorists, you know. Just head back and keep quiet about our presence here."

Under that barrage of commands and the continued influence of the sigils, their resistance melted, and they turned to go on by themselves, slightly dazed. That, I hoped, was at least two lives saved. I hoped we could save the others too, though it might be a bit more difficult.

Connor walked up next to me and shook his head. "Those sigils are amazing. I'm going to have to ask Brighid how she came up with those."

[You can do some pretty amazing things too. I like that camouflage thing. But we should try to catch up and send the others back.] We could still hear the drone of the ATV engines, but they had already disappeared from our sight, as the trail rose rather steeply and curved around behind a stand of eucalypts.

"Yeah, we should."

The dull pop of firearms, the scream of horses, and the abrupt end of engine noise immediately followed.

"We really should. I'm going." He paused only to grab his hatchet from his pack and re-sling it over his shoulder. "Oberon and Starbuck, stick with me." And the Iron Druid sprinted uphill much faster than I'd ever be able to manage. I waved at Rory and Cherise to keep going, and once assured that they would, I broke open a Sigil of Agile Grace and used its power to hoof it uphill after Connor and the dogs. Ya-ping kept pace and withdrew her sai. Buck hoped aloud it wasn't another one of those huge spiders.

"But I think I can help this time, at least. That rest did me good."

When we crested the top of the ridge and saw the summit viewing platform standing next to a radio and weather tower, there was no little amount of chaos in progress underneath it all.

There were two human bodies sprawled on the ground—the officer named Baskin and the SES man named Marcus—and I felt that familiar cold clutch of fear and guilt seize my innards. There were also the bodies of strange creatures, about the size of bulls and mostly built like them, except that below the horns they had the oversized heads of eagles. Two of these had been shot in the head and succumbed to that. One was spinning, trying to keep an eye on Oberon and Starbuck, who were barking and threatening to nip at its legs, while the Iron Druid was in camouflage and taking whacks at its neck. Farther off down the trail, a figure in orange—Thea, I presumed—fled on foot from a fourth eagle bull, and it in turn was being chased by Officer Campbell on horseback, who fired rounds at it with his handgun in an attempt to save her. The eagle bull, to my horror, caught up with Thea and plowed into her from behind, goring her in the back. She flew bodily through the air and disappeared in the ferns. The bull kept going down the trail and Campbell pursued, no doubt to make sure it died and didn't kill anyone else.

Ya-ping crept up to the eagle bull opposite the hounds and darted in, plunging both her sai into its flanks before leaping away. It screeched and turned to confront this new threat, but then its bulk shuddered and dissolved into ash as the sigils of Iron Gall on her weapons disintegrated its magical substance. That left me with nothing immediate to do except check on Thea and see if she could be healed.

I gestured at Buck to keep close, then I jogged over to where I'd seen her disappear into the ferns.

"Wot we daein'? Lookin' for the bird?" Buck asked, and I nodded at him. "Right. I s'pose ye want me tae get searchin' underneath the ferns." Another nod, and he pulled ahead of me and soon disappeared into the leafy cover. It was amazing how quickly he disappeared—anything low-slung could be hiding in there. So far we'd seen only large creatures, but what if that was by design? A swarm of smaller ones could attack us at nearly any point with very little warning and we'd be overwhelmed.

"Found her!" Buck's voice called, and then immediately amended, "Wait. Naw, I didnae."

[What is it?]

The hobgoblin waved his hand over his head so I'd see it sticking up over the fronds. When I got over there, he pointed to a crumpled pile of orange material.

"These are her clothes, are they no? But she isnae wearin' them."

[WTF.]

"Aye, MacBharrais, that's what I'm thinking too, except no in acronyms. Fuck acronyms, awright? Try tae figure this out with me: A huge bloody monster gores ye in the spine and sends ye flyin'. Ye land in some ferns. And instead of callin' for help or even sayin' so much as *Ooyah, ya bastard ye, that hurt!* ye get naked and stroll intae the wild? And quick too. How's that make any sense?"

[It doesn't. Can you hold up the jumpsuit and see if there's a hole in it?]

Buck grunted and did his best to find the back. There was a rather large blood-soaked hole left of center, a few inches above the belt. That would have gotten underneath her ribs. Punctured a kidney, perhaps, or a spleen, ripped up some intestines. Massive shock and pain. There was no earthly way she should be able to shimmy out of the jumpsuit after that in the space of thirty seconds or so and disappear without a trace. Though maybe she did leave a trace. I didn't immediately see a trail of blood leading away from the spot, but perhaps Connor's hounds could be of help.

[Drop it for now. Let's go see if the dogs can track her.]

We walked back to the ambush site, where the Iron Druid was destroying evidence of the other eagle bull corpses by merely laying his hand on them. The cold iron aura that surrounded him and that was lethal to the Fae and all magic broke down the creatures into sodden ashes, and Buck shuddered.

I was about to wave to Connor to get his attention, when I spied movement in the trees past him and a familiar face hovering among the background of trees. It was Gladys Who Has Seen Some Shite, now dressed in a green-and-brown sheath that provided some decent camouflage. As she'd promised, I'd forgotten she was around. I waved at her instead and she curled her fingers in return, grinned affably, and then sort of melted into the forest, her smile fading last, like the Cheshire cat.

Connor, kneeling next to the pile of ash he'd just created, saw me waving and tried to spy who I was looking at, but she was already gone.

"Who are you waving to, Al?"

[My receptionist, who is known affectionately as Gladys Who Has Seen Some Shite.]

Connor frowned and stood abruptly. "Are you joking? Gladys Who Has Seen Some Shite is your receptionist?"

[She is. Do you know her?]

"I know *of* her. Gods below, I remember now—when we met in Rome, you said your receptionist had seen some shite and her name was Gladys, but you didn't tell me you were talking about the actual Gladys Who Has Seen Some Shite. Did you bring her with you?"

[No. She came by herself. I don't know how, though.]

"Oh, Al, this is extraordinarily bad. Are you aware of what she is?"

[She's Canadian.]

Connor blinked. "She's *also* Canadian, yes." My hobgoblin immediately chuckled at this.

[Buck said the same thing. Tell me what else she is, then.]

He shook his head once. "I can't tell you anything except what's in her name. She doesn't go anywhere except to see some more shite, you understand? So the fact that she crossed the Atlantic to take a job as your receptionist means she thinks she's eventually going to see something truly remarkable go down in your office. And the fact that she's watching now tells me something incredibly weird is going on out here, or she wouldn't bother." He looked at his wolfhound and then responded to an obvious query. "Yes, Oberon, even weirder than that time with the adult diapers, the snake, and the marshmallow crème."

I did not ask him for clarification on that statement, because I could tell it would only lead to regret. He shook his head at his dog. "We're not rehashing that time with the goat and the Roman skirt either." He turned to me and said, "I'm going to try to speak to the elemental hereabouts and see if I can't get a clue about the source of these creatures. It might be a while. Can we move a bit and take a small break?"

[Sure. But maybe your dogs can track Thea? We think she's still alive, or was, anyway, a short while ago.]

"Okay. Oberon and Starbuck, will you go with Al and Buck to see if you can find this woman? I need to bury these bodies temporarily. If you wouldn't mind helping me, Ya-ping?"

"No, of course not."

We multitasked and had two separate conclusions at the end of ten minutes: The bodies of Officer Sam Baskin and Marcus Sandford were buried with the elemental's help and marked with a small cairn to make them easy to find later, and Thea had inexplicably left no trail that the dogs could find. She had disappeared into the bush as effectively as Gladys Who Has Seen Some Shite.

Connor relayed to us what they said. "They can't find a trace of her scent more than five feet from where you found the clothes."

"How is that possible?" Buck wondered aloud. "Some kind of magic tae disguise her scent?"

"Possible, I suppose," Connor admitted, "but I don't know

why she'd bother or why an emergency volunteer in Australia would have access to such magic."

[One more thing to ask the elemental?] I ventured.

"Right. Let's find a likely spot down the trail to do that. I don't want to linger here. I hope that officer who ran off is okay."

I hoped so too. But the odds were probably not in his favor.

CHAPTER 11

The Calling of a Crow

The Iron Druid did not share with the rest of us the calculus he used to decide where to commune with the elemental. His binding to the earth was a fact that I accepted but did not fully understand—not unlike the fact that many people on this planet rather enjoy raisins (or at least pretend to). Despite having never visited this area before, he seemed to know precisely where to go. After a brief walk downhill from the summit, he led us about a hundred meters into the bush until we found a spot that was well shaded and quiet, had some handy logs to sit on, and was completely hidden from anyone who might pass on the trail.

"We shouldn't be interrupted here," he said, which was apparently all that he wanted.

But interruptions did come: Ya-ping's phone quacked at her. She was getting text messages from someone that made her huff impatiently and frown. Buck wandered off somewhere after saying he'd be back soon—I assumed to relieve himself. The dogs set up a perimeter and circled Connor while he dropped into a trance-like state. I was thinking about returning to the trail and venturing forward a bit more, following the hoofprints of Officer

Campbell's horse, when Buck tugged on my sleeve. I looked down and raised an eyebrow at him in query.

"Come with me," he whispered. "Ye need tae see something."

[Where?]

"A wee distance in the bush. Don't worry, they'll be fine. The hounds will make noise if there's any trouble."

[What is it? Thea?]

The hobgoblin's lips and brows contorted in an effort to formulate an answer, when a simple yes or no would have sufficed. Finally he said, "I cannae explain. Ye just need tae see for yerself."

He led me into the bush, which grew thicker and rougher, and the hill sloughed away toward the valley where Donnellys Creek ran. There were some thorny bushes mixed among the ferns that caught at my clothing. I saw a couple of brown snakes slithering away from us—I had no intention of provoking them.

Just as I was about to inquire how much farther, Buck stopped and pointed at a tree branch above our heads. A large, sleek crow perched there, and the hobgoblin said, "See?"

I was less than thrilled. [I've seen corvids before, Buck.]

"Look again, ol' man," Buck said. "That isnae yer average crow."

[How'd you even know it was here?]

"She called tae me—in ma heid, I mean."

That was curious. I was willing to give the crow another look. When I did, the crow's black eyes abruptly glowed red, hinting at a volcanic bloodlust, and a cold thrill of fear raced down my spine. A woman's voice, low and scratchy, entered my head.

Do you know who I am, mortal?

Addressing me as "mortal" was a pretty broad hint that the speaker was immortal. [No, but I do know you're scaring the shite out of me.]

That is as it should be, the voice rasped, screeching at my sanity like nails on a chalkboard. *Why do you not use your voice?*

[I am cursed. But perhaps you already knew that?]

I did not, but I see it now in your aura. Ohhh . . . it is a most

delicious aura of death. How delightful. I like you already, Aloy-
sius MacBharrais. We must speak for a brief time, but I can see
that this mental bond is wearing on you. I will take a shape that
can speak aloud.

The crow hopped off the branch, spread its wings, and transformed on the way down to earth into the shape of a white
woman—Thea, if I wasn't mistaken. The SES worker whose body
we never found. She was naked and didn't care, neither slim nor
overweight. Dark hair and naturally arched eyebrows over a long,
thin nose, her lips obscenely red, like raw beef.

[I've seen you before. Thea?]

"You saw this body before," she said, the voice still scratchy
and decidedly lacking an Australian accent. "But I am not she
who used to inhabit it. Thea Prendergast was slain along with
most of her companions by the demon spawn. And just as her
spirit was exiting this flesh, I entered it and took over. I am returned to this plane once more."

[Returned?]

"I am the Morrigan of the Tuatha Dé Danann, Chooser of the
Slain. I have much to tell you, but first you must swear to me that
you will not tell anyone of my return, most especially Siodhachan
Ó Suileabháin and his hounds. Your failure to honor my request
will forfeit your life and your hobgoblin's too." Her eyes glowed
red once more. "Do not think, hobgoblin, that you can escape
me."

Buck knelt and prostrated himself. "I do not, Morrigan, and
would never think so. I swear I will say nothing of your return to
anyone, but most especially the Iron Druid and his hounds."

The red eyes turned to me.

"Well, mortal? What say you?"

The Iron Druid's ending to the previous night's story came back
to me: Sometimes, the dead don't stay dead.

———•———

The Chooser of the Slain

The old treaty between humanity and the Tuatha Dé Danann was not written down for centuries. It was an oral agreement, renewed every so often and tweaked, between the kings of Ireland and those who became known as the Sídhe or the Fae. The Morrigan, however, was always an exception to the general rule that the Tuatha Dé Danann should stay off this plane. She was both a Chooser of the Slain and a psychopomp, who escorted souls to the afterlife. She had to be present to fulfill her function. And nobody even thought about suggesting to her that her movements should be restricted.

Until the nineteenth century, that is, when the first sigil agent was created and binding contracts began to be written. There was an effort at that time to pressure the Morrigan into signing the contract. Goibhniu, the god of brewing, plied her with ale. Manannan Mac Lir, a god of the sea who was also a psychopomp, told her he'd be signing, so that was no excuse. Brighid even called in a favor, and the Morrigan flatly refused on the grounds that it was not a service in kind but rather binding herself to rules she didn't want to follow.

"I will return the favor if it is a favor, but this contract is tanta-
mount to submission, and I submit to no one," she reportedly
said. To which Brighid threatened retribution from many other
deities outside the Irish pantheon, because the peer pressure was
intense; most gods wanted all the other gods off the earth before
someone got photographed and became "the one true God" in
humanity's collective mind. It would be best for everyone concerned if people's faith was never challenged by proof. This threat
of Brighid's—sign the contract or face the combined wrath of
others—successfully brought many reluctant gods to the table,
but the Morrigan would not be cowed. She smiled.

"If any deity wishes to battle me, I welcome them. I will either
live free of all constraints or die."

No one, it turned out, wished to pick a fight with a Chooser of
the Slain—not even Brighid. So the Morrigan lived free until very
recently, when she perished in battle against two other deities,
apparently choosing herself to die.

Why she did that was a mystery. Why she'd want to come back
was not hard to figure: She'd always been one who reveled in pain
and misery. Paradise must have really pissed her off.

CHAPTER 12

The Mother of Devils

Ultimatums and absolutes are dangerous things, and on principle I avoid them. But refusing a goddess of death and battle is also extremely dangerous, especially when she's made clear what a refusal would mean. But perhaps there was some wiggle room to winkle out.

[How long must I keep this oath?] I asked. [For my duties as a sigil agent would make a permanent agreement impossible. I will be required, eventually, to report your presence to other sigil agents at minimum, though I can delay that for a short while.]

"Sigil agents," the Morrigan spat. "Brighid's lever of control. They have never controlled me."

[We have never attempted to control you, since you never signed a contract. And I am not trying to control you now either. I am trying to honor your wishes without compromising my duties.]

"Very well. I can be fair. You will be bound by this oath for a week. The same applies to the hobgoblin. After that time, you may tell who you wish of my return. Now you must swear—aloud, and not on that device."

Using my voice, I said, "I swear to tell no one, for one week, of your return."

"I swear this also," Buck added.

The Morrigan nodded once in acceptance. "Good. Now you may know what it is you face—the source of these creatures that slew this human whose flesh I now claim as my own: It is Caorá-nach, the Mother of Devils. She has escaped from the land beyond the veil in Tír na nÓg. She can summon forth her demon spawn with nine drops of her blood. You have met only a few so far, but more await you on the trail ahead."

"If she's the mother, who's the father?" Buck asked before I could reply. "Wot? That's a legitimate question, in't it? As in, a question of legitimacy? Are these legit devils or bastard devils?"

[I don't think it matters.]

"Course it does! If the father is powerful, then the hellspawn might be powerful too, right? And that's only the first question that popped intae ma heid. I have so many more. Like, how does this summoning thing happen? Does she dribble nine drops of blood on the ground or in a cup or wot? And where do the devils actually emerge? Do they rise from the bloody dust? Or is the 'mother' part of her title a literal thing, and she has a super-fecund, industrial-strength womb with a Slip 'N Slide birth canal so the demons splash out of there like a screaming boatload of kids at the water park?"

[I'm fine not knowing the answer to that.]

"The hobgoblin is surprisingly close. Caoránach is an oilliphéist—a great wyrm accustomed to water."

"Oh, aye? I've heard of them. Sea serpents."

"Aye, but one that can also move on land. She has four legs and talons. The demons are born in water. The blood she drops in the water accelerates their growth to full-grown monsters of varying kinds, and they walk out of the shallows."

"That would mean," Buck said, "that unless there's a big lake around somewhere nearby, she's shitting demons in the creek."

"An apt comparison," the Morrigan agreed.

"Oi, there's a metaphor for evil, eh, MacBharrais? Industrial polluters are shitting demons in the creek. Clear-cutting forests? Also shitting demons in the creek. And if ye put almond milk in ma coffee, ye're definitely shitting demons in the creek. Just say naw tae nut milk is my advice."

[We should focus on the literal demons right now,] I said.

"Caoránach has been dead a very long time," the Morrigan said. "There was no indication that she longed to return to this plane and, beyond that, no indication that she could even accomplish it. She has not been actively worshipped for many years, if ever she was, and her name practically passed out of mortal memory. When she disappeared from Tír na nÓg, I became intensely interested in how she managed to do it. One such as I could have returned at any time—there are many who still pay me my due rites and sustain my powers. But I had no desire to manifest as I had of old and thereby be confined to my accustomed roles. Caoránach showed me that it could be done a different way."

[How?]

"Take over a body at the moment of death. The mortal spirit moves on to whatever hell or heaven it wishes, but the flesh can serve another."

[But isn't it the flesh that died?]

"It's not a problem for one such as myself to heal it. This woman, Thea, perished of intense tissue damage and organ trauma. I repaired it. Of more concern is that, even at full health, this Australian woman's body is nothing like my old one. The muscle tone is middling at best, and the organs are ravaged by age and a wide range of modern toxins. And aside from the dark hair, she looks nothing like I once did. I would change that over time with subtle bindings altering the genetics, except that this body is not bound to the earth. I am, for the moment, possessed merely of my ancient godlike powers but not the powers of Druidry. And while those powers include divination, thus far I cannot divine why Caoránach returned. Especially to this particular place. I cannot begin to imagine how an ancient Irish oilliphéist would have learned of Australia's existence, much less determined that this was where she should stage a return to the living world."

Movement in our peripheral vision drew our gazes downhill, where a familiar face suddenly floated over the bush, her camouflage dress blurring her shape otherwise. It was Gladys Who Has Seen Some Shite.

"Well met, Gladys," the Morrigan immediately said, and executed a small bow. My jaw dropped. An ancient death goddess knew my receptionist on sight and was deferential to her? Who the hell was she?

"It is wonderful to see you again, Morrigan. It has been a long time."

"Indeed."

What someone like the Morrigan would consider a "long time" suggested that Gladys Who Has Seen Some Shite must be much older than she appeared.

"Do you plan to remain on this plane for a while?" she asked the goddess.

"I do."

"Excellent. Let's hope it works out better than last time."

The Morrigan snorted in amusement. "Yes. Let's."

"You know who to contact if you wish to be rebound to the earth?"

"I do. You are kind."

My level of what-the-fuck had, over the past few minutes, ramped up steadily. It had started out on one end of the scale, which was like a mildly bemused Seth Rogen, half asleep in a hammock and wondering how his drink had disappeared because he'd forgotten that he drank it, and quickly accelerated to the other end, which was like a teenager watching their parents peel off their faces to reveal that the reason they acted like aliens sometimes was that they'd been aliens all along. I mean—the Morrigan was back from the dead! And she was telling someone that they were kind! And that someone was my receptionist, who was obviously much more than Canadian!

"Does my aura appear to be divine in this new flesh?" the Morrigan asked, and Gladys Who Has Seen Some Shite cocked her head to the left.

"No, it doesn't. You appear to be human! Well, ain't that a hoot?"

I thought it a hoot that she could see auras. I'd had no idea.

The Morrigan pressed the point. "So I could appear before the Iron Druid and he would not know who I am?"

"Well, not by your aura, he wouldn't. He might figure it out some other way. You kinda have a speech pattern there, you know, and it's nothing like a friendly Australian emergency volunteer. It's more like taking a handful of sharp quartz rocks and wrapping them in cheesecloth made of an Old Irish accent and then dragging them across a sheet of glass. I gotta be honest with ya now, it's a pretty big hint that you might be a Chooser of the Slain. That and whenever you do your glowing-red-eye thing."

"I understand. I may be able to mimic this woman's former voice. The patterns are still in her brain. Let me attempt it now." She closed her eyes and took a deep breath, then opened them again and spoke in a completely different way. I hadn't heard Thea speak before her death, but I had no doubt the Morrigan was pulling it off. All the sandpapery scratchiness was gone, as was the hint of doom that vibrated like a subwoofer in the brain, and what was left was a melodic contralto with a soft Australian accent. "I am not sure if there's an appropriately Australian colloquialism to say at this moment, but perhaps you could help me out, Al?"

I typed out something that would sound utterly ridiculous in my speech app's stilted English accent. [I gotta bail on this arvo, mate, I'm flat out.]

The Morrigan repeated it like a proper Australian. "I have no idea what that means, but I gotta bail on this arvo, mate, I'm flat out."

I nodded in approval, and the Morrigan actually grinned like a normal human might do.

"Excellent. Anything else?" she asked Gladys Who Has Seen Some Shite.

"Yes. Clothes. You should start caring about the fact that you don't have any. Humans these days try not to be naked."

Humans? Was my receptionist not human? I supposed that the chances of that were, at this point, vanishingly small.

"Ah, yes," the Morrigan said, looking down. "An excellent reminder. I believe I can recover the clothes she was wearing earlier. When I shifted to a crow, I obviously had no need of them."

[Both of you can see auras,] I said. [Can you tell who might have cursed me by looking at mine?] Brighid had taken a look at my aura some months ago and had been able to see the curses but not identify the source, except to say that it was masterfully done and quite likely the work of a deity.

"If you wish me to do you a favor, mortal," the Morrigan said, "you will owe me one in return."

[Forget I asked,] I said. There was no way I was getting myself into another deal with her. I was already living under a possible death sentence for the next week. [Gladys, are you able to tell me anything about them?]

"Oh, sure," she said, nodding.

[What? Why haven't you said anything before?]

"You haven't asked me until just now. All you ever wanted was for me to answer the phones and greet people in the office and put out some Danish in the break room. Look, Mr. MacBharrais, those curses were laid on you at the same time, and they're interlocking. But they're two different curses, ya know. So I don't know who did it or how, but it was cast in tandem."

[Tandem?]

"Yep. Two people had to do that together. Each one of those curses represents a whole lot of if/then equations, ya know. Maybe an omniscient type could have done it alone, but an omniscient type probably would have smote you with lightning or something if they were that mad at you. They wouldn't bother with this curse business. Smiting is a very big deal to them."

[So it could have been done by humans? It's not necessarily something done by deities?]

"Hard to say. It's very skilled work, so if it was humans, it's grade-A wizardry. If it was nonhuman, well, then, the possibilities are wider but probably not one of the really big gods, due to the aforementioned lack of smiting. When you find out who did it, that's going to be a very interesting day, I think. Anyway. Just wanted to pay my respects and wish the Morrigan well. Good luck."

The Morrigan bowed again, and Gladys Who Has Seen Some Shite melted from view, the smile lingering in the air and vanishing last.

[Didn't she say we'd probably not see her again until Scotland?]

"Aye, but tae be fair," Buck said, "there's been some shite tae see, ol' man. Demons and goddesses coming back from the deid and whatnot."

The Morrigan nodded and continued to speak in Thea's voice. "And there will no doubt be more to see. We will speak more later, mortal—I mean, Al. I must remember to speak as a human would. I'm going to attempt to discover why Caoránach has returned, but I wished you to know what danger you face. Should we meet again soon, I trust you will keep my identity a secret. In the presence of others, you may call me . . . Roxanne."

[Okay, but why Roxanne?]

"Before I died, Siodhachan introduced me to a song sung by a tantric-sex addict, which implored a woman named Roxanne to neglect displaying her red light. My eyes glow red when I wish to frighten mortals and liquefy their bowels. Choosing this name is therefore my obscure attempt at humor. I recognize that I am not conventionally funny but nevertheless consider myself quietly hilarious." When I didn't immediately respond, her eyes flashed red and her voice returned to the terrifying scratchy rasp. "Do you not agree?"

I nodded vigorously and forced a smile, typing as fast as I could. [Yes! That is very amusing, Roxanne. You don't have to give me the red eye.]

The glow faded and she chucked her chin at a spot behind me, her voice once again modulated and pleasant. "Behind you is a clump of flowers that I believe you require for one of your magical inks. That will provide Siodhachan a reasonable explanation for your absence. He will no doubt be curious, and telling him to mind his own business will only ensure that he does not."

[Am I allowed to tell him that Caoránach is behind this?]

"Can you explain how you know that without revealing my involvement?"

I started to type a response and deleted it, then shrugged.

"When he does that," Buck said, "it means he wants tae say sumhin like *Fuck naw* but is daein' his best tae be polite."

I pointed at Buck and nodded to indicate that what he said was correct.

"Then I guess you'd best not tell him," the Morrigan said. "He will need to figure it out on his own. And he might. He is not entirely without wits, nor without defenses. I thought it best that you know the truth because there is a rough road ahead. Farewell for now."

Without waiting for us to respond, she lifted her arms and transformed into a large crow, flapping over our heads and heading in the direction of where Thea Prendergast had died, presumably to recover her clothes with the huge bloody hole in the back.

Buck and I blinked at each other for a count of ten, and then he said, "Ye want tae know an uncomfortable truth, ol' man? I think I should have packed another pair of pants."

I grunted in amusement and searched for the clump of flowers that the Morrigan had mentioned. It was purple burr-daisy, which indeed was an ingredient for an ink. I tore off a handful and gestured in the direction of the trail. We needed to get back and see what fresh new hells awaited us.

"So what are ye gonnay do about those tandem curses, then?" Buck asked as we began picking our way through the bush to rejoin the others.

[Same plan: Find out who did it. After we get through this.]

CHAPTER 13

The Rite of Passage

The Iron Druid looked irritated by our return. Or perhaps he'd been irritated by our absence, since he was obviously finished communing with the elemental and impatient to move on. His hounds, however, were having a grand old time playing with a wombat, which was chasing them in circles in its rotund, barrel-like fashion, and they barked joyfully to encourage it.

"Where did you go?" Connor said.

I brandished a handful of flowers and Buck spoke for me. "He had to get those ink ingredients. Purple burr-daisy."

"Which ink?"

"Fuck if I know, mate. Wot's that grey creature chasing yer dugs?"

"That's a wombat. And the daisies are for Ink of Mnemosyne," Ya-ping said, looking up from her phone. "It's one of the first Irish-system inks I learned, since the ingredients are almost all native to Australia. The quokka milk is the toughest to get. Have you ever tried to milk a marsupial? It's no picnic."

The Iron Druid shook his head, frustrated at the waste of time. "Let's keep moving. There's no indication from the elemental of what might be causing this. No portals opened. No huge draws on its power, though it says there *have* been smaller draws but cannot say what's causing them. We're going to have to keep going along the Bicentennial Trail, since we have no other solid clues, and put eyes on whatever it is."

The wombat gamboled with us for a wee distance and then disappeared into the bush with a farewell bark from the dogs. The trail from Mount St. Leonard curved east and south, almost looping back on itself for some distance, and we paused for lunch at Monda Dugout, an underground shelter from fire created by workers long ago. The trail itself was now following a ridgeline that would serve as a fire break, and we were heading toward Mount Monda. These mountains were not huge things—they were a smidgen over a thousand meters, barely earning the title of mountain—but still we occasionally saw views of the lands stretching away in all directions, green blankets of treetops hiding the ground underneath.

It was beautiful country, but we could not enjoy it as much as it deserved, since it was at present populated with deadly monsters who'd kill us if they could, in addition to the ordinary dangers of Australia's natural wildlife, adorable wombats notwithstanding. And we still had no idea what happened to Officer Campbell. Was he still alive? Had he used his radio to call for backup? Had Rory and Cherise returned to Donnelly Weir safely, and had they radioed for help? Could we expect a swarm of additional officers soon, or would my ruse of conducting an AFP operation out here hold them off for a while? Were these monsters spreading out along other axes and wreaking havoc elsewhere or only along this specific trail? If they had traveled in other directions from whatever origin point, they could easily reach other population centers and create quite the containment nightmare for us. The cell-phone videos alone would generate weeks of work.

We did note some horse droppings on the trail, and while they seemed to be rather recent, we could not know for certain that they were from Officer Campbell's horse.

Ya-ping gradually pulled me away from such worries, as I became aware that she was marching ahead and staring with utter fury at the cluster of purple burr-daisies clutched in both hands. They're pretty flowers, lilac-petaled with yellow centers full of barbed seeds, but not offensive in any way that I could see. Like all plants, they had no ability to hurl insults, and they did not possess thorns on the stems. So I was having difficulty identifying what might be causing the anger. It had to be something else besides the flowers themselves.

Or maybe the flowers *were* the problem. For just as I was about to say something, Ya-ping gave a strangled scream and crushed them in her fists, then tore them before scattering them to the wind. And once she had finished and realized that she had captured everyone's attention, she looked down at her feet and apologized.

"That felt good for an instant, but it was unnecessary and incredibly rude of me to ruin your ink ingredients."

[There's no need to apologize. Those flowers are much easier to find than quokka milk. But if you feel like telling me at some point, I would like to know why you did that.]

"Okay. Maybe I will share. Let's continue on, however. I don't wish to halt our progress. Sifu Lin is waiting for our help."

Oberon wagged his tail and woofed once in encouragement, and Starbuck did the same, then they trotted on next to Connor, who had taken point. Buck, I noticed, remained silent, exercising some restraint for once. Ya-ping didn't speak for perhaps a hundred meters, but when she did, it was low enough that I could tell she was trying to pitch the words for my ears only.

To his credit, Connor caught the hint and said he was going to scout ahead, jogging forward with his hounds to put some more space between us.

"Did you ever have what they call a 'rite of passage' when you were younger?" she asked.

[Oh, yes. Though I'm aware that what I consider rites of passage are not the same as what others consider them to be.]

"Would it be rude to ask what your rites of passage were?"

[No, no. Not at all. Give me a moment and I'll list some.]

"Okay."

[Thinking about it, I suppose they were tragedies as often as they were triumphs. Getting out of school, falling in love, getting married, and starting a family were great. Becoming a sigil agent was grand. But losing my apprentices, my wife, and all connection to past friends and family was terrible. Bit of a seesaw for me.]

"So the rites were good for a long time, and then they weren't."

[Yes.]

"What does it mean if you're my age and all your rites—except for one, I guess—were bad?"

[Nothing in particular. There is no order or balance to things except what we manage to achieve on our own, and even then, the world outside our control can impose disorder and chaos.]

"But you've had an extraordinary run of bad luck the last few years."

[Yes.]

"Yet you're still optimistic about the future?"

[I am. And it's not just because I'm a white man wearing the robes of privilege. It's because I'm sold on the smooth magic of daily averages.]

"The fuck?" Buck said, but I ignored him.

Ya-ping gave a tiny shake of her head. "I don't understand."

[If you look at long-term market graphs, you'll see daily dips and spikes but a much smoother curve of daily averages running through those spikes and dips. And the thing about those curves is, they never stay high and never stay low. They move up and down just like the spikes and dips. I cultivate gratitude during the highs and patience during the dips.]

"You sound fairly well-adjusted."

[You and I are agents of order in a world of chaos. We have knowledge that most people do not, and that knowledge provides us access to power. Still, we must recognize that we have zero power to sustain our highs, which means we should take delight in them when they occur but remember that we have much power to lift ourselves out of the abyss. Sometimes that power is simply having faith that the trend line of our lives will climb higher once again.]

"It . . . that . . . well." I kept silent and my eyes on the trail ahead, waiting for her to process.

"My big rite of passage," she said eventually, "was supposed to be graduating. Not that it was an especially big deal. Once it was over, I went up to the Gold Coast in Queensland for Schoolies Week with some mates and frolicked on the beaches and watched everyone else get drunk while I stayed sober, but I had cute virgin drinks with little paper umbrellas in them, and I kept those umbrellas to remember the time and they're perfect, because they're thin and flimsy and that summed up the experience for me. I think I was the only one of my classmates who didn't vom on someone else's shoes. Instead, my big rite of passage was losing my parents. And becoming apprenticed to a secret society where the final exam is crafting an ink to draw a Sigil of Unchained Destruction. But now my master is gone and might already be dead. And this boy I kissed once has texted a few times to ask what I'm doing now, and I have to lie, right? I can't tell him I can't come over and play videogames because I'm out killing turtle dragon spiders with a hobgoblin, a Scottish gentleman, and an ancient Druid. So if I lie, I'll feel guilty, and it will be bad if he ever finds out. And if I tell the truth, he'll recommend that I be committed to an institution."

[You're on a hike with friends. That's the truth.]

Ya-ping sniffed and wiped at her eye with the heel of her palm. "Feed him a half-truth, you mean. Yeah, Sifu Lin says that's the way to manage it too. It's easy to rationalize and stay sane with that, because the statement itself is true. But it's still trouble if he ever finds out the full truth."

[That sums up the nature of our business, yes. Trouble if people find out.]

"I wonder what it would be like, sometimes, to not know. To be shouting at people about something on Twitter, as if that was the most important thing we could be doing, or to be looking forward to the next episode of some show that's streaming."

[You would still have problems, just not this particular set of them. Because the chaos is always out there, and the order is inside you.]

Ya-ping snorted. "I'm beginning to sense a theme here. What is that? Scottish wisdom?"

"Naw," Buck said. "Scottish wisdom would be, *The English are always down there, like knobs, so kick a poxy knob before ye fuck off tae the pub.* Practical advice from a practical people."

"Well. The trend line of my life has been sloping down for a while. I hope it curves upward soon, because the grade of this dive only seems to be getting steeper."

A monstrous silhouette skittered onto the trail ahead, setting the dogs to barking and causing Connor to unsling his backpack to get his hatchet.

"Guys, you see this?" he called back. "It's a scorpion with a rat's head. It's like an eighties hair-band demon."

It wasn't easy to kill. The tail was incredibly dangerous and we had to stay out of range, and the claws were likewise difficult to get around. The squeaking of the rat was decibels louder than that of a normal-sized rodent, and it set our teeth on edge. Connor eventually asked to borrow one of Ya-ping's sai and darted in under camouflage to put it down.

He shook his head as it dissolved, then bent to retrieve Ya-ping's weapon. "Do either of you think you can put that Sigil of Iron Gall on my hatchet? I mean, my aura will let me kill these things with a hug if I hold on, but they're not very sweet and embraceable."

A pen nib wouldn't work very well on the steel of the blade, but a brush would do okay. I had my calligraphy brush and a small amount of the proper ink in a pen reservoir.

[I can do it if you will scour the blade clean of blood and dirt.]

"Absolutely."

While he worked on cleaning the blade, the dogs kept alert and I asked Buck to do the same. [I'd just like a warning if something's coming.]

"Aye, that's what yer maw said."

Pretending he hadn't spoken, I selected the proper pen, a burgundy and ivory Pilot E95s, from my field-jacket pocket, along with a brush and the small wax-melting spoon that would serve as a makeshift inkwell for the moment. After unscrewing the nib and connected reservoir from the barrel of the pen (I often called it a reservoir instead of a converter, because I'd decided on my fiftieth birthday that I could call things whatever I wanted), I pulled the reservoir off the nib and upended it over the spoon, using the twist plunger to force the rust-colored ink to dribble out. Connor gave me his hatchet, which still had a faded Sigil of Cold Fire on one side, which he'd not touched. The other side was pristine and dry and ready for a new sigil.

Carefully, taking my time, I painted the Sigil of Iron Gall on there, using all the ink I had. When I was finished, it pulsed and glowed briefly to confirm it was active. I handed it back to him.

"All set?"

I nodded and fished out a small bottle of water to cleanse the ink from my spoon.

"Thanks. This should help out."

We made it to Mount Monda and a little bit beyond as the sun was setting. Since we were exhausted and had no idea how much farther we'd need to go, we decided to make camp. The hope of finding Shu-hua quickly was pretty much gone, so we'd settled for simply finding her. We set up watches, and I was to take the third, meaning I'd get six hours of sleep if I was lucky.

I got it, but an unknown number of those hours were spent in a dream hellscape, the sort of nightmare where you're vividly aware that you're dreaming but unable to wake, so you have no choice but to ride it out.

In the dream I was a walking anachronism, dressed in my modern clothes—my beloved topcoat and derby hat—and wandering the smoky field of an ancient battle in progress, where the combatants were dressed in ring mail and leathers and slick with blood and sweat.

One side of the battle was a Roman legion, with the little pennants on pikes and everything. I was viewing the chaos from the side of the opposition, a seething mass of infantry largely armored in leathers, wearing spangenhelms and carrying round shields, armed with spears and short swords. They were a mixed bag of peoples, but one in particular stood out. It was a familiar red-haired man, except we were obviously in a time when he possessed both arms and wielded a magical sword. He was cutting down Romans with great efficiency, the blade behaving as if armor didn't exist, while a crow circled above him. And just as I wondered if that particular crow was one I had met recently, a voice in my head confirmed:

Yes. It is I.

Where are we, and when?

This is the Battle of Adrianople in 378, in what is now modern-day Turkey. You are witnessing the Goths under the leadership of Fritigern destroying the eastern Roman legions.

And is that warrior I see there the Iron Druid?

Yes, though he was not known as such at the time. He was living with the Goths, still hiding from the god Aenghus Óg and others.

Why are you showing me this? The Goth army was faring well in general, but the Iron Druid's efforts truly broke the Romans and created space for others to take advantage.

Perspective. He has been around a very long time, and I have been around even longer. He has anonymously lifted up empires and brought them down. And I . . . have loved him. I do not wish to see him end his days in Australia.

Is that a concern?

It is. I cannot see his future well, and it troubles me.

What can I do about it?

More, perhaps, than you realize.

She stopped speaking, and the cries and clash of battle filled my head, jets of blood and flashes of steel among teeth bared in agony and rage.

What they were fighting and dying for saddened me so: an empire long dissolved, and a tribe long disbanded. Though, of course, they did not have the same perspective on the event as I did.

There. That thought. That is the crux of your current trial.

It is?

What you are facing in Australia now makes little sense but only because you lack the proper perspective. You must find a way to step back and see it from a distance. As must I. We do not have the proper vantage point to understand why Caoránach has returned. I see much that you do not. And mortals see much that I do not.

All I could see was men dying violently for reasons I could not appreciate. The Romans, no doubt, thought they represented order and civilization. The Goths looked underfed and perhaps thought they were battling oppression, though I didn't know for sure.

Okay, I said, hoping that my acceptance would bring the slaughter to an end. But it didn't. It kept going, and I had to watch these personal struggles and tragedies end in slashed throats and punctured rib cages as the Chooser of the Slain croaked over the Romans shortly before the Iron Druid mowed them down.

Please, I said, *that's enough. I get it.* But my entreaty was either unheard or ignored. The slaughter kept going and going until I said, *Please, Morrigan—stop this!* And the battle crow banked around from the front of the fighting, red eyes blazing, and dove at me with her beak open wide as her chalky, scratchy voice filled my head.

Have you forgotten already, Aloysius MacBharrais? My name is Roxanne.

I screamed myself out of sleep, though in practice it was more of a short "Wha!" as I rose from the dirt. When I did, chest heaving, Ya-ping was standing nearby, staring at me with glistening eyes. The others were sleeping nearby.

"Nightmare?" she asked, her voice low and dull. At my nod, she said, "I've been there. Sometimes I think those are rites of passage too."

CHAPTER 14

———— • ————

Roxanne

Whent the sky slid from indigo to grey, heralding the dawn, the birds began to wake up and call about their urgent need for Wednesday coffee—or so I imagined. I certainly needed some, as a belligerent caffeine-withdrawal headache had taken up residence in my brain and likely had legal arguments against eviction. I got to spend thirty seconds or so dreaming of some heirloom beans from Ethiopia that were grown at a high elevation and prepared with a natural process to preserve their inherent fruity flavors of cherry and blackberries. Silky mouthfeel, brewed at 93.3 degrees Celsius, taken black, perfect with some breakfast haggis and some tatties, maybe a smear of marmalade. It was a far better dream than the one Roxanne had sent me.

But the birdcalls served to wake up the others, and we had our small tents packed up and ready to go by the time the sun peeked over the horizon. That chore was completed in near silence, as no one felt especially talkative before breakfast. We grimly tore the wrappers off protein bars, raised them in mock cheers, and bit into them with more resignation than gusto. Oh, how I missed proper food.

A woman's voice caught us with our mouths full, the way servers in restaurants always manage to ask you how your food is tasting at the precise moment you're unable to answer.

"Hello? Is it okay to approach?"

The dogs startled and barked, obviously annoyed at being surprised, and Connor was instantly on his feet, searching for the owner of the voice. Ya-ping, Buck, and I were close behind, but I already knew who it was: The voice had given her away.

It was Roxanne, dressed in Thea Prendergast's orange threads, smiling winsomely at us and appearing totally harmless.

But Connor was wary. "Hold up there a moment, keep your distance," he said. "Who are you?"

"I'm Roxanne."

"The SES woman who was gored by an eagle bull and disappeared?"

"That was weird. And scary."

I thought those were understatements, but Connor focused on something else. "Your name badge says Thea."

"Oh, yeah. But you shouldn't go around believing what name badges tell you. My name's Roxanne. My uniform wasn't available for this job, so I'm using Thea's."

I realized at that point that everything she had said so far was technically true while completely obscuring the actual truth. Half-truths, like Ya-ping and I had discussed the day before. It was a special skill of the Tuatha Dé Danann, and while I was certain Connor knew that, he didn't know he was speaking to one of them right now.

"Fine. But you sustained a very bloody injury and disappeared for a day. We found your uniform empty on the forest floor. My hounds couldn't track your scent. Now you're here and in no obvious distress, when one would think after an attack like that you'd head back for help, or at least ride one of the ATVs that you abandoned. You have simple explanations for all of that too?"

Roxanne shrugged. "It was a flesh wound. Bled a lot at first, but it's all right now. I thought the noise of the ATV might attract more monsters, so I didn't want to do *that*. I can't explain the tracking thing, though—would a eucalyptus-scented soap fool them?"

The wolfhound actually growled at the insult. I noted that she'd left out some important facts, like the organ damage and her healing it, but, again, she hadn't technically lied.

"No, scented soap wouldn't fool them."

"Oh. So, hey, have you seen the others?"

"Marcus is dead, as is one of the officers. The one named Campbell rode off chasing the creature that gored you and we haven't seen him since."

"Oh, that's terrible. I hope he's all right. So what are you doing here?"

Ya-ping shot a questioning glance at me. "Time to pull out the official ID?"

Connor shook his head and answered before I could. "Not yet." To Roxanne he said, "We're looking for the officer."

I supposed that was true in the same sense that we were looking for a full Scottish breakfast to be delivered any second, along with some of that amazing coffee. It would be nice if it happened, but it wasn't an expectation.

"Mind if I join you, then? Though you really should head back. This area's dangerous."

"Clearly. All kinds of strange things happening." Connor paused and stared at her for a few moments, and Roxanne stared back. "Hmm. You look human."

"You too. What a coincidence!"

"We haven't been properly introduced. I'm Connor. Some people call me the Iron Druid. Would you be willing to shake hands, Roxanne?"

Ah, he'd checked out her aura but was still worried she might be Fae, or some other magical creature that would be disturbed by his cold iron aura. If she was she'd keep her distance, just as Buck was careful to do, but she shrugged. "Sure." She strode forward, extended her left hand to seize his, shook it thrice, and let go. "Satisfied?"

"Not entirely. Why'd you scramble out of your clothes immediately after being wounded?"

"To wash the wound in the creek. That's where I went."

She may indeed have gone straight down to the creek but was leaving out the fact that she had done so as a crow and that's why the dogs couldn't track her.

"And after you washed it, you came back to your bloody uniform, and then you didn't return to Donnelly Weir and get reinforcements or help and didn't even radio?"

"I didn't have a radio—the officers did. And when I got back to the attack site, nobody was there. So, yeah, I went looking for my crew. Because if I went back and told my bosses that I lost everyone, they'd ask me if I looked, wouldn't they?"

"But you were wounded and had no supplies."

"A flesh wound!"

"Do you mind if I see it? I mean, you can't possibly have seen it very well, since it's on your back."

The corners of Roxanne's mouth tugged upward for a split second. She'd been expecting this. "Sure, Connor, you can see it."

It occurred to me that I'd never seen the wound when Roxanne appeared to me yesterday. She'd faced front the entire time and said she'd healed it, so I assumed it must have been fully healed. Now she turned around, and the bloody hole in her uniform was unchanged. Through it could be seen a dark scabbed-over wound, with some seepage of blood and pus, and an ugly purple bruise. We could perhaps question how it had scabbed over so quickly, but she'd dismiss it and say that the wound hadn't been as bad as it looked.

"That, uh. Wow, ouch. You need some antibiotics and a bandage."

"I know, right? But apart from the ache, I feel okay so far. Getting it washed out quickly must have helped, I think."

Connor clearly still had doubts but seemed aware that pushing it further at this point would appear to be more than mere caution. "All right, Roxanne, you're welcome to join us. We're sticking to the trail for now."

"Are we not sticking to it later?"

"We'll see."

Four distant pops that sounded like gunfire made the lot of us look ahead on the trail.

"Sounded like a handgun, eh? I hope that means the officer is alive. Perhaps we'll catch up." Connor took point again with the dogs and murmured reassurances to them that they hadn't screwed anything up and they were very good dogs.

Buck and I walked behind them, while Ya-ping walked with Roxanne. She had no idea who she was really walking with, and I couldn't tell her. She offered a protein bar to Roxanne, who sounded perplexed.

"You just . . . eat this slab of . . . whatever this is?"

"You've never seen a protein bar before?"

"I'm used to a raw whole food diet."

"Oh. Well, yeah. It's got nutrients and all that. Not something you want to eat every day, but when you're on walkabout it keeps you from having to cook."

"Mmf. Um. It's . . . uh," Roxanne said.

"Horrible, I know. But it'll keep your engine running."

Ya-ping's phone quacked, and a rustle indicated she had pulled it out of her pocket. She huffed in annoyance.

"What is the matter?" Roxanne asked.

"This boy. He thinks I'm blowing him off and he's getting impatient with me."

"I see," Roxanne said. "And how is he expressing his impatience? Is he calling you names?"

"No, just asking why I haven't responded to yesterday's texts. I don't know if he's the sort to call names and escalate like that. I suppose this might be a good time to find out."

"If he *does* call you a name, what will you do to him?" The anticipation in Roxanne's voice was impossible to miss.

"Do to him? Nothing. I'll ghost him."

"Oh! You mean, you'll . . . turn him into a ghost? That sounds exciting."

"What? No. You've never heard of ghosting before?"

"Sorry, I haven't."

"It means I disappear like a ghost. I don't respond to anything— I'm just gone."

"Oh, because you actually believe that ghosts *disappear*. That makes sense."

"Yeah, but . . . are you sure you feel all right?"

"I feel wonderful, apart from the injury. There's a modern expression regarding fruit that indicates one's general happiness, but I forget it now. It's lemony or plummy or—"

"Peachy?"

"That's the one! Yes. I feel peachy. So tell me, is ghosting what people normally do now when men become annoying?"

"Yeah, I guess. I don't know, really. I mean, I'm still a bit new at this."

"So there's no flaying or harvesting of eyes, no ear removal, no scarring?"

"No! You're joking, right?"

"Oh, ha ha! Joking."

"Okay."

I marveled at the equivocation. Roxanne hadn't actually *said* she was joking. She only spoke the word *joking* aloud, as in noticing a concept that existed, and let context do the rest of the work for her. Still no actual lies. A few steps passed before Roxanne asked for clarification.

"But you don't even give them a good scratch, just a nice rake of the fingernails down to the bone?"

"What? No! What are you into?"

"What I assume every girl is into. Rending the flesh of men, listening to their agony and fear, reveling in the scent of their blood, existential despair, normal things like that."

Buck and I exchanged a wide-eyed glance of alarm. But Ya-ping laughed, and then Roxanne chuckled along. "You're wild," Ya-ping said, obviously interpreting Roxanne's declarations of what she absolutely, positively was very much into as absurdities.

"Yes, I've been told. Well, I hope the boy will turn out to be the understanding sort."

"Thanks. What about you, Roxanne? You have a significant other?"

"Not at the moment. I was . . . off the market for a while, I guess you could say. But I look forward to starting again."

A faint cry from ahead drew everyone's attention and caused the dogs to bark. Two figures stumbled out of the bush and onto the path, one being supported by the other. The one doing the supporting waved at us.

"A little help?" he called.

"Holy shit," Connor said. "It's Officer Campbell."

———•———

CHAPTER 15

Wherein the Lost Are Found

I had questions. What had happened to his horse? Who was that he was keeping from collapsing to the ground? Why hadn't he called in an air strike or something?

The second question got answered first, when Ya-ping cried, "Sara! He found Sara!" She was off running, and the rest of us trailed after.

Sara was not in great shape. She was dehydrated, scratched, filthy, and probably hadn't eaten well, if at all, for a few days. But she had a blood-encrusted knife clutched in her left hand, and she wouldn't let go of it.

"Who's Sara, again?" Buck said to me.

[Shu-hua's partner, who went looking for her.]

"Oh! Well then, this could be good news, eh?"

[Could be.]

Officer Campbell had questions for us too. "Why are you lot still out here? You were supposed to head back with Rory and Cherise. Are they okay?"

"They're fine, so far as we know," Connor said, as Sara recognized Ya-ping and cried out in relief. They hugged and each asked the other nearly simultaneously if she'd found Shu-hua. The answer was obviously no, and that disappointed them both, but they were glad to see each other.

Sara began to tell a story of being treed by a pack of smaller creatures, like pygmy goats with fanged snake heads. The hooves meant that they couldn't climb up to get her, but she couldn't get down either, and she'd been trapped up there for days. Officer Campbell had come along that morning—on foot, so the loss of his horse must have happened earlier—and shot a few and beat up another with his baton when he ran out of bullets. I was already thinking ahead to what had to happen next and pulled Buck aside.

[We need to get Sara to safety. The car park is most likely due south of here, probably less than ten kilometers. Can you get her there?]

"Ye mean teleport her all that way?"

I nodded, and the hobgoblin winced.

"I suppose I can, stringing some short jumps together, ye know. But I'm gonnay be useless after that, ol' man. Throw me in the bin with a bottle and a bag of snacks, and check on me in a few days."

[You'll be saving her life. Worth it.]

"I cannae fight after this, ye understand? I want tae be clear."

[It's clear.] I withdrew a Sigil of Restorative Care from my field jacket. [But once you get her there and safely into her car, you need to make sure she takes a look at this sigil, or at least takes it with her to use later. It's a healing thing.]

"Got it. Does she need one tae forget everything too?"

[No. She knows about sigil agents already. She's going out with one. The officer, though—I don't suppose you could take the officer too?]

"Naw. Only one, and that's pushing it."

[Okay, we'll deal with him here somehow.]

When we returned to the group, Sara was already looking a little better, because Ya-ping had given her the same sigil I'd asked

Buck to give her. But Officer Campbell was starting to insist that we all leave the area for our own safety—"There's some, like, Dr. Strangelove stuff going on around here"—and I could tell we'd need to use a sigil or four on him to keep things moving.

[Hi, Sara, I'm Al,] I said. [One of Shu-hua's colleagues.]

"Oh, the one from Scotland, right? Nice to meet you."

[Likewise. We need to keep going after Shu-hua but would like to get you to safety first. My hobgoblin can take you quickly.]

"Did that guy's phone just say *hobgoblin*?" Officer Campbell asked, but no one answered him.

"Yes, I guess it would be best. This is . . . too much for me. But you'll find Shu-hua?"

[We'll do our best.]

"Okay. Thank you." She turned to Ya-ping. "I dropped my phone when I climbed the tree. I have it back now, but it's dead. I'll get it charged and then you'll call me if you find her?"

"I will, I promise."

They hugged, and Officer Campbell demanded to know what was going on.

"They're just saying goodbye," Connor said.

"Why? We're all going back together. We should go right now."

[Take her now, Buck,] I said. [We'll wait here.]

"Right. Come on, hen," Buck said, reaching up to take Sara's hand.

"Oh, are you okay?" she asked. "You look sunburned."

"I'm no burnt. I'm just naturally this gorgeous."

They popped out of sight, presumably off somewhere to the south, and that prompted a startled exclamation from Officer Campbell.

"Where'd they go? What just happened?"

I handed a Sigil of Lethe River to Ya-ping and indicated she should give it to the officer. She passed it on with a smile.

"If you'll look at this card, sir, it will explain everything."

"What's this?"

Ya-ping nodded encouragingly, and he popped open the seal on the sigil and took a look. His eyes unfocused as the sigil did its work, and I gave Ya-ping my official ID.

"He has to stay with us but stop trying to get us out of here, right?" she asked. I nodded, and she gave me a thumbs-up. She waited until he blinked and looked up, then showed him the sigils of Porous Mind, Quick Compliance, and Certain Authority.

"Officer Campbell, I'm Agent Chen with the AFP. We're all undercover agents here, and we're trying to reach the source of this threat. We need you to accompany us and cooperate."

He blinked some more but then nodded. "Of course. What can I do?"

Ya-ping lowered the ID. "Did you radio for help at any point out here?"

"No, I lost my radio early on yesterday."

"Why did you continue on without backup and without a radio?"

"I was trying to find the missing park ranger and hikers. He had to be in bad shape. And I had reasons to believe backup was coming soon. It didn't, though, and I made camp for the night. My plan was to head back this morning to take care of my horse."

"What happened to your horse?"

"I . . . I don't know?" He looked around in confusion. Ya-ping glanced my way. If he didn't know, then the loss must have occurred within the last hour, and now the memory was gone.

"You had the horse when you made camp for the night, right?"

"Right. I had the horse then. Can't imagine where she ran off to."

"And when you woke up?"

His face contorted with the effort of trying to recall. He pinched the bridge of his nose.

"Uh . . . I'm sorry. I don't remember waking up. I'm a bit confused as to how I got here. I may have hit my head."

"What's your weapon situation, sir?"

Officer Campbell drew his gun and checked it. "Empty. No

ammunition." This came as a surprise to him because he couldn't remember the goat-snakes.

"Empty?" Ya-ping said, pretending that this was news to her. "What did you fire at?"

"Well, yesterday, right after I saw you lot, there were these wild . . . bulls attacking us. But after that, I'm not sure."

"Will you walk us through what happened with the wild-bull attack?"

"Sure. Well—" He paused, then waved a hand in the direction of Roxanne. "She was there. She could tell you. It was wild."

"Yes, we've established they were wild bulls. Proceed."

"Well, they came at us near Mount St. Leonard, but it didn't seem like a stampede or anything. It was more like they were waiting there to ambush us. One of them took a run at me, and it hit . . . It got my radio, attached to my vest, and between the two I didn't get punctured. Nearly fell off the horse but just managed to stay in the saddle. My partner, Officer Sam Baskin, was killed almost instantly—horn got him in the neck. And they also got the other SES volunteer, whose name was Marcus. And I thought I saw Thea over there—"

"My name is Roxanne," she interrupted.

"What?"

"Roxanne."

"But you introduced yourself as Thea yesterday. And your uniform says Thea."

"Today I'm Roxanne." The Iron Druid, I noticed, was eyeing Roxanne suspiciously, perhaps reviewing her answers in his mind now that he had a statement that as of yesterday she *had* been Thea. It was interesting that the Morrigan wasn't going to let anyone believe she was Thea for a moment. Ya-ping wisely redirected.

"What did you believe happened to Roxanne?"

"Well, I managed to draw my weapon and shoot a couple of the bulls in the head. But I thought one of the bulls had killed her too. I chased it for quite a while—I wasn't able to get a good shot at it and was running low on ammunition. The idea was that it would turn to face me or tire out long before my horse did. But it kept going and even went into the bush for a while. Eventually it did turn, and I put it down with a head shot."

"And then?"

"Then I returned to Mount St. Leonard to find a functioning radio and see if there was anything to be done. Everyone was gone and it was cleaned up—it was like the ambush never happened, except that the ATVs were still there. I reasoned that since there'd obviously been cleanup, some authorities had been there and more would be incoming to find me. The priority was still finding the missing park ranger and hikers, and since I had firsthand evidence that they could be in serious danger, I went on ahead."

"You didn't see anyone on the trail from then to now?"

"No."

We exchanged glances, trying to figure out how he'd missed us, and Connor eventually said, "That time we stepped off the trail and Al went off in the bush with Buck to get some daisies."

That had taken an hour at least, more than enough time for the officer to return to the attack site and pass us again.

"Though it's remarkable you didn't run into Roxanne at some point."

The two of them looked at each other and shrugged.

"He was ahead of you and I was behind you," she said, "so he was obviously ahead of me too."

"We still have a situation ahead of us," Ya-ping said, "so we'd best get going. You'll have to use your baton."

"What's the situation, exactly?"

"Terrorists, possibly with hostages, and wild bulls and other creatures of that sort."

"Foreign or domestic terrorists?"

"We're pretty sure they're foreign but can't rule anything out."

"Are any of you armed?"

"We have weapons, yes, but not guns. If you'd take point with Agent Molloy and the dogs, that would be great."

"Okay. This is pretty weird, though. I've never seen AFP agents like you."

"That's good. You weren't supposed to know about us."

Connor smiled winsomely at him and said, "Come on," and started walking on with his dogs. It was an invitation impossible to refuse. Who wouldn't want to walk with those good dogs?

We waited for them to get out of earshot before Ya-ping spoke freely, handing my ID back. "Was that okay?"

[Perfect.]

"I wonder what happened to his horse."

The incognito Chooser of the Slain spoke up to offer a theory. "He was wakened by a monster attack this morning. The creature, whatever it was, either took his horse or frightened it away. He chased after it and discovered Sara trapped in the tree. We heard him shoot a few of the goat snakes—I'd like to see those— and then we came upon him a short while later." When Ya-ping looked about to ask how she could possibly know that, Roxanne shrugged and added, "Most likely."

Buck reappeared at that point, breathing heavily, as if he'd just finished a high-intensity workout. His skin had edged from pink to red, and he paused for breath between phrases.

"Ye're . . . a bawbag . . . for makin' me . . . do that . . . ol' man."

"Is Sara okay?" Ya-ping asked. My hobgoblin just held two thumbs up and rested his hands on his knees, trying to recover. "Thank goodness." She looked speculatively at Roxanne and then raised an eyebrow at me, leaning in to whisper. "She doesn't seem to be fazed by any of this. Are you okay with her remembering it all?"

[I am.] There would be no positive outcomes for us if we tried to use a sigil on Roxanne, and luckily Ya-ping didn't ask for the reasoning behind that decision.

"Listen, ya gobshites," Buck said, still winded. "There's a bloody army . . . of people . . . at the car park. They're coming."

"What kind of people?" Ya-ping asked.

"Polis and . . . whatever she is," he said, waving at Roxanne's uniform.

"Makes sense. Rory and Cherise returned but none of the others, and they've had no radio contact. It's going to be a big crowd now. They'll bring vehicles. We don't have much time."

I looked off to the right, where Officer Campbell and Sara had originally emerged from the bush. [We need to get rid of the monster bodies if we can.]

Proceeding on the theory that Sara couldn't have been too far off the trail if Officer Campbell had found her and brought her back to it, I found a pine perhaps twenty meters off the path with an unusual collection of bodies underneath it. The bodies would eventually disintegrate on their own—one of them already had, and the rest would definitely turn to ash before the day was through—but the rate at which that occurred varied, and we didn't want them found in the next few hours. Ya-ping stabbed the corpses with her sai to let the Sigil of Iron Gall accelerate the process.

Roxanne shook her head. "I never would have put a snake head on a goat. That's wrong."

Ya-ping frowned at her. "But you'd put other animal heads on the bodies of other animals? Like a platypus on a wombat?"

"Only for science. Science is very popular these days." I recalled that Roxanne thought herself quietly hilarious, and her light tone suggested that she was joking.

"But that's not wrong? Only snake heads on goats is wrong?"

Roxanne chuckled. "Wrongness is almost exactly like quality. Difficult to define, but you always know it when you see it."

"What's wrong right now," Buck said, "is that we don't have one of those wee red wagons that kids have. I could lie down in it and ye could pull me along, ol' man. I in't looking forward tae this hike."

"Would you like to perch atop my shoulder, Buck?" Roxanne asked.

Alarm suffused Buck's expression, and his complaining dried up like a puddle in the Sahara. "Naw. But ye're kind tae offer."

With the Fae monstrosities destroyed, we hurried back onto the trail and followed behind Connor and Officer Campbell. The latter was patting Oberon as they walked and seemed to be in much better spirits than he was a few minutes ago.

"I don't suppose ye have a nice haggis hiding in yer field jacket there, MacBharrais? I need food and a nap."

[If I did, I would have eaten it already.] I tossed him another protein bar as I noted that Ya-ping and Roxanne paired up behind us once more.

"Shite and nuts," Buck declared, delivering his review. "Why can they no make these steak-flavored?"

[Because they're made of shite and nuts. Would you like to use a Sigil of Hale Revival?]

"Is that the one that puts ye tae sleep?"

I shook my head and fished for one in my field jacket until I met success, then handed it over. He broke it open, and after a few steps the trudging improved to a relaxed walk.

"Ah, that's so much better. I don't suppose ye have a shot of salsa in there for me too?"

Hobgoblins, we'd discovered by accident, had the utterly unfair ability to get high from capsaicin. One bite of a jalapeño and he'd be off to a happy place.

[I don't. Perhaps I'll give you a hit of Scotch bonnet sauce when this is over.]

"Scotch bonnet? Are ye sayin' that there's a Scottish chili?"

[Not really. The pepper looks like a tam-o'-shanter hat, and that's how it got the name. I can make some chicken with a Trinidadian marinade and you'll feel fine.]

"Aw, go on with yer sweet talkin'. It gives me hope for the future."

CHAPTER 16

The Present Is
Always a Cusp

We were doing our best to move briskly but there was still plenty of surplus breath to allow conversation, and Roxanne did not wish to let the chance for learning how to live in the modern world pass her by. She knew how to live in the ancient world, as a pagan goddess and a Chooser of the Slain, but navigating it as a supposedly normal human involved a learning curve that she was only beginning to appreciate. We all had learning curves to negotiate.

"So you're on the cusp of adulthood, correct? Becoming this thing you've been working toward, or taking a big step in that direction, anyway," she said to Ya-ping.

"Yeah. I don't like being on the cusp so much. It's like you can't put the old thing down, because you haven't got the new thing in your grasp yet." Ya-ping paused and squinted. "Though I suppose every minute is like that."

"I beg your pardon?"

"Sorry. Getting a bit philosophical. Right now we're on the cusp of the future. We want to get there but we can't leave the past behind us. It gets dragged along, slows us down."

Oh, I felt that hard, as young folk might say. Though it was more likely they would have said it a few years ago and I was already behind on the current vernacular. Might as well go back a few hundred years and quote Laertes in *Hamlet: A touch, a touch, I do confess 't.* I was unable to meet the future because of whatever happened in my past to earn a pair of curses. I wanted an apprentice to live to mastery so I could retire and leave my territory in capable hands; I wanted to talk about football with my son, Dougal, and spend time with my grandchild. I wanted to speak to Nadia without a speech app. And none of those futures was possible until I dealt with my past.

"I can understand that," Roxanne said. "My past was . . . a prison of circumstance. It was a gilded cage, to be sure, but still a cage."

"Oh, I'm sorry. How'd you get out, if you don't mind me asking?"

"Drastic action. I had to stop being who I was, in a very literal sense. It was the kind of action that, normally, there's no coming back from."

"But you're here. So that's good."

Roxanne snorted. "Its goodness remains to be seen. I don't wish to be trapped in such a cage again. I worry about making choices that will box me into another prison."

"Well—you're going to box yourself into something no matter what. Even if you refuse to make a decision, you've made one anyway and boxed yourself into indecision."

"But a new choice can be made anytime."

"Right. But every choice we make entraps us in circles of narrowing probabilities, doesn't it?"

A few steps went by before Roxanne asked, "What do you mean?"

"This boy who's been texting me, for example. Unless he turns out to be polyamorous, choosing to be with him would limit my potential number of partners and guide my future along a certain path—a certain family life and circle of friends, a certain set of problems that comes with their baggage. He might wind up being wonderful. But he could also turn out to be terrible and then I might feel trapped, because getting away from a bad situation can mean you're also throwing away peripheral stuff that's good. But not choosing a partner limits you too, just in different ways. I think it must be difficult—I won't say impossible—to live in such a way that probabilities constantly expand. But you can, as you did, take a drastic step outside your circle of probabilities. You have new choices available! Perhaps too many. Now what will you do with that? Whatever choice you make, it will begin to narrow possible futures. Which is not something to fear, just acknowledge."

It impressed me that Ya-ping recognized it at such a young age. I've heard that hardship can make children grow up quickly, and I think that held true in her case. I thought she was correct about how our choices create circles of probability, whether for good or ill. With Josephine, the circle had been warm and comfortable, and she was the center of it. Her family and friends were mostly kind, like her, and concerned for the welfare of others, though she did have a brother who fell in with some Tories and became a racist bawbag who vomited conspiracy theories. The probability that I might punch him grew every time he spewed another one, but if I'd ever indulged the impulse, that would have changed more than one relationship; I would have been in a future where I had punched Josephine's brother, a narrowed path that would not have been so warm to walk. Ironically, he was the only member of my family who hadn't succumbed to my curse, since I never spoke to him anyway.

But looking back, I could clearly identify where the broad probabilities of my youth narrowed into a career and family in adulthood. The snap decision I made forty years ago to visit Stirling one day and refresh a couple of wards while the weather was fine turned out to be the one that set me on my current path, for it was there I met Josephine. She had a flower in her hair, and the sunlight shone on it like it had never seen anything so pretty. That was how the sun always behaved around her.

And once we were together, I was inside a circle of probability that meant my home would be safe and stable and loving. My job, of course, represented a circle of probability in which gods and monsters might take turns cursing and smiting me or tearing apart my soul.

"I see," Roxanne said. "If I want a different future, I'm required to make different choices."

"Absolutely. And that future may not necessarily be better, because you can't know ahead of time—but if you want different, you can always have it. Just deploy drastic action. I admire you for that."

"I understand you better now. The present is always a cusp. But while you are on the cusp of adulthood, I'm on the cusp of a very different life."

"That's cool. I understand it happens a lot more now."

"What happens? Different lives?"

"Yeah, I mean adults choosing to start over, swap careers and make other significant life changes. Sifu Lin told me—and Sifu Wu as well, actually—that people didn't used to switch things up so much. They'd get a job and stick with it, do that one thing no matter how much it ground down their spirit, because changing meant taking risks and it was easier to be safe and miserable than to take a shot at happiness that might miss. Part of that is systemic, of course."

"Systemic?"

My back was to them, so I didn't actually *see* Ya-ping deliver the side-eye, but I could practically feel it.

"Yeah, systemic. Are you asking me for a definition?"

"I . . . no. It's just an adjective and I don't know what it's modifying."

"Systemic racism is the obvious one. But capitalism itself is a system that has misogyny and other bigotries baked into the recipe. Those systems all represent choices, of course, that people in power made. So when you are going to make a choice for yourself, you have to make that choice in the context of the societal construct you live under. Dismantling systems of oppression are therefore long-term projects we should all work toward, because that would allow everyone more freedom."

"You learned all this in your school?"

"Only some of it. Because education is a system too. To beat it you have to first recognize it's a system and then read outside it— just not on Internet message boards, because that's how you get a diseased brain. Sifu Lin helped with a lot of that."

"I confess I do not know who Sifu Lin is."

"Oh. Right. Because you just joined. Well, she's one of the people that the, uh, terrorists may have taken hostage, and we're trying to find her as well as defeat the bad guys."

"I hope we do. I would like to meet someone so wise."

"Speaking of the bad guys, though—they might be kinda weird. Like the thing that gored you. Or those goat snakes. You look like you're comfortable with weird so far, but they're going to be violent too."

"I assure you that I am extremely comfortable with violence."

"Yeah, I should have realized that from the way you were talking about harvesting ears earlier. I'll take you at your word. But do you have any weapons?"

"You may assume that I am the weapon."

"Oh! You're a martial artist, then?"

"I am. Though I am not well versed in the Chinese martial arts. Choosing to study them would be rewarding, I'm sure."

"What disciplines have you studied, if I may ask?"

"Ancient ones from the European continent, Bronze Age and Iron Age mostly. They've served me well."

"That's fascinating! You feel like these ancient martial arts hold up well against systems that were developed later?"

"I do."

"That is dope as shit, if you'll pardon my language. I'd love to see a demonstration sometime."

"I'm sure we'll have the opportunity soon enough. Is Sifu Lin your martial-arts master?"

"No, she's a master of ink and papermaking."

"That sounds almost arcane."

Ya-ping laughed. "It is."

———•—•———

Paper Is a Phoenix

From pulp—utterly lifeless pulp—new life can be born. Add water and pressure and you no longer have mere pulp but a medium for the miraculous. It can carry the words of one lover to another. Express gratitude for gifts and thoughts. Invoice a client. Threaten death. Bear the light touch of poetry or the weighty prose of novels. It can be folded into an airplane, to annoy your teacher, or folded into origami, an artistic appreciation of nature made from wholesome natural ingredients. And on and on. So much can be built from the ruin of plant life.

Which is not to say that humans are noble. We ruin so much else that never gets a new life, and their dissolution—their extinction—is final.

But paper is one thing we got right.

Thea Prendergast had no doubt been a wonderful person who wished to help others, and her abrupt demise was tragic, but her flesh now held all the effective qualities of paper: Anything could be written on it, and the Morrigan held the pen. Something miraculous and wonderful could result. Something horrific was equally possible, though I had the sense that the Morrigan wished to avoid the paradox of living as a death goddess. She had already followed that story to its end. So now, presented with a fresh sheet, what would she write?

Someone had defaced my sheet of paper and all but ruined it. Was it still salvageable? Could any beauty hold up against the weight of the terrible marks on it? What would I write on the little paper I had left?

CHAPTER 17

———— • • ————

Lend Me Your Ears

While Roxanne and Ya-ping changed the conversation to discussions of ink and paper, I tuned out and focused on how to deal with the problem ahead of me. Somehow—and soon—I needed to let Connor know what we were facing, without revealing that I knew this only because the Morrigan had come back from the dead and told me, except she was called Roxanne now and was walking thirty meters or so behind him. Try as I might, I couldn't come up with a way to slip *oilliphéist* into casual conversation. What would I say?

Dragons are bad, but have ye ever met an oilliphéist? They're the worst!

Naw.

The legends about the Loch Ness Monster have it all wrong, I could say to Connor, because I'm Scottish and that's a thing people who aren't Scottish might expect me to talk about. *I'll tell ye what Nessie is. She's no dinosaur; she's an oilliphéist!*

Naw.

But the way that Oberon and Starbuck kept looking up at Connor as he walked and he looked back, obviously trading mental notes with one another, gave me an idea. It was time to encourage some eavesdropping on our own conversation.

[Buck.]

"Wot?" The hobgoblin looked exhausted. He was trudging again at this point, grimly chewing his protein bar. The Sigil of Hale Revival I'd given him earlier had already worn off, and he was feeling drained. I adjusted the volume on my phone down and played the next message closer to his ear.

[Without shouting it, without being obvious, mention the Iron Druid. We want the dog to hear it but not him. We want the dog to hang back and eavesdrop on our conversation.]

"Mention him how?"

[Something to get the dog's attention. But then just follow my conversation as you would any other.]

"Awright. Now?"

I nodded, and Buck raised his voice somewhat. "Tell ye what, ol' man, I've been wonderin' about sumhin for ages. Does the Iron Druid's aura apply to his cock, and if he cannae perform in the bedroom does he say he's rusty? And that dug of the Iron Druid's: Do ye think he's aware of the double entendre on sausage? I'm bettin' he doesnae, because otherwise he's a legendary straight man and he's the sort who would tell ye he's legendary for sure."

Gods below, that was *much* more embarrassing than I'd anticipated. Though I supposed I was at fault for assuming Buck would be civil because he was exhausted. But the gambit worked. The Irish wolfhound's ears pricked up, and then he wandered to the side of the road to pretend to smell something, a rather obvious ruse to let us catch up to him as Connor, Officer Campbell, and Starbuck kept walking. My reply was a simple redirection, entirely ignoring Buck's questions, but I made sure to crank up the volume on my phone before pressing PLAY. Oberon left off his sniffing as we drew even and kept pace to the side of the road, on our right.

[I've been wondering about these monsters. They're neither demons nor Fae in the normal sense.]

"How so?"

[Normally, demons are summoned or brought through from their plane to this one using a portal. Whenever that happens, there's a detectable draw on the earth's powers.]

"Yeah?"

[That's not happening here. So that rules out normal demons, or the elemental would have noticed that draw on its power and told the Iron Druid.]

"But I thought he said the elemental believed something strange was happening out here, and that's why he was already headed this way when he heard you wanted him to join us?"

[True. But "something strange" is different from "portals have opened." The elemental would say for certain if a portal had opened. It's sensing something else but isn't sure what. And we know from experience that these aren't normal Fae.]

"Naw, that's for sure. Never seen or heard of a turtle dragon spider before, or a rat scorpion."

[But I don't just mean their appearance. I mean how they got here.]

Buck finally figured out what I was doing. I could see understanding break like dawn across his face.

"Oh, ye mean, if they're no normal Fae, then how'd they get here from Tír na nÓg?"

[I mean they never were in Tír na nÓg, or any of the Fae planes, in the first place. If they were, they'd have to get here using an Old Way or a bound tree, or the traditional triangle of oak, ash, and thorn, which aren't found in Australia. The only Old Way is the one we used to get to Melbourne.]

"A bound tree, then, is the only possibility?"

[Possible but unlikely, since, as you've said, they're not your typical Fae. That means they're appearing here some other way.]

"Appearing? Ye mean they're summoned, or wot?"

[Something like that.]

"Well, what could summon all those bloody monsters?"

[That's the question.]

"That's *one* question, ye mean. The other question is about his rusty iron cock."

[Damn it, Buck.]

"Wot?"

I simply shook my head, ending the conversation, and Oberon trotted ahead to catch up with Connor and the others. Shortly after the wolfhound had resumed his position, his head tilted up and the Iron Druid's tilted down. The reporting, as I'd hoped, was happening, though I had no idea how much was being reported or how accurately. Roxanne and Ya-ping were still discussing papermaking and martial arts, somehow conflating the two as a process of refining raw material into something elegant.

When Connor threw back his head and laughed, I knew Oberon must have told him what Buck had said about his aura. Officer Campbell was startled and asked him what was so funny, which I just caught at the edge of my hearing.

"Hobgoblins, man." He hooked a thumb over his shoulder, indicating Buck, and the officer looked back, bemused.

"You mean that little sunburned guy? He's a hobgoblin? Where'd he come from, anyway?" He had, of course, completely forgotten that I'd called Buck a hobgoblin earlier and that Buck had teleported away with Sara, since we'd hit him with a Sigil of Lethe River shortly afterward.

"Yeah, but be honest—he's not the weirdest thing you've seen lately."

"Well, no, that's true."

"Just roll with it," Connor said. "I think you'll be seeing plenty weirder before the day is through."

CHAPTER 18

Yakity-Yak

I didn't know what to expect next on the trail, exactly, except that it would probably be bloodthirsty and a crime against nature. Instead, I got a message on Signal. From Nadia.

Boss. Where you at?

I blinked in surprise and typed a reply: *Still in Australia.*

Right, but where, exactly? I'm coming tae meet ye.

But you're in Scotland.

Naw, I'm in Melbourne.

What?

It's no that hard tae figure. I hopped on a fucking plane after ye left.

Why?

Something's happened with my gift. My battle-seer thing. My semi-divine divination. I can see a bit further into the future— well, at least where you're concerned.

How do you mean?

After you left in the middle of the night, I got a vision of booby traps ahead, and ye cannae avoid them without me there. It's a meat grinder. And some truly dodgy stuff beyond that even if ye

skate through somehow. I got on the first plane and left the fore-
man in charge of the shop. We owe him for this business if we
survive. Unless he steals everything, and then we hunt him down.
So just wait, will you? It'll take me some time to get there, but
you'll be alive. Where are you, exactly?

On the Bicentennial National Trail. Past Mount Monda.

Okay, got it. Stay where ye are, and I'll be there as soon as I can
to get ye through the rest. Ye have to leave the trail there anyway.

We don't have time to wait.

You'll be permanently out of time if ye don't! And I can get
there pretty fast. Car will get me there in a couple of hours if I
approach from the opposite direction on that dirt road you've
been walking.

You can really see where I am?

Not precisely—I did need some help! But the visions keep refreshing and updating. Things are different now.

Right enough, I typed, her words reminding me of Gladys Who
Has Seen Some Shite. I wondered if she was nearby, following us.

But keep an eye out while ye wait, Al. Something's coming for
you.

What?

Heads up, it's coming now!

Something a bit more like what I was expecting erupted from
the bush. It was a trio of bloody yak badgers.

Yaks and badgers are no fun all by themselves if they decide
they don't like your face. But put a giant badger head on a yak
body and you have a one-ton angry juggernaut on your hands.
Or, in this case, three of them—one for each pair of us on the
road, not counting the dogs.

We heard them coming in time for me to shout a warning and
try to get out of the way, but I didn't have time to apply any sigils.
As a result, I narrowly missed getting my throat torn out by badger jaws but didn't miss getting knocked over by a yak shoulder.
My cane, which I'd been carrying in the crook of my arm as I used
my phone, clattered away out of my reach, together with my

phone. And my breath evacuated my lungs and seemed reluctant to ever return.

Falling down as a pensioner, I have noted before, is zero fun. It hurts more than it should, and it contains a nonzero risk of never getting back up again. Especially with murderous Fae creatures on the loose.

Besides my own wheezing gasp for air, I heard the thunder of yak hooves and the furious ratchet growl of irate badgers. One screamed behind me—presumably Ya-ping had scored a hit already—and then another shrieked in front, where Connor had no doubt employed his hatchet. But the one who'd bowled me over halted and turned around for another pass.

I tried to focus on my cane. If I could pull myself to it and extend it in front of me, the Sigil of Iron Gall might convince the yak badger not to trample me or chew my face off.

"Urrk . . ." I managed, and maybe closed the distance a few inches. My strength had left me along with my breath, my muscles refusing to work. Or maybe I had broken bones and my limbs refused to work, the pain on a time delay to my brain while it was trying to think without oxygen.

The hooves trampled closer; the badger snarled in anticipation. Ya-ping shouted a warning, as if I hadn't seen the danger. And then my vision blurred in khaki and pink as something swept through, my cane was gone, and a whoosh of displaced air followed by the dull thud of a blunt force impact tore a cry of pain from the badger's throat. Buck had saved me. The hooves that would have churned my guts into mud rumbled past.

"Here, ol' man," he said, dropping the cane into my grasp. "I don't like yer cane, even tae hold the safe end. The iron vibrates intae ma skeleton. Let's get ye up."

The yak badger was making noises that sounded the way I felt, frustrated and angry and in pain. I wondered if Caoránach wept for these children of hers, being sent out into a world that would try to kill them on sight. Or did the chimeras understand, at some level, that they did not belong in the world and would never be accepted, and as such they should make others suffer like them? Was there a happy place for them—or did they even get the time to think about what would make them happy? It seemed they were unleashed from the bush with the instruction to feed on whatever they found, and I wished it could be different, that they could gambol happily about with the dogs, like a wombat, that we could feed them sausages and comb their badger fur, but their attacks made self-defense a necessity. Except I had no energy to rise, because I was still fighting to breathe. Buck tried to lift me up from my left armpit, but I just gasped and wheezed.

Ya-ping came next to my rescue, first distracting the yak badger from charging me again and then slaying it with her sai. She even popped a Sigil of Hale Revival in front of me, and that gave me the energy to stand and recover my breath.

Buck returned my phone, and I typed out, [Thanks.] The others came to make sure that I wasn't seriously injured, and after reassuring them I would be fine after a few minutes—no bones were broken, though I expected bruises—I told them that we needed to wait.

[My manager, Nadia, is coming from Melbourne.]

Buck brightened. "Nadia's coming? That's good news, by Lhurnog!"

Ya-ping disagreed. "How is it good, Buck? There's going to be police and SES coming through anytime now, according to you. We can't wait around."

"If ye're gonnay be in a fight, ye want Nadia on yer side, trust me," Buck said, while I typed a longer response.

[She says we have to leave the trail here anyway and there are myriad traps waiting for us. She can lead us through them. We can wait off the road, out of sight.]

"How can she lead us through them, exactly?" Connor asked.

[She's a battle seer. She can reliably lead us to the bad guys from here. It's not yet noon, so we can afford to wait a bit. Especially since not waiting and going it alone could be fatal. She's had a vision.]

"We should trust that, then," Roxanne said, and while Buck and I knew she was speaking sincerely, out of a desire to make sure Connor remained safe, I think the others wondered if she was speaking ironically.

Connor looked down at his hound. "I'm being reminded by Oberon that we could all probably do with a snack, at least, after that excitement."

The snacks we had were just more of the same: dry, uninspired mouthfuls of grains and proteins. But if snack time halted our progress and allowed us to wait for Nadia, I was all for it.

[Who's a good boy? You are, Oberon! And you too, Starbuck!]

They each barked once in acknowledgment and smiled up at Connor. They were going to get a snack and they knew it.

Officer Campbell had been silent up to that point, but he twirled his finger around, indicating the piles of ashes in the road.

"So, Agent Chen, those were, uh . . . ?"

"Wild yaks," Ya-ping supplied.

"Wild yaks. Okay. Like those wild bulls. Definitely wild. Yep. We're all on the same page here."

That might be more true than he suspected, for it seemed to me that we were on the same page as the demons: Go forward and kill whatever you encounter. I didn't think that was a healthy place to be for any of us.

CHAPTER 19

The Good Dug's Story

We didn't know exactly what to do except worry. Would the Australian authorities catch up to us? Would something we couldn't handle show up next? How was Nadia going to slip past everyone and get to us before the police did? What if she was delayed and we lost even more precious time?

"Oberon has suggested that we pass at least some of the time with a story," Connor said. "One that he promises is relevant and not about sausage, though he believes to his core that sausage is always relevant."

"You mean Oberon's going to tell us a story?" Ya-ping asked.

"Yes. Through me, of course. If you're willing to hear it. He and I will understand if you're not in the mood."

"Oh, no, I'd love to hear it. A distraction would be good."

"Is this for real?" Officer Campbell asked. "The dog is going to tell us a story?"

"Yes."

"But using your voice?"

"Right. Because his vocal cords and tongue are not capable of reproducing human speech."

"Yeah, I get that. But you can hear him how exactly? In your head?"

Connor waved his hand to dismiss the line of questioning. "Believe what you want, okay? It's a story. But just to be clear, I'm going to tell this in Oberon's voice. Or, rather, the voice I hear in my head whenever he speaks to me. His mental voice given breath, in other words. Don't freak out."

Ya-ping grinned. "I'm sure it's going to be entertaining."

"He usually is," Connor agreed. "Here we go."

 Five billion days or years or seconds ago, I don't know, time is a slippery concept for me, because almost any moment in time you can name is the perfect time to eat or nap or pee on something, and if time is always three things at once, how can you expect me to keep track of it?

Anyway, *six* billion days or years or seconds ago—because six is more than five, right, and some time has passed since I started this, as it does—Starbuck and I were in a place called Portland, and that is a city in a country that is not here. It had zero wombats, for one thing, and completely different smells, most of them coming from food trucks. Oh, delicious food trucks—gyro meat and kielbasas and pulled pork and fried chicken and believe me, I could go on and on and happily list meats for you all day, but I promised my Druid I wouldn't, and Portland had other attractions too. There were, like, *way* more poodles than here, and lots of roses. And some of the poodles were fancy, and Atticus would take us to the dog park sometimes and we could sniff their asses. Those were really good days, you know? But this one time he took us to a park where we uncovered a vast squirrel conspiracy.

I don't mean to say that we were conspiring against squirrels: Conspiracy isn't necessary when the established social norm is to bark at them and chase them on sight. If you don't bark at squirrels, they gradually take over, bit by bit. You get more and more squirrels, until you find yourself overrun and unable to defeat them. We can't have that!

And you might think at this point, what's the harm in one little squirrel? Can't you share? Don't they have rights, and don't they deserve nice things?

Well, I'm all for sharing. I share with my buddy Starbuck all the time. For example: Our human, Atticus—oh, sorry, he goes by Connor now—has only one arm. He can only pet us one at a time. So we have to take turns. We have to share. And that's fine. And those fancy poodles at the dog park? I'll let you in on a little secret: They're perfectly polite and don't mind a good ass-sniffing, but they don't like getting their asses sniffed by more than one dog at a time. That tends to straighten out their curls or something. So we take turns there too. We share.

(But I will add, parenthetically, that you can now buy candles scented with almost anything you want and can therefore buy an ass candle of your favorite poodle and enjoy the scent wafting throughout your whole doghouse.)

But squirrels—they don't share! They look out for themselves and that's it. You see this in the way they hoard nuts. They're just obsessed with nuts and will not share them with other squirrels or anybody. They hide them. They fight over them. And they eat them right in front of you so you not only can't have them but have to watch them removing the mere *possibility* of having a nut. That's why you have to fight squirrels. You can't argue or shame them into sharing or convince them that selfishness is wrong, can't even tell them there's plenty for everyone. Their position is, *All for me, nothing for everyone else.* Negotiation and debate are pointless.

In Portland they let the squirrel problem build. We ran into an army of them and they chased us out of the park—there were too many to fight by ourselves! I'm talking way more than twenty, because that's as high as I can count. There were twenty trillion squirrels. Or twenty dozen. A lot, okay? And Starbuck and I couldn't handle them all, so we ran to the edge of the park and across a busy street. The squirrels lined up on the curb, tails twitching, chattering at us, and our Druid was laughing for some reason. But then he agreed to help us. He organized! It took a while, but he encouraged a whole bunch of Portland dogs and even three civic-minded cats to join us, and together, as a righteous coalition, we charged back into the park to chase those squirrels away.

No squirrels were harmed in our charge, dang it. They all escaped. But they found out that we wouldn't cede that space to them, and we saved Portland from unspeakable evil that day.

Which brings me to my point, but I would first like everyone to notice that I haven't even once mentioned sausage, or its savory deliciousness, its perfect proportions of protein and fat, and how I really deserve some after not mentioning it all this time—and no, that shoutout to the kielbasa food truck didn't count!

My point is that you always have to fight the monsters. It's your duty. You can't let the monsters win, whether they are big beastly things or tiny fluffy things. We don't know why they're doing what they're doing or why they're doing it here. But we have to fight them here so everyone else will be safe.

Thank you for listening, and in lieu of applause, please make sausage donations at your earliest opportunity.

CHAPTER 20

The Alabama Troll Slayer

I admire dogs because they have life figured out. They are here to love and be loved, and that's pretty much it. There are side jobs they attend to with gusto—eating, napping, barking at squirrels, maybe digging some holes in the yard—but loving others and being loved in return is the main gig, and they know it. They ignore most everything that gets us upset and remain laser-focused on why we're all here. They're role models, honestly, and they remind me of what's important.

Ya-ping was quick to assure Oberon that she'd find some great sausage as soon as possible and thanked him for the story, and Buck promised him some too on our behalf, which I emphasized with a thumbs-up.

But Officer Campbell had questions. "Your name used to be Atticus, not Connor?"

The Iron Druid grinned. "Legal name change," he explained.

"And you're a Druid? Did I catch that correctly?"

"I am."

"And you summoned dogs and cats in Portland to chase an army of squirrels back into the trees?"

"Heh! You're not required to believe it. The takeaway about monsters was real, though."

My phone pinged. It was Nadia.

Al, get off the road like you're hobbits dodging a wraith. People coming.

I relayed this to the group and we picked our way into the bush about ten meters or so, allowing the trees and shrubbery to screen us from the road.

"Don't we want to see people? Get some help?" the officer asked Ya-ping.

"Explaining everything would only slow us down. You know by now there's a lot to explain."

"But we're not going anywhere anyway. We're waiting for someone, right?"

"Right. She's got intel on where the terrorists are. But we don't want others getting involved in this."

The rumble of motors silenced us, and we ducked down as best we could behind ferns. Peeking through the fronds, I saw three large open-backed trucks with police and SES workers looking into the bush. With so many eyes pointed in our direction, I felt sure someone would see us, but they motored by without slowing. The puddles of ash left by the Fae yak badgers were not even questioned.

Once they were safely past, Connor asked the officer, "Where do you think they're going?"

"Scouting trip to see if they can find me or the park ranger or, uh . . . Roxanne over there, somewhere on the road or nearby it. Once they travel the length of where they think we could have gone in the time we've been missing, they'll start searching along the roads a bit more thoroughly. Those people in the trucks will walk on either side in a picket line, perhaps as wide as where we are, to see if they can find us near the road or at least find some trace of us to track further. They won't go deep into the bush unless they can get an idea of where we went."

They're past, I Signaled to Nadia.

Good. Stay there. I'm still about an hour out.

[According to Nadia, we have an hour to kill,] I announced. [Anyone else have a story?] My hobgoblin jumped in.

"Aye, I can tell ye a monster story. And before ye say no, MacBharrais, let me assure ye that it's both warm and thrilling, like yer maw."

I sighed and covered my face with a hand. I make mistakes sometimes, and this would no doubt count as one of them.

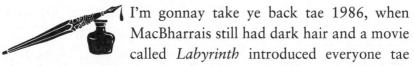 I'm gonnay take ye back tae 1986, when MacBharrais still had dark hair and a movie called *Labyrinth* introduced everyone tae David Bowie's package, courtesy of some insanely tight trousers. Pablo Escobar and his cartel were supplying the world's massive cocaine habit, and word of the human fascination with this powdered recreation reached the Fae planes with disastrous consequences for hobgoblins.

Oi, I see ye there, Officer Campbell. Hold yer questions, ya walloper, and just enjoy the story as a fable if ye want. Nobody needs ye tae believe a word of it is real, least of all me.

Hobgoblins have never had a thirst for power, which I suppose is fortunate for everyone. We thirst, instead, tae hold the powerful in check, tae prevent or avenge abuses of power. Sometimes that's as simple as stealing from the rich and giving tae the poor. And sometimes it's putting ourselves in the service of the powerful so that we can rein them in or sabotage them as need arises. The powerful like tae cast us as fools—the most famous example is Shakespeare's play about the Fae. (Robin Goodfellow is not even *close* to a real hobgoblin name, by the way, but Oberon and Titania weren't real either, so that's poetic license for ye.) But the powerful also like tae use us tae do things they cannae; the ability tae teleport gives them all kinds o' wicked fantasies. We are ever vigilant, therefore, for signs of abuse.

Back in this time, having heard of the human Pablo Escobar, a particularly nasty troll chieftain crafted a plan tae use our strength against us and then use our abilities tae enrich himself. He traveled tae the Morrigan's Fen, where he knew of a swamp hag who could enchant artifacts with magical auras. Somehow—we never found out how, because she died mysteriously soon afterward—he convinced her tae enchant a ring that projected a field thirty feet around it, and inside that field, no hobgoblin could teleport in or out.

The troll used that ring tae embark on a campaign of terror that we will never forget or forgive, all in an attempt tae enslave us.

His basic demand was that hobgoblins serve him and bring him whatever he wanted from the human world. Our counteroffer was that he should insert state-fair-prizewinning vegetables intae every available orifice. And that's when he got nasty. He targeted hobgoblin men, who didnae realize until too late that they couldnae teleport out of danger, and he castrated them, taking their nutsacks as trophies. The ultimatum was tae serve him or he'd keep going and we'd die out. Most of the hobs he caught didnae survive the experience.

He dipped his trophies in resin or sumhin like that tae preserve them and nailed them up all around his den—which was really a warren or cavern—and he even put little plaques under them with the names of the victims. Ma uncle on ma maw's side, Bunk Shitesquirt, was one of them. (And *that's* a real hobgoblin name for ye, get the fuck out of here with that Goodfellow business.)

Well, that troll had himself a war in little tae no time. But we couldnae teleport in behind him or while he was sleeping tae get an assassin in there or even steal his ring. And he had his den warded and protected—there were plenty of other trolls in there with him. We tried tae be sneaky and poison him, but he had tasters, and he retaliated by castrating more of us. We tried a frontal assault, and that didnae go well for us either. Gods below, we even tried diplomacy!

The legendary Holga Thunderpoot herself petitioned Brighid at the Fae Court to intervene, for what this troll was doing amounted tae slavery and attempted genocide. And the First among the Fae made a fancy speech and paid lip service tae civility and all that but ultimately did nothing about the trolls, just like human social-media companies. And Holga's deep disappointment with Brighid is ultimately what led her tae side with Fand years later during that ill-fated rebellion, but that's another story.

At that point Holga realized we'd need tae think radically. We needed human weapons—and more than that, we needed a human willing tae wield them on our behalf, since it was iron that would bring the trolls down and we couldnae touch it.

The first step was tae stop the violence, so she convinced us tae do two things while she worked on a solution: First, capitulate and serve the trolls temporarily, tae buy time. Second, remove the men from danger. That included me. I was sent tae earth with ma heid shaved bald so I could pretend tae be a sunburnt toddler tae some humans we charmed. I was "adopted" by a very kind and sweet couple from Kentucky, who worried about my persistent sunburn and the fact that I often seemed drunk. I spent months watching a lot of terrible eighties sitcoms and secretly drinking a lot of stolen bourbon. I found it was easier tae pretend I couldnae talk if I was nearly unconscious.

But down in Alabama, another hobgoblin-in-hiding gave Holga Thunderpoot the lead she was looking for: a man who liked tae blow shite up and seemed open tae the possibility of magic existing in the world. His name was Cletus Joe Bob MacCutcheon, and he lived a hop, skip, and a jump north of Huntsville, at the base of a forested hill that was too steep tae develop intae rows of identical homes. It served as a broadcast point for a radio station and some weather equipment instead, but the road tae the top of the hill forked intae a private drive, where the MacCutcheons had owned land for years. It was paved but narrow, since it was more of a long driveway through the woods than a road. At the very end of it, there were five buildings that could best be described as "ramshackle" on a good day. There was a house in need of paint and restoration, a separate garage with a huge black truck in it, an old-fashioned privy left over from days before indoor plumbing, a shed for garden tools and that, and an ancient barn with a rusted roof that now served as a workshop for Cletus.

By day, Cletus was a mechanic at a car dealership. He made enough tae get by and fund his hobby, which was blowing shite up. Not like government buildings or political enemies or anything: Mostly he blew up used furniture he bought at thrift stores or found on the side of the road. He'd bring a friend and an ice chest fulla beers, and together they'd drive an old sofa out tae a deserted spot, like maybe some field laying fallow, and rig the sofa tae explode, filming the whole thing with one of those old clunky video cameras with VHS tapes in them. If there was a fire lingering afterward, they'd go out there and roast a marshmallow in it first, then put it out with a fire extinguisher and take off. This was far more entertaining tae them than watching eighties sitcoms, and I cannae find fault with their choices there.

Holga approached him in his workshop on a Saturday afternoon when he was half drunk, half stoned, and playing with highly volatile materials while holding a lit blunt. A radio was playing a song by 38 Special called "Hold On Loosely," which seemed tae be advice he was taking literally regarding his joint, since he nearly dropped it when Holga said hello from the doorway.

"Who're you?" he demanded—oi, that's ma best Alabama accent, so shut it, MacBharrais. Ye cannae expect me tae do it proper, because I've never been there.

"I'm here tae hire ye," Holga said.

"Hire me? For what?"

Cletus was a white man who wore jeans and a white T-shirt with yellow sweat stains in the armpits. He had a thin, patchy brown beard on his face, as if the hair couldnae be bothered to grow evenly on it, and wore a Huntsville Stars baseball cap because they were new in town at the time. (They don't exist anymore, though; the new team is the Rocket City Trash Pandas.) But the light in his eyes was sharp, mind; he was a bright guy who knew how tae have his illegal fun and no get caught by the polis.

"For the kind of work ye're doin' there," she said.

Cletus looked down at his table full of explosives. "This is a hobby. I ain't looking to go pro. That's how ya find yourself workin' on a chain gang all day with no chance of a beer afterward."

"For this job, ye wouldnae have tae worry about human authorities."

"Uh. What other authorities are there?"

Holga grinned at him. "That's a fine question there, fine indeed."

Cletus sat back and took a contemplative drag on his joint, then exhaled a cloud of smoke out one side of his mouth that eventually curled upward in a half-grin. "This shit I'm smoking is turning out to be better than I thought. What's that accent y'all got there? English?"

"Scottish."

"Scottish, eh? I'm s'posed to be Scottish. Pa was into it too. Had himself a tartan and all that nonsense, thought it was rad, but I never saw the big deal. If the old country was so good, why'd our ancestors move here? Whatever. Tell me why a tiny Scottish woman is in Alabama looking for a dude to blow up stuff."

"Well, Mr. MacCutcheon, do ye believe in the Fae?" she asked.

Cletus shrugged. "Can't rule 'em out," he said. He bent down to a cooler at his feet and fished out a cold one. "Want a beer?"

"Sure, that's kind of ye."

He tossed her a Pabst Blue Ribbon and she caught it, then he pulled out another for himself. They paused to enjoy the pop and hiss of fresh cans being opened and chugged down a few swallows. Cletus swiped at his lips with a back of his hand and then pointed at her with the ember of his blunt. "I guess them stories gotta come from somewhere, don't they? Reckon there's plenty of odd creatures I ain't never seen before. See new ones every time they come out with one of them nature documentaries, and I'm sure there's more where they came from. You're pretty odd, to be honest, if I can say that without being mean. I don't wanna be mean."

"No offense taken. I look odd because I'm Fae. I'm a hobgoblin."

"A hobgoblin, huh?" Cletus belched softly and tried to blow the fumes discreetly away from her. "That's cool."

"Ye can tell I'm a hobgoblin. My skin is light blue."

"It is? Sorry. I have a rare condition called tritanopia. You kinda look a bit green to me, but that's okay. Or maybe it isn't. Are hobgoblins ever green?"

"No, that's usually ogres and trolls. Goblins are blue and pink. The point is, I'm a hobgoblin, and all our names sound funny tae humans, maybe even embarrassing. My name is Thunderpoot. Holga Thunderpoot."

Cletus sniggered. "Thunderpoot. That's good, though. Better than a squeaky poot." He took another drag on his joint, down tae just a wee nubbin now. "I gotta remember to get me some more of this shit from Bobby Ray. He was like, 'Sorry, man, all's I got is this stuff my cousin grew in his backyard in Biloxi,' but it is hands-down the best dime bag I've ever scored at this point. Makes me wonder what is up with the soil in Bobby Ray's cousin's backyard."

And that is when Holga realized that Cletus didnae think she was even real. She toyed briefly with the idea of coming back at a later time but reconsidered. Cletus might be in a more receptive frame of mind, so she should take advantage of that.

"We hobgoblins are suffering right now, Mr. MacCutcheon. A band of trolls are killing us and compelling us tae work for them. We need yer help tae be free of it."

"Why would trolls want y'all to work for them? Again, not to be mean, but I bet you couldn't lift a tire."

"We can steal shite for them. Because we can teleport."

"I beg your pardon? You said teleport?"

"Aye. Watch me carefully now. I'm over here by the door. I'm gonnay be on top of yer table in a second. Are ye ready?"

Cletus blinked a few times, then said, "No, wait. Lemme clear off a space. Y'all don't wanna step in this stuff, trust me."

He got tae his feet, extinguished his joint, and put down his beer. In a few seconds, he had a corner of the table clear of debris, and then he sat back down and picked up his beer again.

"All right, Miss Thunderpoot, I'm ready. You can teleport there when—holy shit! Wow! You weren't kidding."

"Naw, I wasnae. Magic is real. The Fae are real. And we have a real problem with the trolls. We need yer help tae blow up a few of them and set ma people free."

Cletus gulped. "Why me?"

"Do ye know what ye're doing with all this explosive shite?"

"Yeah. Got all my fingers and toes and everything."

"And have ye been caught?"

"Nope."

"Are ye an arsehole tae people, like trolls are?"

"I certainly try not to be. Mom would be so disappointed."

"Then that's why we picked ye, Mr. MacCutcheon. One of ma relatives found ye and told me about ye."

"A relative? You mean another hobgoblin found me?"

"Aye. Yer friend Darryl—the one ye blow shite up with sometimes—has a new kid, right? It's no a kid. It's a hobgoblin who's charmed them tae think he's a kid. He heard the two of ye plotting tae destroy a futon. So let's get tae dickering. What's it gonnay take tae get ye tae agree tae help us?"

"Well, I'm not sure what we're even talking about. You just want, what, a bomb or two? Something on a timer or a trigger or a manual detonation?"

"We need sumhin with plenty of iron shrapnel. The iron is key because it disrupts magic, and the troll's den is warded nine ways tae Nancy."

"Who's Nancy?"

"I don't know, but she must be important if there are nine ways tae her."

"What's this troll's name, then, who's causing all the trouble?"

"He is known as Blech Karnage the Nutbane."

Cletus Joe Bob MacCutcheon started giggling at that point and couldnae stop. He wound up falling off his chair after a minute and continuing on the ground until he couldnae laugh anymore.

"That can't be real!" he howled. And it took some time tae get through tae him, but Holga explained that just as hobgoblins tend tae have silly names on purpose, because it lets us get close tae powerful people we wannay take down a few notches, trolls have naming conventions that they think are intimidating but are in fact unintentionally amusing.

"They choose first names tae sound revolting, and Blech is as common as John or Mike. Hork and Plop are also common, and then their surnames often refer tae violence somehow, like Bloodsmear or Limbchop. Karnage with a K is sort of the equivalent of spelling Smith with an i as Smyth with a y." And then she explained that he earned his title for literally being the bane of hobgoblins' nuts, and that's why we needed his help.

That calmed Cletus down, and he apologized for laughing.

"It's awright, ye didnae know. So. How can we make this work?"

"Well, if you can really steal stuff without getting caught, I want two things: First is the jukebox down at this dive bar called Swampy Dick's. It has all the songs I like on it, but I don't like payin' their beer prices to listen to them. Owner doesn't like me anyway, on account of the consensual intimate relations I had one time with his sister. You get that jukebox here and plugged in and you're halfway there. I can build your explosives and listen to my music."

"What's the second thing?"

"A brand-new queen-sized mattress, stuffed full of cash. Fifties, please, not twenties or hundreds."

"Awright, but . . . why fifties?"

"Because Andrew Jackson, who's on the twenty, was pretty much a troll like Blech Karnage. And the one time in my life I tried to pay for something with a hundred-dollar bill was for groceries, and the cashier just stared at me and wouldn't take it. Asked me if it was counterfeit first, and then asked who I stole it from, because I guess I didn't look like someone who'd ever have a hundred dollars to spend. When I insisted it was real then he changed things up and asked me if I thought I was better than him because I had a hundred dollars. Said I was puttin' on airs. And he was just way out of bounds, you know, but people were staring at me like I was some snotty rich guy or something, and I guess that embarrassment kind of scarred me, y'know? Even though I didn't do anything wrong. I just have this negative reaction to hundreds whenever I see them, and I haven't been back to that store since. He probably doesn't even work there anymore but I wouldn't know. I drive all the way up to Meridianville to get my groceries now. And don't worry, I'm seeing someone and talking this through, because it's ridiculous how this random encounter with a total shitbird haunts me and has changed my life. It's been very good for me and I'm getting better. Or maybe . . ." His eyes darted down tae his ashtray. "Maybe I'm not. Because I'm high as fuck and talking with a hobgoblin about blowing up some trolls. I clearly have my issues too, but I'm working on them. Still want fifties, though."

Money is always a thing that humans want, and it's easy enough tae get if ye can teleport intae a vault and back out again. Holga said, "I will get ye a new queen mattress and plenty of cash and ye can stuff it yerself."

"Fair enough."

And so they both got tae work. Holga had three different heists tae arrange—a jukebox, a mattress, and some cash—and that took a day or two. But she delivered everything before Cletus did. He needed tae get some supplies in—which he paid for with a good chunk of the cash Holga gave him—and could only work on the weekends. But eventually he pronounced himself ready, detailed what he'd made, what he'd bought, and how it would work, and Holga started planning the liberation of hobgoblins from Blech Karnage the Nutbane.

Part of it was tae tell all the hobgoblin men that it was time tae sober up and get ready tae return tae Tír na nÓg. Hundreds of humans shook free of the charms we'd laid on them and realized that they hadn't had strange babies after all. Before I left Kentucky, I told the couple who'd been taking care of me that *The Facts of Life* was a terrible show and didnae actually contain any facts about life.

Another part of it was smuggling the iron weapons intae the Fae planes without killing ourselves. They had tae be wrapped and boxed in three crates and then shuttled in using a very stable Old Way, then brought over land slowly, because we couldnae teleport iron at all. That took additional weeks, and all this while, hobgoblin women were stealing fine Islay whiskies tae be crudely gulped, never savored, by mossy troll gobs; diamonds and gold for troll jewelry, which tends tae start at tacky and quickly escalates tae optical nerve damage; and a metric fuckload of cocaine, the abrupt absence of which no doubt caused the deaths of whoever was supposed tae be guarding or transporting it here on earth.

Yet another part—a rather crucial one—was making sure that Cletus was prepared, mentally, tae pull the trigger.

"I want tae check first," Holga said, "because it's no the kind of thing ye should assume: The important bit about being a troll slayer is the actual slaying. Are ye gonnay be able tae do that?"

Cletus thought about it before answering. "Well, these are trolls who are enslaving people, so I don't think it'll be a problem, as long as you give me an out."

"An out?"

"Yeah. If you've misrepresented the situation, I shouldn't be expected to follow through. Liberating folks from slavery is something I can get behind. That's some monstrous shit and deserves a monstrous response. But if I get there, and, like, the trolls are cute and nice, or the hobgoblins still have their nuts, or I find out that anything you've said ain't true—well, I should be able to hold my fire."

"That's fine by me," Holga said. "In fact, I'm pure pleased that ye said that. And ye'll find that I've spoken true about every detail."

When all was in place, we had tae wait for the right moment tae bring Cletus over, making sure that Blech Karnage was in his den and then getting word tae all the hobgoblins tae clear out discreetly in advance of the attack. It was difficult tae figure that part out, because these were some extremely coked-up trolls we were dealing with. They were paranoid as all the hells. If the hobgoblins just all vanished, Blech would realize sumhin was up.

And then, on a Sunday, the moment finally arrived. Holga showed up at Cletus's house as he was washing his truck and detailing it.

"It's time," she said, and presented him with a gift-wrapped box.

"It's time, huh? What's this?"

"A wee sumhin tae help ye confirm I've spoken true."

It was a brass spyglass—a telescope. "Ye can have a look at the den ahead of the attack, and if I've lied tae ye, ye'll have an out."

"All right," he said, and he turned his baseball cap around on his heid. "Let's go."

Holga couldnae take Cletus through tae the Fae planes using a bound tree, so they had tae drive in that huge black pickup tae an Old Way in Tennessee, but once Holga got him tae Tír na nÓg, she was able tae use shortcuts tae bring him a few hundred meters away from the den of Blech Karnage the Nutbane. There were twelve hobgoblin women there, and their job was tae protect Cletus so he could get tae Karnage. One of them was ma aunt, Prissy Shitesquirt, who wanted tae avenge ma uncle, and so I have the account from her. (The hobgoblin men, including me, were out of range for the moment; we were gonnay converge on the spot after we knew for sure that we had Karnage trapped inside.)

There was some cover there, trees and shrubs and the like, and as soon as Cletus arrived, the hobs opened the three boxes of weapons. One of them just contained four handguns with custom ammunition that Cletus had made himself: They fired iron slugs. It was one of the few things that could penetrate the natural armor of troll skin. The boxes were on wheelbarrows, and they'd be pushed alongside Cletus as they advanced, allowing him tae reach in and get whatever he needed. The rest of the hobs had shields tae protect Cletus from return fire, though it wouldnae be gunfire; it would be in the form of spears and arrows.

The telescope got used first, and Cletus had himself a nice long look.

The den was an arched cave entrance of grey stone set intae the side of some low hills. Above the entrance and crawling upward, a thin layer of soil allowed some grass and shrubbery tae grow, but of more importance was a guard platform nestled above the entrance. There were also two towers tae either side and set forward about fifty meters—as soon as we left cover, they'd have a clear field of fire. The trolls in them were not bored and sluggish; they were hyperalert and twitchy, in constant movement, and some telltale white powder could be seen on their upper lips. Some of them were grey-skinned sorts, and some were a light blue to Cletus's eyes but were in fact a light green.

Unaided, Cletus could see some textured bumps around the entrance itself; with the telescope, he could see that these were the grisly trophies Holga had told him about.

"God damn," Cletus breathed. "That there is some evil shit."

"I probably should have mentioned," Holga said, "Blech will try tae take yer nuts too if he can. Just so ye know the stakes here."

Before Cletus could reply, a troll patrol discovered them. They'd been quiet in their approach, and the hobs had no been looking tae the flanks. When the trolls saw the hobs, though, they knew immediately that they were staring down a threat. And the presence of a human was a red flag. They roared, raised their spears, and attacked the nearest hobgoblins. Their spear tips pierced nothing but air, however, as the women ported out of the way; Blech Karnage's enchanted ring wasnae in range.

Cletus dropped the telescope and lunged for a handgun in a

crate. One of the trolls realized he could represent a serious problem and charged. The hobs couldnae stop him—at least no without more time tae prepare. He was eight feet tall and close tae four hundred pounds, and they were two feet tall and maybe fifty pounds on the beefy end.

Demonstrating a coolness under pressure, Cletus snagged a gun and kept moving, flipping off the safety and jacking a round intae the chamber, then squeezing off three quick shots as the troll bore down on him, spear raised.

The iron slugs tore intae his chest, first halting his momentum and then knocking him back off his feet, which surprised everyone, really. Trolls are used tae looking and behaving like juggernauts. Cletus fired a round intae his heid tae finish him and then took leisurely aim at the other troll, who'd frozen in surprise, and placed a round between his eyes.

"No going back now," Cletus said, tossing aside the gun and moving tae a second crate. "Shields up and out, y'all. We're taking the towers first."

Ma Aunt Prissy was part of the shield wall with Holga, formed of nine hobs because the other three were on the wheelbarrows. The shields were fairly wee and made of wood, just enough tae stop an arrow or a spear, the hope being that we'd see relatively few of them and no a huge volley.

The bulk of the money Cletus had spent was on a highly illegal black-market purchase of rocket-propelled grenades. There were three American-made M72s, single-use launchers that mounted on the shoulder and fired with little recoil, though Cletus warned everyone no tae stand behind him when he fired, since the blowback from the rocket was intense. As soon as they emerged from cover, the guards in the towers spotted them—they were already looking in that direction because they'd heard the gunshots. They howled and rushed tae grab their bows. The first rocket whooshed out of the tube and sent the tower on the left up in a glorious orange ball of flame, and at that point the guards in the other towers realized they were in a real scrap.

The arrows came and the women did their best tae meet them as Cletus grabbed another rocket launcher. They formed a little hobgoblin wall in front of his body, standing on shoulders, shields upraised, leaping into the air as necessary. Sometimes the arrows didnae *thunk* into their shields but sank into their flesh; ma aunt took an arrow tae the knee and still walks with a limp. Two others—Anita Goodbang and Bonnie Bedwell—died, sacrificing themselves to the cause. But Cletus took no arrows.

The second grenade destroyed the tower on the right, and that created a little space, since only the platform above the cave entrance remained. They had fewer arrows coming at them, and their accuracy was off since they were farther away. And then the volleys ceased altogether, because a squad of trolls charged out of the warren, wielding giant maces and spears and the like. The mace heads were carved stone lined with bronze, and they did an absolutely smashing job at smashing, in case ye wondered.

But since they saw 'em coming and Blech Karnage wasnae among them, the hobgoblins could do sumhin about it. They ported out in pairs, with a length of rope stretched between 'em, and tripped the bastards as they charged. One would go down and take at least one other with him, if not more. The hobs would port back before the trolls could smash them, then another pair would port out and trip up another one. It slowed down the charge quite nicely and gave Cletus the time tae line up a shot at the platform. Once that shook the hillside and brought all kinds o' debris raining down across the entrance, the alarm was well and truly sounded inside. More trolls started boiling out of there. And Cletus switched tae his guns, slowly advancing as the coked-up monsters tried tae rush him. The hobgoblins slowed them down, allowing Cletus tae take his shots—and he was a good one. Trolls are big targets, tae be sure, but he was pure aces, hittin' them someplace vital, in the heid or their huge necks, and then the iron did the rest. They ran out of trolls before he ran out of bullets, but it wasnae over.

Blech Karnage had no come out of his cave. He was smart

enough at least tae know that if he came out, he could be surrounded. And he might have heard there was a human out there
with human weapons, mowing down his grand gang of bastards,
so sticking his heid out would be unwise. And besides, he was
warded and protected in there. I mean wards beyond the
no-teleportation field. Kinetic ones, designed tae foil things like
explosions and projectiles. They were painted on the floor, walls,
and ceilings. It's why we could never collapse the damn hill on his
heid. But once Holga had explained the situation tae our mechanic, he came up with a plan.

They gathered around the entrance tae the den and peered inside. It reeked, of course, because trolls are no good housekeep-
ers. There were rats squeaking and spiders lurking and plenty of
offal splattered around and flies buzzing about all the offal. Blech
Karnage would be deep down, humping a pumpkin or sumhin.

On the sides of the entrance, they got a closer look at the
mounted trophies. The women were reading the names, and ma
Aunt Prissy cried out, for she found ma uncle's there, and others
found names of people close tae them.

Cletus said, "I'm so sorry. But we need to press the advantage
before more trolls come out. I need the first cave team to come
with me."

Cave Team One was just three hobgoblins in thick-soled
boots—one for the wheelbarrow carrying the crate with the guns
in it, and two more tae serve as a shield or distraction if any trolls
emerged. They carried torches too. The rest remained outside.

They rolled in, illuminating a medium-sized cavern with ten-
foot ceilings that was perhaps forty feet wide and deep before
branching intae two different passages below. They knew from
intelligence gathered by the women who'd worked there that the
right-hand passage led tae the personal rooms of Blech Karnage;
the left led tae all sorts of other rooms, including quarters for
most of the other trolls. Cletus pulled back a sheet of leather that
effectively separated the guns in the wheelbarrow from the goodies underneath. Those goodies were little iron balls, about the size

of the fingernail on yer pinky. He thrust his hand down intae all that iron, which made the hobs shudder, and pulled out a handful. He scattered them on the floor over a painted ward he could plainly see and over a couple of other places the hobs pointed at because they could sense some magic there.

The point wasnae tae create uncertain footing but tae let that iron weaken or even destroy those wards on the floor. He kinda stomped on them and rolled them around all over the wards, until the hobgoblins told him he'd most likely done the deed proper. Then they scooted out of there.

Outside, Cletus reached intae the third crate for the first time and pulled out one of his own creations: a pipe bomb packed full of even more of those iron balls. He lit the fuse with a lighter out of his pocket and tossed it in, warning everyone tae get away from the entrance. The resulting explosion drove the iron shrapnel intae the walls and ceiling, where it could disrupt the wards there. Those wards were keeping the place structurally intact and maybe even fulfilling other security functions—they didnae know the full extent of the magic in Karnage's den, just that it had been impregnable so far. Cletus was making it pregnable.

They waited a bit for the dust tae settle and see if any more trolls came raging out of there. When none did, Holga and Cletus and Cave Team One entered again tae survey the damage. There was a wee crater where the bomb had exploded, and plenty of shrapnel was scattered about and embedded in the walls. Most interesting, there was a collection of those balls lined up at the threshold tae the two passages at the back.

The shrapnel had tried tae travel past it, but its failure tae do so indicated that there were kinetic wards in effect there.

"Huh. Would ya lookit that," Cletus said. "That's pretty gnarly."

"I thought that would have brought some trolls running," Holga mused. "I don't like this. They're planning sumhin. Waiting for us tae come tae them."

"Well, we have plans too."

"Right. Let's be about it."

Cletus repeated the procedure of spreading iron on the floor of the left-hand passage, which would allow him tae explode some more bombs, in turn deactivating wards on the walls and ceilings and making them vulnerable tae cave-ins. It took a total of five pipe bombs tae accomplish it, but eventually the left-hand passage caved in and however many trolls were down there would-nae be coming up again.

The right-hand passage was still open and perfectly sound, its protections fortifying it against all the explosions happening on the other side. That was fine with her: Holga didnae want tae merely trap Blech Karnage down there, because that would allow someone tae dig him up someday and take that ring and dominate hobgoblins again. She wanted the ring destroyed, so they'd be going down there tae find him.

Cave Team Two was three hobgoblins armed with push brooms, and it was their time tae shine. Cletus upended the crate of iron balls ontae the floor of the right-hand passage and the hobs pushed the wee spheres along, allowing them tae disrupt the magic of any wards or enchantments on the floor. Cletus followed behind, hand-gun at the ready.

At first, there was nothing tae worry about. They heard grunts and rumblings in the distance, but nothing seemed close. They peeked intae a couple of rooms that had been carved out and decorated with troll nonsense, confirmed they were clear of anything dangerous except for the smells, and kept going.

They realized after a while that they were no hearing grumbles and roars anymore. It had gone too quiet, ye see.

They arrived at the bottom of the cavern complex and discovered it was lit by a shiteload of torches. It was the final cavern, which had a bunch of satellite rooms protected by actual doors. There was an underground river flowing through there tae the right and a water mill churning, doing some kinda work, and that noise echoed throughout the cavern. There were barrels of stolen whisky and literal crates of cocaine stacked up by the river. Some rats had gotten intae the cocaine and were scurrying about, squeaking like mad, because it's a hell of a drug. But there were no trolls visible, which was weird.

Because of all the noise, they didnae hear the clucking until it was too late.

One of the hobgoblin women in Cave Team Two, Molly Gash-beard, pointed her push broom off tae the left. "Look out!" she said, pointing. "It's a—" and then she turned tae stone. Holga immediately pulled Cletus back out of there, intae the passage, where they couldnae see the cavern except straight ahead, and the other hobs ported intae the hall with their brooms. They still weren't inside the nullification field of Karnage's ring.

"Lord, what happened?" Cletus asked. "Was that, like, a gorgon or something?"

"They have a cockatrice," Holga said. "That's why the bastards are holed up in their rooms. They left a stone-cold chicken snake in there tae take care of us."

Cletus had heard of cockatrices before. Poisonous magical creatures, roosters with snake tails, sometimes confused with basilisks, that can turn victims tae stone with a look. He talked as he moved tae the crate full of pipe bombs.

"We need some of y'all to close your eyes and push iron in that direction to clear out any kinetic wards. Then I'll lob some bombs in there."

The two surviving members of Cave Team Two got on it, keeping their eyes tae the ground, keeping their ears open, and hoping the cockatrice would give a cluck. Shoving the iron balls in that direction did exactly what they hoped: It deactivated wards and alarmed the cockatrice enough tae make some noise.

"All right, that's good, y'all come back," he said. They did so and he lit up a bomb and tossed it toward the sound of the cockatrice, careful tae not look in that direction. A startled squawk followed the explosion, and Cletus grinned.

"Winner, winner, chicken dinner," he said.

A deep troll voice roared, "Bring me their heids!" and all the trolls who'd been hiding behind those doors burst out of there, armed with maces and sporting additional armor on top of their troll skin. It was thick and heavy hardened leather, some of it encrusted with jewels that hobs had recently stolen for them, and a possible impediment tae the iron slugs that Cletus had left.

"Eyes!" Holga shouted, and the hobgoblin women all drew their bronze stilettos and ported ontae the backs of the charging trolls while they could.

There is no way that hobs can match trolls in strength or penetrate the natural armor of their skin. Their only vulnerability is their eyes, so our automatic response tae a troll attack is tae blind them at minimum and shove that stiletto all the way intae their wee troll brains if possible. MacBharrais has seen me do it before—we had a stooshie with a troll not so long ago.

The trolls, of course, are aware of the tactic and expect it. So as soon as they feel us on their backs, they try to dislodge us—or else they whip those maces back and try tae smash us. They drop facedown intae the dirt sometimes tae deny us a target. They'll cover their eyes with a hand, preventing us from stabbing through. There's no standard tactic, because trolls cannae get themselves organized enough for that. So the key, always, is tae move fast and get out of there; ye take yer shot and run, and if ye miss or yer blocked, take off and try again.

Ma Aunt Prissy was actually riding one of the wheelbarrows and couldnae fight, but she didnae want tae miss a thing. There were nine trolls, including Blech Karnage, and nine remaining hobgoblins, including ma aunt, plus Cletus. The one port was all they got, because Karnage emerged from his chamber wearing that blasted ring and the nullification field quickly enveloped the fighters. Four of them, including Holga, successfully delivered stilettos tae the brain. Two of them—Madge Vadgewater and Torie Knobgristle—missed their targets and couldnae port away, and they got smashed deid. Two others missed but jumped free, pursued by the trolls. So focused on the hobgoblins were they, the big bastards forgot all about Cletus.

He coolly pumped a round intae four trolls, dropping each one with a heid shot, and then he was out of ammunition. The only one left was Blech Karnage, and he, at least, realized that he was on the verge of losing everything because of that human.

So he ignored the hobgoblins and charged at Cletus, his mace held high and ready tae strike.

Cletus had no functioning weapons, but he threw his gun at Karnage just tae annoy him, maybe sting him with the iron on the barrel. It bounced harmlessly off the brute's armor, but Cletus stood his ground and roared back at the troll.

The thing is, Karnage really shouldnae have ignored the hobgoblins. There were six fighting women left, including Holga Thunderpoot herself, and while they couldnae teleport ontae his back, they could still jump and scramble faster than any troll.

All six of them attacked Karnage at once, leaping ontae his head and shoulders and making him take notice. He had tae stop and deal with it, dropping his mace and tearing at the women trying tae shove a stiletto intae his eyes. He crushed Wanda Wildbush's ribs in his fist and threw her so far she landed in the underground river. He ripped Kiki Sleekcheeks from his face and threw her at his feet before he stomped on her. He batted Penny Bigbone away—or so he thought. She held on tae his finger, and while he was distracted, trying tae shake her off like a boogie, Holga Thunderpoot, gods bless her, saw her chance. She lunged and thrust her stiletto intae his left eye, shoving it in all the way tae the hilt.

Blech Karnage made a choking noise in his throat—"Hurrk!"—convulsed once, and fell backward, Holga riding him all the way down.

And the first thing she did after pulling out her blade was to take that damn ring off the Nutbane's finger and give it tae Cletus Joe Bob MacCutcheon.

"When ye get back tae earth," she said, "ye must melt this down tae nothing and witness it with yer own eyes. If ye throw it away, it can be found again. It must be destroyed. Promise me."

"I promise," he said, and slipped it intae his pocket.

Well, they celebrated and looted the place, and they mourned the deid and carried the stone figure of Molly Gashbeard out of there tae be returned tae her family, forever a heroine for saving them all from the cockatrice. And once they emerged from the den, ma Aunt Prissy Shitesquirt did sumhin that inadvertently caused a phenomenon in the human world.

Ye see, everyone wanted tae thank Cletus somehow. They gave him a barrel of whisky, which he appreciated, and tried tae give him a crate of cocaine, though he said no thanks tae that. They promised tae steal all his groceries for him for a year and give him another mattress full of fifties. They were gonnay take him tae Mag Mell, the heroes' plane, and let him experience paradise for a day, soaking in healing springs and drinking free beer. Holga was gonnay bring all the Thunderpoots out tae his property and give all the buildings a new paint job and spruce up the place. But Aunt Prissy had nothing tae give him, and she was wounded and couldnae perform any service for him.

So she took down ma uncle's nuts off the side of the den and gave them tae Cletus, who didnae know what tae say. Tae be fair, the gifting of nuts isnae commonplace, bound by well-established rules of etiquette, so we can forgive Cletus for being somewhat adrift.

"Y'all are giving me . . . some green nuts?" he said.

"They're light blue," she pointed out.

"Aw, shit. Sorry. Tritanopia. But, uh . . . I have to admit, I'm not sure what to do with a pair of blue balls."

"They are proof of the kind of human ye are. A man who will ride tae the aid of strangers. My husband will always be a stranger tae ye, but in a way, you've given him back tae me. I've heard ye drive an impressive motor back on earth."

"Naw, it's just a big ol' truck."

"It would be an honor for ma family if this wee bit of Bunk could ride with ye always, a talisman of sorts, so that ma family could look after ye the way you have looked after us."

"You sure? Like, are these going to be okay in the sun and weather and all?"

"Oh, yes, they're sealed and inert at this point. Tanned, cured, whatever."

Cletus gently squeezed them experimentally. "They're kinda tough and tender at the same time."

"That's hobgoblins for ye."

"All right. I'm honored, Mrs. Shitesquirt."

When Holga led Cletus back tae Tennessee through the Old Way, he hung the preserved blue balls of my uncle, Bunk Shitesquirt, from the trailer hitch on the back of his truck, thereby displaying the world's first pair of truck nuts. He had no inkling at the time what cultural insanity this action would inspire; he was merely trying tae honor the wishes of a widow. Humans didnae understand that the first pair of truck nuts was a memorial and a testament tae the debt hobgoblins owed the Alabama Troll Slayer, as he's now known, and Cletus could hardly explain.

He's an ol' man now, like MacBharrais here, but he owns MacCutcheon's Garage and his property's been all fixed up tae look fancy. He still goes out tae his workshop on the weekends and listens tae his jukebox, still drives a truck with ma uncle's wizened nuts dangling on the back, and still wears a ball cap, but it's the Rocket City Trash Pandas now. What Oberon told ye earlier is truth: Ye always have tae fight the monsters, no matter where they are. And sometimes, tae do it right, ye need tae enlist the help of some unlikely allies. Allies like yerselves, is what I'm sayin'. It's grand tae be here on this adventure with ye.

CHAPTER 21

It's a Trap

Ya-ping clapped and beamed at Buck. "Beauty, mate. If any-one ever says to me that they've heard it all, I'll stop them and say they definitely haven't, they really, *really* haven't."

"I've always wondered about how truck nuts got started," Of-ficer Campbell said. "Somehow, that whole thing with hobgob-lins and trolls and cocaine sounds way more likely than someone independently thinking it would be a good idea."

[I have a question, Buck: Why didn't you, or your aunt, join Holga Thunderpoot on Fand's side of the rebellion against Brighid, if Holga was such a culture hero?]

"Because hobgoblins are no a monolith, ya tit, any more than any other group of people are. Admiring someone for their ac-tions on one day doesnae mean I have tae agree with them on everything after that. And besides, ma aunt taught me never tae play with fire. Ye can skate by for about the lifespan of a mayfly, sure, but eventually ye get burned, and Holga did, along with the rest of them. I understand the choice she made, but I didnae agree with it, and I'm damn sorry it turned out the way it did."

A black SUV of indeterminate make and model crunched gravel

underneath its tires, and we ducked down in case it was someone random, but the vehicle parked directly across from us and my manager's spiked mohawk emerged, followed by the rest of her. She wore a black racerback top, black nail polish and lipstick, black jeans, and black Doc Martens. But that wasn't enough. She moved to the vehicle's boot to get something else, looking directly at the ferns and trees we were hiding behind on her way there.

"Awright, Al?" My hobgoblin waved and Nadia nodded. "Hey, Buck."

She opened up the trunk and we heard a zipping noise as she accessed some luggage. The jacket she pulled out of there looked extraordinarily dangerous—even more so once she put it on. It was black leather, of course, but the shoulders, lapels, and forearms were covered with chrome spikes and studs. The spikes weren't modest quarter-inch things either: On top of the shoulders and the forearms, the spikes were easily two inches long, which meant absolutely zero pigeons would be attempting to roost on her today. That it was far too hot for any sort of jacket did not matter: Nadia was ready for a fight. She was a sleek goth avatar of pain.

Whenever Nadia looks a bit over-the-top like this—and I should admit that she frequently looks over-the-top—I take particular joy in introducing her to others.

[Everyone, this is Nadia Padmanabhan, my accountant.]

"Your . . . accountant?" Officer Campbell said with his eyes wide, providing exactly the reaction I relished.

"Most people are scared of taxes," Nadia said as she approached, extending her hand to the officer. "Al keeps me around to scare the taxes away."

"Yeah," Officer Campbell managed, shaking her hand and staring at the spikes on her jacket. "I can see how they would be."

"He's a good boss, ye know. Not every boss considers the exercise requirements of their accountants, not tae mention their mental health. Al gets intae scraps often enough that I can maintain ma fitness and redirect ma anger at the patriarchy in a positive manner. Ye know what I mean, right? Fuck the patriarchy."

"Uh. Right," Officer Campbell said.

Connor and Ya-ping flashed welcoming smiles at Nadia and stated their pleasure at meeting her. Roxanne also grinned and offered the comment that she really liked Nadia's clothes.

Nadia squatted to give the hounds a few scratches. She looked up at Connor. "It's nice tae meet ye. I'm worried about these good dugs, though. There's all kinds of terrible traps ahead, and if they wander, something will get them. Can ye leash them or sumhin?"

"It's not necessary," he said. "Tell them what to do. They understand spoken language."

"Are ye sure? Willing tae bet their lives on it?"

"I'll confirm they understand. Tell us what needs to happen."

"Awright. There's another ridge like this a few hundred meters to the east. Down past that ridge is where ye want tae go—that's the source of the problem. But between here and that other ridge, there are a shiteload of traps. Some of them are magical, some of them mundane. There are ranks of them, and going around isnae an option. The whole area's encircled with traps. So I'm gonnay lead ye through it, and we're gonnay have tae set some of them off. The key tae making it through is tae move single file, step where I step, and be patient. It's gonnay be slow going. The dugs, especially, need tae be careful, because in some cases there are bullet traps called toe poppers out there. We can step over them, but the dugs might hit them with their gait. Can they see yellow spray paint?"

"Aye," Connor said.

"Good. I brought some. We need that, a branch, and a decent-sized rock or two, and we can get going."

She fetched the spray paint from her car, and Ya-ping asked what a toe popper was.

Officer Campbell answered. "They're booby traps where a bullet has been carefully placed above a nail. Step on the bullet—

which is concealed—and it's pressed onto the sharp end of the nail, which acts like the firing pin of a gun. The bullet shoots straight up into the foot and perhaps the leg."

Nadia returned with the can of spray paint and picked up a length of fallen eucalyptus branch, hefting it experimentally.

"Right. This'll do. Okay. Magic Druid man, right behind me and yer dugs behind you. I'm gonnay need ye tae disable some magic stuff if ye can. All the rest of ye follow behind them, single file. Call out if ye're unsure of where tae step next. I'll stop and guide ye. And I may shout at ye if ye're about tae cock up. Stop when I say and do no move until I say. Is that clear?"

Everyone said it was clear, and I wound up trailing behind Ya-ping, with Buck, Officer Campbell, and Roxanne bringing up the rear. But Nadia narrowed her eyes as the supposed volunteer slunk even farther back.

"Sorry, who are you again?"

"Roxanne. Don't let the name tag fool you."

Nadia gestured at the uniform. "And . . . what are ye?" Oh, shite. Here we go.

"This is the uniform of the Victoria SES." That was a true statement but not an actual answer to the question.

"So that's all? There's nothing more tae ye?"

"What do you mean?" Roxanne answered a question with a question.

"I just feel there's something about ye—I'm a bit psychic, if you want tae call it that, and I got a flash of you doing something violent in the future."

"I'd be surprised if you didn't. Have you met men?" Yet another redirection.

Nadia paused before deploying a brief smile and saying, "Fair enough." She turned on her heel and led us into the bush, and I blinked in surprise. In the normal course of events, she would never do that. She must have sensed that she shouldn't push it, that there would be no winning an open confrontation with Roxanne.

Which gave me some hope, honestly. If Nadia's power as a battle seer could show her that truth—vague as it might be—then in one sense she had won already, because she was still alive. She had walked to the cliff's edge, peered over, and walked away. That didn't mean she wouldn't take a running leap at it later and dive off, but at least she had avoided blundering into it, and sometimes, simply avoiding the abyss can be counted as a victory.

I had to wonder what had caused this change in her vision, though, and whether it was a onetime event or a permanent improvement in her abilities. Having a vision of me facing mortal peril days ahead in another country was a significant step up. The emergence of more power didn't usually come without a cost, and it was the cost I was worried about.

For about twenty meters the walk was casual, but Nadia slowed down as soon as the slope steepened, and she lowered herself to the ground, telling us to stop. She set down the paint and extended the branch out in front of her so that it hovered a couple of inches above the ground. She must have triggered an invisible trip wire, for a crack occurred and a heavy ball with blades sticking out to the front and sides swung down from the trees to whoosh right through the space a human torso would have occupied. If it didn't outright kill anyone standing in the way, it would have certainly maimed them. Since no one was there, it swung up and then fell back, beginning a slow sequence of pendulum swings.

"Don't move!" Nadia said to us. "This is just the first of many. There are pit traps tae either side of this. If ye dodge out of the way—if ye get scared by a noise and jump—something else gets ye. This whole area is half Vietnam and half wizard."

"What's Vietnam?" Buck whispered to me.

[A war in which booby traps featured prominently. Thousands of soldiers were wounded or killed by them.]

"Oh, shite."

"Crawl under this, straight ahead," Nadia said, and began inching forward beneath the spiked pendulum. Once past the swing of it, she got to her feet and sprayed two spots on the ground with yellow paint, just to the left of a eucalyptus tree.

"Toe poppers. Tell the dugs, Connor. Avoid the paint. We turn here anyway." She scooched to the right, deployed her branch to trip another wire on the other side of the eucalyptus, and a bamboo whip swung into the unoccupied space, with sharpened sticks ready to pierce anything standing, probably thigh-high. We had to carefully squeeze by that before she held us up and turned to Connor, pointing.

"If we step forward here, sumhin bad happens. A summoning. But I don't know how or why, much less how we're supposed tae get past it."

"Ah. Sounds like a hook binding." Those were nasty Fae traps; trigger one and a creature from another plane was summoned, hooked out of hell or wherever they came from, and invariably in a murderous rage about it.

"Awright. Same thing happens if we go left or right, though slightly different things get summoned. If ye can deactivate them, great. If ye can't, we have tae go back and find another path, or fight whatever shows up."

"Okay. Give me a minute. Where does the hook happen?"

"About two meters ahead, by those ferns."

She pointed again, and we could all see what she meant, but Connor looked up and pointed at a gum-tree branch over that spot.

"Got it. Up there, attached to the burl in the branch."

I saw the burl but nothing attached to it. He must have been viewing it in the magical spectrum. I didn't have the enchanted monocle with me that would let me see what was happening there, but I didn't need it. Connor was busy unbinding whatever was there, softly speaking in Old Irish, and he nodded to himself in satisfaction when it was done.

"Good to go under that now."

"Let me check." Nadia peered forward and took a tentative step in the direction of the magical trap, then shook her head.

"Nope. There's another physical trap just past it. Whole bunch of toe poppers. Maybe we can scoot around them without triggering anything magical to the side. Stay where you are."

She did step forward a little bit past the hook binding, but then drifted to the right and sprayed spots on the ground, which formed a horizontal dotted line, an invisible barrier.

"There's more beyond these, so we cannae just step over," she said, answering a question I'm sure more than one of us were thinking. "I'm just lighting up the edge here." She paused frequently to check what was coming to the right, wary of setting off something in that direction. To me it looked like there was a small clearing downhill for a stretch, almost like a ski run, ferns and grasses growing there but no trees. It looked like the kind of space for a pit trap or something, and Nadia was wary of it too. The toe poppers continued all the way to the trunk of a conifer tree, and past that was open space. Nadia's whole body was tense.

"Sumhin's weird here. Like . . . there's a threat here but I cannae see it yet. I get the sense that if I step in there, I'll be fine. But if anyone follows behind, I'll be doomed somehow. No clear idea of what happens. So that's weird. Okay. I'm gonnay step over there, but don't follow, okay? Freeze."

She stretched out her arm past the conifer, and then her right leg. She planted it at the base of a fern. Nothing.

"Okay, all in," she said, and followed up with her left, placing her whole body past the conifer in fern meadow. Still nothing. She spun and crouched down to the ground. "Awright, Connor, I want ye tae inch forward but be ready tae stop when I say. Get close, but don't actually break the plane of that tree with any part of yer body."

"Got it." He began to move forward, slowly, and once he was nearly past the tree, Nadia held up a hand.

"Stop! Lhurnog's gob, go back. Bloody hell. This is a killing field." She came back across with a visible shudder, considered, and then crooked a finger at Ya-ping. "Come here. I want tae see if it's the same for you."

Ya-ping moved past the dogs and stopped when she drew even with Nadia. Nadia stepped back into the meadow, spun, and instructed Ya-ping to move slowly toward her. The apprentice crept forward and Nadia encouraged her to keep coming, and when she got to the point where moving past the plane of the tree was a given, she paused.

"Keep coming?" she asked, one foot in the air.

"Aye, baby steps."

Ya-ping took a baby step, and another, and Nadia kept encouraging her until they were side by side, safe as could be.

"Huh. Good. Connor, same as before. Approach, but don't cross the plane."

He took a step and she immediately threw up a hand. "Stop! If ye step across, it all goes wrong. What do ye see when you look at this space in the magical spectrum?"

Connor cocked his head to the side and looked around for a few seconds. "Nothing special . . . Wait. Something flickered. That was weird. What was—there it went again! I've never seen anything like it. Almost like a glitch in the Matrix. A flash in the spectrum and then it's gone. I can't . . . I can't isolate it. I have no idea what it is."

"Okay, okay, let's try something else," Nadia said. "Good dugs, stay where ye are, please. Al, come forward, slowly, and let's see if ye're good tae go."

I approached the tree, drew even with it, and took one more step before Nadia shouted, "Stop! Al, oh, my gods—it's you too. What do ye have in common?"

Connor and I exchanged a glance. We had very little in common. He was ancient but looked young. I was younger than he but looked ancient. I was a sigil agent and he was a Druid. The Iron Druid, in fact. Oh.

[Iron,] I typed. [Cold iron.]

Connor's brows shot up. "Cold iron? You have some on you?"

[The carbon steel in my cane is alloyed with a smidgen of cold iron. It helps since I can't pierce with it and poison the blood.]

"Understood. So if that's the working theory, then both Oberon and Starbuck should be a no-go as well, because they have cold iron on their collars. Okay to test that?"

"Sure," Nadia said.

Connor and I stepped back, and Nadia gave very careful instructions to Oberon. He took tiny mincing steps forward and my manager stopped him before he crossed the plane, and the same procedure was repeated for Starbuck. Officer Campbell and Roxanne were able to cross into the meadow without trouble.

"Okay, we can get past this," Nadia announced. "Everyone back and get in the same order as before, and watch your feet. Good. Oberon, may I borrow your collar for a wee minute?"

He woofed and wagged his tail, and she removed his collar and told him what a good dug he was. After making sure everyone was clear, she looped the collar around the end of that tree branch she had and stuck it out into the meadow, making sure to keep all of her body behind the tree. For a few seconds, nothing happened. But then we heard a series of whistles and whooshes, followed by a succession of impacts into the ground. Hundreds of tiny bamboo darts had whipped through the field, leaving zero chance that anything in that space would escape perforation. They were fired from clever mechanisms in the trees surrounding the field, and it must have taken forever to set the trap. One of them even thudded into the branch that Nadia was holding.

"Well. That was impressive," Nadia said.

"May I see that dart?" Connor asked.

"Of course."

Nadia retracted the branch, Connor removed the dart, and Nadia removed Oberon's collar and put it back on him, thanking him for letting her borrow it.

"These are poisoned," Connor said, staring at the tip of the dart. "Fast-acting too. With my healing triskele on my right hand gone, I would have had to ask the elemental for help in healing, and it might not have worked in time. And if it had gotten the dogs too, well . . . I would only be able to save one of us."

"So we probably shouldn't step on any," Ya-ping observed.

"Right. Good point," Nadia said. She led us around the base of the tree, straight downhill between the killing field and the toe poppers, until she reached the other side of the munitions and deemed it safe to dodge back to the left. But I was dwelling on the fact that someone had designed an incredibly lethal trap triggered by cold iron, in addition to all the other traps surrounding the area.

This wasn't the work of an afternoon, or even several afternoons. The layering of the traps and the fact that they surrounded a huge area represented months of effort. And if the source of the demons was in the center of it all, how did the demons get out?

Considering the pattern of their appearance, it did seem like they were portioned out, small-batch-brewed, escorted through the gauntlet, and released in our general direction to keep drawing us toward these lethal ends.

Nadia had us halt and she spray-painted the location of some toe poppers on her left, representing the other side of the bullet field we'd been on earlier. Once she'd done that, she moved two meters to the right and started spray-painting a line all the way back to us.

"Between the dotted line on your left and this solid line, you're safe," she explained. "Toe poppers on the left, and the edge of a rather huge pit trap on the right." She looked at Connor. "Got any ideas how to cross the pit?"

"Yeah. I can ask the elemental to fill it in for us. Give me a few minutes."

He closed his eyes, communing with the elemental, and I took the opportunity to check on everyone. Ya-ping's mouth was drawn down at the corners. The dogs were wagging their tails. Nadia looked like she couldn't wait to meet whoever had set all this up and introduce them to the blade of her razor. Buck's eyes drooped like he wanted a nap. Officer Campbell had a wince on his face and clearly disapproved of all this. And Roxanne appeared quietly delighted, as if this were the most pleasant of walks through nature.

"Okay. Should be good to go," Connor announced. "It's completely filled in."

"Nobody move yet. Let me test first. Safety protocols still apply."

Nadia took two tentative steps across the line, and the ground held. She raised her boot for a third step and then froze, stepping back instead.

"Nope. This is double-trapped. Something magical on top of the mundane. There's another hook binding a few steps ahead that will summon something fiery from hell."

"No shit? Wow." Connor looked up again and spied a eucalyptus branch this time that was home for the hook binding. "Yep, there it is. Give me a sec to unbind it."

He muttered a stream of Old Irish and gave the okay, and Nadia took a few tentative steps forward again.

"Huh. Looks like we're clear for a while. We might be through it all, but I don't trust that. I bet this is to give us a false sense of security. So keep in order as before, stay right behind me, and we'll do this."

We made much better progress after that, but the scale of what we'd come through was sinking in, as was how utterly doomed we would have been without Nadia leading us through it with her foresight.

Once we reached the bottom of the wee valley and started to climb up again, she had us execute an abrupt left turn to avoid another pit trap, but she had us heading uphill again in no time. We dodged two more traps like that, but since they weren't packed together like they had been on the opposite slope, they weren't so difficult to avoid.

Just before we reached the top of the ridge we'd been aiming for, Nadia stopped and turned around. "Good news, everybody! We're past all the traps. Only dangers I see ahead are things that actively want tae kill us deid, rather than sitting there passively waiting for us tae trigger them. So that's refreshing, in't it? We don't need tae go single file anymore, but let me go first, awright, and watch me for developments. Adjust yer expectations accordingly."

"Thank Christ," Officer Campbell said. "Just gimme something to hit already."

The Stain of Blood

I find it significant that of all the varied ingredients required to make magical inks, not one of them, in either the Chinese system or the Irish, is blood. Other bodily fluids of animals make frequent appearances, but never blood. Once I noticed this curiosity as an apprentice, I asked my master, Sean FitzGibbon, about it while he had me scaling skins to make fish glue. It was a nasty, smelly, and necessary business, conducted on a foul patch of land on his estate outside Dublin, which he had set aside for the more toxic and odiferous aspects of inkmaking. Normally he was dressed in a white suit of some kind, signaling that he had no intention of getting dirty and was above all manner of labor, but today he was in a dark-green Aran sweater that suggested he could at least think about work but probably wouldn't do any. And if he did manage to find himself in a situation where work was unavoidable, he'd be sure to do it quickly and efficiently so that not a single sandy hair on his head was displaced. His Irish accent had an amused lilt to it as he answered.

"Ah, good question, Al. That's going to require a pipe to answer," he said, which is precisely what I'd been hoping for, because then he added, "Leave that business for now and come back to it later. Let's go to the library."

I paused inside only to wash my slime-covered hands, and when I joined him in his library, he was already lighting his pipe.

I never took up smoking myself and can't really abide the stench of cigars or cigarettes, but the blend of pipe tobacco FitzGibbon used was a cherry vanilla that I always found pleasant, and his study smelled of it, along with ink and paper and glue and the collected energy of ideas waiting to be absorbed. He gestured to a comfy brown leather chair opposite his and waved out his match before depositing it in an ashtray resting on an end table at his elbow. He puffed a few times, collecting his thoughts, and I waited patiently, because once he'd performed his ritual, he'd explain at length, provide examples, and make sure I understood before leaving.

"Blood magic is powerful stuff. It's full of energy, at least shortly after it's spilled, and very much tied to life force and so on. The fact that someone would be willing to sacrifice a bit of life force to achieve a magical goal is part of what makes it powerful and also a bit taboo. Because the kind of magic one performs with blood has to do with summoning unsavory beings or soliciting favors from the same, it's also frequently used in curses and hexes and whatnot. The whole spectrum of dark magic, in other words, is often achieved with the aid of blood. We therefore don't use it."

"But surely someone does?"

"Oh, aye. Blood inks do exist. Blood itself, raw and undiluted, is famously used to sign infernal contracts. But blood isn't used for any of our sigils."

"Would our sigils be more powerful if the inks included blood?"

"That's a fair question. I don't know for certain, because of course we have no way to find out. The Druidic bindings that sigils form simply don't occur unless the proper ink is used to draw the proper sigil. Alter the chemical composition of an ink by adding blood, and the whole batch will be ruined, and any sigils drawn with it will just be inert symbols. The only way to find out would be to have Brighid make the same sigil and allow it to activate with a recipe made with blood. There is zero chance she'd do that. But, if you're wondering on an apples-to-apples basis if an effect similar to what sigils accomplish is more powerful when created with blood magic, I can answer that."

"Yes?"

"In some cases, they are. Vampires are the easiest example. They're practically made of blood magic. Their strength and speed are still greater than ours when we have sigils in effect. So good for them—they're more powerful than a rhino on the run, aren't they? But the benefits of their blood magic sure come with a high price tag, if ye ask me. An undead existence. Profound lack of sunlight. A liquid diet and, if the rumors are true, an eventual discharge so foul that it's very clear that they offend the ever-loving fuck out of God. Nay, lad, I'll take sigils any day over blood magic. The cost-benefit analysis is much better for one's health. That's not to say we might not get our arses handed to us by an angry god someday, but at least we can walk around in the sun until then. The thing to remember about blood is that any additional strength it gives you is counterbalanced with a weakness. It's potent, but it stains, ye get me?"

"Aye."

"Good talk, lad. Now get back to making that fish glue."

CHAPTER 22

Hammers Versus Lava

We topped the ridge that fell away into a valley that more than likely contained a creek, and quite probably the creek we were looking for, since the approach to it had been so heavily defended. The trees and scrub were no different from what we'd seen so far: plenty of conifers mixed with eucalypts, ferns and shrubs growing between tree trunks and fallen logs. Plenty of birds calling out to warn others of our presence or else shrieking for companionship in the avian equivalent of a singles ad. Nadia paused, held her fist in the air to halt us, then turned.

"Huddle up here for a chat. There are many targets below. From what I can tell, this valley is full of them. I don't recommend sending the dugs ahead."

We gathered together and looked down, but our visibility was limited to fifty meters or so, since the vegetation obscured whatever waited below.

Connor said, "Maybe a stealth recon would be best. But I worry about something down there smelling us before they see or hear us. We shouldn't spend too long here before moving, but I think we should leave our packs. Take only what you need for a fight."

I shrugged off my pack and gave Nadia a Sigil of Agile Grace from one of my pockets, which she accepted with a nod. I plucked out another for me, plus a Sigil of Muscular Brawn. If we were going to start a rammy, I wanted to be prepared this time. I noted that Ya-ping was doing the same, and Connor unhooked his hatchet from his pack and dropped the latter to the ground as Officer Campbell hefted his baton.

"I feel a bit left out here, ol' man," Buck said. "Ye know those bits in action movies where the testosterone is climbing an exponential curve and a bunch of tooled-up sweaty bastards start cocking their weapons and aggressively tying their combat boots? And then the people go, *Aw, yeah, it's gonnay kick off now,* and start frantically stuffing popcorn in their holes? I cannae do that. I have no weapons save for ma legendary wit and smoldering good looks. But there's also a lot of grunting in those scenes. Maybe I can do that for ye. Unngh. Hurrgh. Oomf. Hnnngh."

[Enough, Buck.]

"Aye, that was the perfect amount of grunting. Think I nailed it."

My eyes slid over to Roxanne. She was looking at Buck, a faint smirk of amusement on her face, but I noticed that she did not ask for any weapons or sigils. Whatever waited ahead, she was ready to face it. Which, now that he thought about it, Connor found odd.

"You'd best stay up here, Roxanne," he said to her.

"I'll decide what's best for myself," she replied, not making eye contact, and he let that settle into silence and then shrugged.

"Let's go down, quietly as possible," Connor said, "and hold up if you see something."

There was nothing but the soft rustle and crunch of our passage for close to a hundred meters through the bush, but we stopped once we heard some growls and snorts below and spied some movement between the tree trunks. The hounds lifted their noses to the air and snuffled. In a whisper, the Iron Druid reported what they sensed.

"The dogs hear water down there. There's definitely a creek. And something large is sloshing about in it. They smell weird things but also smell humans that are not us."

"My foresight is useless right now except that I know there's a fight wherever I go. Where is the large thing in relation to us?" Nadia asked. "Straight down, to the left, or to the right?"

Connor consulted with Oberon and replied, "A bit to the right."

"And the humans?"

"The dogs think maybe they're a bit to the left."

"If we can go that way, then," Ya-ping whispered, "I'd really like to see if it's Sifu Lin or the others."

Connor gave a thumbs-up and led us straight left, maintaining our altitude above the valley floor. The dogs stayed near him, their noses in the air, and at some signal from them, after perhaps fifty meters, he halted us again. "The dogs think the humans are directly below us from here."

"Oooookay," Nadia said. "Let's take it dead slow and stop. Couple of steps at a time, wait and listen and see what can be seen."

It was extra slow, but gradually we heard and saw more. And some of what we heard was snippets of Mandarin.

Ya-ping flailed to get our attention. "That's Sifu Lin and Sifu Wu!" she whispered excitedly. "They're alive!"

I checked my phone. We were still close enough to a cell tower somewhere that I got a signal, which meant their phones must have been lost or taken from them.

Ten steps more and we could see the floor of the valley pretty clearly. There was indeed a creek, and on the far bank stood a stockade of sorts, pillars of pine with some space between them but never enough to squeeze through. There was plenty enough space to see through, however, and I recognized Shu-hua, Mei-ling, and Hsin-ye. All were alive and well.

I also recognized that they were pretty heavily guarded by a seething mass of chimeric Fae. They milled about the makeshift prison like the undead, except without the moaning for brains and such. Considering that the ones we'd met prior to this had been keen to slaughter anything human, I thought this behavior to be out of character.

"This is a good time tae grunt again, eh? Uggh," Buck said.

"What do we do?" Officer Campbell asked, wisely ignoring him. "Go down there and start something?"

"Not yet," Connor replied. He laid down his hatchet and curled a finger at me. "Al."

Buck and I kept low and duck-walked over, and the dogs made room as we took up positions on either side of Connor. He pointed down at the captives.

"There they are. Still alive and well after, what, five days? They've been fed and tended to. The question is why. They want you, Al," he said. "This is all to lure you in. Maybe you'll find out who cursed you."

[I think it's far more likely they want you,] I replied.

Connor frowned. "How so?"

[If they wanted me, they could have come for me in Scotland. No, they took Shu-hua and Mei-ling hostage to attract bigger game than yet another sigil agent. They want to bag a Druid, and not just any Druid: They want the Iron Druid.]

"Me? Why?"

"So many reasons!" Buck said, spreading his arms wide but keeping his voice low. "A lot of human violence is committed over the idea of proprietary sex partners. Could that be it?"

". . . Nnno."

"Huh. This doesnae have the feel of a holy mission, so religion is out. Maybe ye have secrets they want?"

"I have plenty of secrets, but apart from the secret of brewing Immortali-Tea, I don't think I know anything worth killing for. They're more like secrets that would make really interesting history documentaries."

"Ah. It's money, then. Either ye owe somebody or they owe you, and they'd rather no have tae pay."

The Druid snorted. "Nobody owes me—oh. Wait. Somebody owes me something that's not money. A favor."

[Those kinds of arrangements can be dangerous,] I noted.

"Indeed. It makes a bit of sense. . . . That could be it, the more that I think about it."

[Can you share the details?]

"Ogma of the Tuatha Dé Danann—the Irish god of writing and learning—owes me a favor. A pretty big one, to be honest—two favors, in fact—and I called them in last year. Since then I haven't heard from him. Maybe he'd rather not be obligated anymore, and this is his way of solving the problem. And if you think back to those traps—the sheer number of them and the magical ones, especially, the hook bindings and that meadow of poisoned darts that got launched in the presence of cold iron—there aren't many people *besides* Ogma who could have done that."

I couldn't figure out the connection with Caoránach but realized that perhaps I didn't need to. All I had to do was ask the question. [What does Ogma have to do with those creatures?]

"I don't know quite yet, but I have a suspicion. I'd like to head back in the other direction and see if I can spot where all these monsters are coming from. Will you wait here? If things erupt, the monsters will come after me, and then you can charge down and try to free the hostages. But I hope to be back to explain after I confirm something."

We promised to wait. Starbuck stayed with us, allowing Ya-ping to pet him, but Oberon crept along the hillside with the Iron Druid, in the direction where they'd smelled something huge in the water. They moved in near silence and we could still hear the captives chattering near the creek, their words carried along the water.

A roar of discordant harmonics and splashing split the air from downstream, but the monsters surrounding the cage didn't seem to be alarmed by this, and the Mandarin conversation resumed after only a short pause. The Iron Druid, however, had disappeared, along with his hound. Either he'd moved out of sight or he'd cast camouflage.

[Can you understand anything they're saying?] I asked Ya-ping.

She listened for a while. "I think . . . they're complaining about the food they're being given. Worried that they're going to get scurvy if they don't get some fruit."

"They're right tae worry. Scurvy is terrible," Buck said.

[But they'd have to go at least a month without vitamin C for symptoms to appear.]

A tear escaped from the corner of Ya-ping's right eye, and when she saw that I spied it, she angrily wiped it away with a knuckle.

"I'm just so glad Sifu Lin is still alive," she explained. "And so worried I'm going to screw this up at the last second."

I felt the same relief and worry—not that Ya-ping would screw up, but that I would. But saying, "Yeah," in agreement was not the appropriate response right then.

[You have done absolutely nothing wrong and won't start now,] I reassured her. [Shu-hua should be proud of you. You are going to be an outstanding sigil agent.] Every word of that was true, and it had the benefit of leaving out my own significant worries.

Buck pointed off to our right. "Hey, look, they're coming back."

Connor and Oberon had reappeared and were keeping low and quiet. Starbuck quivered under Ya-ping's hand, yearning to be reunited with them. When they finally got to us, we huddled so he could whisper what he'd found.

"Okay, it's making at least a tiny bit of sense now. The huge thing making noise over there and giving birth to monsters is the oilliphéist named Caoránach."

My eyes darted to Roxanne and she flashed a quick thumbs-up. He'd finally figured it out, as she'd predicted.

"Did you say *ultra fish*?" Officer Campbell asked.

"No, I said *oilliphéist*. They were great sea serpents, the kind people used to think lived at the edge of maps."

"They're no mere tales!" Buck said, and Connor continued.

"But this particular one is a bit different: She can stay in fresh water too and breathe air if she wishes—like the Loch Ness Monster."

"She's real?" Buck whispered to me, and I gave a tiny nod. The contract with Nessie stipulated that I had to deliver a metric ton of sardines once a year, and in return she wouldn't eat people and would avoid detection. These were things she would have done anyway, because people didn't taste very good to her and she was shy, but she wanted a treat once a year and it was easy enough to arrange. I was glad to do it, in fact, since she gave me absolutely zero headaches. She vacated the lake and hid on land whenever they pinged the waters with sonar to search for her. I tended not to think of her specifically as an oilliphéist but rather as one of the nicest monsters you could ever meet. Buck's jaw dropped wide open, but the conversation continued on.

"How do you know it's Caoránach, specifically?" Nadia asked.

Connor chucked his chin at the milling chimeric figures below. "Because of them. Caoránach was known as the Mother of Devils, or the Mother of Demons. Unlike Nessie or other oilliphéists, she can spawn Fae monsters at a pretty decent clip, and that's why we've seen this disturbance without feeling a draw on the earth's power."

"What's she doing here?"

"Well, that brings us back to what Al was suggesting. She's here for me. Caoránach died in the fifth century in Loch Dearg, her spirit residing somewhere beyond the veil in Tír na nÓg. Ogma had to travel there to convince the spirit of Miach to teach him how to regrow my right arm—that was the favor I required to square accounts. And I can tell by your faces I need to explain who that is.

"Miach was a remarkable healer who in ancient days was able to grow a new arm for an old Irish king, Nuada. And that was necessary because ancient Irish society was horribly ableist, and after Nuada lost his arm, he wasn't allowed to be king. Once Miach fixed him up in a nine-day ritual, Nuada became king again. His brain and leadership skills never changed; it was all ableism, which of course I had absorbed myself growing up in that culture. I called in my favors with Ogma last year when I was still shocked and depressed and hadn't even begun to adjust to my new life. As you can plainly tell, growing a new arm for me didn't work out. Caoránach's appearance here might be Ogma's attempt to get out of the obligation. If you look at it the way a homicide detective might, Ogma had motive, means, and opportunity. Caoránach is the murder weapon he brought back from the land of the dead."

"What the everloving *fuck* are you on about, mate?" Officer Campbell said, and Roxanne chuckled softly, but no one felt like bringing him up to speed on the fact that he was surrounded by people who all used magic to one extent or another. And while Roxanne's laugh drew an odd stare from Ya-ping and Connor, neither of them decided to confront her about it, but rather appeared to tuck her reaction away under a burgeoning mental file labeled "Weird." They had bigger concerns than her strangeness to address at the moment.

"Begging your pardon, Connor," Ya-ping said, "but I'm unclear on the motive part. You're saying Ogma created this situation—the kidnapping of Sifu Lin and all of it—to get out of doing you a favor?"

"Yes. That's the theory, anyway."

"I don't understand. If he couldn't get Miach to teach him anything, why would he not simply return to you and say you have asked for the impossible?"

"An excellent question. If it was truly impossible, he *could* say that and be excused from the request. But I know—and he knows, and others know—that it's not impossible. It's just spectacularly inconvenient, because in order to satisfy his debt to me, Ogma must go into debt with Miach, who—it cannot be stressed enough—is dead. The dead do not typically ask for easily obtainable items like chocolate or videogames or kitchen gadgets. Whatever Miach demanded in return for the knowledge he needed was something Ogma didn't want to do, or it was a price he didn't want to pay. But refusing to follow through on his obligation to me would have real consequences for him. He would suffer an extreme loss of face among the Tuatha Dé Danann and all the Fae if he did so, and we are in fact past the time when I could publicly call him out and dishonor him, because it's been more than nine months."

"Someone skips out on a debt, you have to wait nine months before you can call them on it?" Officer Campbell asked.

"Well, some multiple of nine, depending on the debt they owe you. If it was a very simple request, they'd get nine minutes or hours to make good. Nine days or nine weeks are typical for more-difficult things, and nine months are needed for tough stuff like what I asked for. Nine is a big deal in Irish paganism. But honor is a much, much bigger deal. Without your good name and a reputation for keeping your word, you're basically unable to function in the Fae realms."

"So he did all this instead? How did he manage it? Is he a god of resurrection?" Ya-ping pressed. "Sifu Lin had me study the Tuatha Dé Danann, and I thought Ogma was a god of writing and learning."

"He is—he loves to learn, and he's apparently learned how to bring Caoránach back from the dead. Or someone has, if it wasn't him. But regardless of who's behind it, I think Al's right: This is a trap set for me. I can't shift planes around the world like I used to, so they needed to set up in Australia, where I could travel easily and they could lure the sigil agents in. They knew that something sufficiently weird would eventually draw my attention, and it did."

It occurred to me then that the Morrigan could have also set this trap. She had more opportunity and means, certainly, than Ogma had. The motive, however, was a bit unclear: I'd seen no indication that she'd ever even disliked the Iron Druid, much less hated him enough to plot something like this. She'd even told me she loved him. And the plot itself seemed out of character for her. The Morrigan would come for you in battle, if she was going to come at you. Plus, she'd said she didn't know why Caoránach had returned, so if she was behind it, that meant she had lied to me, and she had been scrupulous thus far about telling the truth—or at least not telling a direct lie. Her honor, like Ogma's, would be tied to telling the truth. And, besides all of that, the arrival of a god on Shu-hua's map predated the death of Thea Prendergast and the rebirth of the Morrigan. That white dot that had set off the Ward of Imbalance and alerted both Shu-hua and Mei-ling had most likely been the arrival of Ogma. He didn't belong to any of the active pantheons in this part of the world and would have an outsized impact.

"So we're pawns to him in this chess game," Ya-ping said. "Or at least the humans he sacrificed to those monsters were. Maybe sigil agents are knights or something, and he knew that if he captured enough of them the king would come running eventually. I am not especially apt at extended metaphors. My point is, he's not a terribly noble fellow."

"No, but he wants to be *seen* as one," Nadia said. "He wants out of his obligation but doesnae want tae pay a price for it. Arranging for it tae happen out of sight would let him save face."

"It's a good thing you came along," Connor said to Nadia. "The more that I think about it, the more I'm sure one of those traps would have gotten me. Or one of my dogs. Especially that meadow of poisoned darts triggered by cold iron. I wouldn't have been able to avoid that, so I'm genuinely grateful to you and say in all sincerity, if I can ever do you a favor, I will."

Nadia nodded in acknowledgment. "Awright," she said.

"So where is this guy, this Ogma? Is he the terrorist leader? Is he down there?" Officer Campbell asked, desperately latching on to something that fit the world he knew. "If he's responsible for . . . all this, we gotta take him in, right?"

We all sort of stopped and blinked at him for a few seconds, processing how ill-equipped humans were to deal with reality. Nothing in popular culture prepared people to confront situations like this. Movies and television trained people to look at such things as fiction. He'd been trained to arrest people, so that was how he would try to solve every problem.

"We're not here to arrest anyone, Officer," Ya-ping said. "The objective is to rescue the hostages and eliminate hostiles."

"Eliminate?"

She gestured at the chimeric creatures milling about the stockade. "The hostiles you see are not human. They're not even natural. There is no zoo that will take them in, because they eat people. And Ogma, if he is here, will not allow himself to be arrested."

"Well, we're not going to give him a choice."

Ya-ping frowned. "I know that if you're a hammer everything tends to look like a nail, but perhaps it would help to recast this. You're a hammer and Ogma is a lake of lava. The only way for you to win is to not fall in."

"He's . . . lava? So not really a terrorist, then. You called him a god earlier."

"Yes. That wasn't a metaphor. He's an actual pagan Irish god. He could crush us. Codes of behavior and the consequences he would suffer at the hands of other gods are the only things holding him back."

His gaze flitted among each of us, and I could almost see the weight of accumulated facts squash the lingering effect of the authority sigils in his mind. "You're not really federal police agents, are you?"

Ya-ping rolled her eyes and let them settle on me, pleading for a measure of patience. I held up a finger to let them know I was going to respond and then typed on my phone.

[We are equipped to handle this situation, and it needs to be handled. You may stay here—in fact, I'd rather you did—and let us engage the targets.]

"No, no. I'm with you. Even though you did something to my head, didn't you? And maybe something to her as well." He gestured to Roxanne at the end and a corner of her mouth quirked in amusement. "She used to be Thea and now she's someone else who is strangely calm about all this."

"Oh, you're profoundly mistaken, Officer," Roxanne replied in a pleasant tone. "I'm quite excited."

"Well, whoever the hell you are, I can see that you're all as ready for this as anyone can be, and I can see that people need to be saved down there, and that's what the job is all about. I'm just trying to understand what's really going on."

"Even if you understood everything, you couldn't report any of it," Ya-ping pointed out. "You'd be referred for a psych evaluation."

"God, you're right. What am I going to say?"

No one had an answer for that, so Connor spoke into the silence. "Hopefully Ogma won't be a problem. If he confronts me directly, he'll do irreparable damage to his reputation. And believe me when I say that is foremost in his mind—I know from personal experience how deeply that conditioning is ingrained. My own obsession with personal honor led me down a path that two gods advised me not to walk and I ignored them and paid the price." His eyes dropped in the direction of his missing arm. "I would have paid a different price if I'd broken my word, and it might have been a smaller one in physical terms, but at the time all I could think of was coming out the other side of things with my honor intact. Right now that's where Ogma's head is at, so I doubt very much he'll wade into things personally."

"But we cannae convince him tae call things off either, right? We still have tae go down there and punch some pieholes," Buck said.

"Right. There's no avoiding this scrap, unfortunately, if we want to get the hostages out of there. I was thinking I'd take Nadia and go after Caoránach. Attacking her will draw off some of the guards. The rest of you can head for the captives, but watch one another's backs. Those guards look nasty."

"Just you two against—all that?" Officer Campbell said.

Connor shrugged. "Gaia's on my side. Pretty much the ultimate silent partner." He looked down at the dogs. "Oberon, I'd like you and Starbuck to remain here. Your teeth won't be able to help me, and knowing you're safe will let me fight freely."

They whined softly, and he gave them each some pats on the

head and no doubt added some additional words mentally before glancing at Nadia.

"Ready to go?"

"Aye. Boss man gave me some sigils earlier." She looked at me to check on something. "That Iron Gall sigil ye painted on my straight razor—that's gonnay work on these creatures, eh?" When I nodded, she favored us with a rare grin. "Then let's order up some carnage with a side of mayhem. Ma favorite takeaway."

Ya-ping was frowning, and I wondered if she was having the same doubts as me. Was this scrap truly unavoidable? That is, if we *could* avoid it, shouldn't we try?

Perhaps Caoránach would be open to negotiation, if she was capable of carrying on a conversation—I wasn't sure about the verbal skills of great wyrms. Nessie never offered more than an affable grunt when I delivered her yearly shipment of sardines, but I assumed at some point she'd communicated to the sigil agent who'd drawn up her contract in the nineteenth century.

It was likely that Ogma would at least *consider* negotiation now. Since we'd successfully worked our way past his traps and he needed to avoid direct conflict with Connor, he might talk if we could just get him to show himself. As far as I could tell, we hadn't fully exhausted our diplomatic options—or ruled out why those options weren't available to us.

Ya-ping raised an eyebrow at me and murmured, "Al, do you think picking a fight is the best way to go here?"

I did not. Fights are messy and often end up spilling blood you'd rather keep contained.

[No, but Connor hasn't shared why he thinks violence is the best option.]

"It's probably because it solves things one way or the other and he tends to win. But there's a lot of unknowns here and a huge risk. We do okay in a fight, but we're kind of unco compared to him. This can go bad super quick."

That was enough for me to suggest some rethinking. My

thumbs weren't fast enough to ask the question, though, because Nadia and Connor had already put some significant distance between us. We couldn't raise our voices without alerting the creatures below that we were up here, so it looked like I'd missed my opportunity to counsel diplomacy.

CHAPTER 23

Jailbreak

My manager and the Iron Druid soon melted from view as Connor cast camouflage on them. They'd move fast, and Caoránach wouldn't know what hit her.

Roxanne finally spoke without being spoken to first. "Wait for the delicious cry of pain, then descend as the monsters are drawn off." That would have sounded like a perfectly reasonable thing to say for the Morrigan, but it struck a strange note to everyone's ears coming from the mouth of a friendly Australian woman who had signed up to find missing persons and pitch in against bush-fires and other disasters.

Officer Campbell bristled, and I could see he considered saying something about how she wasn't in charge here, but since he was doubtful about who was, exactly, and understanding that it definitely wasn't him, he instead asked: "Are you going down there unarmed?"

"It is the purest form of battle." Her lips twisted into a smirk. "Not that I require purity, you understand. Just battle."

"I don't think I can emphasize this enough: What. The. Fuck?"

he said. "Since when do SES volunteers talk about their need for battle?"

Roxanne just laughed at him, low in her throat, and I could practically see the hairs rising on the back of his neck. Ya-ping opened her mouth to say something but reconsidered and shut it. She shook her head as if to dislodge a distraction; her focus was on rescuing Shu-hua, and everything else would be shunted to the periphery until that goal was achieved.

Since the fight train had left the station and there was no emergency brake for me to pull, I crooked a finger at Buck and typed, [Can you pop into the cage and deliver some sigils?]

The hobgoblin swayed on his feet, rocked by the mere suggestion of further exertion. "Aye, maybe. But if I do that, I probably cannae get out again. That would be ma last move."

[A safer one than confronting what's outside the cage. Do it, please. Take these and give them to the sigil agents, with my compliments.]

I handed him three copies each of Agile Grace and Muscular Brawn—all I had left except for a pair for myself.

A pink finger jabbed at my face. "Ye better no leave me in there!"

[I won't. Go when you hear the scream.]

"Wot scream?"

A shriek of agony rose into the air from the right, and the monsters surrounding the stockade paid attention and began to stream toward the noise.

"Oh, *that* scream," Buck said, and popped out of sight.

The Iron Druid must have hit Caoránach pretty well. Or Nadia did—either was equally likely. I saw Buck appear in the middle of the cage and extend his hands with the sigils in them. His voice floated up to us clearly.

"Oi, I have some sigils for ye from Al MacBharrais, but never mind him. What ye need tae remember later is that I'm Buck Foi, a living legend, and I'm saving yer arse right now and I look fabulous."

The captives moved to take the sigils and we started moving too, heading downhill, even as the monsters became aware that something unusual was going on inside the stockade and maybe that scream had been a distraction.

I opened my sigils and felt strength and quickness surge through my muscles, my joints shedding years of wear and tear and becoming limber again. The charge downhill seemed almost joyful after that, rather than incredibly perilous.

Almost.

It was, in fact, incredibly perilous. Especially because we were charging toward creatures who looked upon us as snack food. And as we got closer, we got a better idea of how badly outnumbered we were—for there were four of us, since the dogs stayed behind, plus Buck and the hostages in the stockade.

There were probably two dozen different demons down there, even after some of them ran to investigate what had caused that unholy scream. Caoránach had indeed been busy.

Most of them were on the other side of the creek, where the stockade was; a few were in the creek itself, but these were all cassowaries with cobra heads atop their necks. On our side of the creek were only three chimeras, which looked to be cheetahs with the oversized heads of stag beetles, the ones with the ridiculous mandibles.

We weren't busting out with a war cry or anything, so they weren't really aware of our approach. They were looking instead at the sigil agents in the cage, who had popped open those sigils. The agents' bodies shuddered as strength and uncanny agility flowed through their systems. Then, in a move that understandably drew the monsters' attention, because it certainly drew mine, Wu Mei-ling crouched and leapt straight up to the top of one of the logs in the stockade wall, landing perfectly on an inhospitable surface as if she had been bitten by a radioactive spider recently and was not, in fact, in her eighties or nineties or beyond—I really had no idea how old she was, just that she was of a completely different generation from mine.

Her apprentice, Hsin-ye, followed suit, as did Shu-hua, leaving Buck to admire them and award them some golf claps. He was woozy and extremely low on energy, so the act of looking up and clapping at the same time caused him to fall over backward.

I was quickly closing on a cheetah beetle, Officer Campbell and Roxanne to my left, Ya-ping to my right, and for an instant, I think, I felt every iota of worry and angst that Ya-ping felt. Here was the most mortal of cusps, a battle in which one could emerge triumphant, or wounded, or not at all, cut down due to a misstep or an unseen flanking maneuver or simply being overmatched. I really didn't want to die in Australia, but I could—and so could we all—for sigils did not confer immortality, and if Ogma was truly the shadowy puppet master behind all this, then he clearly intended it to be a mortal end for whoever came to rescue the hostages. It was an instant of horror and hope, a pregnant moment where a miracle or a disaster might be born.

Our element of surprise was ruined by Officer Campbell, who saw the superhero acrobatics of the hostages like the rest of us but was mentally unprepared to witness such feats, or indeed such monstrosities collected beneath them.

"What the fuck!" he exclaimed, and the cheetah beetles heard it and whirled, their mandibles glinting in the afternoon sun.

Officer Campbell's profound disbelief layered on top of the screams of demons was the soundtrack for the next nine seconds, as he cycled through the only phrase he could utter to deal with what he was seeing while he batted away beetle mandibles with his baton. "What! The! Fuck! What! The! Fuck!" he cried, impacts landing with each word, just defending himself from a murderous chimera that he had no hope of defeating. Peripherally, I saw Roxanne and Ya-ping leap into the air, but I had my own cheetah beetle to face.

Cheetah beetles, I discovered, are fast, and when the mandibles come for your torso, you don't want to be there. I spun away from the initial lunge and whacked at the outside of the mandible with my cane, but the creature just swiveled its head to the left and walloped me broadside just above the hip—no way to avoid it. As it pretty much hit my center of gravity, I was tossed off balance and fell onto the hillside, which turned out to feel nothing at all like an air mattress or a field of marshmallows. It followed up by trying to spear me against the ground, but I rolled away and got a deep scratch across the middle of my back instead of a mandible to the heart. The monster's need to pull out of the earth and then lunge again gave me just enough time to stand and wield my cane like a baseball bat. When it tried that knockdown maneuver again to get me on the ground, I brought the bat overhead to smash the mandible down with the cold iron–infused carbon-steel end. It actually cracked, but the creature's strength and momentum still forced the cane back up, and I had to retreat a few steps. The insect head shrieked and the cheetah body danced back, but it was positioning itself to charge at me with the right mandible acting as a lance. I didn't want to give it any kind of running start. So I ran at it instead—just a few steps—and then tried something that was quite frankly inspired by Mei-ling. I forget sometimes that the strength and speed sigils really do wondrous things for a short while, and the limitations of what I can do are more mental than physical. I bunched my legs and launched myself airborne, straight over the cheetah bee-tle's head, which it did not know how to handle. The neck didn't have a lot of vertical mobility, so it tried to back up to get me in front of it again. I just wanted some part of it underneath me when I descended, because I was doing another overhead strike with the carbon-steel end coming down first. It wound up crush-ing the spine, instantly buckling the back legs and ruining its mobility. It wouldn't be charging anymore, so it was effectively neutralized.

I searched for another target—there were plenty—and saw that Ya-ping had efficiently dispatched her cheetah beetle with her sai and Roxanne had somehow defeated the one that had been men-acing Officer Campbell. The officer was standing there gobsmacked as she squared up against a couple of cassowary cobras in the shallow waters of the creek, and Ya-ping was rushing to meet one of them as well.

The three captives were still perched atop pillars of the stockade, looking down at the monsters and being looked at in return by dozens of hungry eyes. That was all to the good: Keeping the bulk of the chimeras occupied gave us a chance to advance without being overwhelmed. And the captives weren't armed, so unless they felt there was some advantage to dropping into a churning mosh pit of death, holding the attention of the monsters was the best possible strategic move while we moved in from behind.

The wound in my back burned, and I could feel blood sheeting down my skin to the waistband of my trousers. I took the opportunity to pop open a Sigil of Knit Flesh before proceeding. It would stop the blood loss and heal up the muscle and even close up any wounds I received in the immediate future.

I targeted one of the cassowary cobras to charge next, since three of them had decided to gang up on Roxanne while one was hyperaware that Ya-ping was inbound and focused on her.

Roxanne was holding her own, dodging their strikes and delivering wild roundhouse kicks from underneath that caught them in the breast and knocked the bird-things backward. Immediately after one of these maneuvers, on the subsequent follow-through she pushed off with both hands from the ground and spun like a figure skater launching herself from the ice, except upside down, so that her legs caught one of the cassowary cobras at the base of its neck. Her rotary motion effectively wrenched the head abruptly to the right and torqued it to the ground with the twin forces of her kinetic momentum and gravity. Once she'd wrestled it to the earth, Roxanne ruthlessly stomped on the cobra head with her booted foot before it could strike, then pivoted to avoid a leaping attack from another. She was grinning.

"What the fuck?" Officer Campbell said. "I know you said you wanted battle, but you fight way better than any SES volunteer should."

The others missed what happened next, but I didn't. Roxanne's grin disappeared and her eyes flashed red briefly, and she said in a deep throaty voice, "You should not have noticed that, Carter Campbell."

Was that his first name? I didn't think he'd ever volunteered it. The two cassowary cobras who'd been targeting Roxanne decided abruptly that the officer was more of a sure thing and charged toward him.

Seeing that he'd be outnumbered and that he had no special strength or speed, I rushed to intercept and did manage to trip up one of the creatures by extending my cane between its running legs. But the other launched itself through the air at the officer, and he was so worried about a bite from the cobra fangs that he didn't block the much more dangerous talons, which have killed more than a few humans. His vest protected his torso, but a talon dragged down below the belt and opened a vertical gash along the top of his left thigh. Campbell cried out and went down.

I thought I could still save him if I could get to him in time, but the cassowary cobra I'd tripped blocked my path and I had to deal with it, which meant swinging like it was the world's biggest cricket ball. I broke its breastbone and it hissed and collapsed to the ground. I was just in time to see the other monster attack again, and this time the talon raked down Campbell's face and neck, tearing open his throat.

"No!" I shouted, and rushed the creature, only to be beaten to it by Roxanne. She caught it by the neck and separated it from the body with brute force, tossing it aside as the carcass toppled over. She knelt next to Officer Campbell, and I searched my pocket for another Sigil of Knit Flesh.

"It's too late," she said. "He's gone. And we have incoming anyway."

I spun around and saw that we'd drawn some attention: Ya-ping's effectiveness and Officer Campbell's cry, coupled with my own, had alerted some chimeras around the stockade that there were soft and meaty munchies within reach. Or maybe they smelled the blood.

"Did you just do what I think you did?" I asked aloud. There was no time for the phone. We had mere seconds before the fight came to us.

"That was a huge mistake," Roxanne said, a phrase very rarely uttered by any deity that I knew of. But it came out all scratchy, and she heard it, then blinked and consciously switched back to the smooth Australian accent. "I don't want to be the Chooser of the Slain. I don't want to be her again."

Which made me wonder if she had a choice.

There were kangaroo lions and monkey lizards, armadillo cats and camel shrikes, a hippo gator and an actual owlbear, who all wanted a bite of Officer Campbell. I held my ground, barely, getting winded and cut up and punctured high in the chest by the beak of a camel shrike even with my advantages, and was only able to hold my ground because of the absolute slaughter that Roxanne unleashed. Ya-ping successfully leapt over most of the opposition to give Shu-hua one of her sai, and then my colleague descended from the pillar to join the fray. Once a tiny bit of space was created, Mei-ling and Hsin-ye also came down and armed themselves with river rocks, but I didn't see much of what they did, since I had plenty to occupy my attention. And somewhere, downriver, Connor and Nadia were still doing something to create a chorus of howls and roars.

The demons fought ferociously, and the number disadvantage nearly overwhelmed us, but the Sigils of Iron Gall helped tremendously, as did an incognito goddess of death who was conflicted about her identity but willing to work through her issues *after* the monsters were dead. The Sigils of Agile Grace and Muscular Brawn faded just after we slew the last one, and we were all exhausted, bloody, and bedraggled. A roar downstream reminded us that we hadn't really won yet. We hadn't even *seen* the true threat.

But Ya-ping, at least, looked mightily relieved. She hadn't screwed up. She'd followed through, done what she was supposed to, and rescued Sifu Lin. With a temporary lull in the action, she beamed at Shu-hua and got a smile and a hug in return. It was genuine affection between them, and it pleased me to no end seeing Ya-ping vindicated and validated. Then she pulled out her phone, presented it to Shu-hua, and said, "Call Sara. She's worried you might be dead."

Shu-hua gestured downstream at the unseen threat, hidden by a bend and some trees. "Well, I might be very soon."

"So tell her that, Sifu. But tell her quickly that you're alive and thinking of her now, and then we'll go."

Rather than waste time arguing, Shu-hua made the practical (and correct) decision to get it done and punched in the number already saved in Ya-ping's phone. I took the opportunity to take a quick look around to make sure there were no other threats, except the unseen one downstream, and made a mental note to come back for Officer Campbell. We gathered together in the creek and decided to proceed as a group as soon as Shu-hua rang off with Sara, which was really twenty seconds of reassurances, a declaration that she was foremost in her heart and thoughts, and a promise to call again later.

"Oi, MacBharrais," Buck said from inside the stockade. He was sitting down and looked half asleep. "That was quite the bumptious brouhaha. Wore me out just watching it. Toss in one of yer bars made of shite and nuts, will ye? I'm really low on petrol here."

I did so and Hsin-ye said, "I appreciate you for getting us out of there, Buck Foi. I know you're exhausted right now, but I think you represent a strong argument in favor of sigil agents contracting hobgoblins to honorable service."

"Honorable service!" Buck repeated. "Ye hear that, MacBharrais? I serve honorably. If ye didnae hear that, I guarantee ye're gonnay from now on, because I'll be reminding ye on a regular basis."

I wanted to ask Hsin-ye about the health of Cowslip, the ailing pixie that we'd left in her care after the poor thing had suffered mightily at the hands of an odious scientist, Dr. Alex Larned, but there wasn't time for that when we still had a situation to attend to downstream.

Mei-ling said, "Speaking of being really low on supplies—how do we stand on sigils?"

"I have some," Ya-ping said.

[I am out of Brawn and Grace but have some assorted healing and memory sigils.]

My answer was obviously not one Mei-ling was looking for, because she turned to Ya-ping and asked, "Do you have Brawn and Grace?"

"Yes. But not enough for everyone. I have three copies of each and there are six of us."

"I do not require one," Roxanne said, and we paused so that Roxanne could be introduced to the former captives. The decision was that we sigil agents would use the sigils; Roxanne and the apprentices would do without.

Tactically our best move was to cross the creek and approach from the opposite side of where Connor and Nadia were attacking. Flanking is the most basic method of outmaneuvering an opponent, and sometimes they were prepared for it. But sometimes they weren't, and so it must be tried.

We crossed the creek and climbed perhaps five meters up the opposite slope to put some ferns and tree trunks between us and the bank. Then we crept downstream toward the sound of chaos, hoping we'd see a quick, clear path to victory.

After seventy meters, we saw the chaos.

And I saw no path to victory at all.

CHAPTER 24

The Oilliphéist

The various Irish legends surrounding Caoránach that I'd surreptitiously looked up on my phone—some pagan, some Christianized with Saint Patrick stepping in as the hero—agreed in general terms that she met her end at Loch Dearg in Ireland, a lake that turned red with her blood. Her death in that place had been confirmed for me by Roxanne, so I discounted the variations of the tale that said she survived.

Her origin, likewise, varied depending on the storyteller, but the one I believed based on what I was seeing was that she had been trapped inside the thigh bone of a hag, and upon the hag's death, people were warned not to break that thigh bone or something monstrous would result. Which meant, of course, some utter git with gelatin for brains broke it anyway—the stories I read ascribed it to one of the Fianna named Conan.

Out of the splintered bone, released from a moist cocoon of marrow, a small hairy worm dropped to the ground and began to grow with unnatural speed into the oilliphéist known as Caoránach. She was naturally quite hungry, after having no sustenance for so long and growing so fast, and so began a binge that consumed most of the cattle of Ulster.

Not a thick steak or a couple of hamburgers, mind: cattle. Her unit of consumption was *cattle,* as in more than a single cow at a sitting. If she had a stomach capable of housing the chewed-up flesh of two whole cows, she had to be pretty huge. And she was.

I don't know how large a creature has to be in order to be counted as a kaiju—bigger than a blue whale, or ten elephants, or what—but I thought Caoránach might qualify. She was certainly in blue-whale territory, easily stretching thirty meters from tail to snout, and I guessed she weighed close to a hundred fifty metric tons. Scaled and glittering, she would not be heaving that bulk about quickly, especially since her legs seemed built more for swimming or, at best, dragging herself along than for high-speed movement.

The scales were mostly greyish but reflected some colors in the sun, with more colors rippling and glinting about the neck and head, which would make her quite beautiful rendered in artwork. She had that elegant sort of dragon's head, with long nostrils and sharp biting teeth that pointed both up and down outside the lips when the mouth was closed, and opalescent eyes with a dark vertical pupil. The hair from her brief time as a worm, if it had ever been hair, was now reduced to the occasional thin spine sticking out between her scales as another line of defense.

Her primary defense, however, was shitting demons in the creek. And that was our problem.

I'd thought earlier that the noise coming from this area had been Connor and Nadia landing a hit on Caoránach, but now it was clear they'd never even touched her. She couldn't move quickly or defend herself well on land, so she surrounded herself with fast-moving monsters to do the fighting for her, and they were engaged with the Iron Druid and my deadly accountant on the other side of the creek, somewhat elevated on the hillside. They needed the advantage of the high ground, for they were barely holding off the attack, much less making any progress toward the Mother of Demons.

Caoránach was producing new monsters quickly, and they in turn had been producing much of the noise, either dying at the hands of Connor and Nadia or being born in the creek. The great wyrm had partially rolled to the left, exposing the right side of her underbelly, and there, with a talon, she had opened up a red line across her chest. Blood oozed rather than dripped from it, dense stuff closer to syrup than water. She regularly swiped at it and then dangled a claw over the creek, letting blood drip from the end like water from a stalactite. Simultaneously, she spoke thickly in a sibilant language while giving birth in the creek at a ridiculous rate, her body rippling and shuddering behind her rear pair of legs. The demon spawn were washed downstream, and then, where her blood dripped into the water, the creatures erupted into unnatural growth and emerged shrieking from the water before charging uphill to fight the Iron Druid and Nadia.

I had no doubt the two of them would not tire—Connor would be supplying them both with energy from the earth. And it was doubtful that Caoránach would tire, but *we* would. We needed to figure out how to get through that horde of defenders—for it was a horde, larger than the one surrounding the stockade, and there was no approach to Caoránach that wasn't defended, except for the space directly in front of her where new demons rose from the water, matured in blood. I found myself wishing we'd had the foresight to bring the arsenal of Cletus Joe Bob MacCutcheon to a fight like this. Some iron bullets would come in handy right now.

Roxanne growled in frustration, then suggested a course of action. "A wedge, perhaps, allowing the people with iron weapons to get close enough to stab her?"

This seemed agreeable to everyone. I took point because my cane could clear some space as we advanced; Roxanne took up position on my right and Mei-ling on my left, with Hsin-ye trailing on the left side. Ya-ping was in the center behind me, and Shu-hua took up the rear position on the right.

We paused only to open the sigils and let the power course through our systems, then we charged down into what might be our deaths.

We did not exactly surprise them, because the chimeras did see us coming before we hit, but they had little time to react before we plowed into them. As such, we almost made it to Caoránach. But I couldn't get past a gorilla elephant that seized on my cane with its trunk and tried to rip it out of my grasp. I barely managed to hold on and felt it slipping from my fingers, but I got it to let go with a swift kick to the solar plexus. It trumpeted in rage and staggered back into Caoránach's flanks, which alerted the Mother of Demons that she was beset from behind. Her massive tail twitched and knocked us all bodily through the air, friend and foe alike, about ten meters back. Our wedge formation was ruined, along with our surprise advantage, and when we got to our feet we had demons streaming toward us to make sure we didn't get that close again.

I kicked that gorilla elephant again, this time in the groin, and followed up with a cane to the skull before whipping it sideways to bat a hyena toad out of the air in mid-leap for Ya-ping's head. I got the feeling that, yes, we could just barely hold our own against them for a little while, but it seemed like Caoránach had sped up her spawning in response to our appearance and more would keep coming and eventually one of us would fall, and then another, overwhelmed with battle weariness and an inexhaustible supply of strange enemies. The thing to do was find a way to exhaust them instead.

And that was when I remembered sitting in my master's library, FitzGibbon's cherry-vanilla pipe smoke swirling in my nostrils, and absorbing the idea that blood magic always exacted a heavy price. I didn't know what toll it was taking on Caoránach, but I did think I spied a possible weakness—and potentially a solution to our wider problem as well as to my own personal problems.

Leaning into the Agile Grace, I dodged a couple of chimeras who wanted a piece of me and charged the tail. Roxanne delivered an assist and punched in the neck a truly strange zebra possum that was rushing to intercept me. A giraffe with the head of an alligator was a rather tall barrier, but I leapt straight at it anyway.

Why did the sigil agent leap over the oilliphéist tail?
To get to the other side.

The gator mouth wanted a bite of me, but my cane met it on the cheek, and I used that impact to spin like a top in the air and come down on the far side of the tail, landing briefly on the back of a startled oryx iguana before leaping again, this time toward the oilliphéist's front end, where she was spawning new horrors every fifteen seconds or so. I was jumping as much for height as for distance, hoping that Caoránach would see me coming and also that the sigils would prevent me from injuring myself whenever I had to come back down. A broken ankle would ruin everything.

She didn't see me on either of my first two leaps, her attention having returned to her demon-spawning activities, but the scream of frustration from the hawk-faced horse who just missed taking a bite out of me drew her gaze my way in midair, and she did not like me at all. Her sibilant chanting ceased, and an actual roar from the oilliphéist vibrated the air and smacked me in the face with a wall of breath as foul as one might expect from eating cattle. That froze almost all of the battle and allowed me to land safely and take out the sigil I was hoping would change things in our favor. Before everything refocused and a giant wolf squirrel could scurry over to snap me in two, I took three steps and leapt as mightily as I could toward Caoránach's face, flicking open the Sigil of Knit Flesh in my left hand and presenting it to her gaze as I traveled.

Work, damn you, I thought, and tried to keep the sigil pointed at her eye even as I fell back to the earth. She tracked my progress, ocular nerve exposed to the sigil, and I splashed down directly in the clear pool where her demon spawn erupted into their cursed existence.

I did not want to be there, and she didn't want that either. She bugled something, and several chimeras converged on me from multiple directions. I did my best to leap over them, away from the oilliphéist, toward the side of the creek that Connor and Nadia were on, while the fight resumed. It took me three leaps to clear away from the worst of the congestion and get to some higher ground, and then I turned to see if I'd had any effect at all. Since I'd vacated her immediate vicinity, Caoránach had gone back to her sibilant chanting to produce new defenders.

But that talon of hers, accustomed to picking up a fresh payload of syrupy blood to complete the spawning ritual, scraped along her breast and discovered that there was nothing there. The wound had healed. And without that ready supply of blood, the demon spawn she was pumping into the creek were just floating downstream, fragile and defenseless without the blood magic to activate them to full-grown horrors. It took her a few precious seconds to realize what had happened. She had to look down, process that the supply of blood had run dry and that her workflow was totally bollixed up now. She'd have to start over. She rent a new gash in her flesh and then ululated when it closed back up again immediately. The sigil was still in effect, and because of it, she'd have difficulty getting the blood flowing again. And that meant we had a small stretch of time where the demon horde could not replenish itself as fast as we could cut it down, and therefore there was a chance for someone to get to Caoránach.

The Mother of Demons was hyperaware of this and wasted another few seconds checking her six and swishing her tail again at our party, who were getting too close. But Ya-ping anticipated the move and leapt straight up to avoid it. Though it was not nearly as high as it would have been if she'd been augmented with sigils, it was still enough for her to clear the tail and come down on top of it—with her sai piercing the scales, plunging into the flesh, and sinking in up to the hilt. I heard Ya-ping cry out, because the spines also pierced her in turn, but Caoránach's eruption of pain followed right afterward and was louder than Mötorhead at the

Glasgow Apollo in my youth. Her mojo was totally thrown off now, the poisoning of Iron Gall shaking like a thunderbolt through her body and disrupting the magic of her existence on this plane. But her tail snapped like a rope at a cross-training event, and Ya-ping was sent flying up into the air. Her training asserted itself and she tucked into a somersault and tried to come down feetfirst, but I could see that she hadn't quite accomplished it and was in danger of landing very awkwardly—perhaps fatally—amongst the rocks.

The giant wolf squirrel I'd avoided earlier was coming to have another try, so I didn't get to watch what happened, except that I saw a flash of Shu-hua moving to break her apprentice's fall. I was in a close fight for my giblets after that, with a creature that matched me for speed and successfully tore through my shirt with its claws before knocking me down. Only my carbon-steel cane in its mouth saved me from getting my throat torn out. It gagged after it bit down on the metal laced with cold iron, and it convulsed as it backed off, allowing me to rise and finish it.

Looking for Ya-ping, I saw that she had survived her fall and was now advancing with Shu-hua against some more chimeras, while Roxanne, Mei-ling, and Hsin-ye were engaged in similar battles. The crowd of creatures attacking Connor and Nadia behind me and off to my right were thinning, and I resolved to go help them out, just as soon as I finished watching Caoránach die. Monsters like her were exactly the sort of thing sigil agents were supposed to take care of, and I figured it was just as well that my second-guessing about the battle was rendered moot. There was no way she would have negotiated peacefully with us.

She was bent nearly double and trying to pull out the sai from her body with her teeth, but a carnivore's choppers are designed like scissors rather than pliers, and therefore she couldn't get a decent grasp on the weapon. She had just figured that she could perhaps grasp it with her lips or gums, pressing her mouth firmly around the hilt, when some critical mass of unbinding was reached and she let go to scream her death song.

I clapped my hands to my ears as she shuddered and crisped into literal tons of ash from her tail up to her head. Much of it fell into the creek to be washed away, but a good portion settled damply on the banks.

The key to defeating the oilliphéist had not been to destroy her so much as to mend. Admittedly, the destruction had followed hard behind, but by mending, the curse of Caoránach on earth had been dissolved once more. And perhaps, by mending whatever rift there was between myself and whoever had cursed me, I could ease my own burdens. Brighid had suggested to me before that I should end whoever did it, but our meeting did not have to be a fight to the death that I would in all likelihood lose; healing could be stitched together from goodwill, if all parties were willing. I certainly was.

CHAPTER 25

Letting It Go

Connor and Nadia welcomed my aid in dispatching the cluster of demons that beset them, and once we had slain the last of them, we hurried down to see if we could help the others, who were on the opposite side of the creek. They had similarly finished their work and were coming to help us, and we all met on our side of the waterway, splattered in blood and ash and too exhausted to feel elated, though we mustered weak smiles of relief for one another.

Curiously, the Iron Druid was surveying the ruins of Caoránach and becoming visibly incensed, his face turning red to match the color of his hair. He shook his head, clenched his jaw, and then bellowed, "Ogmaaa! We need to talk."

He looked like he might say more, but then his dogs came down the hill, barking merrily at him, and he paused to greet them, some of the tension leaving his shoulders.

Buck called from the stockade, his voice faint with distance. "Should I just wait in here for a bit, ol' man? Take a nap, maybe?"

[Damn it, Buck,] I said with my phone, even though I was sure he couldn't hear it. I *was* sure, however, that he could get out without any help if he really wanted to.

"Don't worry, I've got it," Connor said, as I began walking around the bend to Buck's location. A bit of Old Irish and the soil around a couple of the boughs loosened, allowing the dead wood to fall away and give Buck easy egress. The Iron Druid might envy my Sigil of Certain Authority, but his ability to speak to the earth and get it to move on his behalf was beyond impressive.

"Ah, excellent," my hob said, emerging from the prison and skipping merrily downstream to join us. "Let's review, shall we? I was instrumental to our victory; I've performed honorable service; and I'm sexy as all the hells. I've earned a whole *jar* of salsa, ol' man. None o' that mild shite either. I think I can handle a spoonful of medium. Or that Scotch bonnet stuff ye were flappin' yer gums about."

The other sigil agents and Roxanne remained wary, their eyes on the trees all around, in case something else emerged to attack us. I felt the agility and strength sigils wear out, and all the aches and fragility of age returned to weigh me down.

Connor called out for Ogma again, and this time a voice replied, rich and sonorous.

"I am here."

We all turned to witness a tall muscular white man, albeit tanned and oiled as if he was ready for a bodybuilding competition, emerge from the bush on the other side of the creek. He wore only a kilt, though without any tartan pattern; it was a dark green with golden oak leaves. He had shaved his head, perhaps to show off the thick golden earrings dangling from his ears or the thicker golden torc around his neck. In his left hand he carried what looked like a rolled-up length of canvas or oilcloth, which was too thin and lumpy to be a bedroll; he clutched on to a length of rope that wrapped around it, keeping it closed. He had no obvious weapon, but perhaps they were in the canvas. And perhaps, like Roxanne, he didn't really need one.

"You didn't have to do any of this," Connor said, skipping all niceties. "We could have talked. You didn't have to kill anyone."

The god grinned and spread his arms wide in innocence. "I *didn't* kill anyone."

"Let's put a cork in that nonsense right now," a voice with a Maritime Canadian accent said. Gladys Who Has Seen Some Shite abruptly appeared between Connor and me, hands on hips and glaring disapprovingly. She was dressed gorgeously in a golden period outfit remarkably similar to one I recalled seeing Phryne wear in *Miss Fisher's Murder Mysteries,* and her hair was completely different. It wasn't grey, for one thing. And she looked about twenty-five years younger.

A small wrinkle of consternation appeared between Ogma's eyes.

"Who are you?"

"I am Gladys Who Has Seen Some Shite, so you'd better think twice about laying a binding down on me."

"You're Gladys? Well." He raised a hand to cover his heart and bowed his head. "It is an honor to meet you in person."

I reviewed the score: The Iron Druid, the Morrigan, and Ogma had all been instantly deferential to my receptionist, as had my hobgoblin.

Gladys thrust forward her chin and a finger, her tone scolding. "You know the rules. You can't use bindings to cause direct harm. But you sure caused plenty of indirect harm. You brought Caoránach here and knew she'd do all the harm you needed. People are dead because of you. A lot of people."

"No, they're dead because of Caoránach's demons. And I did not bring her here."

"It's easy to connect the dots, Ogma. You taught her how to come back and told her where to go, and you didn't arrange for Caoránach to come back for the peace and goodwill she would bring. You hide behind the letter of the law, but what you've done here is plain to see—and I assure you that I saw it all. I was here to bear witness. You still owe the Iron Druid and remain bound by your oath, but I now declare that you owe me as well. Do you wish to argue your indebtedness and protest your innocence, keeping in mind what I have witnessed and what testimony I can bring to bear on your movements?"

There was a pregnant pause and the forest quieted, waiting for his answer.

"No," he finally said.

Gladys nodded once, curtly. "Wise of you. But let me advise you not to attempt the sort of shenanigans you tried with the Iron Druid. I will not overlook any slight."

"I understand. What is it you wish me to do?" he asked.

"Come see me in Scotland next Monday and we'll discuss it." She hooked at thumb at me. "Come to this guy's office in Glasgow and get proper permission to remain on the plane first."

"I will."

I cleared my throat to indicate I had something to say and typed, [Gladys, I'm getting the idea that it's a bit silly of me to employ you as a receptionist. You're clearly more powerful than anyone here.]

"Yeah, Gladys, what the bollocks is going on?" Nadia asked. "How the hell did you get down here? Where did you even come from just now?"

Gladys just chuckled at Nadia and smiled at me. "Nonsense, boss. I like being your receptionist and putting Danish out in the break room. But you're also right—I'm overqualified, and it's why I'd rather you didn't know what I am. Let me just be that kooky Canadian lady who left a whole lot off her CV. That part's still true, ya know."

I just nodded, since I feared that any attempt at a witticism would fail miserably.

"Well, I'll leave you to do the honorable thing here, Ogma. Like make sure you completely clean up your mess of traps so no one else gets hurt. And keep your word to the Iron Druid. Since I've seen all the shite here I want to see, I've a speakeasy to visit in Melbourne and cocktails to drink and flirtations to indulge. Might as well get in some actual vacation time, eh? Nadia, Buck, boss—I'll see you in Scotland soon. Ladies," she said to the other sigil agents and their apprentices, "I know you only by reputation, but it is a sterling one, and I've seen nothing to besmirch it. You do yourselves immense credit and I'm honored to meet you in person, however briefly."

Shu-hua, Mei-ling, Ya-ping, and Hsin-ye all made thankful noises and gestures, but I could tell they didn't know what Gladys really was any more than I did. They had noted, however, that if Ogma was being deferential, they should probably do the same.

My receptionist leaned backward to catch the eye of Roxanne, who was loitering behind everyone else. "And you—remember to come see me if you want to do that thing we talked about earlier."

"I will."

Satisfied, she finally turned her attention to Connor. "And you, sir. Well. I have watched you, in one way or another, for most of your very long life. I have a message to deliver."

"Yes?"

"It's from Herself."

"From Her—? *Oh!* Yes, I'm ready. Whatever she wants."

Gladys Who Has Seen Some Shite stepped forward, put a hand on his cheek, caressed his jaw, and kissed him tenderly, as if she had known him forever and not just met him for the first time. When their lips parted, she leaned her forehead against his, their noses mashed together. Both of them had their eyes closed, feeling rather than seeing. "She loves you," Gladys said. "And, yes, even now. Especially now, because you are serving her as you should have all along. You have always had your imperfections. That is the essential mortal condition. The number and nature of these imperfections change as you grow and age but ultimately do not matter in themselves. That too is the essence of life, and you are well aware that she unconditionally cherishes all life. You are living yours well, and it is her dearest wish that you continue. I tell you three times." She opened her eyes. "Is that clear?"

Connor opened his eyes then—or, rather, Siodhachan Ó

Suileabháin did—and he was openly weeping, overcome by her words.

"Yes. Thank you," he said, past an obvious lump in his throat.

"Good." She smiled, drew her head back, and the hand on his cheek tapped him three times in affection. "May harmony find you, sir."

And then Gladys Who Has Seen Some Shite began to fade like someone was applying a transparency filter to her body, but her smile lingered until the last. Neither Nadia nor the hostages had seen this disappearing act before, and while most of them simply gasped in astonishment, Nadia provided a running commentary.

"Hey. Hey now, what? Where's she—what's happening? Al? Al! What's the score here? That was not a receptionist just now. Receptionists *do not do* that shite!"

Her increasing alarm and outrage mirrored my own. Because I thought I had a clue now of what Gladys must be, besides Canadian.

Only one entity would command such instant respect and deference from deities: Gaia. That would be *Herself*, if I didn't miss my guess. Gladys couldn't possibly be Gaia, but she could be an avatar, a necessary pair of eyes and ears for Gaia in the human world. She could exist as a fragment of an incomprehensibly vast consciousness and thereby, as a fragment, be comprehended. And as such, on rare occasions, she could serve as a conduit for a message.

I doubted there had been a need for an avatar in the old days. But I imagined that once humans began having a severe impact on the planet—colonialism and the Industrial Revolution serving notice that humans viewed the earth as no more than a thing to be exploited and pillaged—Gaia must have felt the need to understand what was happening, especially since there was only one Druid around at the time. She probably asked an elemental to untether and take human form, walk about the world, learn our language, and report. The avatar would have had to manifest somewhere, and Nova Scotia was as good a place as any.

That was my guess, anyway, based on what I'd seen and heard. Perhaps she would listen to that guess later and tell me if I was right.

[Let's talk about her later,] I told Nadia. Because Connor and Ogma had locked gazes and it looked like the sort of staring contest that might lead to thrown fists.

"I asked you more than nine months ago—more than a year ago, actually—to find a way to grow back my arm," Connor said, "and not a word from you since. I got all this bollocks instead. You know, I could have called you out."

"I am not unprepared for that."

"You did hear Gladys Who Has Seen Some Shite say that you still owe me and you need to keep your word?"

"I did. I merely said I am not unprepared to be called out."

"Ah. Yes. Very prepared. Prepared for me to call you out and prepared to do anything—kidnap sigil agents, arrange for old monsters to come back, set hundreds of booby traps—anything except the one thing I asked you to do."

"I attempted to honor the commitment. I journeyed beyond the veil and contacted Miach as requested. What he demanded in return for sharing his knowledge, however, was unreasonable."

"I don't care about his demands, and I don't even care about my request. What's unreasonable is your response. Trying to arrange my death and make it look like an accident instead of talking to me about the problem is a huge dick move, just so we're clear." Connor pointed a finger and enunciated very clearly. "You. Are. A dick. I risked my life *twice* to do you favors, and this is how you repay me. You absolutely should be called out, but I'm not going to do that."

"No?"

"No. Because life without my right arm has been difficult, and very different, but once I adjusted to my new circumstances, I came to realize my life still had the exact same value. There is no doubt that it's hard and confronting what I've lost is unavoidable on a daily basis, but the core of who I am is unchanged. I love dogs and trees and fish and chips with dark beers; I love poetry and puns and making fun of the Toronto Maple Leafs; but above all, I still serve Gaia. If anything, I serve her better than I have in millennia, now that I'm not running from the gods. I even got an inkling of how selfish I'd been in the past—the desire to steal and hold on to Fragarach, that exquisite sword, created as many problems for me as it solved—and I hoped that I'd learned my lesson. You know, I actually thought that I'd only been doing good in the world since I landed in Tasmania! I lost my arm and unexpectedly found harmony. But now I learn that I set this in motion—your absolutely gross behavior that got innocent people killed—and I feel ill, because it was also born of my selfishness. I want no more of it, and I certainly don't need it. I want to be free of it and free of you. So I'm letting it go and changing the deal."

"Yes?"

"Forget Miach and my arm. The new deal that you're bound to honor to square your debt to me is that you answer my questions honestly without dodging, lead us all past your death traps safely, and never do or say anything in the future to harm me or my associates directly or indirectly."

The god of language waggled a finger. "That's too broadly worded. How many questions, and regarding what?"

"As many as I want, regarding your actions leading up to this meeting, but I only ask them now, not later. I think you'll agree that answering some questions, leading us out of here, and then fucking right off is tremendously easier than whatever Miach asked for."

"Fine. Proceed."

"Did you decide that Caoránach should return to the living world?"

Ogma's jaw clenched. He didn't like the question. "Yes," he finally said, and then I realized what Connor had done. By asking about Ogma's decision, he removed from the table all the wiggle room about how it was done and left the god with nothing but a yes-or-no answer. That was a neat phrasing, and I'd need to re-member it the next time I had some questioning to do.

"Now that she's dead again, will she be able to return else-where?"

"Not by herself. Only with help."

"Did you decide to kidnap sigil agents with the hope of luring me here to investigate?"

"Yes."

"And you decided to set traps surrounding this area?"

"Yes."

"Were chimeras released elsewhere that we need to worry about? In other words, do we have a huge containment issue to confront once we get out of here?"

"No. Once I knew which direction the sigil agents were coming from, I knew that whoever searched for them would follow their path. The demon spawn were given explicit instructions to hunt only along that trail in that specific direction."

"How'd they get there through the traps surrounding this place?"

"I would periodically lead one or more of them past the traps."

"Were the last ones a group of yak badgers?"

"Yes."

Mei-ling cleared her throat and Connor raised an eyebrow at her in query.

"Will you ask what happened to the barghest I sent in pursuit of Shu-hua?"

"What happened to the barghest, Ogma?" Connor said.

"I slew it. If you inform me of the packmaster, I will make sure they are compensated and you are not penalized for the loss of a hound."

Mei-ling nodded curtly in satisfaction, and Connor swept his gaze around. "Any other questions to relay?"

I raised a hand and typed out my query. [Did Ogma decide to have someone take a shot at me in Tír na nÓg near where I emerged from the Old Way in Glasgow?]

Connor gestured to Ogma that he should answer as if he'd repeated the question.

"I did. But it was supposed to be nonlethal, and it was."

"Was it a Fullbritches or a Snothouse?" Buck interjected, but Ogma chose not to answer that, and since Connor didn't insist, it was as if he hadn't spoken. I had a more germane question.

[Why nonlethal?]

"Because killing a sigil agent would have captured Brighid's attention. The hope was that you'd pursue the hobgoblin and be delayed in Tír na nÓg long enough to allow the Iron Druid to proceed on his own. But you brought your own hobgoblin, and then this . . ."

"*Utter badass,* I believe, is the phrase you were searching for," Nadia finished, since he was looking at her.

"Fuck sake," Buck said. "Ye might as well say, *I would have gotten away with it too, if it weren't for you meddling Scots!* But it sounds like ye're gonnay walk away from this villainy with nary a consequence."

"What's your name?" Ogma asked, narrowing his eyes.

"Never mind that. I'm an associate of the Iron Druid that ye're no supposed tae harm. I don't like him either, tae be fair, because he's a walking death trap tae me. But I'd never try tae kill him, and he's right about one thing: Ye're a wee dick, and ye should be ashamed of what ye've done and the innocent deaths ye've caused, but I know ye cannae feel empathy anymore. Ye're too bloody old tae care about mortals or anyone else but yerself, and that is why ye're standin' there now thinkin' I'm givin' ye cheek rather than speaking the truth tae ye and why ye cannae see what an absolute shite bag of bones and fluids ye are. There's abandoned cheese out there, ye know, back at Donnelly Weir. Abandoned cheese that some couple that was building a future was gonnay enjoy, and ye ended it all by bringing Caoránach and her demons here to save what sorry excuse for a reputation ye have left. And that Officer Campbell bloke who's lyin' deid upstream—he didnae deserve that death either."

I noted that Roxanne's eyes dropped to the ground when Buck said that, but I was the only one who had a clue about what had really happened.

Buck continued, "He thought the lot of us were off our heids, and he struggled with the idea that the world still has magic in it, but he was a better man than *you,* ya bastard, because he charged down tae help strangers who needed it, and you are the reason they needed help. I hope ye find that withered husk of a soul inside ye someday and nurse it back tae health so ye can feel a smidgen of the guilt ye should be feeling now, ya fucking wankstain masquerading as a god! Zeus is forever the absolute worst— I think the world can all agree—but ye're a close bloody second. Try tae absorb that and be better from now on."

Ogma visibly seethed, but Connor piled on before he could say anything.

"You deserve every word of that scorn. I think he said it better than I could have."

I nodded and gave Buck a thumbs-up so that he would know I agreed. I was beginning to appreciate hobgoblins' cultural imperative to act as a check on power.

Connor cast around again. "Any other questions for Ogma?"

Shu-hua spoke up. "Our sigils and weapons and phones were confiscated. Do you have them?"

Ogma tossed the canvas-wrapped bundle he'd been carrying to her and said, "They're all in there. Please keep them wrapped up until I leave you."

Shu-hua did not reply to that, except to produce another question. "I am concerned that Ogma is a signatory to the treaty between the Tuatha Dé Danann and humanity yet is here on this plane without permission and apparently suffering no ill effects from the Sigil of Dire Consequence. Has he found a way to circumvent the treaty or to render the sigil ineffective?"

"Have you?" Connor prompted.

Ogma shook his head. "That question has no bearing on my

actions leading up to my presence here. It is outside the scope of our agreement and I will not answer."

"Then I will answer for him," Connor said. "Whatever the Sigil of Dire Consequence does—I imagine it delivers pain—it's working on him now. But he is using Druidic techniques to compartmentalize it into a different headspace, and that allows him to continue to function. I was poisoned with manticore venom once, and I survived by isolating the pain in a different headspace so I could work on neutralizing the toxins."

The tiniest downturn of Ogma's mouth told me that Connor had guessed correctly.

"If that's the case," Mei-ling said, "and if the rest of the Tuatha Dé Danann can do this, that means the contract can be ignored at will."

"Ahahaha!" Roxanne burst out, then covered her mouth with her hand when everyone looked at her. "Sorry. I often laugh at inappropriate times."

Mei-ling had an excellent point. We'd need to investigate and perhaps revise our contracts, for it was a safe bet that the rest of the Tuatha Dé Danann could do the exact same thing. Most all of them were Druids—they were the first ones, in fact.

"Then unless someone else has something to say, that is all," Connor said. "I don't want to know what Miach demanded or how you accomplished Caoránach's return. I only want to serve Gaia from this day forth and do no harm. I'm going to help these sigil agents deal with the aftermath of your bollocks, and then I will go back to Tasmania and hope our paths will never cross again." When no one had anything to add, he nodded once and said, "I understand we lost Officer Campbell in the battle. We're going to make a travois to carry him, then we'd like you to lead us safely out of here."

Ogma didn't speak a word to anyone after that. I couldn't fathom if he felt any remorse or if he would change his behavior after this failure, and I certainly had no idea of what Gladys Who

Has Seen Some Shite might ask of him or whether it would be a penance of any kind for the damage he'd done. But he led us all out of that valley without further harm, directly to where Nadia had parked her rental car on the trail.

Of much deeper interest to me was the fact that Roxanne insisted on hauling Officer Campbell's body out of the valley along with Connor. The travois was really more of a makeshift stretcher, with two eucalyptus branches serving as the supports for a bed of shredded bark that Connor magically bound together to serve in lieu of canvas. He took the left side, and she took the right, and only Buck and I knew that this was the Morrigan walking alongside the man she had professed to love once.

After we retrieved our packs at the top of the ridge, I stole three whole glances back at Connor and Roxanne during the hike out of the valley, during which they didn't speak. Connor's face was expressionless each time, but the Morrigan's—Roxanne's—was different. At first she wore a tight-lipped mask of regret as she gazed down at the body of Officer Campbell, and that alone separated her from Ogma. He had caused many innocent deaths and she had caused one, but only she expressed any guilt over her actions. The horror of what she'd done hadn't left me, but that acknowledgment of wrongdoing gave me hope that she would not be the same terrifying creature of nightmares that she had been in elder days.

The second time I looked back, I caught a tear coursing down her left cheek, which she wiped away as soon as she realized there was a witness. What had that been for? Something from her past life? Mourning Officer Campbell's death in this life? The impossibility of a relationship with Connor? It didn't truly matter to me so much as the existence of the tear itself, for it indicated a basic humanity and a deep well of emotion that Ogma lacked.

And the third time I looked back, she was nearly beaming at some distant thought, her expression suffused with optimism and hope. Perhaps she was imagining someone saying to her how kind and thoughtful she was. Perhaps she was thinking of consuming the heart of some man who offended her. I did not care, in all honesty. What those three separate glimpses proved to me was that Roxanne was a creature of emotion who could feel pain and elation in equal measure, and while her reaction to pain might be wholly terrifying, it might also turn out to be wholly pure. She was entirely unpredictable, but, curiously, I would trust anything she said to me, because she had not actually lied to anyone since returning to this plane.

Technically, Ogma had not lied to anyone yet either, but I would not trust him to boil an egg. What was the difference?

I supposed it was the difference between wishing to be better and wishing to be best. They are not remotely the same thing.

Roxanne clearly wanted to be something better than what she had been yet had made a decision that confirmed her old prejudices and habits. She saw, at least, what she had done and how walking old roads would bring her back to a place she didn't want to be. A tightened circle of narrowed probabilities, to hearken back to her conversation with Ya-ping.

Ogma simply wanted to win. Which was not, in itself, a poor thing to want. But what he was willing to do to win—anything—made me distrust him. His willingness to do what the enemy wouldn't might make him an excellent warrior, but it also made him a terrible person.

Roxanne was willing to lose. Lose everything, in fact, in hopes of winning a different game someday. I didn't know if she would be successful—she'd made a rather huge misstep, and she might be playing a game she couldn't win—but I cherished the idea that she wished to reinvent herself.

Which made me wonder if I could do the same, should it become necessary. If I ceased to be Al MacBharrais in some real sense that didn't mean actual death, perhaps the curses on my head would cease to apply. It was a long shot and probably not a viable proposition but worth a smidgen of investigation. The alternative was to find out who'd done the deed and confront them. If I did, would I behave like Ogma and win at any cost? Would there not be a curse in stooping down to his level to win? What if winning meant I had to cross a line I could never step back over? Would that truly be a win?

It would be for Buck, to be sure. His welfare had to be my priority. But surviving without a family was possible for me—I'd already been forced to do it and had found new family. And there was no great need, apart from my own pride, to train my replacement. Eli's apprentice, or either Ya-ping or Hsin-ye, could very capably take over my territory anytime I wished to retire.

So, for Buck, and to avenge my seven apprentices who'd died from the curse—yes, I'd do whatever it took to win. But I wanted to emerge on the other side, if any emerging was possible, with a soul lighter than the dark one that had cursed me. (Or dark ones, plural, if Gladys was correct and I'd been cursed by two people.)

When we arrived at Nadia's car, Ogma turned and went back into the bush without a word. He was a sulky sort in defeat. I presumed that we'd see him soon, back in Scotland to meet Gladys Who Has Seen Some Shite, and perhaps then he'd feel more talkative.

With his unceremonious exit, Shu-hua placed the wrapped-up canvas on top of the rental car's trunk and unrolled it. Their weapons, sigils, and phones were all in there, and Mei-ling said as they reclaimed them, "Thank the goddess that he had no wish to offend her. He treated us well for her sake and the sake of his own miserable hide."

"How did he capture you?" Nadia asked.

"He used Druidry. The earth sank beneath our feet, immobilized us, and before we knew it, we were up to our necks. He took everything we had, promised to do no harm, and escorted us to that makeshift prison. We never had a chance to resist."

"Why did he no do that tae me, then? Or any of us?"

"You were with me," Connor said. "Any direct action against you, as a member of my party, would mean an action against me. That would be a violation of his oath to repay me a favor, and there were witnesses."

Roxanne gave a tiny nod at this, and it reminded me of another person who had witnessed a past crime—someone I had been worried about—and now I had time to inquire. I waved my hand at Hsin-ye to get her attention and typed up a question.

[I've been meaning to ask: How is Cowslip?]

"Oh, she was having a rough go of it for a few weeks, but she's feeling much better now. Sifu Wu left her in the care of another pixie we contracted for nursing. They had plenty of food in the house—they hardly eat anything anyway—and they are highly entertained by children's cartoons featuring fairies. They spend half their time shouting in outrage and the other half giggling at the inaccuracies."

[Glad to hear it. Thank you.]

The immediate problem we faced next was that there were quite a few of us and only one car, which couldn't possibly carry us all. Beyond that, we had a rather tremendous cleanup operation to do in the wake of Ogma's destruction.

"We will take care of the mess, Al," Shu-hua said, her mind traveling ahead on the same path as mine. "It's my territory, after all, and you need to get back to yours."

[Are you sure? There are quite a few casualties,] I said, looking down at Officer Campbell.

"I know where they all are," Ya-ping said. "At least the ones we found. I suspect there were some hikers out here who got killed and we never saw their remains. Maybe we can track them down with a barghest. And we should try to find Officer Campbell's horse."

"Ye're gonnay walk all that way back tae the car park?" Buck asked.

"We're going to run," Connor said. "Now that we're no longer searching for a threat, or hostages, and don't need to be wary for traps, we can make good time. I'll give everyone who comes along some stamina and speed, courtesy of Gaia, and we'll get there very quickly. After that I can start making my way back to Tasmania." Oberon and Starbuck whuffed and he looked down at them. "After we get you both some sausage, yes."

I tossed the keys to the wizard van to Shu-hua. [You'll need those, then.] Buck's impressive eyebrows shot up in surprise.

"Wot? Aww. Does this mean we're no going with them? I wanted Nadia tae see ma gallus van."

[We'll have you craft another in Glasgow.]

"I'll make sure the van gets returned to the rightful owners," Ya-ping said. "And maybe we can throw in some money to compensate them for the damage."

"Damage!" Buck exclaimed. "I think ye meant tae say *improvements*. Ye're talkin' about givin' them money tae make it a shite tradie van again! If I was the Kaufman who owned Kaufman Electric, I'd be thankin' us for the legendary upgrade and all the fine whisky. Human priorities are bollocks sometimes."

It was time for farewells. [Shu-hua, I have some sigils of yours.] I searched my pockets for all the remaining sigils that I had borrowed from her stores. The Lethe River ones might come in especially handy now. [My deepest apologies for any disorder I created in your sigil room.]

"Please don't worry about it, Al. I'm so grateful for your help. Thank you."

[Welcome. You have a very fine apprentice, who's a credit to your teaching.]

Ya-ping thanked me for my help and my sympathetic ear as well. Mei-ling and Hsin-ye followed up, thanking all of us for coming to rescue them, and of course they were welcome, and we knew they would do the same for us if we needed help. Nadia and I petted the dogs one last time and told them how good they were and that we owed them sausages next time. Oberon gave me a high five for that.

The two apprentices, Ya-ping and Hsin-ye, picked up the stretcher with Officer Campbell on it.

"What's yer story for the polis gonnay be?" Buck asked.

Shu-hua shrugged. "Wild-animal attacks, most likely, combined with the reassurance that the animals have been dispatched.

It's Australia. People buy the killer-creature story every time down here."

[It was an honor to see you again, Connor,] I said.

"Likewise. Take care, Al."

Ya-ping caught the gaze of someone over my shoulder, judging by where her eyes were pointed. "Bye, Roxanne! You're amazing, and I know your new life is going to be great!"

I spun around in alarm, realizing that we'd made a rather egregious error. Roxanne had hung back, said nothing, and gone unnoticed during the farewells. Now she stepped up and waved cheerfully at Ya-ping just before they took off, and then gave a smaller wave to me, a tiny smile on her face.

CHAPTER 26

A Fresh Start for an Old Goddess

I had expected Roxanne to take her leave and embark on new adventures in Australia, eventually becoming Shu-hua's problem when the term of my nondisclosure agreement expired and I was allowed to reveal her return. She defied my expectations, however, and denied me such a convenient denouement.

She instead asked to catch a ride back to Melbourne with us.

I agreed, nervously, which I think Nadia picked up on, judging by the glance she cast my way, but she didn't say anything about it. My hope was that Roxanne would have us drop her off somewhere in the city and we could all finally relax for the first time in days. But that didn't happen either. Once we hit the outskirts of Melbourne, Nadia brought the situation to a head.

"So where would ye like me tae drop you off, Roxanne?" Nadia asked, looking over her shoulder from the driver's seat.

"Oh, I'm going with you back to Scotland."

"You are?"

I froze, and Nadia's eyes flicked to me, a furrow between her brows.

"Yes," Roxanne said. "I assume you're taking a way back that is not an airplane and is in fact much faster."

Nadia's eyes widened in surprise. "Al? Who is she, really?"

[She's Roxanne. That's all I can say.]

"How does she know how we're getting home?"

[I cannot say.]

My manager turned, dangerously taking her eyes off the road, and glared at Roxanne. "You have him under an oath or sumhin?"

"I do. Al, may I assume from all that has transpired that Nadia is familiar with your world and mine?"

[She is.]

"Then I will tell her myself. Nadia, I am now Roxanne, but in my previous incarnation I was known by many names. Most famously, perhaps, as the Morrigan."

"The Morrigan? You're the actual fucking Morrigan? No wonder I got such a strange vibe from ye."

"I *was* the Morrigan. I no longer wish to be her, because that identity comes with certain unsavory baggage. I would like to live a different life. In Scotland."

"In Scotland? With us?"

"In Scotland, but in my own accommodations. Something satisfactory will no doubt present itself. But, Al, I shall require your help to secure my human identity. Papers are necessary in this modern age, and credit histories. Secure me these documents so that I may live as a Scottish citizen under the name of Roxanne Morrigan. I will owe you a favor in return."

"Aw, shite," Buck muttered, echoing my own thoughts. One did not want to become embroiled in the currency of favors. It was why sigil agents strictly limited such trades to contracted agent services.

[It may take some time—weeks, or possibly months—to make that happen.]

"I can be patient, up to a point."

"What are you going to do as a human?" Nadia asked.

"Find employment. Robe myself like a dark queen of ruined hopes. Fall in love, if I can. It was not truly permitted for me to do that before, so that is what I wish most. But I will *not*," she said, raising a finger for emphasis, "cease to eat the hearts of men who truly offend me. Which should make falling in love a dubious proposition, I suppose. Yet I sense that meeting such a robust challenge will provide this new life much of its purpose and joy."

Nadia grinned. "Awright, I like you, Roxanne. If ye want tae go shopping for some dark-queen shite, I know some shops in Glasgow."

"That would be kind. I think . . . Al, if I am passing as human, may I express gratitude as a human without incurring debt?"

[To other humans, yes. The Fae play by different rules.]

"Then thank you, Nadia. Though . . . you are not entirely human, are you?"

Nadia's shoulders slumped and she sighed. "Naw, no entirely. It sounds bloody wild tae say it out loud, but I guess I cannae avoid it when ye're capable of seeing the truth anyway: I'm a demigoddess."

"Excellent. Then I look forward to a shopping excursion in Glasgow. Though I would request that you do not reveal my old identity to anyone until after we reach Scotland. I assume we'll be taking an Old Way?"

[Yes.]

"Coriander will be our escort?"

[Yes.]

"Another excellent test of my disguise, then. Reveal nothing to him; I am merely Roxanne."

"Right."

It took us some time to drop off Nadia's rental and get ourselves back to the hedge near the Fairies Tree in Fitzroy Gardens, during which Buck's thoughts bizarrely returned to the abandoned cheese.

"MacBharrais, do ye think that fancy cheese the lovers were

gonnay eat got imprinted with their love? Like, they bought it to celebrate their relationship, have a fine to-do together, and once they got to the weir, all those pheromones and psychic energy and emotions were swirling about over the cheese, and it was getting infused with their love, and then *blam!* They're deid. Where did the love go, eh? Intae the cheese, I bet. Gods below, I wish I'd tried a bite of it now. I want some love cheese!"

"Ew," Nadia said, delivering a succinct judgment of his desires.

"Ugh, right ye are, um . . . Now that I hear it, that wasnae a thing I should have said out loud. But still, ol' man, have ye ever heard of such a thing—nearby objects or food getting psychically imprinted with emotions at the time of death? What if that cheese absorbed all the potential love they would have shared if they had lived? That would be a powerful dairy product, eh?"

[The only imprinting of objects I've heard of at the time of death are essentially hauntings. Negative emotions rather than positive. And I have yet to encounter a haunted cheese, for which I am grateful.]

"Maybe something more absorbent, then, like a sponge cake?"

[I can't rule it out but have not heard of anything like that. Why the interest?]

"I just wish their love hadnae vanished so completely, that there was an option besides haunting tae leave something pure behind when we fuck off tae another state of existence."

[The love you give while you're alive lingers. I still feel Josephine's love for me, and she's been gone thirteen years. Why are you worried about this?]

"Because, despite ma smoldering appearance and a personal virility that far exceeds ma stature, I'm no a young hob anymore. I'm no gonnay say that every third thought is of the grave, but maybe every fifth would be fair. Especially now that I have a ticking time bomb of a curse hovering over ma heid, and that's on top of all the many and sundry dangers ye have me facing. I'm no used tae thinking of anything but the next heist, so I may no be making any sense."

[You are. I get it. And positive imprints do happen, though I haven't heard of any happening at death. Blessings, lucky charms, wards, talismans—these are all positive. But none of them, alas, is love cheese.]

The hobgoblin only grunted and subsided after that, lost in thought, and didn't speak again until we returned to Fitzroy Gardens and I sent a Signal to Shu-hua requesting that she arrange a pickup. She had some faery working in the city under a visa who acted as a messenger to Tír na nÓg, just as I had Harrowbean in Gin71, and said faery would let Coriander know that we required transport back to Scotland. While we waited, Buck spoke as if no time had passed at all.

"Do ye think maybe ma uncle's blue bollocks are imprinted with good fortune? The Troll Slayer has enjoyed a charmed existence since that time he helped us out, and while I don't begrudge him a lick of it, I'm wonderin' if maybe ma Aunt Prissy unconsciously imbued her gift with some good fortune. What if Cletus MacCutcheon is a jammy bastard driving around Alabama right now with a magic pair of lucky truck nuts?"

[I wouldn't know.]

"Well, I'd like tae know."

[I will ask Diego to investigate, since it's his territory.]

"Will he do it?"

[If I ask nicely, yes. He will use his enchanted monocle and view them in the magical spectrum, and if there is any sort of charm to them, he will see it.]

"Good, good. But if he says naw, he won't do it, tell him from me he can tongue ma fart-box."

There was no way I would ever say that to Diego, but at that point the Herald Extraordinary appeared among us and saved me from having to admit it. Coriander recognized Nadia and greeted her but narrowed his eyes at Roxanne.

"Who is this?"

"This is Roxanne," Nadia said. "She's had a bit of a rough go, as ye can no doubt see by the state of her clothes. She helped us out against the oilliphéist and Ogma, and she knows what's up."

Roxanne nodded solemnly to Coriander. "Hello," she said. "I am expected in Glasgow by Gladys Who Has Seen Some Shite, if you know her."

Coriander's brows climbed up his forehead. "That is quite a name to be dropping. I hope you would not dare to speak it in vain."

"No one would."

That seemed to satisfy him for the most part, though it did not satisfy me at all. I still wasn't sure who my receptionist really was, though I thought my guess a good one. But Coriander did follow up, as Nadia was not bound by any particular oath or bond to the Fae and I was.

"Al? Can you confirm that Roxanne personally knows Gladys Who Has Seen Some Shite?"

[She does.]

"Good enough, then. Follow me, please."

We mirrored his footsteps in a line and ten minutes later stepped onto the cobbled stones of Virginia Court in Glasgow. The temperature was considerably colder and it was nighttime, but Gin71 was still open. Coriander took his leave, citing other pressing duties, leaving the four of us standing there, a bit unsure of what came next. An idea came to me, however.

[May I buy you a drink, Roxanne? A toast welcoming you to Scotland, with no debt incurred or expectation of favor in return.]

"You may."

We found a table, and Harrowbean—or, rather, Heather MacEwan—came over to take our order. I said I'd order from the menu to let her know that I was there socially and not on any Fae business she needed to attend to. We spent some time discussing flavors, tonics, and garnishes with Roxanne before settling on something appropriate for a welcome: Glaswegin, a gin that used

Scottish milk thistle as its primary herbal distillate, garnished with an apple wedge.

The drinks were served with the ice, gin, and garnish in a glass, and bottles of tonic on the side. I pointed at mine and typed, [Roxanne, I know what favor I'd like in return for securing you a new identity here in Scotland.]

"Oh?"

[Yes. If you would please pour my tonic into my glass for me, I would consider your debt to me cleared.]

She narrowed her eyes. "That's all? You could do that yourself. Or have your hobgoblin do it, or your manager."

[All true. But I'd consider it a favor if you would do it.]

"You're certain?"

[Yes. I should be able to get your documents in a few weeks, but if you would do me this favor in the meantime?]

She shrugged, poured the tonic, and set the bottle back down, expecting more to follow. I merely nodded.

"Why'd you release me from a favor so easily? That was nothing."

[We just experienced in Australia what can happen when favors are held too long and called in forcefully. I'd rather avoid that path entirely.]

She chuckled and poured her own tonic into her glass before raising it. "You are a wise man, Al."

I privately disagreed. If I were wise, then I would not have been so clueless as to the true identity of my receptionist. I'd have a better idea of who had cursed me and perhaps avoided being cursed in the first place. The best we can do sometimes, in absence of actual wisdom, is to simply cease being foolish. With this Australian business out of the way and Buck duly informed that we had work to do to save his life, I planned to conduct a thorough review of contracts I'd written eleven years ago and follow up on each and every one to see if the parties involved might have laid a pair of curses on my heid.

I raised my glass, nodding to Buck to indicate that he should propose the toast, and the others all followed suit. My hobgoblin cleared his throat and temporarily committed himself to an air of sincerity and gravitas.

"Tae new friends while honoring the old; tae blazing new trails while remembering the paths of our youth; and tae knowing ourselves better and loving what we see."

Roxanne looked delighted. "Sláinte," she said, and drank deep.

The Necro Crypt

Roxanne turned out to be mightily disappointed that the Glasgow Cathedral was not for sale. She thought it would make a fantastic domicile for a former Chooser of the Slain, and its close proximity to the necropolis made it prime real estate. She demanded that we find her a castle instead and said that when we found an appropriate property, we could find her lurking among the tombs and frightening mortals with ominous croaking.

[If you wish to be a normal human, owning a castle will place you outside the normal range,] I pointed out. She shrugged at this inconsistency.

"I can live with supernormal."

[I should probably mention that we don't have the funds to purchase a castle.]

"Find me a place and then we will discuss the cost."

She went shopping for "dark-queen shite" with Nadia after that, visiting a goth store called the Necro Crypt, which Nadia maintained would be a fantastic new name for an estate if we could find one. Buck and I were left with an unenviable errand on top of my commitment to secure Roxanne Morrigan all the proper identification she would need to live as a citizen in Scotland.

I retreated to the Internet to search for ridiculous real estate and discovered that there was an actual castle for sale—Bardowie Castle in Milngavie, north of Glasgow—for about three million pounds. It rested on the shore of Bardowie Loch, and parts of the building dated back to the fifteenth century; while Roxanne would no doubt need to redecorate to taste, there were enough crooked trees and old stone on the property to satisfy her. It was interesting enough to open that discussion of cost, anyway, because I expected her to simply expect me to produce the purchase price somehow.

When Nadia returned to the office alone a few hours later, I asked her where Roxanne was.

"Oh, I dropped her off at the necropolis. She's gonnay be a spooky crow, like she said, until ye have sumhin tae show her. I'm just holding on tae her stuff until she gets a place."

[Back in the wizard van. I have something.]

It was a very short drive from our office on High Street to the necropolis, but I had to spend nearly an hour walking around the graves before I spotted Roxanne perched on the elaborate tombstone of some long-dead tobacco merchant. I had hailed two other normal crows, who flew off when I called them Roxanne, but the third time was the proverbial charm. She cocked her head and cawed at me, and then her scratchy mental voice entered my head.

I did not expect to see you so soon.

[I may have found you an ideal living situation.]

Show me.

Thus it was that an elderly couple, come to pay their respects to some ancestor, found Nadia, Buck, and me sidled up next to a tombstone, holding up my phone for a crow and swiping through real estate photos as the corvid peered at them intently. They froze, squinting, and the man took off his glasses to clean them, as if a smudge on their surface was somehow responsible for the tableau he was witnessing.

"Pure brilliant, crows are," Buck said, and pointed at Roxanne. "This one predicts football games, so we're just getting a hint for the betting, ye know. Word tae the wise: Put yer money on Inverness to win by a penalty in stoppage time."

That was enough to make them shake their heids and dismiss us as addlepated sorts, but the man could be heard muttering to his wife, "I wish Grandfather had been buried in a nice cozy churchyard in the Lake District. This place gets weirder all the time."

It will require remodeling, Roxanne announced when I got to the end of the photos, *but it will do. How much?*

[Three million pounds should buy it and get most, if not all, of the remodeling done.]

I assume that is a large sum?

[Yes. I would have significant trouble arranging that.]

You will not have to arrange it. I will secure the funds, with Nadia's help. And Buck's, if he wishes it. What say you, hobgoblin? Are you up for a heist?

Buck immediately brightened and blurted out, "Aye!" but then he looked at me. "I mean, would ye mind if I helped with the heist, ol' man, as it may require some time away from ma duties?"

[We have work to do on lifting my curses,] I reminded him.

"I know, I know, but this is a three-million-pound heist tae buy a gallus castle! Ma legendary status would be set in stone—and none of yer shite stone either, no crumbly shale, but smooth, sexy marble, man! A true legacy."

I supposed it would be better to have Roxanne settled sooner rather than later.

[You need to do it quick and in such a way that it doesn't come back to bite us,] I said, and Buck whooped and leapt straight up a good ten feet in the air, demonstrating a joy that was wholly inconsistent with being in a cemetery. He landed and started punching the air in time with his phrases.

"A three! Million! Pound! Heist! And! We're gonnay! Get! Away!"

"Think about what I said," Nadia reminded Roxanne. "*The Necro Crypt at Milngavie* would be a belter of a name. Goths would come from all over the world tae see it when it's fixed up proper."

We took our leave, and I had Nadia drop me off at the train station on High Street. I took it across town to the Mitchell Library, for it was Thursday in Glasgow now and that was my day to visit Mrs. MacRae in the Mitchell Library. Perhaps she could help me find some lore in the occult stacks that spoke of gods working together to curse mortals. Anything might give me a clue at this point or might shed new light on old contracts once I dug them out.

I found myself feeling a twinge of envy at what Connor had accomplished: He had finally worked himself free of the gods. And it only took him two thousand years and a decision to put Gaia's interests before his own.

Which provided me with an object lesson. Living with the curses had in a real sense been easier for me than finding out who was responsible. I had a feeling I wouldn't like knowing the answer. But simply living with it was not an option, now that I knew that others' lives hung in the balance. And the fact was that Connor's problems never got solved until he faced them. When your opposition is (quite probably) immortal, you can't really wait them out, because they're going to win that game every time.

There was a significant chance that I would not survive a confrontation with beings that could craft such an intricate pair of curses, but I knew I could not live with myself if, through my negligence or incompetence, Buck came to harm. I'd pursue any end that saved him from an early exit. I'd prefer an end that didn't involve me actually ending, but if that was the only option, so be it.

The tantalizing clue that Gladys Who Has Seen Some Shite gave me was helpful but did not provide an obvious solution, since twins were mildly ubiquitous in the world's pantheons, often representing opposing dualities or else a harmonious balance of complementary talents. Not that twins necessarily cast the curse on me—it was just one of many avenues to explore.

Maybe I had committed some hubris eleven years ago and didn't realize that I'd offended someone. Off the top of my head, twin deities that resided in my territory included Osiris and Isis in Egypt and Apollo and Artemis in Greece. I did not immediately recall writing or enforcing any contracts that affected them eleven years ago, but perhaps a patient review of my records would illuminate a dark corner of my mind. It was a thorny problem with plenty of fog between now and then, and it was time to walk back through memories with a lantern and see what was hiding back there. Gladys Who Has Seen Some Shite and Ogma wouldn't be bringing their drama to my office until Monday, so I hoped that in the four days until then I could make some progress on my problem.

Mrs. MacRae, the widowed librarian from Oban who'd moved here some years ago, was sitting behind her reference desk and saw me emerge from the fourth-floor elevator. She was wearing her typical somber colors with a bright-patterned scarf draped artfully around her neck, this one white with green clovers splayed festively across it. She smiled and gave me a tiny wave, and I felt a lift in my step and a flutter in my heart. It was good to be home.

ACKNOWLEDGMENTS

Typically, I like to do my own location scouting. Layering the fantastic on top of the real is kind of my jam; I love the travel and I also love providing the vicarious experience to readers. So I was scheduled to go to New Zealand, Tasmania, and mainland Australia in April 2020, but, yeah, the coronavirus pandemic made that impossible. There was some rue and despair and some genuine worry about how I'd do justice to Australia without having laid my own eyes on it, but that August deadline got ever closer. Enter the amazing Amie Kaufman, who really saved my metaphorical bacon here. She recruited her husband, Brendan, plus friends Kate Armstrong and Paul Gablonski, to take some remarkable videos for me in Melbourne and along the Bicentennial National Trail in the Yarra Valley, plus the Healesville Grand Hotel and so much more. I technically *could* have written my book without their contributions, but I would not have wanted to, and it would have lacked many details that it currently has thanks to their incredibly kind efforts. So five billion thanks to them all.

Amie also referred me to spiffy human Nicole Hayes, who performed vital video services in Glen Waverley and told me some of the houses there were very swish, and thanks to her I found a place for Shu-hua and Ya-ping to live.

Thanks go to Karyn Gaffney for providing a bit of Irish language help, and to Angel Giuffra for thoughtful advice.

Any accuracy I've achieved with the Scots language in this book is thanks to a Weegie, Stu West, who's been kind enough to help me out with some pointers. Any mistakes are mine, of course. But just between us, I believe that the Scots word *stooshie* is the cutest name for a fight in the whole world.

My family and friends keep me at least moderately sane. Thanks so much to the Canadian D&D crew, my wonderful neighbors, Alan O'Bryan, Chuck Wendig, Delilah S. Dawson, and my pen pals scattered around the globe. Kimberly & Levi, I love you.

I must thank Sarah Coleman (known as @Inkymole on Twitter and Instagram) once again for the amazing cover art, as well as art director David Stevenson.

The turbo rad peeps at Del Rey do so much behind the scenes to make books happen. Thanks to Metal Editor Tricia Narwani, editorial padawan Alex Larned, Julie Leung, David Moench, Penelope Belnap, Ashleigh Heaton, Megan Tripp, Keith Clayton, and Scott Shannon for doing a boatload of stuff to get this book to a place where you can read it.

But dang, most of all, thank *you* for reading and for saying nice stuff about Al, Buck, and Nadia and spreading the word. You're the best! May you be blessed with happiness and a drink you like and—only if you wish it—a lucky pair of truck nuts.

About the Author

KEVIN HEARNE hugs trees, pets doggies, and rocks out to heavy metal. He also thinks tacos are a pretty nifty idea. He is the author of the Seven Kennings series and the *New York Times* bestselling series The Iron Druid Chronicles and is co-author of The Tales of Pell with Delilah S. Dawson.

kevinhearne.com
Twitter: @KevinHearne
Instagram: @kevinhearne

About the Type

This book was set in Sabon, a typeface designed by the well-known German typographer Jan Tschichold (1902–74). Sabon's design is based upon the original letter forms of sixteenth-century French type designer Claude Garamond and was created specifically to be used for three sources: foundry type for hand composition, Linotype, and Monotype. Tschichold named his typeface for the famous Frankfurt typefounder Jacques Sabon (c. 1520–80).